MURDER AT THE ORPHEUS THEATRE

IRINA SHAPIRO

Storm
PUBLISHING

ALSO BY IRINA SHAPIRO

A Tate and Bell Mystery

The Highgate Cemetery Murder

Murder at Traitors' Gate

Murder at the Foundling Hospital

Wonderland Series

The Passage

Wonderland

Sins of Omission

The Queen's Gambit

Comes the Dawn

The Hands of Time

The Hands of Time

A Leap of Faith

A World Apart

A Game of Shadows

Shattered Moments

The Ties that Bind

To my beloved grandparents, Klara and Naum
Maybe one day I'll find the courage to write your story

PROLOGUE

The theater was full, the stage bathed in gentle gaslight that shrouded the two young people at the center in shimmering golden light. A muffled cough from the back and the gentle rustle of taffeta were the only sounds as Romeo gazed upon his Juliet, a vial of poison in his trembling hand. His handsome face reflected the agony of his loss. Juliet's skin was pale as marble, her features perfect, even in death. This was acting at its best. The sort of performance that received glowing reviews, brought in the crowds, and translated into a steady profit.

Guy Weathers stood in the wings, his eyes on the stage, but his mind on the myriad things that occupied him each day. The run of *Romeo and Juliet* was nearing its end. It had been a resounding success, and the new leading lady was a vision, but after three months ticket sales were dwindling. It was time to begin rehearsing the next play so they would be ready to open in May.

Guy had always dreamed of staging *Macbeth* or *King Lear*, with himself in the lead, but it would make better commercial sense to put on *Othello*. He had an unprecedented advantage over the other companies, and he meant to use it. His Othello would not be played by some pasty, middle-aged thespian whose face was slathered with black grease paint but a real-life Moor, a scion of a royal family. And the boy was handsome too. Oh, not like his Romeo, whose features were the ideal of British masculinity, but in a more sensual, commanding way that was sure to thrill the ladies and unsettle the gentlemen.

Guy pulled out his watch and checked the time. The play was at an end, the prince already on stage, ready to deliver an elegy to the star-crossed lovers. With any luck, the house would clear quickly, and the actors would return to their dressing rooms to change, then head home, leaving Guy to enjoy a well-deserved drink. He loved the brooding quiet of a theater after a performance. It was his own private universe, where he could reflect on a time when he had been young and handsome, he and his Juliet had been the star-crossed lovers, and every woman in the audience had admired his impressive codpiece and wished she were the object of his affections. Sighing, Guy resolutely pushed away his nostalgia and watched as the heavy curtain came down to thunderous applause, another well-received performance under his belt.

The actors lined up on the stage, preparing to take a bow once the curtain was drawn once again, but Romeo and Juliet remained prostrate, their eyes shut and their mouths unattractively slack. What were they playing at?

"Get up," Guy hissed, but Romeo and Juliet didn't stir.

Furious, Guy ran onto the stage, past the row of actors, who suddenly looked nervous and unsure what to do, their eyes darting from Guy to the two young people at their feet. Guy poked Romeo with the toe of his shoe.

"Get up, you stupid little sod," he whispered urgently before bending over Juliet. Guy bit back a cry of horror when his fingers met with cool, lifeless flesh. Unless this was some tasteless prank, Romeo and Juliet were well and truly dead.

ONE

TUESDAY, MARCH 15, 1859

Gemma Tate laid a gentle hand over Mrs. Ramsey's as Colin handed his mother a handkerchief. Anne Ramsey was crying softly, moved to tears by the performance. The older woman's distress was heartbreaking, but it also made Gemma feel a little less guilty about attending the theater. She felt more comfortable being there in her professional capacity as Anne's nurse and not as someone whose only reason for coming was to be entertained.

On any other day, Gemma would have asked that Colin take Anne on his own, but it was Anne's sixtieth birthday and, even if she lived to see another anniversary of the day, chances were she wouldn't enjoy the celebration. Anne Ramsey was no longer cognizant of the passage of time and did not even fully understand that it was her birthday. A little bit of her died each day as her mind continued to fail while her body carried on with the business of living, the physical and the mental completely at odds as Anne's emotions tried to bridge the gap and find a glimmer of hope in a darkness that was growing more impenetrable.

"I'd like to go home now, please," Anne whispered tearfully.

"We'll go after the curtain call, Mother," Colin replied, his gaze returning to the stage.

Gemma interlaced her fingers with Anne's, hoping the gesture would calm her, and Anne looked at her in the way a child looked to its mother for comfort, instinctively realizing that this was the person who'd keep them safe. Tonight, Gemma and Colin had taken on the roles of the parents, while Anne was the child who had been given a birthday treat.

"Did you enjoy the play?" Gemma asked softly, and Anne nodded, her clouded gaze traveling to the fourth member of their party.

Sebastian Bell sat to Gemma's right, his warm hand loosely cradling hers beneath the cover of her voluminous skirts, but his attention wasn't on his companions. Sebastian's gaze was fixed on the stage, where the curtain had yet to rise, and muffled shouts and the sound of running feet could be heard coming from behind the thick folds. Sebastian's jaw tightened, and he gripped Gemma's hand a little more forcefully as his whole body seemed to still. She was just about to ask him if he was all right when a slight man of middle years pushed through an opening in the curtain and stood at the center of the stage, peering into the audience in a manner that could only be described as deeply agitated.

"Is there a doctor in the house?" he cried. "I fear Romeo and Juliet are dead."

Several people chuckled, thinking this was part of the play and the theater director, or whoever he was, was playing up the tragedy for their benefit. The sniggers died away as the audience began to suspect that the plea might be genuine, and something was truly wrong. Gemma looked at Colin, who was a surgeon, but, before Colin could react, Sebastian was on his feet, pushing past the people in their row.

"What the deuce, old boy?" some irate dandy hurled at him. "Something on fire?"

"I'm a policeman," Sebastian tossed over his shoulder as he finally made it to the aisle and strode toward the steps that led to the stage.

Gemma withdrew her hand and began to rise, but Anne grabbed her by the wrist, her eyes wide with terror.

"What's happening?" she cried.

"Everything is all right," Gemma replied reassuringly, but her attention was on the stage, where Sebastian had just disappeared behind the curtain.

The low hum of conversation rose in volume once the audience realized that something was seriously wrong. The majority of the patrons left their seats, gentlemen guiding their female companions toward the exit so they could retrieve their belongings from the cloakroom and leave. Whatever had happened, they wanted no part of it, since it would probably distress them and interfere with their plans for the rest of the evening.

A few people remained, their faces alight with curiosity as they craned their necks to get a better view of the stage and peered through the narrow gap the theater manager had left in the curtain when he had retreated. They were the sort of people who saw someone else's suffering as the best sort of entertainment and would recount the story of their visit to the theater over a drink or at the dinner table to amuse their friends.

Gemma and Colin's eyes met over Anne's head. Colin looked worried, his attention divided between the now-silent stage and the frightened woman between them. He was clearly unsure how to proceed and looked to Gemma for guidance. As a surgeon, he likely felt duty-bound to help anyone in need of medical assistance, but he could hardly leave his mother, particularly when she was already so confused and distressed.

"Would you like me to take Anne home?" Gemma asked softly, but Colin shook his head.

"I really think it should be me. Besides, I strongly suspect

I'll be seeing Romeo and Juliet again before the day is out. You go on," he added, correctly interpreting Gemma's own dilemma.

She was torn between professional responsibility to Anne and Colin and her desire to be of help to Sebastian. No one else had gone backstage, so whatever was happening Sebastian was on his own. He had asked for Gemma's opinion when dealing with a suspicious death before and had welcomed her assessment of the situation. Sebastian would probably benefit from an impartial opinion based on her practical knowledge and years of experience as a nurse.

"Are you sure you don't mind?" Gemma asked, but Colin smiled at her kindly.

"Not at all."

He was already on his feet, adjusting his mother's shawl and offering her his arm once she was ready to leave. Anne still looked lost, the strange ending to the evening and the lingering sadness from the play wrapped about her like a shroud, but she accepted Colin's arm and allowed him to lead her away, her reedy voice fading as Gemma grabbed her reticule and made sure to walk at a measured pace. Her pulse quickened, and her entire being focused on the sounds coming from the stage. She had yet to see what was behind the curtain, but as she drew closer, she heard the one word that changed everything. Murder.

TWO

Sebastian had secretly rejoiced when the star-crossed lovers had finally gone to their eternal sleep. His only reason for coming to see the play had been to spend time with Gemma and to support Colin, who tried to put a brave face on it but was obviously devastated by his mother's rapid mental decline, which had been an unexpected blow so soon after his father's death. Colin seemed to feel a little less forlorn when in the company of friends, and Sebastian was more than happy to forgo an evening at Mrs. Poole's, where he would either keep to his rooms or join the other lodgers in the parlor as Mr. Quince, who was something of a celebrity at the boarding house due to his extracurricular activities, regaled his audience with tales from King's Cross. The busy station provided an endless supply of material, which inevitably made it into new editions of Mr. Quince's popular penny dreadful, published under his nom de plume, B.E. Ware. Beware, indeed!

The play had seemed interminable, and for the life of him Sebastian couldn't see the appeal of two infatuated adolescents resorting to death by suicide after a four-day romance. What did they know of real love or the pain of loss? Romeo and Juliet would have forgotten each other in a matter of weeks had they lived, but then the play would have been long forgotten by now as well, and he would not have had the pleasure of spending a few hours with Gemma or holding her delicate ungloved hand, a rare intimacy.

Their budding romantic relationship had been fraught with death, grief, mourning rituals, and endless hurdles. The most recent obstacle was Colin Ramsey, who had taken to his responsibility to Gemma with all the fervor of an overprotective father. Colin had stipulated that as long as Gemma remained under his roof he would assume the role of chaperone, and had done his utmost to ensure that Sebastian and Gemma never spent any time alone together for fear that they would throw propriety to the wind and give in to their feelings for each other.

With no other place to meet, their courtship had been reduced to wintry walks, occasional meals in establishments Sebastian could afford on a policeman's wage, and trips to the British Museum, where they had visited every exhibit at least twice in order to keep out of the cold. And now the theater, where two young actors lay dead on a dusty stage, their limbs awkwardly positioned and their features frozen in death.

The stage manager, or whoever he was, was blathering on while the rest of the actors stood off to the side, their faces horror-stricken as they stared at the remains of two people who had been alive only minutes ago and had clearly not conspired to pull off a witty prank, as the other actors may have first thought.

Sebastian knelt next to the bodies and pressed two fingers to the woman's neck, then the man's, just to make certain.

"They're gone," he said, addressing the stage manager.

There was a collective intake of breath, the shock of the news followed by sniffling and gasps from the stunned group that had gathered around him. Sebastian couldn't quite make out the number of shadowy shapes that waited in the wings, but he thought he saw at least five silhouettes, the whites of their eyes strangely bright in the dim light as they stared at the deceased like startled owls. One of them had cried out that the two actors were murdered, but Sebastian couldn't tell who had spoken, and it wasn't really important. Not yet.

He stood and faced his audience. "I am Inspector Bell of Scotland Yard," he announced as he pulled out his warrant card and held it up so everyone could see.

The legitimacy conferred on him by the identification usually ensured cooperation, if not respect, and at the moment he needed everyone's collaboration. No one moved, the members of the troupe simply watching Sebastian as if he were about to deliver a soliloquy. Their stage makeup gave their features an exaggerated appearance and made it hard to make out the nuances of their expressions, but their stupefaction was evident.

Sebastian turned to the stage manager. He was a fussy little man, who wore a silk puff tie and a claret-colored waistcoat liberally embroidered with silver flowers, vines, and buds about to burst into bloom. The vines crept up the collar and snaked around the back, making the man's head appear as if it had just emerged from a shrub, the image further supported by the bushy hair that framed his narrow face.

"Are you in charge, sir?" Sebastian asked.

The man nodded vigorously. "Guy Weathers. I can't believe our Romeo and Juliet are really dead," he moaned.

"I will need their real names, Mr. Weathers," Sebastian said. It saddened him that even in death people seemed not to regard them as real people but as the characters they had embodied until their dying breath.

"Yes. Of course. My apologies, Inspector. Esme Royce and

Christopher Hudson," Mr. Weathers supplied. He seemed unsure what to do with his hands, and, after several jerky and uncoordinated movements, he allowed his arms to fall to his sides.

"Were those their given names or the identities they used on stage?"

"As far as I'm aware those were their real names."

Sebastian looked to the rest of the troupe, and everyone nodded, confirming what Guy Weathers had said. Sebastian quickly counted the people on the stage and tried to memorize at least one notable feature about each of them in case someone should slip away and hope he was none the wiser when it came time to conduct interviews.

"I will ask you all to return to your dressing rooms until further notice," Sebastian said. He turned to Guy Weathers. "No one is to leave the premises, Mr. Weathers. Is that understood?"

"Of course. Not to worry, Inspector. I will see to everything." His hands were in motion once again, fluttering like the wings of an enormous butterfly.

"Thank you. Now, please clear the stage," Sebastian ordered.

The actors shuffled off, silently turning to look back at Esme and Christopher as they went, then disappearing from view once they were swallowed by the darkness beyond. The people Sebastian had seen in the shadows went with them, leaving the passage clear. Guy Weathers looked like he was about to say something, then changed his mind and followed the actors. He drooped as if the weight of the world had suddenly settled on his sloping shoulders. Sebastian was in no doubt that Weathers would take this opportunity to go over what had happened and coach his people, but he couldn't be in two places at once, and it was more important that he examine the victims.

He rarely got an opportunity to see the deceased so soon

after death and had hoped that he might observe something important, but the only thing of note was the absence of evidence. There were no visible wounds, contusions, or abrasions. There was no vomit or evidence of a loosening of the bladder or bowels, and there was no foam at the mouth. Nor was there any malodorous smell of gas, and, when Sebastian glanced at the shell-shaped brass footlights, he noted that all ten were still lit and the narrow glass chimneys within seemingly intact. Likewise, nothing seemed amiss when Sebastian looked up. There was no ceiling above the stage, just an open space crisscrossed by wooden beams fitted with pulleys, ropes, and rolled-up backdrops that could be released as needed, but nothing appeared to be broken or out of place. It was as if the two people at his feet had truly expired on cue once their performance was at an end.

Sebastian stood still, taking time to listen. The curtain was down and muffled some of the softer sounds, but he could hear the urgent baritone of the men and the alarmed squawks of anxious ladies in the audience. There was the shuffling of feet, the rustle of fabric, and the click of heels on parquet as the departing crowd stepped off the carpet runners and burst into the foyer. Sebastian heard exclamations of outrage and demands for faster service as patrons waited for their coats and capes, then hurried outside to either hail cabs or summon their waiting coachmen. It was chaotic, but nowhere near the pandemonium that would have ensued had the audience realized that the leading actors had most probably been murdered.

Sebastian hoped Gemma and Colin would keep Anne calm and take her home before she realized that something was seriously wrong, but, if he knew his companions, he was certain that one or the other would appear on the stage within the next few minutes and offer their help. Colin was fluent in the language of the dead, and there was no one else Sebastian would entrust with carrying out the postmortem, but Gemma was more attuned to the nuances of the living and had the medical expertise needed to assess the recently deceased. Sebastian would welcome an opinion from either of them, but he still held out hope that they had done the sensible thing and gone home.

Turning back to the victims, he removed the vial from Christopher's hand, then looked around for the one Esme had dropped when she had slipped into fake death at the end of her scene. The prop had rolled toward the footlights. Sniffing each receptacle in turn, Sebastian didn't detect anything unusual, such as the scent of almonds associated with cyanide or the mildly garlicky odor of arsenic. All he smelled was spirits. Brandy, if he wasn't mistaken, and not the cheap kind. He stoppered the vials and placed them in his pocket to be examined later, then picked up Esme's pale hand and held it to make absolutely certain there was still no pulse before releasing it and cupping her cheek, all his attention fixed on the young woman's features.

Beneath the stage makeup and medieval headdress, Esme Royce was hardly more than a child, her cheeks still gently rounded, her lashes long and thick as they fanned against her cool skin, and her lips full and slightly parted. She looked like she was asleep, and would wake at any moment and demand to know where everyone had gone and why Sebastian was staring at her in such a familiar manner.

Next to her, Christopher Hudson lay just as still, the vibrant colors of his costume violently at odds with the pallor of his face in the flickering gaslight. He was no child, but he was also young, his features finely chiseled, and his body well formed and clearly strong. These two should have had a chance to grow old enough to lament the loss of their looks and bore their loved ones with reminiscences about their days on the stage, when they had been the toast of London and the embodiment of beauty and youth. Instead, their hearts were still, their story finished before its time.

The final line from the play came to Sebastian's mind, and he realized he had spoken aloud as the quote from the play echoed dully on the empty stage.

"For never was a story of more woe than this of Juliet and her Romeo."

THREE

Passing through the opening in the curtain, Gemma walked briskly across the stage, her heels pounding the wooden boards like hammers in the silence that had descended upon the theater. Sebastian turned and smiled at her in a way that suggested that she had been expected. In the glow of the footlights and with two costumed actors at his feet, he looked like a character in a play rather than a policeman who, even on his night off, couldn't seem to get away from suspicious death.

Gemma didn't need to touch either victim to know they were beyond help, just as she didn't need to be told that the deaths had not been natural. The one thing she did notice was the expressions on the victims' faces, or rather the lack thereof. Both looked peaceful, their faces relaxed as if they were in a deep sleep.

Death must have come quickly and silently, and Gemma was relieved that the two young people had been spared the agonizing pain and heart-pounding terror that often accompanied violent death. They had simply slipped away, their lives extinguished like the flame of a candle.

"You should have let Colin take you home," Sebastian said without reproach.

"I thought you could use my help," Gemma replied, and saw confirmation in Sebastian's eyes.

They were well acquainted now, so there was little need to pretend, or disguise their feelings or motivations. Sebastian worried about involving her in a potentially dangerous situation, and, although Gemma was grateful for his concern, she also knew that he valued her input and respected her instincts. She wanted to be of help to him, partly because she cared about him deeply and wanted him to get the recognition he deserved, but mostly because it mattered to her that the dead got justice. Perhaps she had seen too much senseless death in Crimea, or maybe her need for fair play had been stoked by personal loss and bottomless grief that was only now beginning to loosen its hold on her. Whatever the reasons, as a trained nurse she had something to offer, and she had no intention of going home.

"What are your thoughts?" Gemma asked once she was able to tear her gaze from the bodies on the floor.

"I think Esme Royce and Christopher Hudson were murdered," Sebastian said, echoing her own assessment. "Poisoned, most likely."

Gemma nodded. "The poison had to be in the vials."

"Colin will want to examine these."

Sebastian held out the two vials, and Gemma carefully took them from him, turning them over as if they were historical artifacts. One was pearlescent blue and had been handed to Juliet by Friar Laurence, who had offered her the gift of deathlike sleep. The second vial was plain brown glass and was the one Romeo had purchased from the apothecary. The brown bottle had a plain cork stopper, while the blue one had a pretty fitted lid.

"Two vials, two deaths, two poisons," Gemma said as she tried to recreate the timeline in her mind.

"Two poisons? What makes you say that?"

"The poison given to Christopher was fast-acting," Gemma said. "He died as soon as he ingested it. Esme drank from the vial several minutes before Christopher but did not die until after she had stabbed herself with Romeo's knife."

"Could it not have been the same poison but administered in different doses?" Sebastian asked.

Gemma gingerly sniffed each vial in turn but couldn't be certain they smelled exactly the same. "Quite possibly, given that they died in precisely the same way," she agreed. "But whoever poisoned them would have to have known precisely how long it would take for the poison to take effect in order to time the murders so perfectly."

"How difficult would it be to obtain such information?"

Gemma considered the question as she stowed the vials in her reticule. "I can't imagine that someone would simply walk into a chemist shop and ask, particularly as the dose would depend on the victim's weight."

"Would it?"

Gemma nodded. "It's not so different from lager or spirits. A stouter individual will not feel the effects of strong drink as quickly as someone who's much slighter."

"You've clearly never seen Sergeant Woodward put it away," Sebastian replied. "It takes half a keg for him to feel the effects, and he's thin as a rake."

"People can build up tolerance and require more and more to reach the same level of intoxication," Gemma explained, suddenly wishing they could move on to some other theory. Sebastian's prolonged opium use and subsequent withdrawal were still fresh in her mind, and Gemma had no wish to remind him of a time when he'd reached such depths of despair that he'd chosen to remain anesthetized for days rather than face the torment his life had become.

Sebastian nodded but didn't reply, his attention fixing on a scrawny lad who was watching them from the wings. The boy's gaze was glued to the two bodies on the stage. He was dressed in black trousers and a satin waistcoat, and his light brown hair was neatly brushed. It was evident that this wasn't some street urchin who'd found his way backstage while no one had been manning the door, but an employee of the theater. Sebastian beckoned to the boy.

"What's your name, son?" he asked when the boy inched forward, his horrified gaze still on Esme and Christopher. Now that he'd stepped into the light, Gemma thought he might be eleven or twelve.

"Sid," the boy croaked.

"Do you work at the Orpheus?" Sebastian asked.

"Yes, sir."

"Would you be able to do me a favor?"

Sid nodded eagerly. Sebastian took out a coin and held it out to the boy. "I want you to find a cab and take it to Scotland Yard. Tell the desk sergeant that Inspector Bell sent you and ask him to send two constables with the police wagon to the theater. Can you do that for me?"

The boy nodded again. "Can I ride back with the coppers?"

"I don't see why not."

"On the bench?" Sid cried. He was clearly thrilled by the prospect despite his earlier shock.

"Tell the constables I said you could."

"Thank you, sir. Are you going to make an arrest when they get here?" Sid asked, his excitement nearly bubbling over.

"That remains to be seen," Sebastian replied patiently. "First, I need to get the victims to the mortuary."

Sid's face fell, as if he had been hoping the arrival of the extra policemen would lead to a showdown he could have a front seat to. The thought of them ferrying corpses clearly did not live up to his expectations.

"Yes, sir."

"Go on, then," Sebastian prompted.

Sid pocketed the coin, then peered into the dim recesses of the corridor, as though he were searching for someone.

"I have to tell my sister. Rose will be worried if she can't find me."

"Of course. You mustn't worry your sister."

Sid nodded and took off.

"How do you mean to proceed?" Gemma asked once they were alone again.

"I will start with Guy Weathers. I don't know anything about the workings of a theater. Then, I will question the actors. Gemma—" Sebastian began, but Gemma cut across him since she knew precisely what he was going to say and didn't care to be dismissed.

"There's someone I'd like to speak to," she said.

"Who?"

"When I came on stage, I noticed a woman standing in the wings. She was weeping."

"Is she part of the troupe?"

Gemma shook her head. "I don't think so. She wasn't in costume, and I didn't recognize her from the performance. I expect she works at the theater."

"You will be careful." It wasn't a question but a command, and Gemma smiled up at Sebastian and laid a hand on his arm.

"Of course I will. Don't worry about me."

"Come and find me after you speak to her."

"I will."

They walked off the well-lit stage and entered the shadowy maze beyond. Sebastian hailed Mr. Weathers, who was conveniently hovering nearby, his anxious gaze following Sebastian in a way that suggested that he expected the case to be solved that night. Gemma hurried down a narrow corridor before the manager could question her presence and went in search of the weeping woman.

FOUR

Now behind the stage, Sebastian looked around in an effort to orient himself. The Orpheus theater had opened less than three years ago, the two buildings that had previously occupied the lot having been converted into one large space and extensively remodeled. The entrance to the theater was on Russell Street, the frosted glass doors opening onto an elegant foyer done up in pale wainscot and gilt mirrors, and the floor covered in a carpet of saffron and crimson. The main auditorium, accessed through elaborately decorated double doors, was resplendent with red velvet seats, gilded balconies, and a massive chandelier that cast the auditorium in a pool of golden light.

Two horseshoe-shaped balconies ran the length of the walls, each section fitted with a sconce for additional lighting. The first tier was for patrons who wished to watch the play in comfort without paying a premium for tickets. The upper balcony was for those who didn't mind standing for the duration of the performance, and was reached by a separate staircase that offered no access to either the cloakroom or the washrooms on the first floor and exited into a side street. The opulence of the theater was a draw for those discerning patrons who preferred to avoid the older theaters, which, although once splendid, had descended into shabbiness with their worn seats, tarnished light fixtures, and grimy floors.

The area behind the stage was at the back of the building and faced the alley. It was a warren of cubbies and corridors, some outfitted with ladders that led to narrow walkways situated beneath the beams that ran the length of the ceiling and were equipped with pulleys, ropes, and props that could be lowered onto the stage. There were steps that led to a cavity beneath the stage, which was fitted with trapdoors strategically designed for greater access to various parts of the stage. The manager's office was on the ground floor, but the majority of the dressing rooms were on the floor above to make better use of the available space.

"Please, come in, Inspector," Guy Weathers said, and threw open the door to his office.

Sebastian followed him inside and shut the door. The office was furnished with garish purple and gold armchairs, a low table, and a velvet chaise, the pieces arranged on an equally gaudy carpet. There was a bureau topped with a gilt mirror, an oriental vase overflowing with drooping lilies, and bric-a-brac that covered every available surface. A yellow dressing gown embroidered with gold thread had been tossed across the chaise, and there was a screen painted with vivid foliage in one corner.

The room resembled a courtesan's boudoir—not that Sebastian had ever visited one, at least not while the woman was still alive. That case had been one of the first murders he'd worked on after he'd joined the police service, and the cloying scent of lilies always brought him back to that day and reminded him how frightened he'd been at the sight of a fresh corpse that lay sprawled on a blood-soaked chaise, the blood that had pooled beneath seeping through the floorboards.

He was no longer eighteen, nor was he frightened, but he was angry at the loss of innocent young lives and frustrated by the circumstances. To murder two people required daring, but to extinguish their lives before an audience took a special kind of nerve, and cunning. This wasn't a crime of passion. This had been carefully planned and meticulously executed, which spoke of patience and intelligence. Sebastian was in no doubt that the murder weapon was poison. It had to be, but what had the killer used, and how had they timed the deaths so perfectly that no one had suspected a thing? Had Guy Weathers not made his plea, Sebastian would have left along with everyone else and gone home once he'd seen Gemma safely to the door.

Although he was eager to question the actors, Sebastian had no choice but to start with Guy Weathers. He required background information on the troupe and the workings of the theater, and he needed to learn something of the victims before he could delve into the motives and actions of the killer. No one was murdered so publicly and deliberately without good reason, so whatever had happened on that stage tonight had been the result of something vile and secret, something that had been suppurating beneath the surface long enough for the killer to plan their attack and carry it out with such precision. And while Sebastian interviewed the manager, the killer could walk away, never to be seen again and impossible to track down once they'd melted into the panicked crowd of theatergoers, who wanted only to get away from the terrible tragedy and hide behind the safety of their own walls.

Sebastian took an armchair, while Guy Weathers tossed aside the dressing gown and eyed the chaise with longing. He seemed to realize that to recline during an interview with a police inspector would be inappropriate, however, and settled in a chair instead. He sat slightly sideways and crossed his legs, his left boot-clad foot pumping with anxiety and his hands gripping the armrests.

"I'm at a loss, Inspector. I simply can't come up with a

scenario in which any of this makes sense!" Weathers exclaimed.

"The only scenario that makes sense is that your lead actors were murdered tonight," Sebastian replied.

Guy Weathers gasped, his hand going to his heart. "I fear it will be the end of us if the truth gets out," he moaned theatrically. "How? How could this have happened?"

"Why don't we start with the basics before we get to the more complicated questions," Sebastian suggested. "What exactly is your role, Mr. Weathers?"

"I'm the manager and artistic director," Guy Weathers said, his chest swelling with self-importance.

"What exactly does that mean?"

"It's my troupe, Inspector. I make all the creative decisions. The actors are like my children, and I'm their father." Although still bobbing up and down, his foot was moving slower now that his attention was focused on himself.

"And do you own this theater?" Sebastian asked.

"Heavens, no. I leased the theater for four months with an option to renew, which I was planning to do before this catastrophe befell me."

Sebastian chose not to point out that the catastrophe hadn't befallen him as much as it had the two dead people on the stage. Guy Weathers was overcome with emotion, which made him the best sort of witness, one who was reeling with shock and not weighing his answers too carefully.

"How many more performances of *Romeo and Juliet* had you been planning to put on?"

Now that the lead actors were gone, Sebastian wondered if Weathers was going to trot out the understudies or close the play. Presumably, he had at least a few weeks left on his lease and would lose money if he shut the production down altogether.

"We were scheduled to perform *Romeo and Juliet* until the

middle of April, then take a break for Easter and open a new play by the beginning of May. I was thinking *Othello*. Have you ever seen it? Powerful piece of theater."

"No doubt," Sebastian muttered, but his mind wasn't on the play. "How many actors are in the troupe?"

"Ten. Four women and six men. Well, three and five now," Guy Weathers amended morosely.

"Names?"

"Kate Sommers, Serena Winthrop, and Ruth Gregson for the women. Nigel Mowbray, Gregory Gorman, Ishmael Cabot, Lawrence Day, and Hugh Bradley. Lawrence and Hugh are the oldest members of the troupe, followed by Ruth. The three of them have been with me since the beginning."

"But surely there are more than ten characters in the play," Sebastian said once he'd jotted down the names. He wished he'd paid more attention instead of letting his mind conjure up more entertaining scenarios.

Weathers nodded. "Except for the two leads, each actor plays more than one role. The members of the audience don't notice that they are actually seeing the same people again and again. A change of costume makes all the difference, especially for the men, who can be disguised with a beard or a moustache and heavier brows. And for the women, a headdress or a wig can make them unrecognizable."

"Anyone new to the troupe?" Sebastian asked.

"Ishmael Cabot. He's of noble birth," Weathers exclaimed, his eyes shining with excitement. "His father was the ruler of an African tribe. The Oba," he added, clearly proud to have recalled the proper term.

"Is he? And how did Ishmael come to be part of the troupe?" Sebastian asked.

"He was cast out, on account of a rivalry with his older brother, who became the Oba when their father passed. I had just decided to cast Ishmael in *Othello*. It would be the perfect vehicle for him. He'd play the Moor."

Sebastian had never seen *Othello* on stage, but he had read the play and could recall the salient points. It was yet another story in which an innocent woman died as a result of overinflated masculine pride and boundless stupidity.

"Does Ishmael Cabot get on with the rest of the troupe?"

"He tends to keep to himself, but he's an amiable enough chap."

"Can you think of anyone who would want to harm Esme and Christopher?" Sebastian asked. He now suspected that he'd get nothing from Guy Weathers. The man was as slippery as an eel and would give nothing away. After all, his livelihood and reputation were on the line, and he wouldn't be the one to jeopardize them.

"No one at all. We are a family, Inspector, and Esme and Chris were the beating heart of our little clan. Everyone loved them."

"Clearly not everyone."

"I was not aware of any animosity." Weathers bristled.

"Surely there were some tensions within the troupe," Sebastian tried again.

People were people and, in any group of individuals who were forced to spend time together, certain issues inevitably arose. There were always rivalries, frayed nerves, intentional or unintentional slights, and just plain dislike. Not everyone managed to rub along together.

"Whenever you have a tight-knit group of beautiful, talented individuals, desires and tempers will flare, I'm afraid," Guy Weathers conceded. "Such is the nature of the creative personality. We are ruled by our passions."

"Passions that clearly got out of hand," Sebastian replied.

"I refuse to believe that a member of the troupe is responsible."

"How many people were backstage this evening, not including the actors?"

Weathers made an expansive gesture with his hand. "Fewer than ten."

"So, who were the others?"

"There are a number of individuals who work for Mr. Bonneville, the owner of the Orpheus. There are several ushers, who don't go backstage but remain in the auditorium for the duration of the performance, Jimmy and Charlie Milner, who are the carpenters, and other hangers-on."

"Hangers-on?"

"I was referring to Rose and Sid. They don't have a fixed role and go wherever they are needed. Rose sells tickets, works in the cloakroom, and cleans the dressing rooms, and Sid is useful for running errands and delivering messages, and he also fills in as the first-tier balcony usher. Rose and Sid are Bonneville's spies," Weather added spitefully.

"Why would Mr. Bonneville need to spy on you?"

Weathers scoffed. "So he can fleece me, of course. He takes a percentage of the ticket sales. It's part of our agreement. As it happens, Mr. Bonneville was here earlier. He came to collect the rent."

"Did he remain on the premises?"

"He left just as the curtain went up. We had a bit of a disagreement," Weathers admitted.

"What about?"

"The lease. He was happy to renew but he had decided to increase his percentage of the ticket sales from ten to twenty percent."

"Did you come to an agreement?"

"I told him I would not go above fifteen. Mr. Bonneville said he would consider my counter-offer and come back to me by Monday. If you have no objections, Inspector, I have a few questions of my own," Guy Weathers announced. He appeared to have run the gamut of his emotions, and now his mind had turned to more practical matters.

"By all means."

"Are you certain Esme and Christopher were murdered?"

"Unless you can suggest an alternative scenario in which two healthy young people die simultaneously while performing a play, I would have to say yes."

"And how were they murdered?" Weathers demanded. "Surely you must have formed a theory."

Sebastian nodded. "I believe they drank poison while on stage."

"Yes, I know. That's part of the play," Weathers snapped.

"I mean actual poison, Mr. Weathers. Someone had tampered with the vials before they were picked up by the actors."

"Impossible!" Guy Weathers exclaimed. "I'm the one who prepares the vials, and I assure you, Inspector Bell, I had no reason to murder the two people who earned me the most money."

"Surely there are others who have access, unless this is a confession?" Sebastian countered.

"Well, yes. I suppose so," the man blustered.

"What time do you prepare the vials, how is it done, and where do they remain until they are needed on stage?"

"I prepare the vials just before the performance starts by filling them with brandy from that decanter over there." He pointed to a cut-crystal decanter on a narrow sideboard. "It's my way of rewarding the actors for another successful performance. I leave the vials on the prop table in the corridor, right next to the dagger."

"And does anyone have access to this table between the time you deposit the vials and the time they're given to the actors?"

Guy Weathers' shoulders drooped, and he nodded miserably. "Anyone who's backstage."

"Did you see anyone lingering by the prop table at any time during the performance?"

"No!" Weathers exclaimed. "I was here the entire time, and I didn't see anything suspicious."

"Did any outsiders come backstage?" Sebastian asked patiently.

"Well, yes. There are always admirers, you understand."

"And how many admirers were backstage tonight?"

"At least three that I can think of. Sometimes there are more, but tonight was a slow night."

"Do you know their names?" Sebastian asked.

"Lady Argyle came to see Christopher. The woman has been pursuing him for months and visits his dressing room at least once a week."

"What can you tell me about her?"

Guy Weathers smiled humorlessly. "The woman is sixty if she's a day and has a soft spot for beautiful young men. I don't believe for a moment that she meant Christopher any harm."

"So, what did she want?"

Guy Weathers cut his eyes at Sebastian. "What do you think?"

"And was Christopher Hudson open to an affair with a woman who was nearly forty years his senior?"

"I never asked. It's not my place."

"All right. Who else?"

"There was Lord Gilroy, and I thought I saw General Modine."

"And they are?" Getting information from Weathers was like pulling teeth, but at least now Sebastian was getting some names.

"Lord Gilroy is a devoted fan of Serena Winthrop, and General Modine was smitten with Esme. He came backstage at least once a week and brought her flowers and gifts. They occasionally went out to supper."

"Was Esme his mistress?"

"Again, I don't know, Inspector. The actors are entitled to their privacy."

Sebastian's gaze drifted toward the discarded dressing gown. "Do you live here, Mr. Weathers?"

"No, but I do sleep here sometimes. I did last night," Weathers explained. "Had too much to drink and couldn't seem to find the strength to get myself back to my lodgings."

"What about the others?" Sebastian was curious as to where the actors conducted their more intimate business, given that their admirers were unlikely to take them home.

"We all board together at Mrs. Dillane's establishment. I foot the bill," Weathers explained. "The boarding house is a ten-minute walk from the theater, and it's easier to keep everyone together under the same roof; otherwise, they scatter like sheep, and I have to round them up. I don't much relish the role of shepherd."

"And if someone chooses to engage in a dalliance with an ardent fan, where do they take them?"

Weathers smiled slyly, and his gaze drifted toward the purple chaise.

"Is there one in every dressing room?"

"Only in the private dressing rooms, but one doesn't need to lie down, does one, Inspector?" he asked, his mouth curling into a snide smile. "One doesn't even need to remove one's costume. Surely a man of your experience is familiar with all the ways such a liaison can be conducted. I daresay you've seen every sordid thing the mind can conceive of and then some. Perhaps even engaged in a few yourself?"

Sebastian didn't bother to reply since Weathers was obviously goading him now. In his experience, the baring of the claws wasn't an indication of guilt. It was simply the result of frustration and fear, and the person's realization that nothing would ever be the same again. Come tomorrow, the person's life would take a decidedly different course, even if they were completely innocent. No one wanted to get the blame, but they were more than happy to blame someone else, and when they didn't have a ready target they usually turned their anger on the policeman who was trying to get to the truth and accused him of not solving the case on the spot and taking away the culprit in handcuffs.

"I'll need the address for the boarding house," Sebastian said instead, his tone cool and measured. "It must cost a pretty penny to pay for so many rooms."

It was always a helpful tactic to redirect the conversation toward the person's self-interest, and, since Guy Weathers was footing the bill, this had to be a subject that was close to his heart.

Weathers scoffed. "Two women to a room, and three men in each bedroom. Did you think everyone got their own bedroom?"

"Who did Esme share with?"

"Kate. And Serena shared with Ruth."

"Did Esme and Kate get on?"

"Yes. Everyone did."

Sebastian turned to a clean page in his notebook and continued. "Did either victim have family?"

"I don't know. I never asked," Weathers replied. "The others might know."

"I will need the details for everyone who was backstage this evening," Sebastian said. "If you have addresses for Lady Argyle, Lord Gilroy, and General Modine, that would be helpful."

Weathers recited the address for the boarding house, then said, "For the others, best ask Sid. He's delivered messages to them, so he would know."

"I will. Was anyone else here today?"

"Ah, yes. Edward Bannon," Guy Weathers replied after a second's thought. "He's my second in command, so to speak. He keeps the books and sees to a million tiresome details that I have no time to deal with."

"Is Mr. Bannon here?"

"No. He left just after six. An engagement supper for his niece. Oh dear," Weathers exclaimed. "Ned doesn't even know what happened." He clasped his hands before his chest and looked to the heavens, as if about to deliver a monologue. "Oh, who am I kidding?" he cried. "It's all my fault, Inspector." Weathers' face contorted with anguish that didn't seem quite genuine.

"Did you murder Esme Royce and Christopher Hudson?" Sebastian asked, hoping against hope that he was about to hear a confession. That would be a first for him, since no killer he'd ever cuffed had admitted their guilt just after the crime was committed, but perhaps this case would be solved tonight after all.

Guy Weathers shifted in his seat, uncrossed his legs, and recrossed them with the other leg now on top, then sighed with his entire being and met Sebastian's gaze with a tearful one of his own, his unclasped hands clawing at the armrests. "I didn't say it out loud," he cried. "I only thought it."

"Thought what?"

Guy Weathers fixed Sebastian with a terrified look worthy of a prisoner facing the gallows. "The Scottish play, Inspector," he choked out. "One is never supposed to call it by name. It's bad luck. I was thinking about it during the final scene. I as good as killed them both."

"The Scottish play?" Sebastian experienced an overwhelming desire to slap the man but valiantly resisted the urge.

"*Macbeth*," Weathers whispered. "No actor will say the name out loud for fear of invoking the curse."

"Is that so?" was all Sebastian could manage in response. The man was either a complete idiot, or a consummate actor carrying on like a hysterical nitwit in order to deflect suspicion from himself.

"Am I to blame?" Weathers moaned.

"Unless you also added poison to those vials, I highly doubt it."

"But the curse—"

"Another word about the curse and I will slap you in irons and leave you to spend the night in a cell, Mr. Weathers," Sebastian snapped, finally losing his patience.

Looking gratifyingly horrified, Guy Weathers pulled in his neck and stared at Sebastian from beneath his wispy brows. "I told you everything I know, Inspector."

Sebastian doubted that was true, but to spend any more time with Guy Weathers seemed a waste. He closed his notebook and stood, then asked one last question.

"Is there anyone here who has knowledge of poisons?"

"I beg your pardon?"

"Is there anyone here who has studied chemistry?" Sebastian reiterated.

"For the love of God, Inspector. We're actors. What do we know of chemistry?"

"Possibly nothing. But you certainly know all about devious ways to commit murder," Sebastian said, and walked out of the room.

FIVE

Given the number of individuals milling around backstage, Gemma expected at least one of them to stop her and ask where she was going, but no one paid her any mind. People stood in small clusters, talking quietly, and asking all the usual questions those left behind tended to ask when tragedy struck unexpectedly. How? Why? And most important, who? A few were crying softly, while others wore expressions of shock and kept looking around as they waited for someone to tell them what to do. One never knew how to behave in such a situation. Gemma recalled only too well her own bewilderment when she had learned that Victor had died. She hadn't known whether to sit, stand, grab her things and race to the scene of the accident, or simply curl into a ball and weep until there were no tears left in her body.

She didn't know how close the members of the troupe had been or who would grieve for Esme and Christopher once the initial shock wore off, but tonight they were all united by sadness and loss and joined in fear for the future. The loss of the lead actors was sure to affect each and every one of them, possibly even those who weren't part of the troupe. No one knew what tomorrow would bring, and sometimes that was the most terrifying thing of all.

Gemma hurried down the dimly lit corridor, careful not to catch her skirts on protruding objects or trip over coiled rope or props that had been carelessly left either lying about or stacked against the walls. She hoped the woman she had seen wasn't upstairs, since Gemma would have no cause to be up there or to barge into the private rooms of the actors, especially if the doors were shut.

She found the woman at last, in a small room at the rear of the building, huddled in a wingchair, her arms wrapped around her middle, her gaze fixed on nothing in particular. The room was cluttered with hanging garments, a dressmaker's dummy dressed in a half-finished gown, and a large table covered with swathes of fabric, shears, skeins of thread, thimbles, and pincushions. It had a large window that would provide natural light during the day, but now the glass panes were lit by moonlight and the woman was bathed in a silvery glow that made her look like a specter. She was no longer weeping but had the haunted look of someone who'd lost the most important thing in their life and didn't know if they could go on.

Gemma knocked on the doorjamb, and the woman's head jerked in surprise.

"May I come in?" Gemma asked.

The woman nodded, but the response was mechanical; she was probably just either too polite or too stunned by grief to ask Gemma to leave. As Gemma advanced into the moonlit room, she could make out the woman's features more clearly and realized she was younger than she had originally thought, probably no more than twenty-five. She had wide blue eyes and ginger hair that was loosely braided and pinned atop her head. Her face was as pale and round as the moon beyond the window, and even though she was seated it wasn't difficult to tell that she was short and plump.

"Who are ye?" the woman asked.

"My name is Gemma Tate. I'm a nurse, and I'm here with Inspector Bell."

"Inspector Bell?" The woman's Irish lilt was soft and lyrical and her gaze not quite focused as she no doubt tried to recall where she'd heard the name. "Where's Esme?" she asked, and sat up straighter, her expression suddenly fierce.

"Inspector Bell will have Esme and Christopher moved to a mortuary."

Gemma couldn't bring herself to refer to the beautiful young people as remains, especially not when the woman was so obviously grief-stricken. She didn't need to know that the victims would undergo a postmortem, most likely in Colin Ramsey's cellar, where their bodies would be taken apart and sewn back together like Frankenstein's monster. But unlike the monster, they would never be reanimated and given another chance at life. Colin would cover up the ugly seams with clothes and arrange their hair so they could look like themselves one more time before their caskets were nailed shut and lowered into the ground.

"I'm sorry for your loss," Gemma said as she inched into the room. "Did you know the victims well?"

Perhaps she should have asked only about Esme, since the woman hadn't mentioned Christopher Hudson. She and Esme had similar coloring, but it was unlikely that they were related, given that this woman was obviously Irish and Esme had been English; but, whatever their relationship, they must have shared a close bond.

"Victims?" the woman asked confusedly.

"Esme and Christopher did not die of natural causes."

"Was it murder like?"

"It would appear so."

"I knew it. That's diabolical, that is."

"What's your name?" Gemma asked gently.

"Mona. Mona Grady. I'm the sempstress."

"The costumes were stunning," Gemma said.

Mona nodded. "Esme's costume took weeks to make, but she looked like an angel, so she did."

"You obviously cared for her," Gemma said.

"She was..." Mona wasn't able to finish whatever she was about to say. Her face crumpled and she began to cry again, her anguish painful to behold. "I'll never get me miracle now," she whispered. "He's lost to me forever."

"Who's lost?" Gemma asked, but Mona waved her away.

"I'd like to be alone," Mona whimpered. "I can't help ye." She brought up her knees and buried her face in the fabric of her skirts, her shoulders quaking with sobs.

"Forgive me. I'm sorry to have bothered you, Miss Grady," Gemma said, and left the woman to her grief.

As she made her way down the corridor, Gemma spotted a girl of about sixteen. Her fair hair was tied back with a velvet ribbon and, although her pale blue gown was outdated, it looked clean. A wide strip of darker blue was sewn onto the hem, as if someone had used whatever they had to hand to make the skirt longer so the gown could last a few more years. The girl was sitting on a trunk and appeared to be lost in thought.

"Hello," Gemma said.

"Hello," the girl replied.

She was studying Gemma quite openly, so Gemma studied her in return. The girl's heart-shaped face was very pale, probably from lack of sunlight, and her brown eyes were wide with fawnlike innocence. She looked tired, and her sharp cheekbones and twiglike wrists spoke to a lack of proper nutrition.

"You're with that policeman," the girl observed.

"Yes. My name is Gemma Tate. I'm a nurse."

The girl nodded. "I reckon the play will close now. Shame that, since it was such a success."

"Are you part of the troupe?" The girl seemed eager to talk, and Gemma wasn't going to pass up an opportunity to learn something that might come in handy.

"I work for Mr. Bonneville. It's his theater."

"What do you do for Mr. Bonneville?" Gemma was genuinely curious, since she knew nothing of how a theater was run and what went on behind the curtain.

"I clean mostly, but I also sell tickets and work in the cloakroom. Just a dogsbody, really," she added with a shrug. "It's part of the arrangement. In return, Sid and I get to live here."

"You must be Rose," Gemma said, and the girl nodded.

It seemed odd that the children lived at the theater, but perhaps these were live-in positions, like those of domestic servants. Or maybe Rose and Sid's parents were somehow associated with the theater and lived on the premises as well.

Noting Gemma's confusion, Rose said, "Mr. Bonneville knew our father and took us in when he died. He lets us stay in the attic, so we don't have to spend money on lodgings. It suits us fine, but it does get cold in the winter."

"You must see everything that goes on backstage," Gemma said.

"We do," Rose said with a proud smile. "No one pays us any mind. Sid and I may as well be props."

"Can you think of anyone who'd want to harm Miss Royce and Mr. Hudson?"

Rose scoffed. "Who wouldn't want to harm those two?"

"Why do you say that?" Gemma asked, taken aback.

Rose's face took on a wistful quality. "There are many beautiful people in the world, Miss Tate, but they all wear their looks differently."

"What do you mean, Rose?"

"Well, take Miss Royce. She was lovely, no doubt about it, but her beauty was her weapon."

That was a surprising comment from one so young, but Gemma supposed Rose had seen more than most girls her age.

She didn't just watch the performances; she also saw what went on behind the scenes. If one was a student of human nature, the theater was certainly a fitting classroom.

"How did Esme use her beauty?" Gemma asked.

"She used it to get what she wanted," Rose replied simply.

"And what was it she wanted?"

Rose was about to reply when Mr. Weathers came striding down the corridor.

"Go outside and wait for the police, Rose," he barked. "Send them round the back way. I won't have a police wagon parked outside the front door."

"Yes, sir," Rose said, and slid off the trunk. It was only as she walked away that Gemma noticed the limp. Rose's right leg appeared to be shorter than her left, and she listed like a ship in a storm every time she put weight on her right foot.

The condition might be congenital, or the result of a fracture that hadn't been properly set at the time of the injury and had led to an unbalanced gait that put undue stress on the spine and hips. No wonder Rose looked so worn out. Gemma felt a wave of pity for the orphaned girl and hoped she had a comfortable place to sleep after she'd been on her feet all day. Somehow, living in a theater attic did not conjure up images of feather beds and warm blankets. At best, Rose probably slept on some lumpy cot or discarded prop that had found its way upstairs. Mr. Bonneville might have saved the children from living on the streets, but he didn't appear to have cared enough to look after them or make certain they got enough to eat.

SIX

Gemma had just spotted Sebastian, following Mr. Weathers closely, when a commotion by the back door signaled the arrival of the police. She was glad to see the tall form of Constable Meadows, who strode toward Sebastian with all the determination of a man eager to get an unpleasant task over with. Constable Forrest trailed behind him, his eyes round with wonder as he took in his surroundings. His gaze stopped on Serena Winthrop, who had taken off her stage makeup and costume and had come downstairs in nothing but a dressing gown, the middle-aged woman she'd portrayed in the play replaced by a beautiful young lady.

Serena had seen Constable Forrest looking, but her attention was all for Sebastian, whose scowl and barely suppressed irritation told Gemma all she needed to know. Serena's eyes were narrowed and her lips slightly parted, and she gazed at Sebastian with the rapture of a woman who'd never seen a more fascinating man. Gemma thought her admiration was feigned and wondered what she really wanted and why she had come down in a state of undress. Sebastian's gaze swept over Serena as if she were nothing more than a coat rack and returned to

Constable Meadows, who'd taken off his tall hat and was holding it under his arm as he addressed his superior.

"I'm sorry it took so long, Inspector. There was an over-turned carriage in Tavistock Street, and we couldn't get round."

"Where is Sid?" Sebastian asked, glancing toward the door.

"Stayed with the wagon," Constable Meadows explained. "The lad was eager to help, and if we had left the horses unat-tended we'd likely come back to an unhitched wagon."

Sid could hardly prevent a horse theft, but he could at least raise the alarm should someone be brazen enough to try, and Gemma thought he probably relished the task since he'd been so eager to ride with the constables.

"What would you have us do?" Constable Meadows asked.

"Retrieve the victims' bodies from the stage and deliver them to Mr. Ramsey," Sebastian said. "And take Miss Tate with you."

"What?" Gemma cried, outraged to be spoken of as if she were unclaimed baggage.

Sebastian turned and smiled apologetically, then walked over to her and took her hands in his. Gemma's anger dissipated when she saw the concern in his eyes. "Gemma, it's close to midnight, and Constable Meadows will see you safe."

"But you're not leaving," Gemma protested.

Constable Meadows raised a dark eyebrow, and Gemma felt heat rise in her cheeks. She sounded like a nagging wife, and was putting Sebastian in an awkward position, since he could hardly argue with her in front of the men. She forced her features to relax and drew her shoulders back. Her mother had always told her to be mindful of her posture, and just then she had been standing hunched over their joined hands in a manner that was most unbecoming.

"Thank you, Inspector," she said coolly. "I will leave with the constables as you suggest."

Sebastian nodded, and Gemma could sense his relief. He

had been bracing for a confrontation at a time when she should be the least of his worries.

"I will be leaving shortly as well," Sebastian said as he released her hands. "The actors are hungry and tired, and I can hardly interview everyone tonight."

"The super will be wanting a briefing first thing," Constable Meadows reminded him. "You know how he gets."

Sebastian nodded and turned to Mr. Weathers, who'd just come striding down the corridor. "Would you have anything to wrap the bodies in, Mr. Weathers?"

"I can spare some old curtains," Weathers said. "Will that do?"

"It will have to."

The manager went to fetch the curtains while the four others walked toward the stage. Sebastian walked ahead, with Constable Meadows behind him. Gemma and Constable Forrest brought up the rear.

The young constable's breathing was so ragged, Gemma couldn't help but ask, "Are you ill, Constable?"

"Just stuffy, miss, and my head feels awful heavy."

"You might want to try a hot toddy, and Dr. Greely's Nasal Douche is most effective for nasal congestion," Gemma said.

"My mother is a devotee of Cigares de Joy. She says they help with stuffiness and clear the lungs right up as well. A miracle cure."

"You may as well bend over and have your mother blow smoke up your arse," Constable Meadows quipped. "You'll be cured in no time."

Constable Forrest turned an angry red and seemed ready to respond to the insult, but the words died on his lips when he caught sight of the victims. Esme Royce and Christopher Hudson had been beautiful in life, but now, after nearly two hours lying on an empty stage, they resembled what they were—human remains. The bodies looked like they had fallen off the back of a wagon and brought back memories of the carts Gemma had seen through the hospital windows in Scutari, the creaking conveyances piled high and moving slowly as they took the fallen soldiers on their final journey to the yawning mass grave at a nearby burial ground. If a body rolled off the cart, the two porters whose job it was to dispose of the dead simply stopped, picked up the corpse, and tossed it on top of the pile as if it were nothing more than a sack of turnips.

Of all the things Gemma had seen during those dark days, that was one of the saddest and most sobering, since it had forced her to see just how little anyone cared or how inconsequential an individual really was, especially once they were no longer of any use. The trappings of a decent burial were not for the dead but for the living, meant to make those left behind feel better about what awaited them when their time came, but in Scutari feelings weren't taken into consideration. As Gemma stared at Esme and Christopher, their still faces bathed in flickering gaslight, she wondered if anyone would bother to organize a funeral or if the bodies would be consigned to the dead house once Colin was finished with them and all that was left was to put them in the ground before they began to putrefy.

The men remained silent as they spread the curtains on the floor, then lifted each body and wrapped them in their makeshift shrouds. Gemma offered to help, but Sebastian shook his head and called over Guy Weathers, who took hold of Esme's ankles while Sebastian hefted her by the shoulders. The two constables lifted Christopher Hudson's body, and the four men carried their burdens off the stage and toward the door that led to the alley. Gemma followed and watched as the victims were loaded in the wagon, side by side.

"Inside or outside, Miss Tate?" Constable Meadows asked once the constables were ready to leave.

Rolling up to Colin's house on the bench of a police wagon was probably not the most dignified way to arrive, but to ride in the back with the deceased with just a narrow grille to offer a glimpse of the night sky was even less appealing, so Gemma hitched up her skirts and accepted Sebastian's help as he handed her up. Sid, who she was happy to see wore a shabby coat and woolen cap, reluctantly surrendered the reins to Constable Meadows, while Constable Forrest climbed into the back of the wagon. The hinges squealed as Sebastian shut and bolted the wagon door.

"I want to be a policeman when I grow up," Sid said as he looked up at Gemma from the ground. He didn't seem in any hurry to go inside, and patted the rump of the horse closest to him affectionately.

"It's a very worthy profession," Gemma said. "But until that happens, isn't it time you went to bed?"

Sid shrugged. "Rose doesn't care when I go to sleep. She's not my mother."

"Inside with you," Sebastian said, then, once the boy had disappeared through the door, reached for Gemma's hand.

"I will see you tomorrow," he promised.

Gemma nodded and squeezed his hand. "Goodnight, Sebastian."

She glanced back when the wagon reached the mouth of the alley, but Sebastian had already gone inside, and she heard the heavy door slam shut behind him.

SEVEN

When Sebastian finally got home, all the windows were dark and the front door securely locked. Mrs. Poole didn't furnish her lodgers with individual keys, but she did keep a spare hidden behind a loose brick by the back door, a trick Sebastian had taught her. After unlocking the door, Sebastian returned the key to its hiding place and trotted up the stairs in the dark.

As usual, his rooms were cold and damp, and tonight they reeked of cat piss since Gustav had been on his own since Sebastian had left that morning. Gustav was nowhere to be seen, and, as Sebastian hung up his hat and shrugged off his coat, he hoped that the cat hadn't retaliated against him for this slight by fouling his bed. Without bothering to light an oil lamp —there was enough moonlight to see by—he removed the reeking newspaper from the litter box, shoved it into a bucket he kept for that purpose and closed the lid, then lined the box with clean newspaper and walked through to the bedroom.

Sebastian always left the curtains open, since entering a pitch-dark room made him feel like he was walking into a tomb. The white bedlinens were the only bright spot in an otherwise dark interior, and Gustav, damn his eyes, was stretched out on

Sebastian's pillow, his furry backside right about where Sebastian's face would be, his pale eyes reflecting the moonlight like shards of green glass.

"Get off," Sebastian growled, and smacked the cat gently on the rump. Gustav gave him the stink-eye and emitted an outraged meow in return, but graciously moved over.

Sebastian was hungry, but there was nothing to eat since Mrs. Poole strictly forbade her lodgers from keeping food in their rooms. The only exception was the occasional fish for Gustav, who received special treatment because he was so proficient at hunting mice. Although sorely tempted to help himself to some of the brandy Mrs. Poole had given him for Christmas, Sebastian resisted the urge, knowing he'd probably finish the bottle and then feel awful come morning. He hadn't had a drop in nearly three months and only kept the bottle on display to test his resolve and prove to himself once and for all that he had conquered his demons, and spirits and opium no longer held any sway over him.

Instead, he turned over the pillow, divested himself of his clothes, and climbed into bed. Gustav immediately fitted himself to Sebastian's side, a clear indication that he was forgiven. Although physically tired, Sebastian was fully awake. He was always like this at the start of a new case, his mind buzzing like a hive as he tried to make sense of what he'd seen and heard and arrange the information he'd gathered into some sort of discernible pattern. It was too soon to determine which bits were relevant and which were just random facts that had nothing to do with the case and would only distract him from getting to the truth.

Letting everyone leave the theater had been a risk, and he would no doubt have to justify his decision to Superintendent Lovell tomorrow, but Sebastian could hardly keep everyone there all night. He had taken down the names of everyone present and made a mental note of which face went with which entry. He had then searched the dressing rooms of the deceased but found nothing to arouse his suspicion. That was all he could have reasonably done, since he had been working blind without the postmortem results and was miles away from establishing a motive. He didn't believe that the deaths had been the result of a freak accident, since he'd seen nothing to support that supposition, but there was one possibility he'd failed to consider. The double murder could in fact have been an elaborate suicide, which would explain the lack of evidence and account for the impeccable timing; but deep down, Sebastian couldn't quite embrace that theory.

Could the two young actors have been so skilled at their craft and so emotionally detached that they could have performed a nearly three-hour play before finally dying on stage? Sebastian had met people who'd given in to despair. He'd been one of those people himself not so long ago, and he thought he could recognize the haunted look of someone who'd lost all hope. In the two actors, he hadn't noticed any dead-eyed stares or the slow movements that were a symptom of complete apathy and a lack of energy or motivation. He couldn't fathom going through the motions or summoning the emotional reserves required to perform for hours before reaching the final act, and still going through with the plan. Esme had been luminous, her face animated and her gaze reflecting whatever feeling she was meant to evoke during a particular scene. Christopher had been passionate, obsessed, and burning with lust for the woman before him. The two actors were probably more alive for the duration of the play than anyone in the audience, whose pleasure in the performance was utterly passive.

Still, it was possible that what the audience had witnessed had been suicide. Despite every major religion branding self-murder a mortal sin, there were those who saw suicide as romantic, the ultimate expression of feeling that was to be admired rather than condemned. A conversation Mrs. Poole had engaged in with the now-deceased Herr Schweiger suddenly came to mind. Helmut Schweiger had liked to talk about his native Germany and had sometimes used literary examples to make a point. Grieving and completely numb to everything around him after the deaths of Louisa and their baby boy, Sebastian had paid little attention to Herr Schweiger's ramblings, but he now recalled that the man had mentioned suicide clusters. He'd called it the Werther effect. Sebastian must have absorbed more than he'd realized because now that he thought back, he also remembered that the phenomenon had been named after Goethe's novel *The Sorrows of Young Werther*. The story had been deemed responsible for a drastic increase in suicides among young men who had believed themselves unlucky in love.

Sebastian thought it not only ludicrous but highly dangerous to romanticize the taking of one's life, but he supposed it was possible that some young people might become enamored of the idea of tragic death, the same way they embraced the ridiculous dictates of fashion or threw themselves into newfangled pursuits. And who better to fixate on the deaths of tragic young lovers than the actors playing tragic young lovers?

And there was another possibility as well, Sebastian thought as he absentmindedly stroked Gustav's silky head. Rather than double suicide, the deaths could have been the result of a murder–suicide, where either Esme or Christopher had decided to take matters into their own hands and end whatever unhappy relationship the two stars had become embroiled in. Somehow, this scenario seemed even sadder and was probably more difficult to prove, unless one or the other had made verbal threats that might have been overheard by someone at the theater.

But although these theories were viable and definitely worth exploring, Sebastian's copper's instinct told him he was dealing with a double homicide and the victims had not had a say in anything that had happened tonight. As he gazed upon the moon that cast the rooftops of London in a silvery haze, he couldn't help but feel crushing sadness for the two people whose bodies now lay in Colin's cellar, wrapped in dusty old curtains. They had been so gloriously alive only a few hours ago, their passion and skill keeping the audience rapt as they acted out a centuries-old tragedy, both completely unaware that within minutes they would go the way of the doomed lovers.

Despite his sorrow and the helpless rage he felt when faced with senseless death, Sebastian had to admit that he felt a minuscule degree of admiration for the killer. The majority of killers were stupid, unimaginative, inherently violent, and surprisingly predictable, which was why they were ultimately caught, but a select few were truly brilliant, their acts of malice so Machiavellian that Sebastian had to give credit where credit was due. Whoever was responsible for the deaths of Esme and Christopher was in a class by themselves, a killer so cool it would take all Sebastian's experience and skill to unmask them.

Tired of thinking about death, Sebastian turned his thoughts to life, namely Gemma, whose birthday was in a few weeks. He wanted to get her a gift, but the more he weighed his options the more paralyzed with indecision he became. What did one get a woman who was beautiful, intelligent, fiercely independent, and not quite his? The gift had to be something uniquely personal yet not too forward or inappropriate. It also had to express Sebastian's deep regard without causing Gemma to feel uncomfortable or beholden to him in any way. Sebastian knew the answer would come to him, but at the moment he had no idea. When he finally fell asleep, it was with the image of Gemma front and center in his mind, her green eyes luminous with affection and her smile absolving him of his every shortcoming.

EIGHT

WEDNESDAY, MARCH 16

The morning dawned stormy and frigid, and by the time Sebastian arrived at Scotland Yard he was cold, wet, and feeling unusually short-tempered for so early in the day. The duty room was quiet, just Sergeant Woodward sipping his tea and reading the morning edition of the *Daily Telegraph*, as he did most mornings until the daily assortment of riffraff was hauled in and things got lively. For a moment, Sebastian wondered if he might like Sergeant Woodward's job, but he immediately decided he would be bored to tears within a week, a realization that dramatically improved his mood.

"Quite a hullabaloo last night, eh?" Woodward said by way of greeting.

"Is it in the papers already?" Sebastian asked.

He had passed at least three newsboys on the way to the Yard, but the headlines had made no mention of the Orpheus, which was to be expected since the morning editions would have been typeset by the time the deaths had occurred last night. The earliest the stories would make it into the papers would be the evening editions, and that was only if someone got wind of what had happened and brought it to their editor in time.

"Nah. Not yet," Woodward replied as he folded the paper and set it aside. "But Constable Forrest was here bright and early, regaling anyone who would listen with his morbid tale. Rather fortunate you happened to be in the audience."

"Is it?" Sebastian asked as he took off his dripping coat and draped it over his arm.

"Lovell can hardly assign the case to someone else. And a high-profile murder will keep you in the game, so to speak."

"What game is that?" Sebastian asked in an indifferent tone. He knew precisely what Sergeant Woodward was referring to and had decided he didn't care to get into it.

Rumor had it that Lovell was to be replaced by Inspector Ransome, who'd recently married the commissioner's daughter and was now Sir David's golden boy, but the gossip mill had been going full tilt since December, and they had yet to hear anything definite. Until Sebastian was presented with fact rather than conjecture, he wasn't going to comment publicly or align himself with either man.

"I know you like to keep your cards close to your chest, Seb, but you'll have to show your hand eventually," Woodward said. "There's strength in numbers, you know."

"In a democracy, maybe. Is Lovell in?" Sebastian asked, thus preempting Woodward's pitch.

He had no time to waste, not when he had to interview a dozen people and obtain the postmortem results, which probably wouldn't be available until later in the afternoon. Colin had to autopsy two people and wasn't the sort to rush through a postmortem for the sake of expediency.

"Lovell's in his office and looking rather down in the mouth," Woodward replied. He clearly hadn't given up on drawing Sebastian into a discussion, but Sebastian didn't take the bait and strode down the empty corridor toward Superintendent Lovell's office. The door was closed, so he knocked and waited.

"Come," Lovell called. "And shut the door behind you," he instructed as soon as Sebastian had entered the office.

"Good morning, sir." Sebastian hung his coat and hat on the coat rack in the corner and turned to face the superintendent.

"It may be for some," Lovell replied glumly.

A few months ago, this sort of remark would have been out of character, but since then Lovell's usual brusque efficiency had been replaced with sarcasm and angry outbursts that he didn't even try to control.

"Have a seat, Bell."

Sebastian settled in the guest chair and waited. If Sergeant Woodward was aware of what had happened at the Orpheus, then so was Lovell, but the superintendent, who normally went directly to the crux of the matter, leaned back in his chair and fixed Sebastian with a speculative look instead.

"I suppose you already know," he said.

"Know what, sir?"

"Don't play coy with me, Bell. There isn't a man at this station who doesn't know and hasn't expressed his opinion on the matter, albeit behind my back."

Sebastian waited, since anything he said at this juncture would be the wrong thing.

"I met with Sir David on Monday. It has been decided. Ransome will succeed me as superintendent as soon as he returns from his rather lengthy wedding trip. It would appear that nepotism trumps loyalty and experience every time. I really shouldn't have expected anything else, not when the previous Home Secretary's clodhopper of a nephew had already been forced on me and given credit for cases he never could have solved on his own."

"I'm sorry, sir."

"I can either announce my imminent retirement or air my

grievances, which would be bad form." Lovell smiled bitterly. "If I am to be replaced by a younger man, I'd rather it be you, Sebastian, but you're not mercenary enough to marry the commissioner's daughter in order to move up the ranks and, if you were, I probably wouldn't back you."

"I have no desire to become superintendent, sir," Sebastian said.

"Whyever not?"

"I'm not the sort of man who would be happy to sit behind a desk."

"No, I don't suppose you are," Lovell agreed. "You're a man of action, not a sniveling weasel who relishes wheeling and dealing and getting his name in the papers. I hate to admit it, but Ransome is probably the right man for the position, since the better part of my job is putting a good face on our failures and courting favorable public opinion in order to assure funding for the Metropolitan Police. Ransome has what it takes to walk that line between policing and politicking, and at least half the men in this station wholeheartedly agree. Out with the old and in with the new, especially when the new is someone who comes from their ranks and understands their plight."

Sebastian was growing weary of Lovell's bellyaching, which he'd been subjected to several times over the past few months. Lovell had to either fight back, or accept defeat and walk away with his head held high and his reputation intact. To ask his men to choose was neither gentlemanly nor fair, since the men had no say in the appointment and would have to accept whatever was decided with good grace. There were those among them who genuinely cared about order and justice, but most had joined the police service because it was a better alternative to becoming clerks or laborers or joining the army. They needed to support their families and couldn't afford to rock the boat too hard for fear of falling overboard, something Lovell didn't fully understand since he had come from money and had never had to worry about putting food on the table.

"About the case, sir," Sebastian interjected.

Lovell's demeanor changed instantly, the superintendent having seemingly realized that his rant was neither appropriate nor appreciated. "Tell me what happened last night."

Sebastian relayed the facts and watched Lovell's reaction. He appeared surprised at first, then became a little dubious.

"Are you sure it was even murder, Bell?"

"Are you suggesting that two young people died within moments of each other due to natural causes?"

"Well, perhaps there's some other explanation. Do you recall the couple in Clerkenwell that died by asphyxiation? Gas leak in the bedroom."

"Eight other actors shared the stage with the deceased over the course of several hours, and there were a dozen or more people in the front row, and no one else was affected. I did not smell gas when I came up on stage, and none of the light fixtures appeared to be damaged. Unless it was an elaborate suicide, which I doubt, it was murder, sir."

"Hmm," Lovell said. "I'm not fully convinced."

The superintendent's reaction was so odd that Sebastian suddenly wondered if there might be another reason for Sir David's decision. Perhaps it had become apparent that Lovell had lost his edge, or maybe Lovell didn't want his last well-publicized case to prove an embarrassment and wanted to hand-pick a case he could feed to the newspapers in order to safe-guard his reputation. Such maneuvering wasn't really in keeping with Lovell's character, but neither was his lack of interest in what had to be double homicide.

"So, what are your thoughts?" Lovell finally asked when Sebastian failed to agree with his assessment and see himself out.

"I think Esme Royce and Christopher Hudson were poisoned."

"Which means it had to be one of the other actors. Professional jealousy," Lovell announced with the finality of someone who'd just solved the case and wasn't open to any other possibilities.

"Not necessarily," Sebastian argued.

"What other reason would someone have to murder two actors? What would they have to gain?"

"That's what I intend to find out."

Lovell smirked. "You're assuming it's your case, Bell."

"I was there when it happened, sir. Who else would you assign it to?"

"I could give it to Inspector Reece," Lovell mused.

Sebastian bit his tongue. Inspector Reece was a bungling idiot, but Lovell could take the case away from Sebastian just to spite the men who had made him feel old and expendable. Perhaps he was now willing to sacrifice his reputation and that of the service for petty revenge.

Lovell made a show of thinking, then said, "No, you take it. Until I walk through that door for the last time, I am still in charge, and I want my best man on this."

"Thank you, sir."

"And Bell," Lovell said, the warning in his tone unmistakable, "I don't want Miss Tate anywhere near this."

"She was at the theater, sir."

"Yes, I'm aware, but that doesn't mean you have to involve her in your investigation. The men don't like it, Bell."

"What is it they object to?" Sebastian asked, doing his best to keep his anger in check, since he knew precisely what the issue was.

"That business at the Foundling Hospital left some questioning your judgment and feeling denigrated by your cheap stunt. Scotland Yard is no place for a woman. Bringing Miss

Tate here was an insult to the hardworking men who risk their lives daily to fight crime in this city."

"May I remind you that it was Miss Tate who apprehended the killer, sir?"

"To your everlasting shame," Lovell snapped. "Miss Tate is a clever woman, I'll grant you that, but her meddling in matters that don't concern her will not be tolerated. Make no mistake, Bell, I'm still your superior, and I can render you unemployable should I choose to do so. Do you understand?"

"I do," Sebastian ground out.

A sly smile tugged at Lovell's colorless lips. "If you are so enamored of the chit, marry her, and give her something to occupy her time besides snooping and engaging in unseemly physical altercations. Respectable women feel most fulfilled within the bounds of marriage, Sebastian. I daresay you could use the love of a good woman, given your recent past. I trust Miss Tate is not too old to bear you children?"

Blood pounded in Sebastian's temples, and his hands unwittingly balled into fists. How dare Lovell speak of Gemma that way, and how dare he belittle her contribution to cases that had earned Lovell a pat on the back from the commissioner? Gemma was more intelligent and intuitive than half the inspectors on the Yard's payroll but, because she was a woman, her experience and ability were not only dismissed but made to sound as if she were somehow unnatural, a condition that could only be remedied by marriage and motherhood.

Sebastian took a deep breath and forced himself to relax, splaying his hands on his thighs before Lovell could notice his reaction and turn it against him. The superintendent was angry and bitter, and lashing out at Sebastian because he felt helpless and unsupported. To sully the character of an innocent woman was beneath him, but it wasn't Gemma he ultimately took issue with; it was Sebastian. Perhaps Lovell was right, and Sebastian had allowed his judgment to become clouded. Gemma had been in very real danger, and it was Sebastian's job not only as a policeman but also as a man to protect her from harm. He'd have a word with Gemma later, but right now he had to get away from Lovell before he said something he would later regret.

"If that will be all, Superintendent."

Lovell made a dismissive gesture. "I expect an update by the end of the day."

"Yes, sir."

Sebastian took his things and left the office, passing Sergeant Woodward on the way out.

"Did he tell you about his meeting with Sir David?" Woodward asked sourly.

"He did. Perhaps retirement is not such a bad idea," Sebastian replied.

"I never took you for a turncoat," Woodward snapped.

"And I never took you for a man who's intimidated by intelligent women."

Sebastian was in no doubt that Sergeant Woodward was one of the men who'd spoken out against Gemma and her involvement in the Foundling Hospital case. Woodward was a decent sort, but like most men he held a firm opinion on the role of a woman. Unless the woman was a mother, a wife, or a daughter, he had no use for her, and even if they were family their claim on him was limited, since he didn't spend much time at home.

"Be careful, Sebastian," Sergeant Woodward said, his tone grave. "You're skating on thin ice."

"Then you'd better keep off the ice, or we'll both go down."

Woodward's nostrils flared with anger, but Sebastian turned away, unwilling to continue their argument. "Constable Bryant, you're with me," he said when the young man entered the duty room.

Constable Bryant snapped to attention. "Yes, sir."

"Let's find a cab," Sebastian said as they stepped outside and were immediately assailed by gusty wind and lashing rain.

"Yes, sir," Constable Bryant said again. Despite the weather, he had a twinkle in his eye and a spring in his step, and his dripping top hat sat at a jaunty angle. "I was hoping you'd ask for me, Inspector Bell," he said happily. "I won't let you down."

"See that you don't." Sebastian smiled at the young man, recalling the eager young bobby he himself had been fifteen years ago. "Let's go, then. We have a case to solve."

NINE

Gemma felt sluggish when she awoke, in both body and mind. She was partial to tea in the morning, but now she asked Mabel for coffee, and had to drink two cups in quick succession before the brain fog started to lift and she felt more alert. Anne had been terribly agitated when Gemma had arrived home with the constables, and, while Colin had gone to see to the morbid contents of the wagon, Gemma had spent nearly two hours trying to get her charge to bed. She had been so tired when she'd finally crawled under the sheets herself just before three o'clock that she had fallen into a dead sleep, only to be woken by Anne at seven, when the older woman had rung the bell and asked for help with her morning routine.

Thankfully, Anne seemed to have no recollection of how the previous night had ended and had suffered no adverse effects. She was in good spirits, talking animatedly about the play and praising the actors' performances over a hearty breakfast of eggs and kippers accompanied by buttered toast with marmalade and several cups of tea. Gemma applied herself to a soft-boiled egg and toast and, after much deliberation, poured a third cup of coffee and added cream and sugar for good measure.

Colin was uncharacteristically quiet, his gaze thoughtful as he met Gemma's eyes across the table. He was clearly eager to discuss the tragedy but didn't care to do so in front of his mother or Mabel, who'd just brought a fresh pot of tea and more toast. Tossing his napkin on the table as if he were throwing down a gauntlet, Colin excused himself, pushed away from the table, and hurried off, no doubt impatient to begin and either prove or disprove his theories.

Gemma would have liked to join Colin in the cellar, but she had a job to do, work that was necessary but at times mind-numbingly dull and surprisingly difficult. Had the weather been fair, she would have taken Anne for a walk, but it was bucketing down, so they would have to remain indoors. Anne didn't have the patience to listen to Gemma read to her, prob-ably because she could no longer follow the plot, so they usually played cards to while away the hours.

Reversis or Old Maid were Anne's favorites. The card games were simple enough that Gemma didn't have to concen-trate too hard and could allow her mind to wander, which at times was even worse than answering endless questions or repeating the same explanations over and over until Anne finally grasped her meaning. When given free rein, Gemma's thoughts inevitably returned to the same worries and arguments that plagued her during the interminable hours of darkness when she couldn't sleep and fretted endlessly about the future, which now seemed more uncertain than ever.

Looking after Anne and helping her to navigate her cruel illness gave Gemma purpose and allowed her to support herself at a time when she was alone in the world. But the temporary security of her position and the gratitude she saw in Anne's eyes weren't enough to satisfy her longing, not only for more exciting work but also for the emotional contentment that continued to elude her. Although Gemma had forbidden herself to think of Lucy, the little girl she had come to love while working at the Foundling Hospital, Lucy was frequently in Gemma's thoughts, and she had once even gone so far as to walk past the hospital during the children's daily walk in the hope of catching a glimpse of the child. Gemma had never since given in to this weakness, despite feeling her loss so keenly, and had sworn never to go near the hospital again. If Lucy saw her, she would run to the gates and either demand an explanation for Gemma's abandonment or beg Gemma to take her away, a scene neither would walk away from with her heart intact.

Gemma kept Lucy in her prayers and hoped that she had forgotten Gemma and was adapting to her situation, but, having treated the child for malnutrition due to severe anxiety, Gemma feared that Lucy might be ill once again, and felt that this time it was Gemma's fault. What she wouldn't give for an update on Lucy's condition but, since her involvement in a murder investigation, Gemma was persona non grata at the hospital and could hardly march up to the gates and demand to speak to Matron or approach one of the mistresses, who weren't likely to speak to her.

Despite the long hours and strict rules of the institution, Gemma missed the Foundling Hospital and the children she had helped to care for, and she longed for the sound of laughter and the sweet innocence of the boys and girls who had brought life into her otherwise lonely days. She also missed the company of other employees and the camaraderie that developed between them, unmarried women in need of adult companionship. She hadn't grown as close with the teachers as she had with the nurses at Scutari, but it had been nice to join the others for meals and have a cozy chat with Miss Landry, who had always managed to shock Gemma with some titillating tidbit of hospital gossip.

Spending hours with Anne left Gemma feeling lonely and

frustrated, but she couldn't seek a new situation again so soon, not when Colin had been so kind to her and depended on her to look after the one person he loved most in the world. Besides, Gemma had come to care for Anne and couldn't justify causing her any more suffering than she was already enduring. Colin did his best to offer Gemma easy, undemanding companionship, particularly once Anne had retired and it was just the two of them for the rest of the evening, but the tenderness Gemma saw in his eyes when he thought she wasn't looking only served to remind her that perhaps she had been too hasty in accepting his offer. She couldn't help but wonder if Colin's motives when it came to protecting her reputation had to do with his feelings for her, which would eventually make it impossible to remain in the Ramsey household once her mourning period was at an end and she could finally permit Sebastian to court her openly.

In the meantime, she had to do her job and wait for an opportunity to speak to Colin in private. By midmorning, the lack of sleep had caught up with Anne, so Gemma escorted her to her room and helped her to bed, then locked the door behind her. It broke her heart to have to lock Anne in like a prisoner, but it was for her own safety and Colin's peace of mind. He still talked about the time Anne had walked out into a December afternoon wearing nothing but her nightdress and wandered all the way to St. Paul's Cathedral, where Sebastian had found her in front of the memorial to John Donne, barefoot and freezing as she gazed upon what she'd thought was her husband's likeness. Anne had no recollection of that day or of the panic she had caused, but Colin wasn't going to take any more chances with his mother's health and safety.

As Gemma returned downstairs, she wondered where Sebastian was at that very moment and if he had made any progress on the case. She hadn't had a chance to speak to him privately last night and wanted to tell him about her conversations with Mona and Rose. Neither had imparted anything that seemed important, but one never knew what might become relevant in the course of an investigation.

"May I come in?" Gemma asked once she'd knocked and pushed open the heavy door to the cellar.

Death had been part of Gemma's every waking hour while nursing in Crimea, but the odor that hit her when she entered the cellar was like a punch to the gut. In Scutari, the deceased had been carted off almost immediately, not only to prevent contamination but also to make room for incoming patients, who had often been left lying on the floor and in the corridors due to a shortage of beds. Colin's *patients* were rarely as fresh, and the stench of putrefaction had wormed its way into the very walls, making the cellar smell like a dead house. Colin didn't seem to notice. All his attention was for the bodies that found their way to his dissecting table, and his need to understand and learn from them overrode any physical discomfort.

Colin glanced up from his work when Gemma called out to him. He hastily pulled a sheet over Esme, covering her entirely, but not before Gemma caught a glimpse of a yawning chest cavity and Esme's still face, her eyes mercifully closed. Gemma hated to see Esme that way and looked away, willing herself to remember the young woman as she had been last night before she had tipped the contents of the vial into her mouth and been transformed from a living, breathing person into this silent husk. Christopher was still wrapped in his shroud, the body laid out on a cot by the wall, but now that Colin was almost finished with Esme he would be opening the young man up as well.

"Did you discover something?" Gemma asked as she approached the table.

She thought Colin might ask her to leave, since tender regard for women was ingrained in his nature and he always tried to protect her from anything she might find distressing, but Colin clearly resisted the urge, and shook his head. It was obvious to Gemma that he wanted to discuss his findings, and until Sebastian arrived there was no one else he could talk to, since he didn't allow private students to practice on the cadavers until Scotland Yard got the postmortem results and had no further use for the corpse.

"Esme Royce was a healthy young woman," Colin said, his sorrow for Esme etched into his features. "You and I both know that her death wasn't a result of an undetected illness or accidental injury. Someone murdered her, and the killing was almost certainly premeditated. The only kindness the killer did her was to spare her the agony that comes with other forms of execution. Esme would have known something was wrong, but she wouldn't have had much time to dwell on what was happening. She would have slipped away before she realized there was no hope."

Gemma nodded. She had been thinking the same thing. "Esme and Christopher were poisoned, and the only substance I can think of that would cause such a quick, non-violent death is morphine."

"Yes," Colin agreed. "Any other toxin would elicit an obvious physical reaction."

"Precisely. There would be convulsions, disorientation, vomiting, and loosening of the bowels."

Colin nodded. "But a lethal dose of morphine would present as airway obstruction, flaccid limbs, and finally slowed breathing and heart rate, which would eventually result in death. Physical manifestations that the audience would attribute to Juliet dying of a knife-inflicted wound and Romeo succumbing to poison."

Colin turned toward a worktop where he kept surgical tools and bowls of various sizes, and picked up one of the two vials Gemma had brought from the theater last night. It was the plain brown one that Romeo had purchased from the apothecary. "Before I share my findings with Sebastian, I would like to test my theory."

"And how do you intend to do that?" Gemma asked, a shiver of apprehension running up her spine.

"It is my assumption that Christopher died first, even though he drank the poison some minutes after Esme. This would mean that his dose was considerably higher and faster-acting. Christopher drained the contents in full view of the audience, but there's bound to be residue in the bottom of the vial."

"Have you found a way to test it?" Gemma asked.

The Marsh test was frequently used to check for the presence of arsenic, particularly in cases where arsenic was believed to have been used as a murder weapon, but she hadn't heard of any test that would isolate morphine and didn't see any items in the cellar that might be used in an experiment. Colin mostly used scalpels, saws, and clamps that helped him get a better look inside the body.

"I think I have," Colin replied, and smiled ruefully. "But it's not a scientific experiment you would have heard of."

He set the vial on the worktop, then went to a cabinet and rummaged inside until he found a dropper. He then poured a spoonful of water from a bottle he kept on the counter into a shallow bowl and returned the bottle to its place.

"What do you mean to do?" Gemma asked, alarmed.

Colin filled the dropper with water, added a few drops to the empty vial, then pressed his thumb over the opening and shook the contents almost violently.

"I've had a terrible headache since last night. I think it was the stress of the situation combined with the onset of stormy weather. I tend to get headaches when there are sudden changes in atmospheric pressure," he explained. "If this is indeed morphine, then my headache will begin to improve within a few minutes."

"And if it isn't morphine but some other highly dangerous

poison?" Gemma asked, surprised that Colin would so cavalierly ingest an unknown substance.

"Then I will get ill," Colin replied matter-of-factly. "A few drops will not kill me. The worst that might happen is that I will feel nauseated and get stomach cramps."

"That's reckless and uncalled for," Gemma cried. "And I will not be party to it."

Colin seemed gratified by Gemma's concern and smiled warmly. "My dear Gemma, it would be reckless if I were on my own, but I will conduct my experiment in the presence of a highly competent, well-trained nurse. Should the worst happen, which I very much doubt it will, you will know what to do."

"You mean stick two fingers down your throat," Gemma replied, her mind instantly supplying the unwelcome image and its aftermath.

"Precisely. Vomiting will expel the toxin from my body. Will you help me? I can't undertake this trial without your consent."

"That's not fair," Gemma retorted.

"Perhaps not, but it will go a long way toward helping Sebastian solve this case."

"I can't believe I'm even considering this," Gemma muttered, but deep down she knew she would agree. This was the only way to test the poison, and, if Colin was willing to take the risk, the least she could do was make certain he didn't suffer any ill effects. "All right, but if the results are inconclusive you have to give up this madness and promise me you won't try again."

"You have my word."

Colin tipped the contents of the vial into his mouth and swallowed, then smacked his lips. "Tastes a bit like laudanum, but laudanum would put the victims to sleep. A small amount wouldn't kill them."

"How do you feel?" Gemma asked after several minutes

had elapsed. Colin didn't look any different, and she didn't see any cause for concern.

"I feel fine," Colin said as he reached for the skein of silk thread and curved needle that he needed to close the body. He threaded the needle but didn't pull back the sheet. "I would prefer that you didn't watch this."

"I won't leave you alone."

"I'm all right," Colin said. "In fact, my headache is all but gone."

"So quickly?"

"Morphine is a very powerful drug. When used properly, it can offer unequaled pain relief, but like any drug it can also be fatal." Colin shook his head and sighed heavily. "Hundreds of people witnessed a heinous crime but had no idea that was what they had seen."

"Do you think the killer has a keen understanding of poisons?" Gemma asked, her mind leaping ahead to the person instead of focusing on their crime.

"They would have to be knowledgeable enough to understand what would happen once the poison was ingested, and which substance would best serve their needs."

"Unfortunately, that theory doesn't point to a suspect," Gemma said.

"No, it does not. Whoever did this will not readily admit to a knowledge of poisonous substances, not if they're as clever as I think they are." Colin cocked his head and looked at Gemma. "Sebastian must be told."

"He is probably at the theater."

"I would go, but I'm expecting my pupils. This is a teaching opportunity not to be missed. They can observe Christopher's postmortem."

"How did they know you would be performing a postmortem this morning?" Gemma asked.

Colin smiled guiltily. "I invited them. I won't allow them to touch the remains, but there's much they can learn by observing."

"I'll go," Gemma said.

They both turned at the sound of the cellar door opening. Mabel put her head around the door but didn't venture inside. "I'm sorry to interrupt, but Mrs. Ramsey is calling for you, Miss Tate," she called out.

"Not to worry," Colin said. "Sebastian will find his way here soon enough. Best see to Mother."

Gemma nodded and left Colin to it.

TEN

When Sebastian and Constable Bryant arrived at Mrs. Dillane's boarding house, they were greeted by a friendly, pink-cheeked young woman who turned out to be the proprietress. Mrs. Dillane informed them as soon as Sebastian introduced himself that the entire troupe had departed after an early breakfast. She made no mention of the deceased lodgers and seemed eager to get back to whatever she had been doing.

"Where did they go?" Sebastian asked, suddenly worried that he'd made a grave mistake by allowing the actors to return to the boarding house. Perhaps they were all complicit in the murders and were now miles away, traveling one of the many roads that led out of the city or already aboard a train bound for God-knew-where. If that were to happen, Sebastian would face dismissal and professional disgrace; but the alternative would have been to herd the entire troupe, including all the other individuals who had been present backstage last night, to Scotland Yard and lock them up without a shred of evidence. The choice had been obvious.

"Mr. Weathers asked me to convey that they'll be at the

theater," Mrs. Dillane replied. "I believe they have rehearsal this morning."

"Rehearsal?"

"It will be a full house tonight, Inspector," she stated proudly, as if she were a member of the troupe and the success of tonight's performance hinged on her efforts. Sebastian supposed that Mrs. Dillane was understandably invested in the continued success of the troupe, since she would lose all her lodgers at once if they were to pack up and take their show on the road.

"Thank you, ma'am," Sebastian said, and tipped his hat.

"Good morning to you, Inspector," Mrs. Dillane said, and shut the door in his face.

The deluge had finally stopped, and the air was thick with moisture. The trees were weeping rainwater, and gauzy tendrils of mist veiled the buildings in a nearly impenetrable shroud. The dark outlines of horses materialized out of the fog, their manes damp and their ears pressed back as they trotted down a road they probably couldn't quite see. The wagons and carriages they pulled moved silently, the squelching of wheels in the mud and the creaking of wood muted by the heavy air.

Sebastian gestured to Constable Bryant to follow, then dashed across the road just after an omnibus had passed, leaving a break in the traffic. He hurried toward the theater, praying all the while that Guy Weathers hadn't skipped on the bill for the troupe's accommodation and taken off, despite what he'd told the landlady. She would have noticed trunks and valises, but perhaps the actors kept the majority of their possessions at the theater and would be able to leave unnoticed once they'd packed up their costumes and props and sent them to the station.

The door to the foyer was unlocked, but the elegant space that had teemed with well-dressed ladies and gentlemen and had buzzed with the hum of conversation last night was now empty, silent, and nearly dark, the only source of light the gloomy daylight diffused by the frosted-glass doors. The ticket booth was empty as well, and a calligraphed sign displayed behind the glass partition proclaimed that the evening's performance was sold out.

Constable Bryant's face was ruddy with cold, and he shook his head like a wet dog, droplets of rainwater flying from the brim of his hat onto his shoulders and the carpet.

"What will you have me do, guv?" he asked once he'd removed his hat and tucked it under his arm.

Sebastian took out his notebook, wrote down several names, then tore out the sheet and handed it to Constable Bryant. There were constables at the Yard whom he wouldn't trust with such an important task, but he had worked with Constable Bryant before and knew he could rely on him to get the interviews right. Constable Bryant was not only conscientious but also intuitive and observant, and would note unspoken clues such as nervousness, evasiveness, or obvious attempts to shift suspicion onto someone else.

"Until last night, the troupe consisted of ten actors, four women and six men. Start with the names on the list," Sebastian said. "Ask them if they saw anything suspicious or noticed anyone lingering near the props table during last night's performance. Also, I would like to know if there had been any change in behavior in Esme or Christopher over the past few days. Did they exhibit signs of melancholy, or were they angry or upset? Had there been any arguments within the troupe, or between actors and the individuals who'd come backstage? Do they suspect any member of the theater crew of tampering with the vials? Note everything down. No detail is too small."

"Understood," Constable Bryant said, and looked at the list. "There are only five names here."

"I'll speak to Ishmael Cabot, Kate Sommers, and Serena Winthrop myself."

Constable Bryant nodded and followed Sebastian backstage, where the two men parted ways. Unlike the evening before, when a horrified hush had hung over the area and the actors had congregated in groups of two and three and whispered urgently to each other as they tried to make sense of what had happened, the space was now better lit and more chaotic. Several people were hurrying along the narrow corridors, two men were carrying an unwieldy plywood cutout, and Guy Weathers was berating a young girl for not cleaning his office thoroughly enough. Weathers stopped midsentence when he spotted Sebastian coming toward him.

"Away with you, Rose," he hissed, and the girl, who was clearly lame, hobbled away and disappeared around the corner.

Guy Weathers smiled at Sebastian as if he had just arrived at a party rather than come to interview potential murder suspects. "Inspector, I do apologize for disregarding your orders, but I'm afraid waiting around at the boarding house simply wasn't an option. With our leads gone, I had to reassign the parts and get in a full rehearsal before tonight's performance."

"Who is to replace Esme and Christopher?" Sebastian asked.

"Kate Sommers and Nigel Mowbray."

"Are they the assigned understudies?"

"Nigel is."

"Who is Esme's understudy?"

"Serena Winthrop."

"So, why did the part go to Kate Sommers?"

"It was a creative decision, Inspector."

"Based on what? You clearly thought Serena Winthrop was the right person to play Juliet before. Has she not already learned the part?"

Guy Weathers huffed irritably and glared at Sebastian in a way that suggested he was being obtuse and such things happened all the time in the theater. "Frankly, Serena has been a thorn in my side these past few weeks, and I wanted to punish her. Petty, I know, but there it is. And to be perfectly frank, she's too old to play Juliet."

"Was she not exactly the same age when you cast her as Esme's understudy?" Sebastian asked.

"She was, but I didn't think she'd ever have to step into Esme's shoes, so I wasn't overly concerned."

"Was there rivalry between Serena and Esme?"

"Are you suggesting that Serena murdered Esme so she could get the lead?" Guy Weathers exclaimed. "What utter poppycock!"

"People have killed for less," Sebastian pointed out.

"And Christopher? Why would Serena murder him?"

"Were they ever involved romantically?" Sebastian asked.

"Not that I know of."

"Would you tell me if you did?"

"I would. Contrary to what you might think, I want to see justice done," Guy Weathers snapped.

"Even if said justice might cost you your livelihood?"

The man smiled unpleasantly. "Now that's where you're wrong, Inspector. The troupe will benefit from the publicity these murders generate. People are prone to morbid curiosity and will come to see the performances in the hope that someone else will get bumped off."

"You don't think much of your patrons."

"I don't think much of humanity in general," Weathers replied. "The plays we put on have retained their popularity for centuries. Do you know why? Because they reflect the worst of human nature, and our audiences can relate to that. They understand the pain of having their romantic hopes thwarted, or the desire to murder their brother so that they might steal his inheritance. They know hopelessness and despair, and long for the grand passion Romeo and Juliet embody. They want to believe that love will prevail, even if it ends in death, and even if there are those who would do anything to destroy it."

"Well, we have a death. Two, in fact. Now we need to figure out if there was love and who was hell-bent on destroying it."

Guy Weathers rolled his eyes in exasperation. "People don't kill for love, Inspector. Not in real life. Jealousy. Greed. Power. But not love. Now, if you don't have any more questions for me, Kate and Nigel are on stage now, so I really must be going."

Sebastian nodded in dismissal, and Guy Weathers hurried off. Sebastian did not agree with him for a moment and thought the man had probably never loved anyone so completely that he could see love as a motive for murder. People killed for love all the time. They killed because they lost love and couldn't bear someone else to have it, because they thought they might find love by murdering a rival, and, most often of all, they killed to protect those they loved. And despite what many believed, everyone was capable of murder; they simply needed the right reason or a valid excuse.

Those who killed often felt absolved of guilt because they simply couldn't allow someone who'd mortally wounded them to live another day. That person drawing breath would be an affront to everything that was right and holy and morally acceptable. Sebastian knew what the latter felt like and had carried out his vengeance, even though he understood that he would be sentenced to death if caught. It didn't matter. He had not felt any remorse for ending the life of the man who'd murdered his family and would have gladly taken his place next to Louisa and their boy if it came to that. And even though he didn't think he'd ever willingly take a life again, he also knew that if he had to, he would, and he would accept the consequences if he believed his actions to be morally right.

"Where would I find Serena Winthrop?" he asked Rose, who had appeared in the corridor with a dustpan and brush.

Rose pointed toward the stairs. "She's been in her dressing room all morning. Sulking."

"Why did Mr. Weathers really give the part to Kate Sommers?" Sebastian asked.

He could see a physical resemblance between Rose and Sid and noticed the same awareness in the girl's eyes that he had spotted in her brother. They might be orphans, but the theater was their home, and they were privy to everything that went on, even if they weren't part of it and would be left behind once the troupe moved on and someone else took over the lease.

Rose shrugged. "Mr. Weathers doesn't share his reasons with me."

"But I wager you have a theory." Sebastian smiled at the girl. She was eager to talk; she just needed to be prompted.

"Serena's been all high and mighty of late. Mr. Weathers passed her over to put her in her place," Rose said, lowering her voice so only Sebastian could hear.

"Did the casting news come as a surprise, or had Serena expected as much?"

"Oh, it was a surprise, all right," Rose scoffed. "Serena had a go at everyone in the cast before she stormed off."

"Why do you think she was acting high and mighty?"

"I expect her prospects suddenly looked brighter," Rose replied.

"Brighter how?"

Rose shrugged again. "There's only one thing that can alter a woman's prospects, isn't there?"

With that, she shuffled off, leaving Sebastian to ponder what she had said. She either knew more than she was letting on or had simply arrived at her own conclusions based on what she thought she had seen and heard. There was only one person who could prove or disprove Rose's claims.

ELEVEN

The upper floor was a stark contrast to the downstairs area. The dressing rooms were situated on one side of the corridor since there was no ceiling directly above the stage, and the beams and walkways stretched all the way to the roof. Given the number of doors, the rooms had to be fairly small, and faced the alleyway that ran between the theater and the adjacent building. A rickety staircase led upward, presumably to the attic, where Rose and Sid made their home. The corridor wasn't carpeted, and the doors could have used a fresh coat of paint. The wallpaper was still intact, but the pattern was tawdry and faded, and there was a faint smell of damp and wood rot.

The renovation had not extended to the upper floor, since the actors were not the ones Mr. Bonneville needed to impress. Sebastian hoped that the attic wasn't musty and overrun with rats—no one should be expected to live in such conditions—but, given the number of children he'd seen hovering in doorways and sleeping on the ground dressed in nothing but rags during the coldest months of the year, he also acknowledged that Rose and Sid's situation could be much worse. They were likely grateful to their benefactor for providing them with a dry place to sleep, serviceable clothes, and probably a wage to cover their food and other expenses.

The doors were fitted with narrow brass frames where a card with an actor's name could be inserted. Serena Winthrop's door was locked, and she ignored Sebastian's request to let him in until he was forced to threaten her with arrest. The scrape of a key in the lock was followed by Serena herself. She looked Sebastian up and down, then turned and walked away, tossing a sly look over her shoulder once she had reached the center of the room.

"Well, don't just stand there glowering, Inspector. Come in."

Sebastian stepped inside the room and shut the door behind him. Serena did not utter a word of protest. She seemed unbothered to be alone with a strange man.

As expected, the upstairs rooms had not been updated, and the space was small and shabby with just enough room for a vanity table with a large mirror, a chair, and a velvet chaise, much like the one he'd seen in Guy Weathers' office but significantly older and more worn. Several lamps were lit, since there was no window, and the room was nothing more than a plaster box.

Now that Sebastian could see Serena clearly and without stage makeup, he took a moment to study her, since he hadn't had the opportunity to look at her more closely last night. Everything about Serena Winthrop was dark. Her raven-black hair was pulled back from her face with a jeweled clip but hung down her back in glossy waves. She had dark eyes fringed with sooty lashes, and her winged brows gave her face character. Serena's gown was dark red satin trimmed with black velvet, but, where the crinolines should have fanned the skirt away from her waist, the fabric hugged the curves of her hips and cascaded to the floor, creating a much narrower silhouette. Serena Winthrop had to be in her early twenties, but the knowing look in her eyes belied her years, and something about her expression put Sebastian in mind of a wild animal, the sort that would only feel free in the jungle or a dense forest where a hunter would soon become the hunted.

Serena smiled humorlessly when she saw him looking and sank into a sweeping curtsy, as if she had just finished a performance and was ready for applause, then straightened and plopped onto the chaise. She pointed toward the chair in front of the vanity, so Sebastian turned it around and sat facing her. He was mildly impressed with both the woman's lush looks and her bravado. If Esme Royce had looked sweet and innocent, Serena Winthrop had the look of a woman who was guilty of every sin known to man.

"Am I your prime suspect?" Serena asked when Sebastian failed to speak quickly enough for her liking.

"You could be," he replied. "You were Esme's understudy."

Serena laughed throatily. "Except I didn't get the part. It went to that silly cow, Kate Sommers."

"So I heard. If playing the lead was the objective, then your efforts would be a dreadful waste of a double murder."

Serena laughed again. "I had no reason to murder them. Esme and Christopher were no threat to me."

"No? Esme was cast in the lead, while you were given an insignificant part and forced to wear a costume that made you look old and dowdy and hid your beauty from the world."

"You think I'm beautiful?" Serena teased.

"You know you are."

"And that makes me guilty, does it?"

"I didn't say I thought you were guilty. But I am sure you're in possession of information that can help me."

"And what makes you say that, Inspector?" Serena cocked her head and licked her lips in a way that made Sebastian feel very warm.

"In my experience, women are much more observant than

men, and clever women who're driven by ambition are never to be discounted."

"Beautiful and ambitious," Serena mused. "You make me sound like a royal courtesan."

"Are you not Lord Gilroy's mistress?"

"In all ways but one."

"What does that mean?" Sebastian asked.

"It means I'm holding out until we agree terms."

"And he's willing to offer terms in advance?"

"Oh, he's had a little taste, Inspector," Serena replied, a small smile playing about her lips. "A preview, I like to call it."

"And what of your acting career?"

Serena laughed. "Acting career? Surely you jest."

"Enlighten me." Sebastian leaned forward and fixed Serena with a look of his own that was returned with a smile of feminine appreciation.

"If you were in a position to offer generous terms, I wouldn't say no to you, Inspector," Serena purred.

"I'm spoken for."

"Who's the lucky lady? Was it that crow that came with you last night? Surely you're not courting a woman who's in mourning. Did she top her husband, and you helped her to cover it up?" Serena asked, and laughed merrily.

"We're not here to talk about me," Sebastian countered. "And I'm rather pressed for time, so can we dispense with the games, Miss Winthrop?"

"All right." Serena leaned back in the chair. "I will answer your boring questions."

"Did you want the part of Juliet?"

"I did, but not for the reasons you imagine. I suppose there are those who go into acting because they genuinely care about the art, but people with sense do it to ensure their future. I was blessed with looks, brains, and talent, but not with a fine lineage. My mother was a maidservant, and my father was some silver-tongued Romani who promised her the moon but gave her a full belly instead. Lucky for her, her mistress didn't turn her out, but she was punished in other ways." Serena looked desperately sad. "I would rather die than waste my life scrubbing pots or laundering some matron's unmentionables. Acting gave me a way to display my attributes and attract the right sort of man."

"And that man is Lord Gilroy?"

"That man is anyone who can offer comfort, independence, and a tidy sum besides."

"Insurance, is it?" Sebastian asked, impressed with Serena Winthrop's honesty.

"Precisely. There isn't a man out there who won't tire of his mistress and eventually replace her with a younger, prettier rival, and when that happens I mean to be set for life."

"And is Lord Gilroy willing to offer such generous terms?"

Serena's smile was slow. "He's willing to offer something even better. He means to marry me."

Sebastian highly doubted that but wasn't going to argue the point. "So, you will leave the troupe?" he asked instead.

"I might have stayed had I got to play Juliet, I might still if I am cast as Desdemona in *Othello*, but if I'm not, then I don't suppose there's anything holding me back."

"Did you resent Esme for getting the part of Juliet?"

Serena made a dismissive gesture. "Of course I did, but if it were up to me I'd have chosen her as well. She was perfect to play innocent, insipid Juliet. Unfortunately, there are no other good female parts in that play. Lucky for me, Peter Gilroy saw me out of costume when he came backstage, so it all worked out in the end."

"You'd make a memorable Desdemona," Sebastian said.

Serena inclined her head in acknowledgement. "Peter would enjoy knowing that every man in the audience wanted me for his own. It would fan his already flaming ardor."

"And if you didn't get the part and Lord Gilroy decided to move on?"

Serena shrugged. "You see, Inspector, there are only three parts a woman can play. The beauty, the mother, and the crone. I can still play the beauty, but by casting me as Juliet's mother Guy reminded the audience that I'm no longer in the first flush of youth. It's time I made alternative arrangements before I'm asked to play the hag. If Peter shoves off, then I will simply find another patron. That's how this works."

"Why would Guy Weathers, who stands to benefit from your continued ability to play the beauty, want to remind the audience that you're past your prime?"

"Because he's petty and cruel," Serena replied, and Sebastian saw a flash of anger in her dark eyes.

"Surely there's more to it than that?"

"Do you know what *droit du seigneur* means?"

"I don't, but I'm sure you're going to tell me."

"It translates to *the right of the lord*. It was a medieval tradition where the lord of the manor had the right to have any woman on his estate, particularly on her wedding night, to assert his power over his subjects."

"And is Guy Weathers the lord in this instance?" Sebastian asked, suddenly seeing the fussy little man in a new light.

"Guy never openly demands submission, but he drops subtle hints and makes snide insinuations meant to remind the women that they can be easily replaced."

"And is every woman in the troupe susceptible to such manipulation?"

"Some are and some aren't. Esme pretended to misunderstand him, but Guy didn't push her. She was his star and, despite his overblown ego, he was always more interested in his purse than his pleasure."

"What about the rest of the women in the troupe?" Sebastian asked.

Serena's laugh was low and bitter. "What do you think?"

When Sebastian didn't immediately reply, she went on, "Guy no longer takes an interest in Ruth—she's too old—but he has had Kate on occasion. She didn't please him," Serena explained with a knowing smirk. "Too timid for his taste. I admit that I had fallen for his antics when I first joined the troupe and worried constantly about finding myself on the streets, but I have not allowed him to lay a finger on me since meeting Peter."

"And this is his punishment for you."

Serena raised her chin defiantly. "Guy gave Kate the part to spite me, and to remind me that she now has his favor."

"But I thought Kate didn't please him," Sebastian said.

Serena shrugged. "She'll do until he finds an adolescent ingenue to replace Esme and browbeats her into submission."

"And does he not mind when his women lavish their affections on their benefactors or other members of the troupe?" Sebastian asked.

"Why should he? He has no interest in a permanent arrangement."

"That doesn't mean he doesn't get jealous."

Serena made a dismissive gesture. "One has to care to get jealous. Guy collects sexual favors the way the Crown collects taxes. He simply feels they are owed to him."

"So, tell me about Esme. Was she looking for a benefactor as well?"

"Of course she was, only she was terribly unlucky."

"How so?"

"Her most ardent admirer, General Modine, had scared away every lily-livered dandy who might have offered Esme a life of security and comfort." Serena chuckled. "That man is like a wild beast. A predator to the bone."

Sebastian made a mental note of the turn of phrase. If

anyone could recognize a predator, it was Serena Winthrop, and this man clearly intimidated her.

"And was Esme flattered by his pursuit of her?"

"Flattered, yes. Comfortable, no. General Modine is not the sort of man who can be trifled with. He sets forth the terms, and he decides when the association is over."

"Was Esme his mistress?"

"I don't know. We didn't talk of such things."

"And what about Christopher Hudson? I believe he had an admirer of his own."

Serena grinned again. "You mean dotty old Lady Argyle?"

"Is she dotty?"

"She's not as easily duped as you might imagine, but Christopher was too much a man to realize that. He truly thought the pot of gold at the end of the rainbow was between the lady's thighs and applied himself diligently to securing his reward."

"And would the lady wish to murder him if he rejected her?"

"I wouldn't be surprised. You know what they say, Inspector. Hell hath no fury like a woman scorned."

"Did Esme and Christopher have feelings for each other?"

"Are you asking me if they were lovers? Such delicacy from one so rough," Serena purred. "You are an intriguing man."

"Let's get back to the victims, shall we?" Sebastian replied smoothly. "*Were* Esme and Christopher lovers?"

Serena shrugged again.

"Was Esme close with anyone in the troupe?"

"Not really, but Mona adored her. Panted after her like a dog."

"Mona?" Sebastian couldn't recall anyone named Mona.

"Mona Grady. She's the sempstress. She'd do anything for Esme. A sad case of hero worship."

"And was this devotion reciprocated?"

"Lord, no. What would Esme want with the likes of Mona?"

"And what about Kate Sommers?"

"What about her?"

"Surely you have an opinion that goes beyond *silly cow*?"

"I do not. That's the best I can say for her."

"And Ruth Gregson?"

"Ruth likes to mother everyone. I suppose it's because she never had children of her own and now feels the lack of a family. She's a good woman, Inspector Bell. Kind."

"What about the men in the troupe? Anyone consumed with lust, professional jealousy, or a need for vengeance?"

"Not that I know of. They're all dull as dirt and completely incapable of such feats of the imagination."

"Thank you for your time, Miss Winthrop," Sebastian said, and pushed to his feet. "This has been extremely illuminating."

"If you get tired of your lady love, come find me, Inspector Bell. If it's illumination you seek, I can be your moon and your stars."

"But the moon and the stars pale next to the sun, Miss Winthrop," Sebastian replied, and left Serena to stew.

TWELVE

Sebastian would have liked to speak to Kate Sommers, but she was currently on the stage rehearsing with Nigel Mowbray and Ruth Gregson, who was playing the nurse. The trio were being harangued by Guy Weathers, whose commentary was loud enough to raise the proverbial dead. Mona Grady was busy sewing costumes for that night's performance, since Esme and Christopher had been wearing theirs when they were taken away and Kate and Nigel would be requiring new costumes within a few hours. Mona's mouth was full of pins and her eyes red-rimmed with either crying or lack of sleep, but she clearly couldn't take the time to speak to him, so Sebastian decided to interview some of the men instead.

"Where can I find Ishmael Cabot?" Sebastian asked Sid, who appeared at his side as soon as Sebastian descended to the ground floor and looked all set to follow Sebastian around like a puppy.

"Ishmael likes to watch the rehearsals," Sid replied. "I reckon it's an excuse not to talk to anyone. How old does a body have to be to join the police service?"

"Older than you," Sebastian replied.

"But how old?"

"Sixteen at least."

"I want to become an inspector," Sid exclaimed, his eyes shining with excitement.

"You'll have to work your way up," Sebastian said as he strode toward the door that would take him into the auditorium.

"How long?" Sid asked as he trailed Sebastian.

"About ten years, unless you have useful connections, in which case you could become an inspector right now," Sebastian replied sarcastically, and was instantly ashamed of himself. The boy was sincerely interested, and Sebastian had no right to discourage him or tarnish the reputation of the police service.

"Can you be my useful connection?" Sid asked, his tone wheedling. "Maybe I can watch you and learn."

"Sorry, Sid, but I'm rather busy at the moment."

Sid's face fell. "All right. Find me if you need anything. I'm happy to deliver a note or go for the police wagon, should you decide to arrest someone."

"I'll keep that in mind. Now scram!"

Sid bounced off, leaving behind a momentary silence that was soon filled with Guy Weathers' scathing review of Kate's performance and Kate's quiet sobbing. Nigel Mowbray gallantly came to the rescue.

"Steady on, Guy," he said. "Kate's doing her best, and this is her first crack at the part. There's no call to be so harsh."

"Well, her best is not good enough, is it?" Guy Weathers snapped. "Should I get Serena, Kate?"

"Serena wouldn't play the part now if you begged her," Nigel retorted angrily. "And neither will I if you don't apologize to Kate."

Backed into a corner, Guy Weathers instantly altered his belligerent demeanor. "I'm sorry, my dear, but I only want you to shine."

"The way Esme shone?" Kate sniveled.

She was about twenty, with light brown hair wound into a loose bun and pale eyes that glittered with tears in the diffuse haze of the footlights. Although pretty, she was nowhere near as striking as either Esme or Serena and was clearly very sensitive, not a useful trait for someone who had chosen a profession in which they were constantly judged. Sebastian noted that no one had mentioned any of Kate's admirers, but he could see how Nigel Mowbray would appeal to the ladies. In last night's performance he had played several roles, including that of the prince, and would make a fine Romeo—if the performance actually took place tonight.

"Esme was sublime," Guy said wistfully, "but you can become just as good as she was. You just need a little confidence. Don't sound so apologetic when you deliver your lines."

"How should I sound?" Kate whined.

"Like you are the most beautiful woman to ever grace the stage."

"But I'm not," Kate protested.

"That's the whole point of acting. You're not playing yourself, dear."

Guy Weathers draped a paternal arm around Kate and led her off the stage, his voice soft and apologetic as he tried to build her up after tearing her down. Unsure what to do, Nigel and Ruth followed, leaving the stage empty.

Sebastian hadn't paid much attention to Ruth Gregson last night. In her role of nurse, she'd worn a wimple-like headdress that showed only her face, and a shapeless brown robe beneath a white apron that fell to her feet. This morning, she was wearing her own clothes and her hair was pulled back into a simple knot. Ruth was the oldest of the actresses in the troupe and was probably just the other side of forty. She was attractive, but no longer of an age to play the beauty, and the role of mother had been given to a younger actress. The hag, Serena had called Ruth's role. Unless Ruth Gregson was one of those actresses who were on the stage for the love of the craft, she had failed to find an admirer who would look after her in her twilight years, or had found someone and had been discarded when she was no longer wanted. Would Ruth Gregson have a motive to murder Esme and Christopher? Not that Sebastian could see, since she wouldn't gain anything by their deaths, but he couldn't rule her out. Not yet.

In the auditorium, the chandelier wasn't lit, but several wall sconces gave off meager pools of light. The empty seats looked forlorn, and shadowy balconies loomed out of the darkness. A theater was just a shell, the audience the soul that supplied the emotions to bring it to life. The seats closest to Sebastian looked worn, and the wainscot was dull without the glow of the lamps to soften its patina. The chandelier that had glowed golden last night now revealed itself to be brass, and the parquet floor was scuffed where a carpet runner did not cover it.

Sebastian found Ishmael Cabot in the first-tier balcony, his boot-clad feet propped on the seat before him, his gaze fixed on the empty stage. He looked to be in his mid-twenties, a tall, lithe man with warm brown skin and thickly lashed dark eyes accentuated by strong brows. His woolly curls were very black, and deep dimples flanked his generous mouth. Sebastian hadn't had a chance to speak to him last night and had seen him only in passing, but the young man had struck him as a loner, an outsider, and outsiders tended to be keen observers.

"May I join you, Mr. Cabot?" Sebastian asked.

"If you like."

"So, what African nation do you hail from?" Sebastian asked once he was seated.

He didn't put his feet up on the chair in front of him but made himself comfortable and sat sideways two seats over from Cabot so that he could see the man's face. Facial expressions and body language provided answers of their own, and Sebastian wouldn't be able to read them if the two men sat side by side.

"Algeria," Ishmael replied. "I came to England a few years ago, after my father died."

"Your English is flawless."

"I had an English tutor when I was a boy. My father thought it was important that we spoke several languages. I was always eager to learn."

"*À cœur vaillant rien d'impossible*," Sebastian said. Nothing is impossible for a willing heart. It was the only phrase he knew in French, having heard it from his father, but he thought it would serve his purpose.

"I don't know what you just said," Ishmael replied sulkily.

"Don't they speak French in Algeria?" Sebastian asked conversationally.

"So I hear." Ishmael turned to face Sebastian, his face tight with anger. "I have never been to Algeria, nor any part of Africa, as you have clearly already deduced."

"So, why did you lie?"

"Why do you think?" Ishmael retorted. "Idiots like Guy Weathers are willing to believe anything when it suits their purpose and can make them money. And besides, I'd rather be thought of as an African prince than a mulatto. Did you know that means mule?" he ground out. "Or tar baby, which is even worse than being called brownie."

Sebastian had heard the term *tar baby* before. It usually referred to situations that were hopeless, but there was a nastier, crueler meaning that had originated at the London docks and referred to the skin color of children who had been fathered by black sailors who'd come into port. The insult was meant to denigrate individuals who were already struggling to fit into a society that had no use for them and to insult the mothers who'd brought them into the world.

Brownie was no better. Louisa, who'd had a Scottish nurse

when she was a child, had entertained Sebastian with tales of Highland folklore and had told him all about the fairy folk and the creatures who were believed to inhabit the homes of the mortals. A brownie was wrinkled and brown and was generally helpful to the family unless mortally offended, in which case it could turn into a boggart and create chaos for the poor folk who'd angered it.

"Was your father a sailor?" Sebastian asked, but he thought he could anticipate the answer.

Ishmael shrugged with indifference, but Sebastian could see the pain in his eyes. "I don't know who my father was. My mother abandoned me shortly after I was born. Left me on the riverbank. Like Moses," he said bitterly. "Perhaps she'd hoped I'd be washed away and drown, but someone found me and brought me to St. Magnus the Martyr. So I was called Magnus."

"And Cabot? How did you come by the name?" Sebastian asked softly.

He didn't want to feel pity for this bitter, wounded man, but it was difficult not to imagine the terrified child, whose chances were even worse than those of an English orphan. The color of Ishmael's skin ensured that he'd be treated no better than a dog.

"No idea," Cabot replied. "The surname was probably given to me at the orphanage, but I didn't remain there long."

"Where did you go?"

"When I was around seven, I ran away. Anything was better than daily beatings and starvation rations. I lived on the streets for a while, then took to sleeping in an alley behind a tavern since I could always find scraps to eat. The owner tripped over me one morning on his way to the privy," Ishmael said with a wistful smile. "He invited me inside, gave me some bread and cheese, and asked if I wanted a job. I took out piss buckets, washed the floors, and cleaned up vomit in exchange for room and board. It was the first time I'd had a home."

At least someone had been kind to a child no one wanted,

Sebastian reflected. Even if the publican most likely hadn't paid Ishmael a farthing. But when cold and starving, a place to sleep and some food was payment enough, so he couldn't really fault the man too much. He'd probably saved Ishmael's life.

"How did you become an actor?"

"Years later, I saw a street performance and asked the actors if they might take me along. I was willing to do any job that needed doing as long as I could be a part of their world," Ishmael said. "Eventually I changed my name."

"Call me Ishmael," Sebastian said, but the young man looked blank, the quote from *Moby-Dick* clearly not ringing any bells.

"I thought Ishmael sounded appropriately foreign. No one would believe that someone called Magnus came from Algeria."

"That's a valid point. Ishmael suits you."

"I didn't murder them, Inspector," Ishmael said quietly.

"Do you know who did?"

"No."

"Surely you have a theory." Sebastian tried again.

"I heard Esme and Chris arguing the other day."

"When was this?"

Ishmael shrugged. "Last Wednesday, I think. Maybe Thursday."

"What did they argue about?"

"I don't know, but Esme seemed really upset. She said time was running out."

"And what did Christopher say to that?"

"He told her to have patience," Ishmael replied.

"And you have no idea what he was referring to?"

"None, but knowing Chris he was probably trying to swindle someone out of something."

"Was he that dishonest?" Sebastian asked.

"I've never met a bigger fraud," Ishmael replied, and smiled at Sebastian in a way that suggested he was well aware of the irony of that statement.

"Will you remain with the troupe now?"

Ishmael's jaw tightened, and his gaze slid away from Sebastian's face and back to the stage, where Kate, Nigel, and Ruth had taken their places once again. Several others followed, then Guy Weathers trotted onto the stage and stood at the very edge, peering toward the balcony.

"Ishmael, take your place," he called out.

"I will stay with the troupe for now," Ishmael said, and stood.

"A moment, Mr. Weathers," Sebastian called out as he pushed to his feet.

Guy Weathers' annoyed expression seemed to say, "What now?" but Sebastian didn't care. The two people on stage were suspects, and he had yet to speak to either lead.

THIRTEEN

"You do realize we're on a tight schedule," Guy Weathers snapped as soon as Sebastian walked onto the stage.

"You do realize two people were murdered last night," Sebastian countered.

The manager had the decency to look chastised. "Please, can you make it quick?" he asked. "They need all the practice they can get."

"I will do my best," Sebastian replied, and pulled Kate aside. She had the look of a lamb being led to the slaughter. "You and Esme shared a room at the boarding house. Were you close?"

Kate shook her head. "None of us were. We spent so much time together during the day, we wanted nothing to do with each other at night. We hardly talked after supper or when we returned after a performance. But I liked Esme," she hurried to add. "She was a lovely person. Much nicer than Serena."

"Did Esme have any admirers besides General Modine?"

"Gentlemen came backstage from time to time, but Esme politely dismissed them."

"Did anyone take offense?"

Kate shook her head. "I don't think so."

"Do you have any admirers, Miss Sommers?"

"Not yet, but maybe now I will," Kate said nervously. "I'm not looking to be someone's mistress, you understand, but it would be nice to be noticed."

"Was Esme close with any male members of the troupe?"

"She looked up to Mr. Bannon. He tends to be more reasonable than Mr. Weathers and talks him down when he gets upset. They're old friends."

"You benefited directly from Esme's death."

Kate inhaled sharply and went red in the face. "Serena was the understudy. I had no idea Mr. Weathers would give the part to me."

"You could have easily accessed the two vials when you weren't on stage."

"What reason would I have to murder Esme and Christopher?" Kate cried.

"What reason would anyone have to kill them?" That was a rhetorical question, since Kate either didn't know anything or wasn't saying.

Sebastian couldn't think of anything else he wanted to ask her, so he went to speak to Nigel Mowbray, who seemed surprised that Sebastian wanted to speak to him since he'd already been interviewed by Constable Bryant. Mowbray's answers closely mirrored Kate's. He didn't know anything. He wasn't close to the others, and he had no reason to cause them harm. Without any evidence to go on, there was nothing more Sebastian could do.

"How did you get on?" Sebastian asked Constable Bryant once they had met up in the foyer and stepped outside, where they could speak privately. Thankfully, the rain had stopped, and watery sunshine had dispelled the mist, leaving behind a world that glistened with moisture. The air smelled damp and clean, the usual odors of rotting fruit and vegetables and raw meat wafting from the market replaced by the intoxicating scent of spring.

Constable Bryant scratched his head, then plopped his hat atop his ginger curls. "Everyone swears blind they heard nothing and saw nothing, and Esme and Christopher were both fine, no signs of despair. Christopher were making plans to spend Easter with some friends in Slough, and Esme were looking forward to the time off so she could order a new wardrobe, courtesy of General Modine. They all seem sad and frightened."

"Is that all?" Sebastian asked. He hadn't expected any confessions, but this was extremely disappointing.

"I did have a word with Walt Dickie. The old geezer's a night watchman, but I think the only thing he watches is gin disappearing. He did tell me something interesting about this place, though."

"Oh? What's that?"

"The backstage area used to be a brothel before the current owner bought the building and the one next door and converted them into a theater. Walt used to be a heavy at the brothel in his younger days, but when he'd outlived his usefulness the madam took pity on him and kept him on as a watchman."

"How is that relevant?" Sebastian asked, giving the young man his full attention. Constable Bryant wouldn't have brought it up unless he'd learned something useful.

"The dressing rooms were where the girls took their punters. Walt said there's a narrow walkway behind the wall, like a servants' corridor." Constable Bryant grinned, clearly pleased with himself. "All the rooms are fitted with discreet peepholes. The owner of the brothel would charge blokes as couldn't afford to pay for sex sixpence to watch. They'd get their own private show so they could pleasure themselves."

"What does this have to do with what happened last night?" Sebastian asked.

The constable's lopsided grin grew even wider. "It seems our Walt likes to patrol the walkway while the ladies are changing into their costumes. He's very diligent when it comes to his work, Walt is. He saw Esme and Christopher at it."

"At it?" Sebastian took the constable's meaning, but he had to be sure.

Constable Bryant chuckled. "Walt said, 'She were riding St. George.' It seems our Esme liked to be on top, so as not to ruin her costume."

"How many times had he seen them?"

"More than once."

"Had Mr. Dickie seen Esme with anyone else?"

Constable Bryant nodded. "General Modine, and once he saw her with Ishmael Cabot."

"Ishmael? Is he sure?"

"Well, as sure as a drunk peering into a darkened room can be," Constable Bryant replied.

"Does anyone else know about these peepholes?"

"They're Walt's dirty little secret."

"Let's keep this to ourselves for now," Sebastian said.

"What'll you have me do now, guv?"

"Get something to eat, then get back to the theater and make sure no one leaves."

"Don't worry. No one will leg it on my watch."

Sebastian thanked the constable and left him to it.

FOURTEEN

By the time Sebastian got to Blackfriars, it was nearly two o'clock. Two young men had just emerged from Colin's house, but rather than take their leave they lingered on the doorstep, one of them, a fair-haired youth, making cow eyes at Mabel and inquiring about her afternoon off. Mabel looked annoyed but could hardly be rude to Colin's students, whose fees likely paid her wages. Instead, she gave the young buck a tight-lipped smile and told him that her afternoons off were already spoken for.

"Are these gentlemen bothering you, Mabel?" Sebastian asked as he walked up the steps and came level with the men.

"No, *Inspector*. They were just leaving."

Mabel put undue emphasis on his title, and the students tipped their hats and hurried down the steps, the cloying scent of cologne hanging in the air as they passed.

"I'll have a word with Mr. Ramsey if you like."

"Oh, no. Please don't," Mabel exclaimed. "It was nothing. They weren't so bad."

"That fragrance alone is enough to cause offense," Sebastian joked, but Mabel shook her head.

"They use it to mask the smell," she explained. "The new students in particular. They're not accustomed to *real bodies*."

Mabel whispered that last bit as if Sebastian wasn't aware what Colin got up to in the cellar. He couldn't blame the young men for dousing themselves in cologne. There were some things one never got used to and, for students who had so far only been allowed to learn from books and watch from a safe distance sitting in the operating theater, the sights and smells had to be a shock.

"Yes, I expect the scent of violets is preferable," Sebastian agreed. "Is Mr. Ramsey finished for the day?"

"He's still in the cellar," Mabel replied. "Excuse me, Inspector. I have a pot on the boil."

Sebastian descended the steps and pushed open the door. The cellar offered the usual array of unpleasant odors. Esme's body was covered with a sheet, but Christopher's was still on the table, the sawdust beneath the funnel-like opening in the table damp and brown with bodily fluids. The air was so close, Sebastian's breath caught in his throat, and he tried to focus on the lingering scent of violets that overlaid the smell of death. Colin was in the process of closing Christopher's chest, his hand wielding the needle with the precision of a master tailor. He smiled apologetically when he heard Sebastian's sharp intake of breath, and yanked open the door that led to the alley to allow a rain-scented breeze to air the fetid space.

"You're just in time," he said as he tied off the thread, pulled up the sheet to cover the body, and looked up from his work.

"I met your students as they were leaving," Sebastian said as he approached the table.

He would have preferred that Colin wait to expose the murder victims to his students, but he supposed it was too much to ask that the man waste such an opportunity. Colin never mentioned money, but now that he had to employ a live-in nurse for his mother his expenses had to have increased significantly. He needed to take on more private work—the Yard's fees were negligible and Lovell could always utilize the services of the staff surgeon. Mr. Fenwick was rarely sober enough to make a straight incision, much less glean anything of importance from the deceased, but most inspectors were not overly interested in the results of the postmortem. All they needed was the cause of death, which was usually obvious.

Sebastian could pinpoint the cause of death quickly enough himself in most cases as well. It wasn't difficult to spot a bashed-in skull or deduce that the victim had been stabbed and had hemorrhaged to death, but, in situations where the motive wasn't obvious, the postmortem sometimes provided clues that were not immediately visible. Sebastian hoped that would be the case with these murders, since he had yet to come up with a single valid motive that fit the facts and accounted for such malice.

"My students are not privy to the identity of the victims," Colin said apologetically. He must have sensed Sebastian's disapproval, or more likely realized that he had overstepped his remit.

"They'll make the connection once the newspapers get hold of the story. It's bound to make the evening edition," Sebastian replied.

He didn't think there was too much the students could do with the information, but it still galled him that Colin had not waited.

"You have my word that I did not share any confidential information," Colin said defensively.

Sebastian nodded, ready to end the argument. With the door open, he could see Colin's face more clearly. The harsh daylight had highlighted his pallor and obvious fatigue, and Sebastian realized that Colin's cheekbones and jawline had become more pronounced, and his eyes appeared wider in a face that was now gaunt. He'd lost weight and had been more distracted of late. Colin was under a lot of pressure, Anne's rapid decline having pushed him over some invisible line of forbearance. As a doctor, Colin understood the ramifications of Anne's condition and knew what to expect, but as a son he was heartbroken and lost. How did one come to terms with cognitive decline in the person who had been one's guiding light one's whole life? And how did one reconcile one's own needs with the needs of an ageing parent who could no longer be trusted to be left on their own, even for a few minutes?

Anne was Colin's only remaining family, and, once she was gone, he'd be alone. Perhaps that was the reason he had grown so close to Gemma, who not only offered friendship and support but was also on her own and living under the same roof. Gemma was the closest thing Colin had to a wife, and the situation was sure to give him ideas. Had Sebastian made a terrible mistake by suggesting that Gemma move in with the Ramseys? It seemed a selfish thought, particularly when Colin had been at it since early morning, working tirelessly to have the post-mortem results ready for Sebastian by the time he arrived. Sebastian was just about to thank Colin when the door opened and Gemma walked in.

"Sebastian, I thought I heard your voice," Gemma exclaimed, and smiled as happily as if she hadn't seen him for weeks, not mere hours.

Sebastian felt an answering pleasure and grinned like a besotted schoolboy, while Colin muttered something about star-crossed lovers under his breath.

A capacity to feel was the one thing that never changed as long as people were still alive. No matter what had happened and regardless of what horror they had been exposed to, human beings were still capable of joy and could smile and exchange pleasantries as they stood over the remains of those who could no longer feel anything. It was that ability to compartmentalize tragedy that allowed them to set aside their personal feelings to focus on the task at hand, which anyone else would find indescribably gruesome.

"Is Mrs. Ramsey all right?" Sebastian asked.

What he really wanted was to inquire about Gemma. She looked exhausted and had probably not been able to sleep after last night's unexpected final act, her mind whirring with thoughts and theories that she no doubt longed to share with him. That conversation would have to wait since he had to discuss the postmortem results with Colin, then return to the theater to resume questioning the suspects.

"Mother is tired today," Colin replied in Gemma's stead. "It had been months since she'd been out in public, and although she enjoyed the performance it took a lot out of her."

"Yes, I'm sure it did," Sebastian said. "Does she recall what happened?"

"She thought it was part of the play," Gemma said.

"The mind will sometimes protect one from painful memories," Colin said with a sigh. "Small mercies."

Sebastian's gaze slid toward the sheet-covered remains of Esme Royce. He wished his mind would protect him from painful memories, but every time he was faced with a young woman whose life had been cut short all he could see was Louisa, her face the only part of her that had been left undamaged by the attacker's knife. That was the only memory he could not manage to shut away in some inaccessible compartment of his mind. It haunted him and would probably remain with him for the rest of his days, no matter how his life turned out. Some things one never forgot or forgave. And some crosses had to be borne alone, the burden too heavy for a loved one to carry.

Esme looked nothing like Louisa, but all young female victims had something in common. There was still that innocence that had yet to develop into life experience, or sometimes distill into the bitterness and awful sense of waste that squeezed the heart like a closing fist and ate away at one's soul. Esme had been robbed of years, decades even, her life extinguished before it had truly begun. She was hardly more than a girl, whose beauty and talent were beginning to blossom as she gained awareness of herself as a woman. And now her beauty was already fading, death starting about its work as it mercilessly destroyed the perfect vessel created in life.

"What have you got for me?" Sebastian asked, suddenly eager to get back outside, where he didn't have to stare death in the face.

"I'm certain the cause of death is morphine overdose," Colin said. "In fact, Gemma and I have conducted a little experiment, just to be sure."

The two exchanged looks that were entirely too smug for Sebastian's liking, but he pushed his personal feelings aside. This wasn't a social call. He was there in his professional capacity, and his duty to the victims came before anything else.

"What sort of experiment?" he asked, looking from Colin to Gemma.

"A taste test, if you will," Colin said.

"You plied Gemma with morphine?" Sebastian balked, his resolve to remain impartial instantly forgotten.

"Of course not," Colin replied, clearly affronted by the very suggestion. "I took it myself in Gemma's presence, just in case I should need assistance. But all it did was cure my headache, and very quickly too."

"How did you obtain it?" Sebastian asked.

"I added a few drops of water to the brown vial and allowed it to become infused with the residue," Colin explained. "And I also have physical proof."

He turned back to the worktop and picked up a square glass slide that appeared to be stained with congealed blood. "I scraped the bottom of the blue vial and was able to extract a small amount of sediment that had settled and dried. Raw morphine presents as a resinous brown substance." He held the slide out to Sebastian.

"How much morphine would it take kill someone?"

"When I worked at a hospital in Edinburgh, a dose of twenty to thirty milligrams was administered in cases of extreme pain. One hundred milligrams would be enough to induce coma and possibly death in a subject who was underweight and weakened by illness," Colin said. "Since Esme and Christopher were neither ill nor malnourished, it would take considerably more to achieve the same result."

Gemma nodded in agreement. "There was an ongoing shortage of morphine in Scutari, but when it was available we were instructed to administer no more than twenty milligrams to patients whose need was greatest."

"And how much did you ingest?" Sebastian asked, turning back to Colin.

"By my calculation, less than five milligrams."

Colin and Gemma looked at each other and a silent conference took place before Colin announced, "If it was my intention to murder someone quickly, and if my victim was a strong young man, I would administer two hundred milligrams just to be sure."

"And if it was a woman?" Sebastian asked.

"Half that," Gemma said. "Possibly even a quarter. Fifty milligrams would be enough to render Esme senseless, but if the killer wanted to ensure that she died they would most likely give her at least seventy-five."

This time Colin nodded in agreement. "The poison was mixed into the brandy, and the presence of alcohol would amplify the potency of the morphine, making the dose even more lethal."

"How could the killer ensure that Esme woke and was able to finish her scene?" Sebastian asked.

"They couldn't," Colin said. "The fact that Esme didn't slip into a coma right away is a testament to the strength of her will to go on, not proof of the killer's intention."

"How well versed in poisons would someone have to be in order to achieve the desired result?" Sebastian queried.

"Enough to know that a high dose of morphine would lead to death," Colin said. "And that they had to give two different doses to make certain Christopher's acted faster."

"So not as knowledgeable as you two?"

"I don't know," Colin said. "Maybe, but one could also argue that it's a matter of common sense to work out that a high dose would work faster."

"Which means it could have been anyone at that theater," Sebastian concluded.

Colin and Gemma nodded in unison.

"Could this have been suicide?"

No one had said that Esme and Christopher had suffered from melancholia or had become embroiled in a situation in which a quick exit would be the only alternative, but Sebastian still needed to ask, if only to rule out the possibility of self-harm.

Colin considered the question. "I suppose so," he said at last, "if the objective was to be remembered for their very public deaths, but, having watched them on stage for several hours, I saw nothing that would lead me to that conclusion."

That assessment lined up with Sebastian's own conclusion on the subject, and he was glad that Colin agreed.

"I concur," Gemma said. "Suicide is the last resort of a person who believes they have no other options or any hope for the future. Do you have reason to believe that either of them was that desperate?"

"No, I don't," Sebastian replied. "Which is why I'm treating their deaths as murder." He turned to Colin. "Were you able to learn anything from the postmortems?"

He hoped that Colin had not invited Gemma to watch the dissections, but, when presented with evidence of their newly formed professional bond, he couldn't be sure and didn't think he should inquire. Gemma was a grown woman and could decide for herself whether she wanted to attend a postmortem.

"There were one or two surprises," Colin said, and paused as he looked at Gemma expectantly.

"I would prefer to remain," she said with a defiant lift of her chin.

Colin turned to Sebastian, who immediately realized that the wrong answer would cost him dearly and it wasn't worth it to argue over something that was a foregone conclusion.

"It's fine with me," he replied.

Gemma's shoulders relaxed, and she shot him a look of gratitude.

"All right. Let us begin with Mr. Hudson." Colin pulled back the sheet and the linen pooled modestly around the man's hips. "Christopher Hudson was a healthy male in his mid-twenties. He was well nourished and probably took regular exercise."

"You mean beyond strutting across the stage and engaging in pretend swordplay?" Sebastian asked, and earned a look of reproach from Gemma.

"Given his well-toned upper body, I would venture to suggest that he either boxed or engaged in some form of recreational swordsmanship. There are no recent injuries, but I did find evidence of a broken wrist and a scar on his ribcage, just here, which is telling."

"Telling how?" Sebastian asked.

"At first, I thought the mark was the result of a knife wound or even a nasty scratch, but during the postmortem I discovered that the wound went quite deep. No scratch, this," Colin added thoughtfully. "Christopher Hudson was stabbed at some point, and not with a knife."

"How can you tell?" Sebastian inquired as Gemma leaned forward to see the scar for herself.

"The blade entered just here," Colin said, touching the scar tissue gently, "then encountered the sixth rib, glanced it, and slid above and out the back."

Colin carefully rolled the body onto its side, and Sebastian and Gemma were treated to a glimpse of firm white buttocks as the sheet slid forward.

"Note the exit wound," Colin said, and pointed to another strip of scar tissue on Christopher's back.

"The only weapon long and narrow enough to penetrate the body and leave this sort of scar is a cavalry saber or a bayonet," Sebastian concluded.

"Precisely. Had Christopher sustained this injury during a fencing match, for example, the scar would be considerably narrower."

"Which means that he was in the army, and, given his age, most probably stationed in Crimea."

"Perhaps he was treated at Scutari," Colin suggested, and looked at Gemma expectantly. "What do you think, Gemma? Is that a possibility?" he asked when she didn't immediately reply.

"I really couldn't say just by looking at a historic wound."

"Would you not remember him if he had found his way to your ward?"

"Thousands were wounded and treated at Scutari. I can't recall every patient who passed through the hospital, not even someone as handsome as Christopher Hudson."

"He was very handsome, wasn't he?" Colin agreed wistfully. "The perfect specimen of English manhood."

"Yes," Gemma agreed. "Dressed as Romeo last night, it was like he'd stepped down from a painting. An Arthurian knight." The two seemed transfixed by Christopher's chiseled features.

"Was there anything else?" Sebastian asked, sounding more annoyed than he'd intended to but impatient with the pointless fawning nevertheless. The man was dead. How handsome he had been in life was no longer relevant unless it was his looks that had cost him his life.

Colin rolled Christopher onto his back and adjusted the sheet for Gemma's benefit before replying. "Christopher had fish and potatoes for his last meal. As did Esme. It was most likely at luncheon, since the contents of their stomachs were well digested by the time they died."

It was possible that Esme and Christopher had eaten together, just as it was possible that the entire troupe had shared the midday meal.

"Is there anything else?" Sebastian asked.

Colin shook his head. "Christopher's autopsy didn't yield anything too unexpected."

"And Esme's?"

"Esme is quite a different story."

FIFTEEN

After he had finished with her, Colin moved Esme's remains to a table that stood flush with the back wall. He didn't usually work on more than one cadaver at a time, and the table was used to hold various implements and deformed organs that floated in jars of formaldehyde. The offending specimens had been moved to the top of a cabinet to make room for Esme, who looked like she was sleeping peacefully rather than waiting to undertake her final journey.

Colin pulled back the sheet, but only as far as the shoulders, conscious as ever of propriety because there was a lady present. Esme's face was pale as moonlight, her features so delicate they might have been carved out of stone. Her hair cascaded off the table, the waves reminiscent of a waterfall lit up by the setting sun. Her skin was smooth and supple, and her form, clearly outlined by the thin sheet, was perfectly proportioned.

"Esme was in excellent health when she died," Colin said, his sadness for the woman on full display. He laid a gentle hand on Esme's shoulder as if he could reassure her that she would be treated with respect. He couldn't protect her once she was taken away for burial, but, as long as she was in his custody, he would treat her with all the care he would afford a living person.

"As you can see, she was adequately nourished, still in possession of all her teeth, and her skin was clear and smooth. Her hair was lustrous, and she didn't have any historic injuries or scars."

Gemma's eyes shimmered with tears. "She was so young, and perfect," she said quietly. "It's so unfair. Esme had so much living left to do. They both did."

"Esme wouldn't have remained perfect for long, nor was longevity guaranteed," Colin replied, taking Sebastian by surprise.

"What do you mean?" Gemma asked, and Sebastian was gratified to note that whatever Colin was about to reveal would come as a surprise to her as well.

"Pregnancy and childbirth leave their mark even if the woman is well looked after, and there are the risks associated with labor and delivery," Colin explained.

"Esme was with child?" Gemma asked. Her face looked pale in the flat white light streaming through the open door, and she was shivering.

The smell was barely noticeable now, but the cellar had grown cold and damp, and Gemma didn't have a coat or a shawl to keep her warm. Sebastian removed his coat and draped it over Gemma's shoulders, which left him in his shirtsleeves and waistcoat. Gemma shot him a grateful look, but then her attention immediately returned to Esme.

"She was about twelve weeks along," Colin said.

"Would she have known?" Sebastian asked.

He didn't say so aloud, but it was a relief that the child hadn't suffered, and that Esme had simply gone to sleep without experiencing any of the agony she would have endured had a different, more toxic substance been used. There were blessings even in death, if one chose to look for them.

"It is possible that she was unaware, if her menses were not regular, but she probably would have realized by this point. And if she was engaging in sexual congress, she would have been mindful of the possibility." Colin's cheeks turned pink, and he made it a point to not look at Gemma.

Sebastian would have preferred that Gemma return upstairs so Colin could speak freely, but Gemma looked like she had no intention of leaving until she had heard every last word. He had no choice but to proceed, despite Colin's obvious embarrassment at discussing such intimate subjects in front of a woman, even though the woman in question happened to be a trained nurse and was familiar with the workings of the female anatomy, being one herself.

"Are there any signs of sexual violence?" Sebastian asked.

Gemma didn't seem disturbed by the question, but Colin resolutely avoided looking at either of them.

"Violence, no, but there is evidence of recent sexual inter-course. There were traces of semen on the thighs and on Esme's drawers. I do beg your pardon, Gemma," he hurried to add, his neck and cheeks now turning a mottled shade of crimson.

"Not at all," Gemma replied coolly.

"Esme clearly had a lover, who might have been the father of her child," Colin said.

"Esme had been enthusiastically pursued by General Modine, who was at the theater last night, and, according to the night watchman, Esme and Christopher were romantically involved. He'd seen them together," said Sebastian.

"Seen?" Gemma asked, her brows lifting in astonishment.

"You mean *in flagrante delicto*?" Colin asked, the tips of his ears now flaming as well.

Sebastian nodded.

"That must be the motive, then," Gemma ventured.

"You think someone murdered them because they were sleeping together?" Colin asked.

"Both Esme and Christopher had ardent admirers who would have felt betrayed had they found out."

"Enough to kill?" Colin asked.

"Romantic jealousy is the world's oldest motive," Gemma said softly.

"I don't know that I would classify their jealousy as romantic," Sebastian said.

"What would you classify it as?" Gemma asked.

"Sexual."

"Isn't that the same thing?" Colin asked, looking from Sebastian to Gemma.

"Far from it," Sebastian replied, but didn't belabor the point.

Colin and Gemma both clearly associated physical affection with emotional love, but in Sebastian's experience the two didn't always go hand in hand. The countless brothels that did a brisk business in London were a testament to that; most punters did not become emotionally invested in the women they paid to see. Sexual jealousy was more about possession, and the loss of something one felt they owned could very easily result in murder. Sebastian had seen it a number of times and didn't care to recall the damage that had been inflicted on the victim in the heat of the moment. The killers, unable to allow the object of their jealousy to remain beautiful even in death, had needed to disfigure them. Esme and Christopher's killer had not felt the need to go that far, but they had murdered them all the same and had probably derived extreme pleasure from watching them die before an audience of hundreds.

There was one more indelicate question Sebastian needed to ask, and he would have preferred not to do it in front of Gemma, but she left him little choice.

"Colin, did you examine Esme's baby?"

"What do you mean? Examine it for what?" Colin asked.

"The baby is the size of a lemon at this stage, so it's difficult to say if there were any developmental abnormalities."

"That's not what I was going to ask. Is there any evidence that the child was of mixed race?"

"Why would it be?"

"It was suggested that Esme had been with Ishmael Cabot as well, who is of mixed race himself."

"Had she indeed?" Colin asked, shaking his head in obvious disapproval. "How many lovers did she have?"

"Three, as far as I'm aware," Sebastian replied.

There could easily have been more, and Gemma seemed to be thinking the same thing because she looked utterly scandalized. Colin sighed and lifted his shoulders in the universal sign of not knowing. "I really couldn't say when it comes to the fetus. It's possible, I suppose, but it wasn't immediately obvious. Do you think someone would murder Esme because she had taken Ishmael Cabot as her lover?"

"I don't know," Sebastian said. "I don't even know if any of it is true, but I do have to ask."

Colin pulled the sheet over Esme and stepped away from the body. "Forgive me, but I have a pupil coming in a few minutes. A private session."

"Of course. Thank you, Colin," Sebastian said. "I will let you know when the bodies are to be collected."

"I would appreciate that," Colin replied. "I'm afraid I don't have the room to keep them for too long."

There didn't seem anything more to say, so Sebastian and Gemma left Colin to it and returned upstairs.

SIXTEEN

"Where will you go now?" Gemma asked once they reached the ground floor.

"Back to the theater, and then I must return to Scotland Yard to provide Lovell with an update."

"Have you eaten?"

"I haven't had time."

"You must be famished. Let me make you a cup of tea and a sandwich," Gemma offered.

"Thank you." Sebastian followed her to the kitchen. He was hungry, and grateful for the offer of food, but he also looked forward to spending a few minutes alone with her and hoped they could speak uninterrupted.

Mabel wasn't about, but a covered pot stood on the hob and the savory aroma of mulligatawny soup filled the kitchen. Sebastian settled at the pine table while Gemma fetched a soup plate and a spoon, ladled a generous serving of soup, and set the plate before him. She then pumped water into the kettle, set it on the hob, and disappeared into the larder. While Sebastian ate the soup, Gemma made a ham sandwich, and, once the kettle boiled, she brewed the tea. She poured him a cup and fixed it the way he liked it before making a cup for herself.

"You're an absolute treasure," Sebastian said as he pushed away his empty soup plate and started on the sandwich.

"It's only soup and a sandwich," Gemma said with a smile, but it was obvious she was pleased with the compliment. "I enjoy looking after you."

Seeing Gemma move about the kitchen with the assurance of someone who was used to doing things for herself reminded Sebastian of the time she had invited him to dinner when they had first met. It was the only time they had been truly alone together, and they had taken their time over the meal, talking with surprising ease and feeling their way forward in that way people did when they had just met but realized they'd made a connection. Gemma had insisted that Sebastian have another helping of stew, probably because she had realized that he was still hungry and too embarrassed to ask for more. And she had baked a wonderful apple charlotte that had been the best thing he'd tasted in years after primarily eating meals prepared by Mrs. Poole, whose culinary skills bordered on a method of torture.

Sebastian wished they could share more meals like that, but such simple intimacy wasn't possible since neither had a home of their own. Everything they said and did was observed by others, who judged them and took it upon themselves to monitor their conduct. But it wouldn't always be so, Sebastian reminded himself. He took a sip of tea and smiled at Gemma over the rim of the cup. A lovely blush stained her cheeks, and he was certain that her thoughts had been running along the same track, a realization that made this grim day seem just a little bit brighter. Sebastian had never seen Gemma in anything other than mourning attire, and for a moment he imagined her in a gown of emerald-green satin or sumptuous burgundy silk. How vibrant she would look, and how young. The relentless black leached color from her skin and did its best to dull the fire in her eyes, but to him there was no one more beautiful or more desirable.

"Penny for your thoughts," Gemma said, and cocked her head to the side as she awaited his answer.

Sebastian could hardly admit to what he was thinking, and he did want to speak to her about the case, since they hadn't had an opportunity to talk last night. He decided to ease into it before the conversation turned to more difficult subjects.

"The general's name sounds vaguely familiar, but I am not able to place it," he said.

"General Modine distinguished himself during the Battle of Balaclava, in October of fifty-four. You might have read about him in the papers," Gemma supplied.

"That must be it," Sebastian replied, although he had been too distracted to pay much attention to news from the front. "Did you know him in Crimea?"

"Not personally, but I heard things."

"What sort of things?"

"The man was accused of committing nearly all seven deadly sins."

"Was he, indeed?" Sebastian asked, genuinely intrigued. "Which one was he not guilty of?"

"Sloth," Gemma replied promptly.

"So, what exactly was said about him?"

"I heard him described as a cruel, prideful man who was dangerously competitive and prone to lining his pockets at the expense of others."

"Sounds like a charmer," Sebastian said. "He was at the theater last night, which makes him a suspect."

"Mona Grady, the woman I spoke to last night, mentioned that General Modine had been pursuing Esme for months."

"She seemed very distressed. Was she close to Esme?"

"I didn't really get that impression. It was more like she had personally lost something irreplaceable."

"Such as?"

"Mona said something about not getting her miracle now that Esme was gone."

"What sort of miracle?"

"I don't know, but the very thought of it sent her into floods. She said that someone was now lost to her forever."

"Why didn't you tell me last night?" Sebastian asked. "I would have made a point of speaking to her."

"You never gave me the chance. You bundled me off home before I could tell you anything."

"I had to be sure you got back safely."

"I don't think five minutes would have made much difference," Gemma said reproachfully.

"You're right. Please forgive me. It wasn't my intention to dismiss you," Sebastian said, doing his best to sound contrite.

"Water under the bridge," Gemma replied graciously.

"Is it possible that Christopher Hudson and General Modine had known each other during the war and now found themselves in pursuit of the same woman?"

Gemma considered the question, but her expression was dubious. "Given his occupation and lifestyle, I doubt Christopher Hudson was an officer, since officers generally come from well-to-do families that can afford to buy their sons a commission, but he may have been promoted. If he was a foot soldier, he might have heard of General Modine. He might have even served under him, but I wouldn't expect the general to remember a lowly soldier or a low-ranking officer years after the war." She paused, her gaze narrowed in thought. "But having a lowly soldier romance one's mistress is motive for murder if I ever heard one," she added.

"Yes, but we don't know that General Modine knew of Esme's relationship with Christopher. Or Ishmael Cabot. No one besides the night watchman mentioned it, and I'm not inclined to take the word of an old drunk as gospel."

"She had a relationship with at least one man," Gemma pointed out. "If the rumors about the general were true, then he's a shrewd, ruthless man who would do anything to protect his interests. Perhaps he had a mole at the theater."

"That's an interesting theory. I suppose the general could easily afford to pay for information if he questioned Esme's loyalty."

"Anyone spring to mind?" Gemma asked.

Sebastian nodded. "If I was in the market for a spy, I'd tap Sid."

"Sid? Why?"

"Who better to spy on the actors than a boy no one pays attention to?"

"Yes, I suppose you're right," Gemma agreed. "Children are so often overlooked."

Sebastian saw a veil of sadness pass over her eyes and knew she was referring to Lucy. It'd been several weeks since Gemma had left the Foundling Hospital, but she still missed the child and probably thought of her constantly.

"Do you want news of Lucy?" Sebastian asked, and hoped he wasn't tearing a scab off a healing wound.

Gemma stilled, her breath catching in her throat at the mention of Lucy's name. "How would you...?" She trailed off, overcome with emotion.

Neither of them was welcome at the Foundling Hospital, and Sebastian was in no doubt that Matron Holcombe wouldn't let him past the front door, but he would find a way in if it would help Gemma make peace with leaving Lucy behind.

"Never mind how," Sebastian replied. "I will find out, but only if you want me to. Do you?"

Gemma clasped her hands on the table, fidgety now where

before she had been calm. "I don't know," she admitted, and blinked tears away. "Do you think I should?"

Sebastian wanted to tell her she should forget Lucy, but bit his tongue. What right did he have to judge Gemma's feelings? She had so few people left to love, and Lucy had touched a part of her that no one else could reach. Gemma's heart was broken, and, until she knew that Lucy was thriving, she wouldn't be able to let her go and look to the future.

"Yes," he said at last.

Gemma breathed a sigh of relief, as if she had needed his approval. "Please," she said. "I only want to know Lucy is well."

And if she's not? Sebastian wanted to ask.

There was nothing Gemma could do if Lucy were ill again. The child was lost to her, and the sooner she admitted it, the better; but he couldn't bear to hurt her. All he could reasonably do was offer his help and hope that the news would soothe Gemma's aching heart.

"Give me a few days."

Gemma nodded. "Thank you. Is there anyone beside General Modine that you intend to interview?" she hurried to ask, clearly eager to change the subject.

"I'd like a word with Mr. Bonneville, the owner of the Orpheus."

"Why? How is he involved?"

"Guy Weathers had an argument with the man just before the curtain went up. Money is always a motive for murder, and according to Weathers Mr. Bonneville was demanding a higher percentage of the ticket sales if the contract was to be renewed for another four months. I don't see how Bonneville would benefit by killing Esme and Christopher, but he was at the theater, so he's a suspect. I'd also like to ask him about the peep-holes. According to the night watchman, every dressing room is equipped with a peephole that can be accessed via a narrow walkway situated behind the rooms."

Gemma looked scandalized. "Do you think he was aware of this irregularity?"

"If it was just one hole, maybe not, but if each room has one then he must know. It's his theater, after all."

"Curious," Gemma said under her breath.

Sebastian decided not to tell her what the holes were for or explain that the building used to be a brothel. Gemma probably wouldn't be shocked, but he saw no reason to reveal the sordid details. Instead, he took out his watch and checked the time. "I had better be going if I hope to get back to Scotland Yard before Lovell leaves for the day. He's on the warpath now that his replacement has been made official."

"So, you'll be reporting to Ransome now?" Gemma asked.

"So it would seem."

"How do you feel about this development?"

Sebastian sighed. "Lovell and Ransome are two sides of the same coin. They're driven by self-interest and will sacrifice anyone who gets in their way."

"A plague on both their houses," Gemma quipped, and Sebastian chuckled, grateful for a moment of levity since it was likely to be the last in a day that was nowhere near over.

"I'll see you out," Gemma said, and went to fetch his things.

"Perhaps I can call on General Modine," she offered once they'd reached the front door. "I can allude to our Crimea connection."

Sebastian sighed heavily. He didn't want to argue with Gemma, especially when she only wanted to help him, but she left him no choice.

"Gemma, please, you need to stay out of the investigation."

"I'll be safe," she hurried to reassure him. "Where's the harm in speaking to the man?"

"Where is the harm?" Sebastian exclaimed, dismayed by her cavalier attitude. "For one, the man might have just murdered two people. For another, your continued involvement will cost me my job."

Gemma stared at him. "Your job?"

Sebastian had not mentioned the snide comments and nasty jokes that had been made at his expense these last few months. The ridicule he'd opened himself up to had been his own fault. He had wanted to give credit where credit was due, but bringing Gemma to Scotland Yard and openly admitting that she had been instrumental in solving a case had undermined his position and made him look weak and ineffectual in front of men who saw women as overly emotional, intellectually inferior, and unbecomingly mannish if they tried to assert their independence. The men were moreover inherently suspicious of any woman who had willingly gone to Crimea to nurse wounded soldiers, assuming that no respectable woman would choose to be surrounded by hundreds of men and that she had ulterior motives that had nothing to do with nobility and compassion but were all about satisfying her unnatural desires.

Inspector Reece had gone so far as to publicly invite Sebastian to consult with *Inspector Tate* and had been heard to say to Sergeant Woodward that Gemma carried Sebastian's bollocks in her reticule, and he had to ask permission to use them. Lucky for Reece, at the time his uncle had still been the Home Secretary, or Sebastian would have beaten him to a pulp in some back alley. Sebastian had graciously allowed him to live, but had made certain to remind Reece and anyone within hearing distance that his uncle was the only reason a man with Reece's lack of breeding, below-average intelligence, and pitiful solve rate was still on the police service.

Taking Gemma gently by the shoulders, Sebastian looked down at her with what he hoped wasn't a patronizing expression. "Gemma, you are clever and brave, but it's not only irresponsible of me to allow you to act on your own, it's also dangerous and highly inappropriate. You know I welcome your insights, but I would prefer to keep our collaboration to the safety of the drawing room."

"I see," Gemma said, and stepped away from him.

Sebastian allowed his hands to fall to his sides, but his innards twisted with guilt. He had hurt her feelings and belittled her contribution, but he had to get his point across. Gemma had grown too comfortable in the role of investigator, and, although he was to blame for encouraging her efforts, he had to put a stop to her snooping before she got seriously hurt.

"Gemma, I won't risk the life of another woman," Sebastian said, hoping the plea would make his case, but Gemma's eyes flashed with anger.

"I will not be forever compared to Louisa. I know you feel responsible for what happened and think it's your job to protect me, but you're not my husband, Sebastian. I am my own person, and I don't answer to you."

"I meant no disrespect. Please try to understand," Sebastian tried again, but Gemma cut him off.

"I understand. And now I must go. Mrs. Ramsey should be awake by now."

Gemma turned on her heel and walked away, her hips swaying seductively as she hurried up the stairs. Sebastian would have liked to follow her and make things right between them, but he had a murder to solve, and prioritizing his personal needs was just as inappropriate and irresponsible as allowing Gemma to help him work his cases. He resolutely pushed the guilt away and walked out the door. Perhaps news of Lucy could serve as a peace offering.

SEVENTEEN

Gemma felt ashamed of her outburst as soon as she heard the door close behind Sebastian. She had been wrong to lash out, but it was too late to go after him and apologize. She had been grateful and proud when Sebastian had introduced her to the men and had admitted to her part in apprehending the Foundling Hospital killer, but she should have realized that he'd pay for his chivalry, given the strictly masculine nature of the establishment. Men of their generation, or any generation really, did not look kindly upon women who upstaged them or the men who not only allowed women to get away with it but condoned their involvement and praised them for it. The very idea that a woman might possess the wits and skills necessary to apprehend a killer was so shocking and threatening to the members of the profession that it was a wonder Sebastian had not been sacked on the spot.

Gemma should have realized that Sebastian's standing among the other detectives would suffer, and that Superintendent Lovell would have no choice but to warn him about her interference now that she had become unwittingly involved in another murder investigation and threaten him with dismissal should he ignore the decree. The possibility of Sebastian losing his place at Scotland Yard drove home the gravity of the situation and forced Gemma to confront the reasons for the panic that enveloped her. For one, she had never met a man better suited to his profession, and she would never wish to be the instrument of his undoing. And for another, if Sebastian were to be dismissed he might leave.

He hadn't mentioned his plan to go to America in months, but Gemma was sure the pull was still there and thought that he might thrive in a country where his temperament wasn't straitjacketed by social expectations and departmental politics. The Pinkerton Detective Agency was focused on results, not social standing or public approval, and she had heard—and maybe this was nothing more than salacious tittle-tattle—that they employed women and treated their female agents with courtesy and respect. For a fraction of a second, Gemma allowed herself to imagine a life in which she could be a gun-slinging vigilante who rode astride through dusty American plains and primitive frontier towns while hunting fugitives for a bounty.

The idea was ludicrous, but she could understand the attraction such a life held for Sebastian. He was different from any man Gemma had ever known, driven by needs few understood and desperate to break through the walls of convention that imprisoned him and crushed his spirit. A man couldn't outrun his past, but he could shape his future, and to Sebastian America was synonymous with freedom. In a place that was as wild as it was vast, there was always a demand for men who were looking for adventure, and the Pinkertons would snap up a man with his qualifications in a heartbeat. Sebastian longed to be free, to sail away from a place that held nothing but painful memories and endless recriminations, and, although Gemma didn't dare say it out loud, she suspected that he had only chosen to remain in London because of her.

And if she were honest, she had to admit that her eagerness to help him wasn't just a need to see justice done. She wasn't naïve enough to believe that her intentions were purely altruistic. She was driven by her own feelings, as well as her shameful need to be validated and seen. And by her longing for Sebastian. Her desperate desire to spend a few moments alone with him made her cheeks burn with shame, but she was a woman on the brink of thirty, a spinster who might never again glimpse the promise of marriage and family. The notion of spending her days in other people's homes, not quite a servant but not one of the family, left her feeling hopeless and depressed. She wouldn't be the first woman to wind up an old maid, but, unlike so many others, who accepted their fate, Gemma chafed at the prospect of living a barren life when Sebastian's mere presence made her long for more. So much more. And Lucy had reminded her how desperately she wanted to be a mother.

It was perhaps that longing that had made her snap at the mere mention of Louisa. She knew Sebastian still grieved for his wife and son, and it was right that he should, but there were times when Gemma thought he was comparing her to Louisa and was afraid he'd find her lacking. Perhaps if she had known Louisa, or had at least seen a photograph, she might feel less threatened, but Louisa loomed large, the perfect woman who had been murdered in the prime of her life.

Recalling the details of Louisa's death made Gemma sick with shame. Sebastian was terrified about unwittingly putting her in danger and only wanted to keep her safe. Any woman would be grateful beyond words to be courted by a man who was so concerned with her well-being, but Gemma wasn't any woman, nor did she think staying at home would keep her safe. After all, Louisa had been murdered in her own home, an innocent victim of revenge. She had not involved herself in Sebastian's work, nor had she gone out alone or made herself known to individuals who might use her as a pawn to further their own agenda. Louisa had been murdered only because she was married to Sebastian, and, unless he meant to remain alone for the rest of his days, any woman who dared to love him might meet the same fate. Since any possibility of marriage was remote, especially now that they had quarreled, Gemma decided to focus on the more immediate problem.

A sensible woman would honor Sebastian's request and settle for waiting for news, but there were other ways she could help without doing anything to jeopardize his standing with Scotland Yard or back him into a corner. And it would be best to present him with tangible evidence rather than forewarn him that she intended to do a bit of harmless investigating. After all, it was always better to ask for forgiveness than seek permission and take the risk of being denied.

Anne was still sleeping peacefully and would probably remain abed until dinnertime, so Gemma locked the door, fetched her bonnet, cape, reticule, and gloves from her room, and returned downstairs. She knew precisely where she was going and if she took a cab would be back before Colin finished with his student. As far as she could see, the most important aspect of this case was the method of murder. Poison was the perfect weapon for a killer who thought themselves too smart to get caught and had no desire to witness the result of their handi-work. It could be administered in advance and from afar and spare the killer having to watch their victim die. Although lethal, it wasn't as intimately personal as a physical altercation, where the killer and the victim came face to face at the moment of struggle and there was the possibility of things going wrong.

Arsenic in particular was extremely popular, since the victim could be poisoned over a period of time and eventually succumb to the effects without anyone realizing they had been murdered. If the killer were patient and clever they could commit the perfect crime, and no one would be the wiser. After all, spouses, in-laws, and even abusive employers and meddling neighbors died all the time, and of natural causes. So why would anyone suspect that the victim had died of slow poisoning if the killer hadn't done anything to draw attention to themselves?

Death by poisoning had become something of an epidemic in recent years, and chemists were now required to keep a book of poisons, in which they recorded every sale of toxic substances and the name and address of the buyer. Of course, they could intentionally forget to record a particular purchase, or the buyer could give the wrong name and address, but as a rule chemists knew their regulars and tended to comply with the law, if only to protect themselves and their livelihood. There was also the fact that, unless an individual came prepared with an alias and a false address, they tended to freeze with indecision when asked for the information, thereby giving themselves away. Most people simply bought reasonable quantities of poison and provided their real names and addresses, and if questioned by the police claimed that the poison was needed to get rid of rodents.

This murder, however, went against every logical reason a killer might decide on poison. They'd opted for an obvious and dramatic death, a double murder that would be written about in the papers and shouted about from every street corner. This suggested to Gemma that the killer was not someone who feared getting caught, either because they believed themselves exceptionally clever or because no one would ever associate them with the deaths of Esme and Christopher. Gemma didn't think they would have given their name when purchasing the morphine, but, if they were connected with the theater, chances were they had obtained the poison from a local shop. Her efforts might come to nothing, but she thought it was a theory worth testing. As a nurse, she was practically exempt from undue scrutiny, so no one would question her if she asked for a small amount of morphine.

Gemma had just reached the bottom of the stairs when she came face to face with Colin.

"Are you going out?" he asked.

She couldn't bring herself to lie, so she filled Colin in on her plan.

"Would you like me to accompany you? I can ask Mabel to keep an eye on Mother for a few hours. My pupil is running late. Perhaps he won't show at all," Colin explained.

"I'm sure your pupil will be here soon. Imagine his disappointment if he's had a wasted journey," Gemma replied.

In truth, she didn't want Colin to come along. For one, they would probably draw more attention if they questioned the chemists together, and for another, she needed to do this on her own so that neither Sebastian nor Colin could be held responsible by anyone at Scotland Yard. Colin relied on the fees, and Gemma wasn't about to endanger his position as well.

"Well, let me at least jot down a list of chemists located near Covent Garden. I believe there are three in the immediate vicinity."

"I would appreciate that. It will save me a great deal of time."

Colin walked into his study, pulled out a clean sheet of paper, and wrote down the names, then handed it to Gemma, who had remained by the door. As she glanced at the list of names, then folded the list and stowed it in her reticule, Colin shot her a searching look and shook his head in a manner that suggested he couldn't even begin to verbalize what he was thinking.

"What is it, Colin?" Gemma asked.

"It's nothing."

"No, please, tell me."

Colin sighed, his shoulders sloping as he exhaled heavily. "Gemma, far be it from me to comment on your choices, but I really do think you're becoming addicted to danger. Some would say that it's the result of an unsatisfactory personal life or the tedium of your profession, but in your case I think it's something quite different."

"Oh?" Gemma asked, doing her best not to appear affronted or give in to the desire to agree that her decisions were none of Colin's affair.

"You're entirely too intelligent for a woman, and, like any thinking person, you crave intellectual stimulation. Involving yourself in murder inquiries is a way to exercise your powers of deduction and feel like you're making a difference, but it's also something else. It's a way to earn Sebastian's respect."

Gemma suddenly wished she hadn't been quite so forthcoming about her plan. Colin's analysis made her deeply uncomfortable and reminded her that she was clearly more transparent than she had imagined. Even though Colin wasn't entirely wrong in his estimation, his unexpected bluntness made Gemma feel violated and unfairly judged. Instead of replying, she mumbled something about getting back before dark and fled, wishing only to be on her own before she could get into an argument with someone else.

EIGHTEEN

Mindful of wasting time, Gemma hailed a cab and asked the cabbie to drop her at the corner of James Street and Long Acre, near the entrance to Covent Garden Market. Normally the market was a hive of activity, especially early in the morning, when the vendors had just arrived with their laden wagons and set up their stalls, and discerning housewives and kitchen maids came out in full force to fill their baskets with meat, produce, and fruit. By midafternoon, the pickings grew less appealing and the offerings were not as fresh, and by late afternoon many of the vendors had packed up and gone, leaving behind broken crates, rotten produce, and a terrible stench.

This afternoon the market was nearly empty, with only a few stragglers packing up the last of their wares and gangs of barefoot street children picking through the trash and begging for a handout. The rain had washed away blood spilled by the butchers, bits of straw, and the squashed fruit and vegetables that had fallen from the stalls and been trampled underfoot, leaving behind glistening cobbles and deliciously clean air. The rain had now stopped, and the clouds that raced across the heavens offered brief glimpses of yellow-gray sky that reminded

Gemma of a healing bruise. She tried to avoid the deeper puddles as she walked down James Street, checking the signs until she spotted the Drug Emporium.

Despite the grandiose name, the place was small and dingy, with dusty counters, scuffed floors, and windows that probably hadn't been washed since the Flood. The man behind the counter had to be in his seventies. He was almost completely bald, his scalp and hands dotted with brown liver spots. His nails were long and yellowed, and he smelled strongly of stale sweat and tobacco. Gemma's stomach heaved with revulsion, but she forced a friendly smile onto her face as she approached the counter.

"How may I be of service, miss?" the man asked, smiling to reveal stained teeth.

"I would like to purchase a small quantity of morphine. For pain management," she added when the man's eyebrows lifted in surprise.

"I don't carry morphine, but I can offer you a tincture of laudanum or Bond's Rejuvenating Elixir. It cures all manner of ills and is guaranteed to put pep in your step. Says so right there on the label." The man's smile grew wider. "I take it myself. A spoonful every morning. I can assure you, I've never felt better."

Gemma strongly suspected that the pep in the elixir came from the cocaine it was laced with, which made Bond's health tonic very popular with people who felt listless and fatigued, but she wasn't about to take it herself or give it to Anne, since individuals who took it tended to form a dependency and couldn't get through the day without several doses.

"Er, I'll take the tincture of opium," Gemma said.

She didn't want anything from this filthy shop, but she needed to see the book of poisons, and she couldn't very well ask the man to show it to her. He wasn't obligated to do so and would only become suspicious of her motives if she asked without a reason, which she intended to keep to herself.

"All right, but you're missing out," the chemist said, then turned around to take down a dusty brown bottle from the top shelf. He used it to fill a small vial, stoppered the vial with a cork, and set it on the counter, after replacing the bottle on the shelf. "You'll have to sign the register," he said. "Not my idea, you understand, but rules are rules."

"Of course," Gemma replied.

The chemist produced a ledger from beneath the counter and opened it to the current page. The entries went back to the beginning of the year, and there were only seven. None of the names sounded even remotely familiar, so Gemma dipped the pen in the ink and signed her name as illegibly as she could manage, and provided her previous address. If anyone went looking for her at Mrs. Bass's boarding house, they were sure to be disappointed, since Mrs. Bass had never asked for Gemma's new address.

Stowing the vial in her reticule, Gemma walked briskly through Covent Garden arcade, her steps echoing in the empty space, until she came out in Russell Street. Driscoll's Drugs was the next shop on her list and was the closest chemist to the Orpheus theater. The shop was nothing like the Drug Emporium and was the sort of place Gemma would frequent if it were within walking distance of the Ramseys' home. The gold letters shone bright against the dark green of the sign, the windows reflected the sun that had finally broken through the storm clouds, and the interior smelled of beeswax polish and lavender.

The man behind the counter was closer to Gemma's age and something of a dandy. His hair was artfully arranged, his face clean-shaven, and his nails clean and buffed. He wore a splendid satin waistcoat with a matching tie, and the chain and fob of his pocket watch gleamed in the light of the gas lamps that were lit throughout the shop despite the early hour. There were several carefully arranged displays, and the drawers behind the counter were neatly labeled. A boy of about four-teen was arranging hair pomade on a shelf, and nodded to Gemma solemnly before returning to the task.

"Good afternoon, madam. Herbert Driscoll at your service. How can I help?" Mr. Driscoll asked politely and smiled.

He had a lovely smile, and Gemma found herself smiling back. She liked the fact that he had referred to her as madam and not miss. She didn't care for people who made unfounded assumptions about her marital status or treated her with brusque tolerance because she was on her own and not accom-panied by a husband or a male relative.

"Do you carry morphine, Mr. Driscoll?"

"Morphine is a dangerous substance, madam, and not to be administered by someone unfamiliar with its effects," the chemist said. He still looked friendly, but his guard was up, and it was clear that he wouldn't simply sell the drug to anyone who asked.

"I'm a trained nurse, Mr. Driscoll, and it's for my patient, who's in the final stages of stomach cancer. The morphine is to alleviate her pain, and I administer it twenty milligrams at a time." Gemma hated to lie, but she needed to convince the man that she was familiar with the dosage and understood the ramifi-cations of administering the drug.

"A terrifying illness," the man agreed. "I can offer you sixty milligrams. Anything more and I will have to report it to the authorities."

"Really?" Gemma asked, her shock genuine. She had known she'd have to sign the book, but she had never heard of a chemist volunteering the information to the authorities without being asked.

"I'm afraid so," Mr. Driscoll said. "I don't know if you've heard, but Buxton's in the Strand was closed down by the police last month."

"On what grounds?" Gemma asked. She had never been to

Buxton's but had walked past it when she had come to meet Victor near the offices of the *Daily Telegraph.*

"It seems they sold large quantities of arsenic to a Mrs. Singleton, who then used it to poison her entire family, including her two small children. She was hanged last week."

Gemma had heard about the case, but the articles had made no mention of Buxton's. Perhaps the decision to close down the shop had come about after the trial.

"Mr. Buxton, who I happen to know personally, thought it suspicious that Mrs. Singleton wished to buy such a substantial quantity, but did not report the sale. Mrs. Singleton said that the arsenic was needed to deal with an infestation of rats, and he believed her," Mr. Driscoll said, his indignation bubbling just beneath the friendly façade. "There are those who feel that Mr. Buxton bears moral responsibility for what happened and should be treated as an accessory to murder."

"Goodness me," Gemma exclaimed. "That does seem a bit extreme."

"That's exactly what I said," Mr. Driscoll cried. "The merchants are not responsible for what the public does with the merchandise. After all, can a blacksmith be held liable for making a sword that was used to kill someone, or a stonemason for cutting a stone that bashed someone's skull in? Surely what's important is the intent and not the tool."

"I couldn't agree more," Gemma said, wishing Mr. Driscoll would tire of the subject and allow her to complete her purchase; but the shop was empty of customers, and he clearly relished an opportunity to talk to someone of like mind.

In theory, Gemma did agree with him. Mr. Buxton should have notified the police, but, if Mrs. Singleton had actually used the arsenic to kill rats, he would have looked foolish and would have been ridiculed and forever treated with mistrust by his customers. Gemma had heard of nurses and doctors standing accused of the death of a patient when it was clear that they weren't at fault. Patients died, even those whose conditions were not very serious or who appeared to be on the mend and then took a turn for the worse. Mr. Driscoll was right; it wasn't always about the outcome but about intent.

"As I'm sure you understand, we have to do our utmost to protect ourselves from baseless accusations," Mr. Driscoll said, but his anger had seemingly burned out.

"Indeed you must," Gemma agreed.

"You will have to sign for the morphine," Mr. Driscoll said as he pulled out the poisons register and set it on the counter between them.

"Of course. And if I should require more?"

"You can purchase a further sixty milligrams in a few days, or, if you require a steady supply, then I will have to ask that the treating physician make the request directly to me."

"Sixty milligrams will be sufficient for now, and I will have a word with the doctor."

"Very well. Please sign the register, and I will prepare your order," Mr. Driscoll said, and disappeared into a back room.

Gemma felt the boy's gaze on her as she opened the register. He was probably charged with keeping an eye on the customers when Mr. Driscoll stepped away, in case someone decided to avail themselves of the opportunity and take something from an unguarded shelf. Gemma ignored him and scanned the entries. There were considerably more purchases of poisonous substances at Driscoll's, probably because the shop inspired confidence in the quality of its merchandise and attracted a more discerning customer. There were more than two dozen entries since the start of the year, but only one jumped out at Gemma. An F. Modine had purchased a packet of arsenic and a bottle of laudanum three weeks ago. There was nothing suspicious about the quantity, but Modine wasn't a common surname—perhaps there was a connection?

What was the general's Christian name? John, she seemed

to remember, or possibly Jonathan, but definitely not a name that began with F. Of course, he could have used a false initial, but Gemma didn't see General Modine as someone who would lie. From what she knew of the man, he was too prideful to feel the need to hide behind a false name. Unwilling to provide her own name for fear of drawing suspicion or getting reported to the police for inquiring about morphine, Gemma signed with her mother's maiden name instead. *E. Milton.* Then she jotted down an address in St. John's Wood that filled her with sadness. No Miltons had lived there since her grandparents had passed, and Gemma's father had sold his wife's inheritance and invested the money in the haberdashery business he had still co-owned at the time of his death.

Gemma paid for her purchase, thanked Mr. Driscoll for his help, and left the shop. As she walked down the nearly empty street, her mind returned to her conversation with him. Was it possible that the murder weapon had been a combination of substances rather than pure morphine? That would make sense if the killer had hoped to avoid detection and had put together a lethal mix that was potent enough to murder two people; but, if that were the case, Esme and Christopher would have had a more violent physical reaction. Since neither had experienced obvious convulsions, noticeable disorientation, or a loosening of the bowels, Gemma had to concede that her theory had to be wrong. Someone had managed to acquire a large amount of morphine; but unless the chemist who had sold it to them alerted the police, there was no way to trace the purchase. And given what Mr. Driscoll had said, no one would be foolish enough to come forward, since they could be held complicit in a double homicide.

But perhaps they could be flushed out.

NINETEEN

Gemma consulted the list Colin had given her and quickened her step. There was only one shop left to visit. It was in Tavistock Street and seemed a respectable establishment that was neither as elegant as Driscoll's nor as seedy as the Drug Emporium. Harbor's Drugs was neat and tidy, with a discreet sign, gleaming bay windows, and a welcoming interior. There were no prominent displays or the clean scent of lavender, but it smelled as a chemist's should, of medicinal substances and pungent herbs.

The woman behind the counter was in her thirties, and, although she was not conventionally attractive, her dark coloring was striking in its own way. She wore a gown of black bombazine, and her hair was parted in the middle and scraped into a tight knot but not covered by a cap. She had an air of brisk efficiency and competence, and greeted Gemma with a nod before turning her attention back to an elderly woman, who explained that her husband was costive. The saleswoman advised her to try castor oil before resorting to more aggressive alternatives, and produced a bottle that was large enough to unbind a small elephant. The customer then asked endless questions about various other ailments for which she was not seeking a remedy and took another ten minutes to leave, carrying the bottle of castor oil in front of her with both hands.

"Good afternoon," Gemma said as she finally stepped up to the counter.

"Good afternoon," the woman replied, and fixed Gemma with an expectant look.

"Are you the proprietor?" Gemma asked, curious if she was addressing the chemist or a salesperson.

Gemma had never met a female chemist but had once met a woman who had taken over her husband's shop after he passed. Mrs. Smith had employed a male chemist to reassure the customers who didn't think a woman could be trusted to prepare their medicines, but Gemma was certain that she understood every aspect of the business and made some of the compounds herself.

"I'm Mary Harbor. My husband is the chemist," the woman replied peevishly. "I can help you with whatever you need."

"I require sixty milligrams of morphine," Gemma announced.

The woman shook her head. "Sorry, miss, but we're all out of morphine. We have yet to replenish our stock since the break-in."

"Break-in?" Gemma echoed. She couldn't believe her luck, but was careful not to show her excitement.

Mrs. Harbor nodded. "A week ago. Nothing was taken except the morphine. It's like the culprit knew precisely what he wanted and where to find it."

"Did you keep the morphine on display?" Gemma asked. The break-in couldn't be a coincidence, given the timing and location of the murders.

"Heavens, no," Mary Harbor replied. "We kept it in the back, under lock and key. They picked the lock but didn't take anything else, not even the laudanum, which to my mind is more profitable if one hopes to sell it."

"How much morphine was taken?"

Mrs. Harbor sighed heavily. "We'd just replenished our stock, and they took it all. Nearly three hundred milligrams."

"That's quite a lot," Gemma exclaimed, astonished by the magnitude of the theft.

"Know much about poisonous substances, do you?" the woman asked, her eyes narrowing in suspicion now that she had likely realized that she had revealed too much to a stranger who seemed unusually interested in a lethal drug.

"I'm a nurse," Gemma explained. "I administered morphine during the Crimean War. Of course, we never had enough, but when we did receive supplies it provided highly effective pain relief."

"You're one of Florence Nightingale's girls," the woman exclaimed, a warm smile lighting up her stern features. "A pleasure to make your acquaintance, Miss...?"

"Tate." Gemma was reluctant to give her name, but lying to someone's face was vastly different to scribbling down a false moniker.

"My sister was in Scutari. Perhaps you knew her. Penelope Bright."

"Yes!" Gemma exclaimed. "How is Poppy?"

"She's well. I wager she'd like to see you, Miss Tate. She talks about her time in Scutari all the time. Drives us to distraction. You'd think she was on a seaside holiday the way she reminisces about that Godforsaken place."

"I would love to see Poppy again. We lost touch once we returned to England."

"It was difficult for her," Mrs. Harbor said. "An adjustment."

"Yes," Gemma agreed. "For us all."

Mrs. Harbor nodded, her gaze sliding over Gemma's

mourning weeds and her eyes warming with sympathy. "I'm sorry for your loss," she said, but thankfully didn't ask for any details. "Here," she said. She pulled out a sheet of paper, dipped a pen in the inkwell that stood on the counter, and wrote down an address. "Mr. Harbor and I assumed that Poppy would come and live with us once she returned, but she wouldn't hear of it. She said we were worse than our parents, and she wasn't having it. So instead of living in safety and comfort with the only family she has left, she prefers to live in a mean little boarding house in Blackfriars. Imagine that! She needs her independence, she says." Mrs. Harbor threw up her hands in obvious incomprehension. "Independence to do what, I ask you? A woman needs to have her family about her, especially an unmarried woman, who can fall victim to unscrupulous men and greedy landlords. But she won't listen to me. I'm only her sister, so what do I know?"

"Thank you," Gemma said. "I will call on Poppy at the first opportunity."

Mrs. Harbor nodded. "Maybe you can talk some sense into her, Miss Tate. She's at home in the mornings. Works the evening shift at an infirmary in Lambeth," she added with a shake of her head, then seemingly recalled that Gemma had yet to purchase something. "Was there anything else you needed, Miss Tate?"

"Some headache powders, and if you have any hand cream. Perhaps something light." Gemma's hands were reddened and dry, and she hoped the woman might offer something that wasn't scented lard.

"Have you tried Constance's Creations?" Mrs. Harbor asked. She took out a simple white jar and set it on the counter. "It's made with lady's mantle and aloe, and a dash of rosewater. Smells lovely and doesn't contain any animal fat. Here, try it."

Mrs. Harbor unscrewed the lid and held the jar out to Gemma, who took a tiny dab of the cream and rubbed it into her hands. The cream absorbed easily into the skin and didn't make her hands feel greasy.

"Oh, this is nice. I'll take it."

Mrs. Harbor smiled. "I shall apply a discount since you're a friend of Poppy's."

"Thank you. That's very kind. Did you ever report it to the police?" Gemma asked as she took out her coin purse.

"Report what?"

"The theft of the morphine."

"And what were they going to do about it?" Mrs. Harbor asked with obvious scorn. "Not like anyone would admit to breaking in. What's done is done, I always say. I told Mr. Harbor, perhaps this was a lesson to us, and we should invest in better security." She leaned forward and lowered her voice. "No chemist is safe these days, Miss Tate. I blame the Chinese. They brought their filth into our cities, and now there's no getting rid of it. Have you ever met an opium eater? Disgraceful. They will do anything to get their fix. Anything, I tell you. And women too. But you can hardly blame the women."

"Why wouldn't you blame the women?" Gemma asked, curious to hear Mrs. Harbor's views on the subject.

"The women are innocent victims, Miss Tate. They're given laudanum by their physicians and fed the stuff until they develop a craving for it. And it's usually the husbands that ask for it. I suppose it's the preferable alternative."

"Preferable to what?"

"To a hysterectomy, if the woman becomes unmanageable, or putting their wife in an asylum. Imagine the scandal, and the expense. Why, a respectable place can cost a fortune. Much easier to dose the poor woman with laudanum and leave her in a stupor all the long day. And if the poor wretch has children, at least they still have their mother, and she's as docile as a lamb."

"Are there any physicians you know of who are open to persuasion from desperate husbands?" Gemma asked.

"There are a few, but the one with the most questionable reputation, in my opinion, is Dr. Lederer. A butcher of women. It's either the laudanum or the scalpel, or both. He doesn't recognize any other form of healing. You beware, Miss Tate, if you ever come across him."

"I doubt our paths will ever cross," Gemma said.

"Never say never. You're a nurse, so you know how it goes. One patient meets their Maker, and you're on to the next. And it's a small world, isn't it? You know our Poppy, and she knows Dr. Lederer. See what I'm saying? Small world."

"I do," Gemma replied. "And thank you for the warning."

"I tell you, Miss Tate. Sometimes it's safer to remain unwed. At least there's no disappointed husband to wish you away. Thank the good Lord I'm such a help to Mr. Harbor, or who knows what he'd do, given his occupation." Mrs. Harbor smiled at her own joke—if it was a joke and not an articulation of her fears.

Gemma was relieved when two men entered the shop and their presence put a stop to Mrs. Harbor's tattle. Gemma paid for her purchases, stuffed them and Poppy's address into her reticule, and bid Mrs. Harbor a good evening before stepping out into the street. It was high time she returned home and faced Colin, who would either be contrite for his earlier criticism of her or still riding his high horse, which would make for an awkward evening. As she hurried toward the nearest cabstand, she realized that, although she wanted to smooth things over, she wasn't prepared to admit to any wrongdoing on her part. As far as she was concerned, she was a free agent, and Colin had no right to censure her personal choices.

Normally, Gemma tried to avoid conflict, but today she had stood her ground, and she had quite liked how it felt.

TWENTY

Sebastian had intended to return to the theater, but changed his mind and made his way to Bedford Square instead. He wanted to speak to General Modine before the evening edition of the *Telegraph* and the weekly edition of the *Illustrated London News* hit the streets on Saturday and the printed accounts and the journalists' inflammatory speculation afforded the general an opportunity to explain away any careless revelation or remark by saying that he had read about the case in the papers. Sebastian wanted to gauge the man's reaction for himself and also ask some difficult questions that he was sure the general would not wish to answer.

Esme Royce had been nearly three months pregnant, which meant the child could be General Modine's if the relationship had started shortly after the play had opened in December. Had the general known about the pregnancy? How would he react if his lover were to tell him she was carrying his child? More important, how would he feel if he thought the child had been fathered by someone else? Sebastian had yet to meet him, but the picture Gemma had painted was of a man who would not take kindly to sharing a woman he probably thought of as his chattel. Infidelity would certainly be a motive, and, if General Modine had known about Esme and Christopher, a double murder would make perfect sense, particularly if the general lived up to his reputation for competitiveness and cruelty.

But had Esme been romantically involved with Christopher, and had she engaged in secret trysts with Ishmael Cabot? Sebastian had no reason to accuse Walt Dickie of lying to Constable Bryant, but he needed someone to verify the watchman's claims, since no one else had mentioned Esme's involvement with the two men. He thought that he should have a word with Sid. A curious child who lived at the theater had to be familiar with every nook and cranny of the place and might be able to verify or refute Walt Dickie's account. Sebastian found it odd that Mr. Bonneville had decided to keep on a gin-soaked watchman and two orphaned children and allowed them to live at the theater. He was either a kind, generous man who took pity on those less fortunate, or someone who took advantage of others' desperation and paid them a pittance instead of hiring employees who'd demand a fair wage.

When he located the correct address, Sebastian was surprised by the grandeur of the Modine residence. A three-story house in Bedford Square spoke to wealth and influence. It was possible that General Modine was a scion of a wealthy family who'd purchased himself an officer's commission and then risen through the ranks—or perhaps he'd made his money in other ways. Sebastian had heard much about profiteering during the Crimean War during his investigation into the murder of Jacob Harrow, and, given what Gemma had said about the general's character, it was also possible that the general's current standing was the result of brazen double-dealing. He certainly wouldn't be the first high-ranking officer to engage in fraud.

The door to the Modine residence shone with fresh black paint and was fitted with an iron door knocker in the shape of a snarling gargoyle that gripped a ring between its pointed teeth. One didn't have to be a student of symbolism to deduce that the knocker wasn't a token of welcome. The twisted face that stared back at Sebastian seemed to say, "Enter at your own risk." When Sebastian knocked, a smarmy butler who oozed pomposity and would have looked down his nose at Sebastian if they weren't of a comparable height opened the door.

"Tradesmen's entrance is round the back," the butler intoned, not bothering to hide his annoyance.

"Inspector Bell of Scotland Yard to see General Modine."

"As I just said," the butler repeated. "Round the back."

"I'm not a tradesman, and the general will want to hear what I have to say," Sebastian replied patiently.

"I'd say that's debatable. On both counts," the butler replied, his face twisting into an ugly sneer that resembled the gargoyle's ferocious expression.

This man, who had devoted his life to answering the door, browbeating footmen, and guarding his master's silver, clearly thought himself better than Sebastian and believed that he'd climbed a few rungs higher on the ladder of success, but Sebastian couldn't imagine anything more demeaning than a life of servitude. Perhaps he simply wasn't suited to such a role, but he would sooner return to his parents' farm than spend years of his life catering to the whims of some jumped-up cretin who used young girls to satisfy his lust.

"Are you going to let me in, or do I have to come back with reinforcements?" Sebastian barked.

He'd never yet had to make good on his threat, since a police wagon at the door was a fate worse than death for a butler who had allowed his master to be thus humiliated in front of his neighbors. It was easier and much more discreet to simply let the policeman in, thwart him in every way possible, then send him on his way with a flea in his ear and a stern warning to not come back.

"What is your name?" Sebastian asked when the butler failed to budge.

"Richardson," the man answered with all the snootiness he could muster.

"You had better announce me, Richardson, or I will come back with half a dozen constables and break down this door. I doubt your master would thank you for your diligence on his behalf then."

Richardson looked conflicted, but was astute enough to realize that challenging Sebastian would not end well. He finally stepped aside and allowed Sebastian to step into the foyer, but didn't tell a passing maid to take his things. The omission was clearly meant to reiterate that he wasn't welcome and would not be staying long. Good manners dictated that Sebastian wait until he was invited into the drawing room, but he followed Richardson when the butler went to announce him, and stopped only when he could see into the room beyond.

The drawing room was beautifully appointed, the Prussian blue walls matching the embroidered gold-and-blue motif of the cream curtains and the damask upholstery. The marble-topped fireplace gave off a pleasant warmth, and a porcelain tea service painted with delicate blue flowers was set out on the low table along with platters of tea cakes and bite-size sandwiches.

A man in his forties, presumably the general, sat in a wingchair, his legs crossed, a steaming cup halfway to his lips. With curling dark hair that was gently threaded with gray, hooded blue eyes beneath strong brows, and an aquiline nose, he resembled a Roman bust, but the similarity ended there. Whereas sculpted faces usually wore an expression of heroic fortitude, General Modine's mouth had a cruel cast, and his expression was one of intense displeasure that bordered on anger. Sebastian could sense Richardson's apprehension and could understand why the butler felt so intimidated. General Modine looked like a man who wasn't interested in excuses or explanations and would exact punishment on anyone who failed to follow his orders.

A woman of around thirty was perched on the settee. Her fair curls framed a heart-shaped face, and she was attired in a gown of blue-gray silk that was liberally adorned with silver lace. There were jeweled combs in her hair, and she wore a delicate sapphire and diamond necklace and matching earrings that swayed when she turned to look at the butler. Despite her carefully arranged expression, the woman's posture radiated coiled tension, and Sebastian thought he'd caught a flash of fear before she cast her eyes down at the empty plate before her. When she lifted her teacup, he noticed a bruise on her wrist, which she instantly tried to cover with the lace of her cuff. She was like a damaged ornament that someone had turned to hide a crack that marred its beauty.

"What is it, Richardson?" the general demanded.

"Forgive the interruption, General, but Inspector Bell of Scotland Yard has requested an audience. He insists the matter is of the utmost urgency."

The woman's obvious fear and the deferential phrasing and slight quiver in Richardson's voice were telling, and Sebastian felt a twinge of sympathy for them both. It was as if General Modine were a monarch who had the power to harm those who depended on him in ways that were truly terrifying, rather than simply a husband and an employer. Given that the general was a military man, it wasn't beyond the realm of possibility that he whipped his employees as well as his wife as if they were foot soldiers who could earn twenty lashes just by looking at their superior officer the wrong way.

"Send him away," the general snapped.

Richardson looked like he was going to be ill, and Mrs. Modine set down her cup, her hand shaking so badly that a bit of tea sloshed out onto the skirt of her gown, and the cup clattered loudly against the saucer in the silence that ensued. Sickened by this display of terror, Sebastian marched into the drawing room.

"Inspector Bell of Scotland Yard," he said, and held up his warrant card. "A word, sir."

Unless the general intended to physically remove him from the premises or instruct Richardson to wrestle him out the door with the help of the footmen, Modine had no choice but to speak to Sebastian.

"Leave us," the general barked at his wife, and Mrs. Modine scurried toward the door. She seemed relieved to be dismissed but also nervous, as if this interruption were somehow her fault.

"Take everything away," General Modine instructed the butler.

Richardson quickly placed all the items on the tray and practically sprinted from the room, managing to shut the door behind him while balancing the heavy tray on one hand.

The general didn't invite Sebastian to sit, so he advanced further into the room and stood at the center, his feet planted firmly on the thick rug and his arms at his sides. The general did not intimidate him, but he was curious. Few people Sebastian had met elicited such a visceral reaction, and he couldn't help but wonder if the general had treated Esme Royce harshly or if there was a softer side to the man when his affections were engaged. He had brought Esme flowers, but that didn't mean a thing. The flowers and gifts were material things that couldn't replace affection or kindness.

"Well, what do you want?" the general demanded.

"You paid a visit to the Orpheus theater yesterday."

"What of it?"

"Esme Royce and Christopher Hudson both died on stage last night."

The mask slipped, and for just a moment Sebastian saw what he thought was genuine sorrow, but he couldn't tell if it was grief for a woman the general had loved or the sort of sadness one might feel at losing an elderly dog or a beloved horse. But although the initial shock had seemed genuine, the sadness was instantly replaced by cold fury.

"What happened?" General Modine demanded hoarsely.

"The victims were murdered."

"How?"

"The brandy in the vials was laced with a large dose of morphine," Sebastian replied. He was watching the general intently, alert to every change in tone and expression.

"Who would do such a thing?"

"That's what I'm tasked with finding out," Sebastian replied. "How well did you know Esme Royce?"

"Are you suggesting that I had anything to do with her death?" the general exclaimed, clearly outraged.

"I am not suggesting anything. I'm asking a fairly simple question, which you have yet to answer."

"You are impertinent," Modine ground out.

"And you're evasive," Sebastian countered.

Annoyed and tired of standing, he walked over to the settee and sat down. He didn't have to pander to this man, and if the general wished to lodge a complaint he was welcome to do so. Sitting down uninvited would be the least of Sebastian's offenses during his time with the police. He was surprised to glimpse a spark of respect in the general's eyes, and felt as if he'd just passed some test he hadn't known he was taking.

The general leaned back in his chair and placed his hands on the armrests. "You wouldn't be here if you didn't know of my relationship with Esme, so you may as well hear my side of the story."

"So there's a story, is there?" Sebastian asked as he flipped open his notebook and fished for the stub of a pencil in his pocket.

"Everything is a story," General Modine replied.

"And the details vary according to the teller."

"I first saw Esme three months ago, when I took my wife to see *Romeo and Juliet*. I thought she was the most beautiful creature I had ever seen. I returned the next day, by myself, and went backstage after the play."

"What was the nature of your relationship?" Sebastian asked, curious to see how the general would classify his affair with an adolescent girl.

"I've had plenty of conquests over the years, but I have never been in love. Until now." General Modine's expression softened, and Sebastian caught a glimpse of the young man he must have been before life, or the army, had hardened him into the despot he had seemingly become. It seemed inappropriate to offer condolences, so Sebastian continued with his questioning.

"What was it about Esme that attracted you?" he asked, too cynical not to question whether the man was sincere or playing the part of the bereaved lover for Sebastian's benefit.

"Her youth and beauty, but, most of all, her modesty. I suppose if she had given herself to me right away, I would have tired of her and moved on to someone else. I always keep a piece on the side," the general added. "Keeps things interesting. But Esme truly intrigued me."

"How soon did you consummate the relationship?"

The general scoffed. "You don't mince words, do you, Bell?"

"In my job, mincing words can have dire consequences."

Modine nodded. "Esme made me work for it, but I won her over. We were lovers within a few weeks. She was a virgin," the general said with obvious pride. Sebastian thought he was a man for whom it was important to be the first, and probably the last. He might not find his wife desirable anymore, but God help any man who tried to romance a woman he considered his property. The poor sod would probably be singing like a ten-year-old soprano and about as much of a sexual threat to any woman.

"Were you making plans for the future?" What Sebastian really wanted to ask was whether the general had suspected that Esme had been cuckolding him, but he had to tread carefully and keep the man talking.

"I asked Esme to leave the troupe and allow me to maintain her. That's all I can reasonably offer, being a married man."

"And did she accept?" Sebastian asked.

"Not at first. She said she wished to maintain her independence, and I respected her spirit. But then, a fortnight ago, Esme found out she was with child and realized that her independence would soon be curtailed unless she placed the child in an orphanage."

"So she changed her mind?" Sebastian asked, new scenarios taking shape in his mind as he imagined the general's fury at discovering that the innocent he'd thought he loved had actually been lining him up to be her meal ticket while carrying on with other men.

"She did, but only after I promised that she could keep the baby and I would provide for the child's future, regardless of the duration of our liaison."

Any decent man would offer to provide for his child's future, but such sentiments rarely applied to spoiled, wealthy men who fathered bastards indiscriminately and didn't give their offspring a second thought. Adultery was common, particularly in marriages where the husband could afford to visit exclusive brothels, or keep a mistress if they preferred something more permanent and didn't fancy sharing their paramour with other men. The orphanages were overflowing with children whose fathers were alive and well and could easily afford to support them, but felt that the children had nothing to do with them and were not worth the cost of their upkeep.

"Did you see the child as an impediment?" Sebastian asked.

"The situation wasn't ideal, but these things happen," the

general said with a minute shrug. "I certainly wouldn't murder my mistress because I didn't want the child."

"What would you have done?"

"The world is full of beautiful young women, Inspector. I would have been disappointed had the relationship turned sour, but I would have moved on. I'm not a child," the general said with a sardonic smile. "I don't break my toys once they no longer please me."

But would you destroy the toy if someone else wanted to play with it, or had played with it without permission? Sebastian wondered.

"Do you and Mrs. Modine have children, General?"

"We do not. Sadly, my wife was unable to provide me with an heir."

"That must be a disappointment to you."

"A man needs a son he can mold in his own image, or a daughter who will dote on him and devote herself to his comfort in his twilight years."

Sebastian couldn't imagine anyone doting on General Modine, but kept his counsel. Any daughter of the general's would probably be as frightened as his wife, so perhaps she would devote herself to his happiness only to prevent him taking a strap to her if she displeased him.

"Did you recognize Christopher Hudson?" Sebastian asked, changing tack.

"Recognize him?"

"I have reason to believe Christopher Hudson was in Crimea."

"So were thousands of other men. I had no interest in him," General Modine retorted. He seemed too riled up for a man who had nothing to hide, so Sebastian pushed harder.

"He would be worthy of your interest if he were Esme's lover."

The general let out a bark of laughter. "Christopher

Hudson was of no account. Esme wouldn't waste her time on the likes of him."

"But according to an eyewitness, she did just that, which would give you a motive to kill them both," Sebastian pointed out. "Especially if the child you thought was yours was actually your rival's."

The general's expression turned stony. "Inspector, if you were even remotely proficient in your chosen profession, you would realize that I would never stoop to tampering with props. If Hudson had laid a finger on Esme, I would kill him in a way that was honorable and worthy of my military rank."

"Pistols at dawn?" Sebastian asked. "As I'm sure you're aware, dueling is illegal, General."

"A duel to the death is the only way to defend one's honor. It might be illegal, but it's not prosecuted when the duel is between two officers."

"I never said Christopher Hudson was an officer."

The general's dismay was fleeting, but it was evident that he'd realized he'd said too much. He waved his hand in dismissal. "It doesn't matter if he was an officer or a foot soldier. No judge would try me, Inspector, even if I killed him."

"And Esme? What would be an honorable way to murder a woman who had betrayed you so thoroughly?"

Sebastian had clearly struck a nerve, because the general's eyes flashed with fury and he gripped the armrests until his knuckles turned white. "I've answered your inquiries, and now it's high time you were on your way."

"I'll go when I'm ready," Sebastian replied. The tone of the conversation had changed, and he didn't intend to leave when he was about to get some answers.

"I can have Richardson evict you from the premises," General Modine threatened.

"Yes, you can, but I can return with reinforcements, which

would be quite embarrassing for you. So, if you have nothing to hide, I suggest you answer my questions."

"I should call you out and put a lead ball through your heart, you insolent pup," the general snapped.

"And I would refuse the challenge," Sebastian replied calmly. "I'm simply doing my job, General, and I should think you would be eager to help me discover who killed the woman you profess to have loved. Unless that person was you."

The general seemed to acknowledge the truth of this and nodded, his temper apparently cooling as quickly as it had flared. "I did not murder either Esme or Christopher Hudson. I give you my word as an officer and a gentleman. Ask what you will, then leave my house and don't come back. You will not be admitted a second time."

"What time did you get to the theater?"

"Around six."

"But you didn't stay for the performance."

"I was on my way to a regimental dinner. I only stopped by to bring Esme flowers and a gift."

"What gift?"

No one had mentioned a gift, and Sebastian had not seen anything in Esme's dressing room that might have been a present from her lover.

"A brooch. A rose of rubies surrounded by emerald leaves and set in rose gold. I had ordered it specially to commemorate Esme's role in *Romeo and Juliet*."

"A rose by any other name..."

"Precisely."

"And was Esme pleased with this gift?"

General Modine smiled sadly. "She cried when I gave it to her. She said she had never owned anything so beautiful or so precious. She said she would treasure it forever."

"I did not find such a brooch in Esme's dressing room or on her person."

"Then that must be the motive," General Modine replied. "Theft."

"Why kill Christopher Hudson if that were the case?"

"Perhaps his death was accidental."

"I doubt it. What time did you leave the theater, General?" Sebastian inquired.

"A quarter past. The dinner began at seven."

"And can anyone confirm your alibi?"

"Every officer who was in attendance, including the servers. The dinner was held at Knightsbridge barracks."

"Thank you for your cooperation," Sebastian said. He shut his notebook and slid it into his pocket once he stood to leave.

"I would like you to keep me apprised of your progress," General Modine said.

"To discuss my findings would be unethical."

General Modine chuckled. "You don't strike me as someone who's concerned with ethics, but I'm sure that's to be expected, given that you're not bound by a code of honor."

"I live by my own code, General. One you wouldn't understand," Sebastian replied, and strode from the room.

TWENTY-ONE

Before he returned to the theater, Sebastian decided to call on Mr. Bonneville, whose residence in Hanover Court was in the general direction of Covent Garden. The door to the Georgian townhouse was opened by a very young uniformed maid, who smiled at Sebastian in a friendly, open manner he so rarely encountered when turning up unannounced. Not that he was greeted with more enthusiasm when he was expected. Such was the lot of the policeman.

"May I help you, sir?" the young woman asked.

"Inspector Bell of Scotland Yard to see Mr. Bonneville."

"Mr. Bonneville is not at home, sir."

"Not at home, or not at home to visitors?"

"Not at home," the maidservant clarified.

"Is there a Mrs. Bonneville?"

"Mr. Bonneville is not married, sir."

"When do you expect him back?"

"Not until tomorrow evening," the maidservant said. "You actually just missed him."

"Where has he gone?" Sebastian asked. He knew he was taking advantage of the young woman's inexperience by asking her to reveal the whereabouts of her employer, but he wasn't about to pass up an opportunity to learn as much as he could.

"He went to Lakeview Lodge sanatorium," the maidservant explained. "He goes every month. Mr. Bonneville suffers terribly with his—"

"Not another word," a stern voice cut across her. "Step away from the door this minute, you foolish girl."

The maidservant looked terrified, and with good reason. She was sure to be chastised for her lack of discretion, but she really should have known better and closed the door as soon as she'd informed Sebastian that Mr. Bonneville wasn't at home.

A woman of late middle years, presumably the housekeeper, replaced the maid and fixed Sebastian with an icy stare. "What is your business with Mr. Bonneville, sir?" she demanded.

"I'm Inspector Bell of Scotland Yard, and I'm investigating a double murder that occurred at the Orpheus theater last night."

The housekeeper's distress at the news was plain to see, but the shock did little to undermine her admirable aplomb. "And what has a double murder to do with my employer, Inspector?"

"As the proprietor, I thought he should be informed," Sebastian said. There was no point in alarming the woman any further by telling her that he had hoped to question Mr. Bonneville in connection with the case.

"That's very thoughtful of you, Inspector, but as you have already been told, Mr. Bonneville is away. If you would care to leave your card, I will make certain he gets the message."

"Thank you." Sebastian handed the housekeeper one of the cards he carried expressly for that purpose. "Kindly ask him to send a message to Scotland Yard if he returns earlier than expected."

"Of course," the housekeeper said, and shut the door in Sebastian's face.

TWENTY-TWO

Sebastian checked the time. It was half past five, too late to return to Scotland Yard to give Lovell an update, which was just as well, since he had little to report. He did have to relieve Constable Bryant, who'd been at the theater for hours and would be eager to get home.

On his way to Covent Garden, Sebastian encountered no fewer than five newsboys, who occupied their assigned corners and were quickly going through freshly printed stacks of the evening edition of the *Daily Telegraph*. Two boys were in Russell Street, and one near enough to the Orpheus to be heard by the well-dressed ladies and gentlemen who were alighting from hansoms and private carriages and making their way inside for the evening's performance. The child was yelling himself hoarse, his ringing voice inviting the passersby to read all about the tragic murders of Romeo and Juliet, which made for a more shocking headline than the deaths of two relatively unknown actors.

As Guy Weathers had predicted, the news seemed to have no adverse effect on the quickly swelling crowd. Several men speculated excitedly, suggesting possibilities that were inappropriate for mixed company. The women pretended to be shocked, but were clearly lapping up the details of the scandal and most likely storing the information away to be discussed over bottomless cups of tea as they paid and received social calls with friends. The deaths of two young people did not touch these people in any personal way. It was entertainment at its best, which was the reason murder always made the front page and crowds still gathered for public hangings, despite claims that these were enlightened times and modern-day Londoners were much more civilized than their bloodthirsty ancestors.

After all, what better way was there to spend the morning than watching someone die, particularly if the poor sod's neck failed to snap during the drop and the crowd got to enjoy their suffering for a little while longer? If they got lucky, the condemned managed to free their hands and clawed at the rope, or got a stiff prick, which was always a crowd-pleaser. The ladies giggled and pointed, and the men commented on the size of the dying man's member and made crude jokes at his expense. Some parents hoisted their children onto their shoulders so they could have a better view and jeered loudly if the condemned soiled themselves in their final moments. After the execution, men lined up to purchase bits of the hangman's rope to carry as a talisman, and the ladies splurged on hangman's lockets, which were meant to guarantee good luck and came complete with a tiny metal skeleton and bits of hemp from the rope. Sebastian had attended several hangings as part of his duties, and, as he had watched the immense pleasure of the crowd and seen the onlookers stuff their pockets with hemp, he had decided that there really was no hope for humanity.

That view was reaffirmed when a well-dressed gentleman who had yet to reach the door of the theater loudly expressed the opinion that all actresses were whores and should offer their services after the performance, particularly as the place used to be a whorehouse and the rooms were outfitted with the clients in mind. Several ladies hissed with outrage, since the offender had gone too far for their delicate sensibilities, but a few individuals nodded in agreement, their leering faces a testament to their depravity. A number of outraged husbands hurried their wives through the double doors to spare them further embarrassment, while one patron who was there with his adolescent daughter threatened to knock the man's block off if he didn't shut up. Sebastian was certain that, if the man who'd made the offending comment didn't pipe down, a brawl would break out and people would get hurt. Thankfully, he decided to keep quiet.

An usher checked tickets as quickly as possible in order to avoid further unrest, and within minutes the crowd had thinned, and Sebastian went inside. He found Constable Bryant backstage, sitting with his back to the door that led out into the alley.

"Sorry it took so long," Sebastian said.

"Not to worry," Constable Bryant replied calmly. It took a lot to rattle his chain, which made him the perfect partner for jobs that required time and patience.

"Anything worth reporting?"

The constable shook his ginger head. "Everyone was on their best behavior, and no one tried to abscond."

"Thank you, Constable. Get on home."

Constable Bryant heaved himself to his feet and plopped his hat onto his head. "Goodnight, guv."

"Goodnight," Sebastian replied, and watched as the young man disappeared into the night.

With the play soon to begin, there was no time to speak to the actors, so Sebastian decided to start with members of staff who had been backstage during the performance, starting with Mona Grady, who'd clearly had a personal relationship with Esme

Royce. As he walked toward the area immediately behind the stage, he encountered Sid. The boy was dressed in a clean shirt and wore a black bowtie that matched his satin waistcoat. His trousers appeared to be freshly pressed, and his shoes had been shined.

"Hello, Inspector," Sid called out excitedly.

"Hello, yourself. You look smart," Sebastian remarked.

"I'm to be an usher in the main auditorium tonight," Sid said, his chest swelling with pride. "I'm just on my way."

"Is someone ill?"

"No, but it's a full house, and Mr. Weathers needs an extra pair of hands in the rear mezzanine."

"Do you have a moment to speak to me?"

Sid smiled. "Only a moment, but then I have to go. The doors to the auditorium open in five minutes."

Sebastian studied the boy's eager face. "Sid, I wager you know every inch of this place." Sid nodded. "Did you know about the peepholes in the dressing rooms?"

Sid's eyes grew wide with surprise, and he looked like he wanted to deny it but then saw the futility of lying. "Yes," he admitted. "I knew."

"And you have looked through them." It wasn't really a question, but Sid nodded again.

"Did you ever see Esme with anyone?"

Even in the dim light, Sebastian could see Sid's cheeks redden, and he thought that the boy probably spent more time spying than he was willing to admit.

"Yes," Sid whispered.

"Who did you see her with?"

Sid looked nervous, his gaze straying toward the door that led to the auditorium. "I saw her with Christopher," he admitted after a few moments had elapsed.

"What were they doing?"

Sebastian hated to put the child on the spot, but he needed

to know, and Sid probably understood more about relations between men and women than an average boy his age. He had watched every play staged at the Orpheus and had seen love, hate, jealousy, and betrayal. Sid looked like he was going to be ill, but Sebastian couldn't afford to back down.

"Esme was..."

"Esme was what?" Sebastian prompted.

"She was..." Sid swallowed hard. "She was astride him."

"Was that the only time you saw them together?"

Sid shook his head. "I saw them a few times. And I heard Esme tell him that she loved him and would do anything for him."

"What about Ishmael? Did you ever see him with Esme?"

Sid's surprise that Sebastian would know that was evident, but then he nodded. "Yeah, I saw them," he admitted. His earlier embarrassment had dissipated, and his lip curled. "She was a right leading lady, Esme was. Leading everyone by the prick."

"It's not nice to speak ill of the dead," Sebastian said.

"Even if it's the truth?"

That was a good question, and Sebastian did not have an equally good answer. "Run along."

"I'll see you after the show?"

"Maybe."

Sid hurried off, and Sebastian advanced deeper into the mayhem that went on backstage before a performance. He supposed that for the members of the troupe tonight was no different from opening night, since there were new leads, whose performance would impact the rest of the troupe and directly shape everyone's immediate future. No one mentioned Esme or Christopher or alluded to the murders; their attention was fixed on Kate and Nigel, who were clearly on edge. Kate was muttering under her breath, and Nigel paced back and forth and recited his opening lines. He gesticulated with his hand to punctuate the words and seemed oblivious to everyone around him.

Ishmael Cabot looked calm. His demeanor did not change when he spotted Sebastian, and he raised a hand in greeting. Sebastian decided he'd speak to Ishmael later, since he didn't appear to pose a flight risk, and continued toward the sewing room. Mona held a white garment in her hands, but her gaze was on the rectangle of sky beyond the window, her expression one of untold misery.

"Miss Grady?" Sebastian asked as he entered.

Mona started and nearly dropped the shirt she was holding, then bunched up the fabric and set the garment aside before nodding slowly.

"I'm Inspector Bell," Sebastian said, and removed his hat.

"I know who ye are," Mona whispered, her voice quavering.

"I'd like to ask you a few questions, if you don't mind."

Mona looked so frightened, Sebastian thought she might faint.

"You were close with Esme," he said.

"Not really."

"But you were very distressed by her death."

"Esme was kind to me, so she was," Mona cried.

"Are the others not kind to you?"

Mona glared at him. "Mr. Weathers pays me half the wage an Englishwoman would get, that bleeding miser."

"Why did you take the job?"

"Because I have to eat, Inspector." Her fear had turned to anger, which suited Sebastian's purposes much better.

"Did Esme ever confide in you?"

Mona shook her head. "Why would she?"

"Did you not talk during the fittings?"

"We did yeah, some."

"What did you talk about?"

"The weather."

He was getting nowhere, but he was certain Mona was hiding something and she was fearful for some reason.

"What miracle were you hoping for, Mona?"

Mona's reaction was instantaneous. Her already fair skin went even paler, and her eyes filled with tears.

"It's nothing. Just silly talk," she said. "I don't know what yer woman told ye, but I was just upset when I said that."

"I don't believe you, Mona. You told Miss Tate that you would never get your miracle now and someone was lost to you. Whom did you mean?"

Tears slid down Mona's cheeks, and she looked like a person who'd just lost their last shred of hope. She reached for a handkerchief and blew her nose, then wadded up the fabric in her fist.

"Me wee one was taken from me," she said at last. "Me Brendan."

"Who by?"

"Father Mackie. He took him while I slept, and I never saw him again. He was two days old," Mona wailed.

"Why did this Father Mackie take your son? Surely a child is better off with his mother."

Mona looked away, but not before Sebastian saw both shame and defiance in her gaze. She didn't want to explain, that was clear, but her feelings for her child seemed to compel her to tell the truth.

"I was a nun, Inspector, at St. Mary's Priory in Ballycotton. I entered the convent when I was sixteen and was expelled at twenty-two. I lost not only me child, but me home, and me only family."

"And the child's father?"

"A visiting priest. The fecker forced himself on me down in the cellar. I tried to tell Father Mackie when I discovered I was with child, but he accused me of seducing a man of God with me wanton behavior and told me to do penance. And then he took me boy away."

Sebastian was in no doubt that Mona was telling the truth. The pain was raw in her voice, and her anger burned bright, against both the priest who had forced himself on her and Father Mackie, who'd taken his side and had not offered Mona a choice. It was a bit surprising that Mona would feel such fierce love for the child of a rapist, but then Sebastian supposed she didn't see the baby as an extension of the lecherous priest. She simply saw him as an innocent who needed her love, and she probably needed his love as well, the way Gemma had needed Lucy's. Mother and child were two souls who were connected on a deeper level, and their bond would never be broken, even if they never saw each other again.

"Where did Father Mackie place Brendan?"

Mona shook her head. "I don't know, do I? He said I had no right to him, and Brendan was better off without such a wicked mother who could do nothing but shame him." Her bitter smile was more of a grimace. "Father Mackie said I was dirtier than shite and that I was no longer welcome at the convent, so I'd better shut me gob and be on me way before he had me excommunicated."

"How old would Brendan be now?"

"Six next week," Mona said softly.

Sebastian felt deep pity for this poor woman who'd been in hell for six long years, wondering what had become of her son. What sort of man would punish a nun who'd been raped and take her child? But of course, Father Mackie would sooner shield a lascivious priest than an innocent girl who'd never had any say in the matter. It was the easiest way to make the problem go away and avoid embarrassment for the Church. Mona and her child had no value and could be disposed of at Father Mackie's discretion, the two torn asunder without a second thought.

"Did Esme promise to help you find Brendan?" Sebastian asked.

Mona sniffed and nodded. "She said she'd make me a loan once she received her wages."

"And how would this loan help?"

Sebastian thought that perhaps Mona wanted to go back to Ireland so she could continue the search, but then the money wouldn't be a loan, since she wasn't likely to pay it back.

Mona's eyes suddenly lit up, and when she smiled her face was transformed, making her look young and radiant. She clasped her hands before her as if in prayer and said, "I would go to Lourdes."

"You would go to the Lord?" Sebastian repeated. Was she warning him that she intended to commit suicide? But then why would she need money?

"Not to the Lord, to Lourdes. It's a town in France," Mona hurried to explain.

"Do you have reason to believe Brendan is there?"

Mona shook her head. "It's a holy place, Inspector Bell. Our Heavenly Mother came to a child in Lourdes last year. She has been seen many times since, and she's performed glorious miracles. Father McDonaugh said so. If I go to Lourdes on a pilgrimage, Our Lady will help me find me Brendan."

Sebastian studied Mona's shining face and was struck by the determination in her eyes. Mona truly believed that the Virgin Mary would help her, and it seemed she was willing to do anything to get to her, and Esme had been willing to lend Mona her hard-earned wages to facilitate her pilgrimage.

"Why would Esme, with whom you claim not to have been close, lend you money for this?"

"Because she understood, she did. Esme was Catholic, Inspector. We attended Mass together at St. Stephen's on Wednesdays. She heard all about the miracles, and she believed."

"Was Esme Irish?"

Mona nodded. "A bonny Irish girleen, but she didn't want anyone to know. She thought she would be discriminated against, and rightly so, but I knew as soon as I saw her, even though she made a show of going to an Anglican church on Sundays with all the rest of them."

Sebastian wasn't really surprised to learn that Esme had been Irish. There had been an influx of Irish immigrants since the famine and, for the first time in centuries, Catholic dioceses had been established in London and churches were openly holding Mass for the quickly increasing number of worshippers. Esme must have been a talented actress to be able to mimic the English so effectively and allow no trace of accent to slip through, but someone like Mona would spot a fellow Irishwoman, no doubt about that, and exploit the connection.

"Was Esme her real name?" Sebastian asked.

"Course not," Mona scoffed. "It was Erin, but she preferred Esme. She said it made her sound like a proper Englishwoman."

"Is it possible that Esme committed suicide?" Sebastian asked.

"No!" Mona cried. "Suicide is a mortal sin. She would never."

"And Christopher Hudson?"

"He had everything to live for. Why would he kill himself?"

Sebastian studied Mona's tense features. On the surface, she appeared to be telling the truth, but Sebastian's gut instinct warned him that there was more to the story and Mona was holding something back, something vital that she didn't want him to know.

"Miss Grady, lying to the police is a criminal offense," Sebastian said. He could hardly throw Mona in jail for withholding information, but she didn't know that; and, judging by her reaction, he'd hit a nerve. Her earlier exaltation had been replaced by palpable fear once again.

"I'm telling ye the truth," Mona protested feebly.

Sebastian hated to use her faith against her, but she seemed to be the only one who knew anything of the real Esme Royce and could help him separate the wheat from the chaff when it came to rumor and innuendo. He needed to get to the truth.

"You can lie to me, but you can't lie to the Heavenly Mother. Will she grant you a miracle if you come to her by way of dishonorable means?"

Mona began to cry again, and her skin turned blotchy and damp. "I threatened Esme," she confessed at last. "I guessed she was with child, and I used it for me own gain."

"What did you threaten her with?"

"I said I'd tell General Modine the child wasn't his. She'd lose him for sure, and he'd promised to set her up in her own house, hire a maidservant, and give her an allowance. I didn't want to ruin her prospects, honest I didn't, but it was me only chance, so it was," Mona cried. "I would do anything to see me wee boy again."

Sebastian nodded. He'd suspected there was blackmail involved, but he couldn't find it in his heart to blame Mona. She was so obviously desperate that all he felt was pity.

"Where is Ballycotton?"

"County Cork. Why?" Mona asked, clearly thrown by the question.

"Just curious. Was Esme from Cork as well?"

"No, she was from a village near Limerick. She lost her family during the famine. She was just a child then, but she'd decided to leave Ireland as soon as she was able. She called it the Land of Tears."

Sebastian fixed Mona with a piercing look. "Did you tell General Modine that the child wasn't his?" If she had, the general would have a solid motive for murder, and Mona Grady would be an accessory.

Mona shook her head violently. "I swear, I never said a

word. I wouldn't have either, even if Esme refused to pay. I just wanted to frighten her into helping me."

"It seems you'd scared her senseless, if she was willing to give you enough to get to France. Did Esme ever confide in you?" Sebastian asked again. "She was your friend," he added softly. "She deserves justice."

Mona sniffled loudly and blew her nose again. "She told me about her arrangement with General Modine. She loathed him, but he was willing to do anything to have her, and she wasn't going to pass up a chance at a better life."

"Would it be a better life?"

"He'd tire of her eventually, she knew that. But if she was careful, she'd have enough put by to live on for years."

"And what about Christopher Hudson? Was Esme involved with him as well?"

Mona smiled through the tears. "She loved Christopher, but she was too sensible to imagine she could have a life with him."

"Why?"

"Because Christopher would always love himself first and spend his wages on his own pleasure."

"Was the child his?"

"I don't know," Mona said. "Esme never said. Maybe she never knew who the father was."

"What about Ishmael Cabot?" Sebastian asked.

"What about him?"

"Did Esme have relations with him as well?"

Mona's mouth fell open with shock. "With Ishmael? She would never."

"Because he's black?"

"Because she loved Chris, and because she didn't trust Ishmael," Mona replied.

"Why not?" Sebastian asked. This contradicted what he'd heard so far and he was curious to hear Mona's explanation.

Mona shrugged. "Esme said he was a thief. And she said the young one knew it too."

"Who, Sid?"

"No, Rose. That one notices everything. Ask her."

"I will. What about the other members of the troupe? Is anyone else keeping secrets?"

Now that Mona had confessed to blackmailing Esme, she didn't seem to care what else she revealed. Perhaps she truly was afraid to ruin her chances with the Heavenly Mother, or maybe she didn't feel a sense of loyalty toward any other members of the troupe since they probably treated her no differently than a servant.

"Serena had a fling with Christopher. He threw her over when Esme joined the troupe."

"And how did Serena take that? Was she angry enough to want to punish Christopher and his new love?"

Mona looked nonplussed. "I shouldn't think so. She was fixing to fleece Lord Gilroy."

"And what about the rest of the men in the troupe?"

"They're sound. Nigel Mowbray fancies Kate, but she thinks he's an eejit, and Gregory Gorman loves only strong drink. Lawrence and Hugh are harmless old fellas. They wouldn't hurt a fly."

"What about Ruth Gregson?" Sebastian asked.

Mona shrugged. "She's a good woman herself."

"She's the oldest female member of the troupe. She must be worried about her future."

"If she is, she never told me," Mona replied.

"Thank you for your candor, Miss Grady."

Mona looked at him, her eyes shining with hope. "Do you think the Heavenly Mother will forgive me now?"

"I'm sure she will."

"There's no greater pain than the loss of those ye love," Mona said.

"No, there isn't," Sebastian replied, and left the room.

TWENTY-THREE

It was a good while until intermission, so Sebastian knew Rose would be on her own in the cloakroom. He found her sitting on a three-legged stool. Her head drooped like a wilted flower. Her shoulders were slumped in a way that suggested she wasn't comfortable, and her back was probably aching. Rose instantly tensed when she saw Sebastian, and sat up straight.

"Are you leaving, Inspector?" she asked. "Shall I unlock the door for you?"

"The doors are kept locked during a performance?" Sebastian asked.

Rose nodded. "There've been some thefts from the cloakroom in the past, so the doors are locked once the performance starts in order to prevent someone from wandering in off the street."

The cloakroom was close enough to the main entrance to be easily accessible should someone decide to help themselves. Even if Rose were there when that happened, she could hardly be expected to deter someone bent on theft.

"I'd like to ask you a few questions, if you don't mind," Sebastian said.

"Of course. Anything I can do to help."

Rose perked up, and Sebastian thought that she was probably very lonely and scared. She was no older than sixteen and had her brother to look after. What would happen to them if Mr. Bonneville dismissed them or if she needed to find other employment? Rose's infirmity would prevent her from finding a position as a domestic servant. No housekeeper would employ a girl who had difficulty walking, since it would interfere with her duties. If she was handy with a needle, she might find a place in some backroom workshop or failing that, get a job in a seedy tavern, where she'd mop up sick and take out piss buckets. The better places wanted able-bodied, alluring barmaids who appealed to the patrons.

And what would become of Sid? He'd probably find some menial job or take the Queen's shilling and join the army, but, even if he survived whatever conflict he engaged in, he'd be on his own as soon as he left the army, since military service did not provide a pension for those who'd been discharged. Perhaps if Sid really was serious about joining the police service, Sebastian could have a word with Ransome once the dust of the transition had settled. Sid was too young now, but in a year or two they could surely find something for him to do. He could run errands and deliver messages, and once he was of age he could become a proper constable.

Tearing his thoughts from the children's prospects, Sebastian asked, "What did you think of Esme and Christopher?"

"They were nice enough, I suppose, but it's not like we were friendly."

"Were they having a relationship, do you think?"

Rose nodded. "They didn't want anyone to know, but it was obvious, at least to me."

"Obvious how?"

"They tried too hard to avoid each when they were around the others, to make sure they didn't suspect."

"What about Ishmael Cabot? Was Esme involved with him as well?"

"Esme didn't trust him," Rose said.

"Why not?"

"Because he's a liar and a thief."

"What did he steal?"

"Money. Esme saw him sneaking out of Mr. Bannon's office one night and told Mr. Bannon the next time she saw him."

"Did Esme tell you this?"

Rose shook her head. "I heard them talking. And she told Mona that she saw Ishmael hiding something behind his back."

"When was this?"

"'Bout a month ago."

"How did Esme know it was money?" Sebastian asked.

"That's where the strongbox is kept."

"Did Mr. Bannon ever acknowledge that something was taken?"

"Not to the rest of us, but he and Ishmael had words. In private. And Mr. Bannon got a pistol. For protection. He didn't tell anyone, but I saw it when I was cleaning his office."

"Where is it kept?"

"In a drawer, in his desk."

"Why were you looking in his desk?"

Rose squirmed in her seat when she realized she'd said too much and had admitted to snooping, but recovered admirably. "I was looking for a boiled sweet. Mr. Bannon keeps them in his desk, and he said I could take one after I finished cleaning."

"Thank you, Rose. You've been most helpful."

Rose looked pleased with the praise but relieved to see him go.

As Sebastian returned backstage, he reflected on what Rose had told him, but also on the girl herself. Based on her manners and speech, it was clear that Rose had been born to well-heeled parents. Rose and Sid weren't the first or the last children to find themselves in reduced circumstances when their parents died, but it seemed odd that there had been no relation to take them in and provide for them until they were of an age to fend for themselves. How had they come to Mr. Bonneville's attention, and what were the terms of their arrangement? Sebastian fervently hoped that the proprietor was not abusing the children. Rose might be lame, but she was young and pretty, just the sort of sweet, vulnerable girl an unmarried older man might take advantage of if she was desperate enough to do anything to survive. Sebastian had some questions to put to Mr. Bonneville; but just then, he needed a word with Ned Bannon, whom he had yet to meet.

TWENTY-FOUR

Sebastian found Ned Bannon in his office with an open bottle of Scotch whisky and a half-full glass on his desk as he looked over a stack of papers. He was in his mid to late forties and, even seated, it was obvious that he was tall and very slender. Ned's light brown hair was thinning at the front, and he had a long, nervous face and pale blue eyes. His nose was narrow and pointy, and his full lips were completely devoid of color. He looked like he hadn't slept in a week and would benefit from a hearty meal.

"Mr. Bannon?" Sebastian asked when the man failed to acknowledge his presence even after Sebastian had shut the door behind him.

"Yes. Come in. Sorry," he muttered. "I leave for one evening, and the unpaid invoices somehow multiply on my desk."

Ned Bannon made no mention of the two people who had been murdered in his absence, but perhaps it was easier for him to focus on something more practical, like unpaid bills.

Getting up, he shifted some items off a guest chair and invited Sebastian to sit. His room was nothing like Guy Weath-

ers' and had most likely been a storage space before he took it
over. The furniture was mismatched, the carpet was threadbare,
and a narrow cot stood against one wall, the mattress covered by
a plain wool blanket. There was also a faded screen in the
corner that might have once been crimson but was now a faded
mauve.

"I'm Inspector Bell of Scotland Yard," Sebastian said once
he had sat down.

"What can I do for you, Inspector?"

"I have a few questions."

"Well, make them quick. I have work to do."

"Who would have reason to murder Esme Royce and
Christopher Hudson?"

Bannon looked perplexed. "I've been asking myself that
since Guy told me what happened, and I honestly don't know. I
will not insult your intelligence by telling you they were blame-
less human beings, but I can't think of anyone who'd want them
dead. I simply can't conceive of a motive."

"Can't you? Serena Winthrop was jilted by Christopher
Hudson, who then began a relationship with Esme. Esme was
also involved with General Modine, whose child she might have
been carrying, unless the child was Hudson's, or Ishmael
Cabot's. Christopher Hudson was stringing along a wealthy
widow, and, by her own admission, Mona Grady was blackmailing Esme over the pregnancy. As far as I'm aware, neither
Kate, Nigel, Ruth, nor Gregory had any romantic dealings with
either victim, but it's early days yet."

Ned Bannon looked stunned, his mouth going slack. Sebastian thought the surprise at these revelations was twofold. First,
Bannon had had no idea that quite so much had been going on
beneath his twitchy nose, and second, he seemed worried that
Sebastian had gleaned so much in such a short time and realized
that Sebastian now posed a very real threat to the troupe's
future. Bannon stared at Sebastian and blinked several times,

reminding him of a confused owl, then grabbed the glass of whisky and tossed it back, much like Romeo had done with the poison that had killed him.

Once he'd regained his composure, he said, "Inspector, when a small group of people lives and works together for years on end, romantic entanglements are to be expected. But people don't generally murder each other when the liaisons come to an end. They simply move forward."

"As you have just pointed out, Mr. Bannon, these liaisons take place between people who live and work together. It's difficult to move forward when one is forced to see someone they might still love with their new partner day in and day out. Such proximity can foster murderous sexual jealousy and create opportunities for blackmail, particularly when wealthy, influential patrons have the power to change the actors' lives, and the loss of their regard could be the difference between a comfortable retirement and the workhouse."

"Trading affection for financial security is nothing new, Inspector. People have done that for as long as there have been those who have more than others and can afford to look after someone less fortunate. But in all my years in the theater business, I have never before witnessed a murder."

"Well unless Esme and Christopher committed suicide, someone killed two people in plain sight, Mr. Bannon."

Bannon shook his head. "If you had known them, you'd realize that suicide wasn't a possibility."

"Which is why I'm treating this as murder. It was an act both brutal and utterly controlled since the killer had obviously planned it very carefully."

"I can't see any of our people resorting to such savagery."

"How well do you know your people?"

"We don't pry into their past, but we do take an interest," Bannon retorted.

"Did Christopher Hudson fight in Crimea?"

Ned Bannon seemed taken aback by the question but answered right away. "He did. He was wounded early on and was sent back to the front once he was sufficiently recovered."

"Do you know anything of his background or family?"

"He was an orphan, as are most of our actors. This profession tends to attract people who crave attention and love, something they never had as children."

"And Esme?"

"She was orphaned as well. I thought she might be Irish, but I never asked, and she never said. She had the looks and talent necessary to bring in the crowds, and that was enough."

"Guy Weathers mentioned a disagreement with Mr. Bonneville. What can you tell me about that?"

"If you're suggesting that Mr. Bonneville murdered two people to get back at Guy, you're barking mad, Inspector. They didn't agree on the terms of the new contract, but eventually they came to an understanding, and Mr. Bonneville left the theater. In fact, we walked out together. He's a good man," Bannon said. "He took in Rose and Sid when they had no place to go, and he kept on Walt Dickie. I would have sent the old drunkard packing years ago."

"Did you know there are peepholes in all the dressing rooms?" Sebastian inquired.

"Who told you that?"

"Walt Dickie."

Bannon nodded. "No, I didn't know, but I'm not surprised now you mention it. This side of the building used to be a brothel."

"Is that a standard feature?"

"It's an additional source of revenue," Bannon said matter-of-factly.

"And speaking of revenue, have there been any thefts in the past few months?" Sebastian asked.

"Thefts?"

"You keep the strongbox here, do you not?"

"Yes, but nothing was taken."

"What was Ishmael Cabot doing in your office, then?"

Ned Bannon's eyes widened with shock. "How do you know about that?" he exclaimed.

"He was seen, and he reportedly hid something behind his back."

"It was lavender oil," Ned Bannon said, and sighed with resignation. "I sustained an injury to my back some years ago, and I suffer from chronic pain. Ishmael is good with his hands. He massages my back and hips to relieve the tension."

"Why do you feel the need to keep that a secret?"

"If someone comes in and finds Ishmael bent over me when I'm lying naked, they will arrive at their own conclusions, which would endanger us both."

Sebastian drew his own conclusions from Ned Bannon's reasoning. A man who had nothing to fear wouldn't work this hard to hide something that was of no account, but Ned Bannon clearly feared being arrested on a charge of sodomy and likely had good reason to be worried.

"Do you take anything for your pain, Mr. Bannon?"

"I take morphine when the pain gets bad. Why do you ask?"

"Because Esme and Christopher died of a morphine overdose."

Bannon's reaction to the news was more than mere surprise. He went white to the roots of his hair, and his hand trembled. For the second time that night, Sebastian's instinct vibrated like a tuning fork, and he knew he'd finally hit on the right question.

"Do you keep the morphine here at the theater?"

Bannon nodded and sprang to his feet, then hurried over to a cabinet fitted with nine narrow drawers, three per row. He yanked the top right-hand drawer open with such force, there was the sound of splintering wood as the knob came off in his hand, throwing him off balance. He caught himself, tossed the knob aside, then pulled out a small brown medicine bottle. He clutched it triumphantly, as if he'd just unearthed a buried treasure.

Sebastian held out his hand, and Ned Bannon handed over the bottle. Holding it up to the light, Sebastian studied the contents. The bottle was about three-quarters full, but, although the liquid inside appeared to have a viscous consistency, it wasn't as dark or opaque as the substance he'd seen on Colin's glass slide. Sebastian opened the bottle and sniffed the contents, then dipped in one finger and tapped it lightly against his tongue.

"This is treacle," he said with disgust. "How much morphine did you have left, Mr. Bannon?"

"Close to one hundred milligrams," Ned Bannon replied. He looked utterly devastated. And frightened.

"When was the last time you took any?"

Ned looked up at the ceiling as he tried to remember. "It's been a while. At least a fortnight."

"Who knew about the morphine?" Sebastian asked.

"Only Ishmael and Guy."

"When was the last time Ishmael gave you a massage?"

"Yesterday, around five o'clock."

"Was he ever left alone in your office?"

"I went behind the screen to dress after he was finished," Ned Bannon replied, his gaze shifting to the screen. It was tall enough that Ned wouldn't see what Ishmael was doing, only hear him.

"So, he could have switched the bottle. It would have taken but a moment."

"Yes, I suppose he could have, but why would he do such a thing?" Ned asked.

"If Ishmael had feelings for Esme, he might have been consumed with jealousy and murdered Esme and the one man she seemed to actually love."

"No," Ned cried. "Ishmael is a gentle soul. He would never hurt anyone."

"Sure, are you?"

Sebastian could see the internal struggle as Ned Bannon returned to his seat. He wanted to protect Ishmael, but he wasn't sure of the man's innocence.

"And Guy Weathers? Might he have taken your morphine?" Sebastian asked.

"Esme Royce and Christopher Hudson were magic together. Our sales have never been as steady. Why on earth would Guy murder the two people who assured the continued success of the troupe?" Ned's gaze slid toward the stack of unpaid invoices, as if to illustrate his point.

"Does anyone else have access to your office?"

Bannon shook his head. "I lock the door whenever I leave. Not even Guy has a key."

"Rose comes in here to clean. Does she have a key?"

"No, I let her in. And anyway, Rose didn't know about the morphine."

"She knew about the pistol."

Ned Bannon's face registered shock once again. This man was clearly oblivious to everything that went on right under his nose.

"Why did you acquire a gun, Mr. Bannon?"

"I didn't acquire it, Inspector. It had belonged to a dear friend and was left to me in his will when he died last month. I swear I have no intentions of shooting anyone."

"Can I see it?"

Ned Bannon nodded and pulled open the top drawer of his desk. He handed Sebastian a plain wooden box that contained a Colt 2nd Model Dragoon pistol and a full box of paper cartridges. The pistol was in excellent condition and appeared to have been cleaned and oiled since it was last fired. Sebastian took out the gun and examined it more closely. He was impressed with both the craftsmanship and the economical beauty of the weapon. It was the sort of gun a Pinkerton agent might be issued with and would wear in a specially made shoulder holster.

"This is American," Sebastian remarked as he replaced the pistol in the box, closed it, and returned it to Ned.

"Yes. My friend bought it in Texas, from someone who had fought in the Mexican War. It came loaded and with a full cartridge box. I admired it, so he left it to me. Surely that's not a crime."

"No, it isn't. Neither is having morphine, but when these items fall into the wrong hands they can be deadly."

"Like I said, Inspector, I always locked the office when I wasn't here."

"Does anyone keep a spare key?" Sebastian inquired.

"Mr. Bonneville has a key for every door in the theater, but he seldom comes here."

"Were there any signs of forced entry in recent days?"

Bannon shook his head. "No. I'm certain no one broke in."

"Thank you, Mr. Bannon," Sebastian said, and pushed to his feet. He walked to the door and examined the lock and the jamb for himself. Bannon was right. If someone had broken in, they had done so with the aid of a key.

TWENTY-FIVE

Even though she was hungry, Gemma wished she could skip dinner and retire to her room. Colin had not alluded to their earlier conversation, but he clearly felt contrite for chastising her, and the tension was still there, particularly since there was no one besides Anne to act as an intermediary.

When Colin asked Gemma over dinner if she had discovered anything, she realized she didn't care to discuss her findings with him and told him that her mission had been a waste of time. She might have changed her mind eventually, particularly since the conversation was unusually stilted and they were both grasping for a safe topic to discuss when Anne mistook her plate of consommé for a finger bowl and washed her hands in the soup. Her symptoms tended to worsen once the sun had set, and the hours of darkness were the most difficult to get through, not only for her but for those around her.

When Gemma went to clean Anne's hands, Anne looked up and smiled with gratitude, then asked, "Are you my daughter, dear?"

"No, Mrs. Ramsey, but I am your friend," Gemma said, and saw the light go out of Anne's eyes, as if she had lost a daughter in that moment and felt the crushing grief one would experience at losing a child.

Accustomed though she was to Anne's disorientation, the conversation nearly broke Gemma's heart, especially when she saw Colin tear up and stare into his soup plate until he felt safe to meet her gaze. As difficult as it was for her, it was a thousand times worse for Colin, who had to watch the mother he loved disappear day by day and revert to childlike behavior and complete ignorance of the world. And perhaps he feared for himself as well, Gemma thought as she resumed her seat. Who would look after him if he began to display symptoms of the illness, and would it come for him earlier if this was something that ran in families, like madness, and afflicted generation after generation?

Gemma forgave him then, attributing his earlier irritation to a difficult day. Colin meant well; she knew that, just as she meant well when she tried to advise him on how to deal with his mother and he became upset and didn't want to discuss Anne's condition anymore. Gemma could understand his grief. To lose so much of oneself was a fate worse than death. It was easier to die of a fever or succumb to fatal cardiac infarction than face this cruel decline that left one so helpless and lost. For the first time since her parents had died, Gemma was grateful for the manner of their deaths and relieved that they had at least been spared such degeneration and suffering, and that she and Victor had not had to helplessly watch their daily decline.

Once the interminable meal was finally over, Gemma helped Anne to her room and into bed, then hurried down the corridor to her own bedroom instead of joining Colin in the parlor as she did most evenings. She breathed a great sigh of relief as she undressed, set aside the hoop pannier, unhooked her corset, and unpinned her hair, letting it cascade over her shoulders in rippling waves. She lay on her bed in nothing but her cotton nightdress, feeling wonderfully unencumbered after a day of being constricted, both physically and emotionally. What a joy it would be to throw away her cumbersome clothes and wear garments that were light and comfortable and didn't restrict her range of movement. To even think such a thing was scandalous, but Gemma was tired of being bound by convention and constantly told what she could and couldn't do. Even Victor had corrected her on occasion, having taken on the role of guardian once their father had passed.

And now both Colin and Sebastian were doing their best to hem her in. She readily acknowledged that they both had her well-being at heart and would risk their own safety if she were in trouble, but neither of them was really in a position to question her behavior or prevent her from investigating on her own if she had a mind to do so. They carried on as if she were some helpless damsel.

Pfft! Gemma thought irritably. She had spent nearly three years in Scutari, living and working in conditions so appalling, no one who hadn't seen the hospital and the nurses' lodgings for themselves could possibly begin to imagine. She had frozen in the winter, sweltered in her crinolines and wool gown in the summer, and stepped over rats as big as kittens to get to her patients, some of whom had been barely holding on after being blown up by Russian shells or repeatedly skewered with bayonets. Now that she was back in England, everyone liked to pretend that she was just another sad spinster whose only value lay in nursing others. She enjoyed helping others and felt that she had made a difference to those who could no longer care for themselves, but she was about to turn twenty-eight, and she longed for a life of her own and a purpose beyond making someone comfortable.

Tomorrow, she would take Anne for a walk, and they would call on Poppy Bright. Gemma longed to see her old friend and to spend time with someone whose undemanding company would be a balm to her soul. And if Poppy happened to remember Christopher Hudson, or knew something about General Modine, then Gemma would simply pass the information on to Sebastian. He could hardly object to that, could he?

Having settled on a plan, Gemma climbed under the covers, turned out the oil lamp, and allowed herself to sink into the mattress. She'd earned her rest.

TWENTY-SIX

While waiting to question Ishmael, Sebastian decided to interview the carpenters. The men were employed by the theater, so would have no reason to protect any member of the troupe or the admirers who came to see them backstage. And being on the scene, they might have observed something the others had failed to spot.

He found the two men in a storage area at the back of the building. The space was a jumble of random furniture, painted columns, backdrops, and other bits that might be useful to a theater company. Jimmy and Charlie Milner sat across from each other. The plush armchairs they occupied were clearly stage props. A fat-bellied bottle stood on the low table between them, and the smell of strong spirits permeated the dusty air.

The Milner brothers were both dark-haired, dark-eyed, and stocky, with biceps that stretched the fabric of their shirts and well-muscled chests that strained against the black waistcoats they both wore. Though they weren't very tall, the men gave off an air of competence and strength. The older one, who looked to be around thirty, radiated insolence, while the younger one, who was clearly still in his twenties, appeared more watchful, his eyes following Sebastian as he approached.

"Drinking on the job?" Sebastian asked without reproach.

"Just toasting another successful performance, aren't we, Charlie?" the older one said.

"As ye say, Jimmy," his brother agreed.

Jimmy raised the bottle in a salute, then took a swallow before passing it to Charlie, who drank deeply.

"I'd like to ask you lads a few questions."

"Fire away, guv. We live to assist the police." The brothers sniggered at this witticism, then Jimmy gestured to a wooden stool that stood off to the side. "Make yerself comfortable, Inspectah. This is likely to take a while."

Sebastian pulled up the stool and sat down, looking from one man to the other. It was obvious that Jimmy was the leader of this two-man gang, so he turned his attention to him.

"You are employed by Mr. Bonneville, is that correct?"

"Ye got it in one." *Clever you* seemed to hang in the air between them.

"And how long have you worked at the Orpheus?"

"Since it first opened its gilded doors."

"What did you think of Christopher Hudson?" Sebastian asked.

The men seemed surprised by the question, possibly because Sebastian had asked for their opinion. Both appeared to give the question some thought.

"He were a good bloke," Charlie said, breaking with protocol and speaking before his brother. "Kind," he added.

"Kind how?"

"Just treated us like people, ye know," Charlie said. "Never turned up 'is nose."

Jimmy nodded. "'E bought us a pint from time to time. Like we was mates."

"He ever talk about his time in Crimea?" Sebastian asked.

Charlie nodded. "'E said it were the worst time in 'is life and 'e'd never risk 'is life for someone else's gain ever again."

Jimmy cocked his head to the side and gave Sebastian a narrow-eyed look. "What's this got to do with 'is murdah?"

"Some resentments run deep, Jimmy," Sebastian replied.

"So ye think 'e were snuffed cause of somefink 'e'd done in Crimea?"

"That's what I'm trying to find out," Sebastian replied nonchalantly. "Did Christopher ever mention General Modine? I heard he spent a lot of time backstage."

"Nah," Charlie said. "Chris avoided the general like the clap. Disappeared into 'is dressing room as soon as Modine turned up."

"You think he was afraid of General Modine?"

"Not afraid, just wary," Jimmy said. "And who could blame 'im? That cove's bad news."

"Why do you say that?" Sebastian asked.

"'E 'as a reputation, don't 'e?" Jimmy replied. "Whipped 'is groom bloody cause the poor sod didn't muck out the stables quick enough."

"How do you know that?"

"'Ad a palaver with 'is coachman while 'e were waiting on '*Is Majesty*."

"And how did Esme Royce feel about the general?" Sebastian inquired.

"I think she were afraid of 'im," Charlie said.

"And rightly so," Jimmy concurred. "'E's the sort to beat 'is whores for the sheer pleasure of it."

Sebastian nodded. He could believe that. "Think Modine killed them?" he asked.

Both men shook their heads in unison.

"Not 'im," Jimmy said. "'E ain't the sort to creep about. If 'e were to kill 'em, 'e'd do it in the open, and still get away wif it."

"How?" Sebastian asked.

"Our esteemed judges don't send war 'eroes to the gallows, do they? It's the likes of us that get to dance the dead man's jig if we take matters into our own 'ands."

Sebastian couldn't argue with that either. The Milners weren't nearly as thick as they looked. "You see anyone backstage the night of the murders? Anything odd?"

Both men shook their heads again.

"Nuffing unusual—" Charlie said.

"No, wait," Jimmy interrupted. "There was that fancy baggage as come backstage."

"What fancy baggage?" Sebastian asked.

"A lady. She wore a black cloak with a hood, but ye could tell right off she were posh."

"What time was this?"

"Right before intermission."

"And what did this woman want?"

"She wanted to speak to Esme Royce," Jimmy said.

"And did she?"

"Yeah," Charlie said. "But only for a few minutes like. Then she left."

"And no one else saw her?" Sebastian asked, surprised that no one had mentioned this woman until now.

"They probably thought it were Lady Argyle. She wears a black cloak, but this bird were much younger. And fair," Charlie added. "Lady Argyle 'as dark hair."

"And how did Esme seem after the conversation?"

Jimmy shrugged. "'Ow should we know? We're 'ere to work, not to muck about with the star o' the show."

"She seemed all right," Charlie said. "Quiet like."

"Anything else that stands out about that night?" Sebastian asked.

Jimmy and Charlie exchanged looks. "Some cove come to the back door, asking for Ishmael. Wanted to wallop 'im."

"Is that so? Did he say why?"

"Nah," Charlie said. "But 'e were raging."

"Can you describe him?"

"'E were a darky, like Ishmael. A sailor mebbe."

"And he just left, did he?" Sebastian asked. This was all news to him.

"Ishmael went out into the alley with 'im during intermission, then came back in."

"Did they settle their differences?"

Sebastian hadn't noticed any evidence of a fight when he'd spoken to Ishmael, but the man might have hit him where the bruises wouldn't show.

Jimmy and Charlie shrugged again. "They must 'ave since Ishmael still has all 'is teeth."

"Did you ever see anyone going into Ned Bannon's office when he's not there?"

The men shook their heads.

"'E keeps it locked," Jimmy said. "It's by invitation only, innit?" he added with a smirk, and shot Sebastian an impatient look meant to convey that he was done answering questions.

"Just one more question," Sebastian said. "Where is the entrance to the passage that runs behind the dressing rooms?"

He had intended to ask Walt Dickie, but Jimmy and Charlie had to know every inch of the building and probably had a fairly good idea even if they never used the passage themselves.

"Know 'bout that, do ye?" Charlie asked, clearly impressed. "Walt tried to keep it a secret, but we saw 'im sneaking up there, didn't we, Jimmy?"

Jimmy nodded. "There's a cupboard next to Ned Bannon's office. The back panel opens onto a staircase that leads to the second floor."

"You ever been up there?" Sebastian asked.

Charlie shook his head and Jimmy shot Sebastian a look of derision. "Charlie and I don't lack for female company, guv, and before ye ask, we ain't making time with anyone 'ere. All that drama leaves us limp, if ye know what I mean."

Sebastian knew precisely what Jimmy meant and thought he was being truthful. "Thank you," he said, and stood. "You were surprisingly helpful."

"Like I said, we lives to serve," Jimmy said, and pretended to pull at his forelock.

TWENTY-SEVEN

Having finished with the Milners, Sebastian was just in time to corner Ishmael Cabot as intermission began.

"A word, Mr. Cabot," Sebastian called out when he saw Ishmael's tall silhouette melt into the shadows.

Ishmael Cabot looked less than pleased to be hailed but sauntered over to Sebastian. He looked dashing in his costume, but his face looked different, and it took Sebastian a moment to realize that his skin had been heavily dusted with rice powder to make him look whiter and more in keeping with the other actors.

"This way, please," Sebastian said, and directed Ishmael to an out-of-the-way corner where they could speak privately.

"I told you all I know, Inspector—" Ishmael began, but Sebastian cut across him.

"I don't think you did."

"What is it you think I'm hiding?"

"What did you do with the morphine you took from Ned Bannon's office?"

Cabot looked stunned, myriad emotions passing over his

face as he weighed his options. "I didn't kill anyone," he said at last.

"That's not what I asked."

The young man sighed deeply, his shoulders drooping with resignation. "I used it to repay a debt."

"To whom?"

"Harold Lively. I hadn't seen him in years, but when he heard I was at the Orpheus he came to claim what was owed to him."

"And what did you owe him?"

"I knew Harold from the tavern where I worked. He spotted me a few quid when I was at my lowest a few years back, but then he joined the navy and shipped out, and I never saw him again."

"And he was happy to accept a vial of morphine in lieu of a cash payment?"

"You can't put a price on oblivion, Inspector."

No one understood the value of oblivion better than Sebastian, but he moved toward Ishmael, forcing the other man to take an involuntary step back. "I don't believe you."

"I'm telling you the truth."

"No, you're not. You had a bottle of treacle at the ready. That doesn't square with a visit from a mate you hadn't seen in years. You were prepared."

Ishmael's face fell as he realized his mistake. He clearly couldn't think of a clever comeback quickly enough and remained silent.

"What did you do with the morphine?"

"I put it in a cabinet near Esme's dressing room," Ishmael confessed with a sigh of defeat.

"Why?"

"Someone left me a note on Monday, threatening to accuse me of sodomy. They wanted the morphine in exchange for their silence."

There it was again, the fear he had seen in Ned Bannon's eyes. Sebastian would wager good money that the two men got up to more than a mere massage in that office.

"Who was the note from, Mr. Cabot?"

"I don't know."

"Do you still have it?"

Ishmael shook his head. "I burned it."

"Was this the first time, or have there been prior threats?"

"This was the first time."

"If your blackmailer knew about your visits to Mr. Bannon and the morphine, they must work at the theater."

"I thought so too."

"Any guesses?"

Ishmael's face twisted with distaste. "Serena Winthrop. She's always watching everyone and making nasty digs meant to imply that she knows more than she's saying."

"Tell me about the note," Sebastian invited.

"I just did." Ishmael looked confused, and Sebastian was forced to spell it out for him.

"What sort of paper was it written on? Did the handwriting look masculine or feminine? Did it smell like anything? How was it worded?"

Ishmael made no pretense at not remembering. He'd admitted too much already, and now his only option was to help the police. "It was written on the back of a leaflet advertising the performance, and the words were uneven and spelled out in block letters. It said, 'Leave morphine in china cabinet or I tell the police you're a molly.'"

Taking a shaking breath, Ishmael added, "Morphine was spelled with an f, and molly was spelled with one l."

"What did you make of that?"

"I thought it was done on purpose, to disguise the writer's identity."

"Is the accusation true?"

"Does it matter? No one will believe me anyway," Ishmael snapped.

"I will believe you, but I need to know the truth," Sebastian replied.

Ishmael's expression was pained. "When I was living on the streets, I sometimes had to pleasure men in order to survive. I never did anything illegal," he hurried to assure Sebastian, making it quite clear how he'd earned his bread.

"And do you pleasure Mr. Bannon?" Sebastian asked. "Anything you tell me will remain between us. You have my word."

Ishmael looked away for a moment, clearly embarrassed. "I have pleasured him on occasion, but I never let him bugger me."

"Do you think someone saw you?"

"I don't know how they could have. The door was locked, and there are no windows in that room."

"Is there anyone else who knows about your visits to Ned Bannon's office?"

"Esme knew."

"Could she have sent the note?" Sebastian pressed.

"Maybe."

"Did you two ever engage in sexual congress?"

"What?" Ishmael looked stunned.

"You heard me."

"No," Ishmael said. "Never."

"Did you ever go to her dressing room?"

"Yeah, once."

"Why?"

Ishmael sighed deeply. "I was upset, and Esme invited me in for a drink. And before you ask, it had nothing to do with Ned. I was just feeling low, that's all."

"Did you touch her?"

"She embraced me. There was nothing in it. Just a bit of comfort."

"When did you switch the bottles?" Sebastian demanded.

"Last night, around five o'clock, while Mr. Bannon was getting dressed."

"And when did you put the bottle in the cabinet?"

"During intermission," Ishmael said.

"Did anyone see you?"

"Everyone was downstairs except Esme. A woman came to see her, and they went to Esme's dressing room."

"Who was the woman?"

"I don't know. I've never seen her before, but I heard Esme call her by name."

"Well, what was it?" Sebastian snapped when Ishmael went quiet.

"Frances."

"And who was the man who came to see you last night?"

"I told you. Harold Lively. I really did owe him money, and I gave him everything I had." That sounded like the truth.

"May I go now, Inspector Bell?" Ishmael pleaded. "I need a moment before the next act."

"Go on," Sebastian said.

He went upstairs and examined the cabinet, which was just a cheap replica of a piece that would be valuable if authentic. It was empty. He then returned downstairs and went in search of Walt Dickie. He wanted to question the man for himself. Perhaps there was another passage that ran behind the offices of Guy Weathers and Ned Bannon, which would explain how someone had known about Ishmael and Ned.

When he found the watchman, the old man was slumped against the wall in the back alley, an empty bottle of gin loosely clutched in his gnarled fingers. His nose and cheeks were criss-crossed with broken capillaries, dried drool flaked on his chin, and his entire body reeked of spirits and urine. Sebastian first thought that the man was in a drunken stupor, but he was too quiet for someone who was merely drunk. Drunks snored, wheezed, grunted, and farted in their sleep. Walt was suspiciously silent.

Bending down, Sebastian placed two fingers against the man's scrawny neck, but all he felt was loose, bumpy chicken skin. No pulse throbbed against his fingertips and, although the body was still warm to the touch, he was certain Walt was gone. Given the foul reek of the man and his unhealthy appearance, he'd most likely died from alcohol poisoning, but until Sebastian solved this case he had to consider the possibility that someone had helped Walt to shuffle off his mortal coil. He lifted the bottle to his nose and sniffed, but all he could smell was juniper with a hint of citrus. If something had been added, the odor of the poison was thoroughly masked by the flowery scent of the gin.

Setting the bottle back down, Sebastian considered Walt Dickie's mortal remains. Given the state of the body and the lack of blood or any visible wounds, Sebastian didn't think Colin would be able to learn much from the postmortem. He decided not to subject his friend to the grisly task of dissecting someone who was so filthy and thoroughly pickled in gin. There was nothing Sebastian could reasonably do for Walt other than inform someone of his passing, and, if he didn't leave the theater now, he'd probably arrest the lot of them and leave them to stew in the cells until they were ready to confess to their sins.

Just then the back door opened, and Charlie Milner stepped outside.

"Walt Dickie is dead," Sebastian told the young man. "Please see to his remains."

"What ye wants us to do with 'im?"

"Did he have any family that you know of?"

"Nah."

"Then take him to the nearest dead house."

Charlie wrinkled his nose in disgust but didn't argue that it wasn't his responsibility to deal with the corpse. The Milners probably had a wagon and would deliver the body to the dead house, where Walt would continue to decompose until he was buried in a pauper's grave.

"Yes, sir," Charlie muttered and began to unbutton his trousers. His stream hit the wall mere inches from Walt's head and pooled near the body. Sebastian turned on his heel and walked away.

When he got home he skirted the parlor, where Mrs. Poole was giggling at something Mr. Quince had said, and hurried up the stairs. If he stopped in to say goodnight, Mr. Quince was sure to invite him to join them for a drink and quiz Sebastian about the case. Quince had been lodging with Mrs. Poole for a mere three months but had already established himself as the man of the house and never passed up an opportunity to corner Sebastian and put the screws to him. And he'd be hungry for information tonight, given that the story about the murders had just been published and Quince would correctly assume that Sebastian knew more than the papers were reporting.

In his bedroom, Sebastian checked on Gustav, who was snoozing peacefully, then undressed and climbed into bed. He'd missed dinner again, and wished he had bought something to eat, but he hadn't seen any vendors on his way home and wasn't in the mood to go to a pub or a chophouse alone. He conceded that it had been a foolish decision, since his stomach was rumbling with hunger and he wasn't going to get anything to eat until morning. He would have liked a chop or bowl of rich stew, but what he wanted more than food was to talk to Gemma and share his impressions with her. Then he remembered that Gemma was angry with him and would likely not wish to speak to him until he apologized.

Normally, as he lay in bed, Sebastian would have reviewed

everything he had learned and tried to force the information into some sort of order, but his thoughts failed to crystalize, and he began to drift, his mind turning his findings into a series of dark, menacing dreams that plagued him throughout the night.

TWENTY-EIGHT

THURSDAY, MARCH 17

Despite a difficult evening, Anne had slept soundly and was feeling stronger by the time she came down to breakfast and asked Mabel for a soft-boiled egg and toast with butter and marmalade. Gemma was happy to have the same, and they enjoyed a companionable breakfast with Colin, whose day didn't begin until he had had his fried eggs and kippers. The tension of the previous day had dissipated, and they talked easily, remarking on the weather, which looked pleasant.

"I would like to call on an old friend today," Gemma said once Colin had excused himself and disappeared into the cellar, leaving the two women to enjoy a second cup of tea. "Would you care to accompany me, Mrs. Ramsey?"

There were days when Anne longed to get outside and days when she wouldn't budge from her spot by the window, even if the weather was fine and a walk would do her good. Gemma hoped this was one of her good days and Anne would agree. She could ask Mabel to keep an eye on Anne and pop out for an hour, but she thought it would do Anne good to get out of the house and get some fresh air and exercise.

Anne's face instantly brightened. "Oh, I do love paying

morning calls. I will wear my new bonnet, the one with the silk violets."

The bonnet was at least five years old, the violets now faded and misshapen, but Gemma wasn't about to point that out to Anne. "Of course. It goes well with your blue cape."

The cape was as old as the bonnet, the deep-blue velvet worn in places, but it was Anne's favorite and would keep her well insulated from the chill wind that was so prevalent at this time of year.

"Don't you have anything else to wear?" Anne asked, casting a judgmental eye over Gemma's gown. "Black is so unbecoming."

"I'm in mourning, Mrs. Ramsey," Gemma replied.

"I don't want Colin to mourn me when I'm gone," Anne suddenly said. "He's mourned me already, the poor boy, and his dear papa too. It's time he got on with his life."

"Shall I bring your boots here?" Gemma asked, hoping the question would redirect Anne's thoughts.

"Yes, do."

Anne turned in her chair and stuck out her legs, kicked off her kid slippers and wiggled her toes. Gemma brought Anne's walking boots to the breakfast room and helped her to button them, then guided her to the foyer, where she draped the cape over Anne's shoulders and tied the ribbons of the bonnet beneath her chin, before getting ready herself. She called out to Mabel that they were stepping out for a walk and escorted Anne outside into the watery March sunshine, which made Anne squint despite the wide brim that shielded her eyes. Gemma slid her arm through Anne's in case the older woman should become distracted by something on the other side of the street and veer into the road, and they set off. Poppy lived in New Bridge Street, which wasn't very far.

"It's been such a long while since I've paid a morning call," Anne said excitedly. When she looked at Gemma, her gaze was clear and bright, and Gemma knew it for what it was, another rare moment of lucidity. "When Colin was a boy, he'd get an attack of collywobbles every time I left the house. He was so attached." Anne smiled at the memory. "And look at him now, a grown man."

She smiled at Gemma, her manner ingratiating. "Forgive me if I overstep, my dear, but I daresay you and Colin couldn't be better suited. And I know Colin has feelings for you. A mother can always tell when her son's in love."

"Colin and I are friends, Mrs. Ramsey," Gemma said softly. "I hold him in great regard, but that is all."

Mrs. Ramsey sighed dramatically. "It's that policeman, isn't it? What's his name again?"

"Inspector Bell."

"That's right. Bell. I could have sworn he was married."

"He lost his wife three years ago."

"And the child?" Anne asked, clearly recalling that Louisa and Sebastian had been expecting a baby.

"The child as well."

"Oh, the poor man," Anne exclaimed. "But these things happen, don't they, and people have to move on, otherwise their life will pass them by."

She stopped walking and peered at Gemma, her gaze so alert it was as if she could see into Gemma's very soul. "He might make you happy at first, Gemma dear, but in the end he will break your heart."

"Why do you say that?" Gemma asked, shaken by Anne's unexpected prediction.

"Because he's that sort of man."

"What sort is that?"

"The sort who'll make you feel more alive than you ever thought possible when he wants you and then will push you to the brink of despair. Colin will make you feel cherished and safe, and security is so important in a marriage. Extremes of emotion are exciting, to be sure, but in the end, they do nothing but give one bouts of indigestion and a sallow complexion."

"Inspector Bell and I are not courting, Mrs. Ramsey, and Colin is my employer," Gemma reminded her. She was deeply uncomfortable with the direction the conversation had taken and longed to change the subject.

"You don't have to be courting to be in love," Anne replied wistfully. "I was in love once."

"With Colin's father?"

Anne shook her head. "No, Clive. He was an officer in the Queen's Guard. He was so charming and handsome. He said he would gladly claim every dance on my dance card, propriety be damned, but we could only dance together twice or tongues would begin to wag."

"How old were you?" Gemma asked.

"I had just come out, so sixteen. Clive gave me my first kiss," Anne said dolefully. "He told me he loved me and would speak to my father and ask for my hand, but he never did. I was absolutely crushed."

"Why didn't he?" Gemma asked. She knew virtually nothing about Anne's past and was curious to hear about her youthful experiences.

Anne suddenly looked furiously angry, bright spots of color blooming on her cheeks. "A girl I trusted and believed to be a friend wanted Clive for herself, so she poured poison in his ear. She made him believe I had loose morals and he wasn't the first man I had been affectionate with."

"And he believed her?" Gemma exclaimed.

Anne nodded. "Not only did he believe her; he married her. Seemingly artless young girls can be vicious and calculating when it suits their purpose."

Gemma knew this to be true based on her own adolescent heartbreaks and the vicious gossip and ruthless character assassinations she had witnessed in Scutari. Women might be the weaker sex, but they could hold their own when it came to back-stabbing and covering their tracks.

"And then you met your George?" Gemma asked in an effort to redirect Anne's attention to happier times.

"I met George years later. He was my last chance at marriage and a family of my own. I did come to love him in time," Anne said softly. "Colin is so like him. He's not dashing or charming in that effortless way some men have, but he's loyal and steadfast, and that's what matters in the end, isn't it?"

Anne's gaze slid toward Blackfriars Bridge, where a sleek carriage pulled by a pair of magnificent grays was outlined against the pale blue sky.

"Beautiful," she said softly. "I always liked pretty horses."

When she turned back, her gaze was no longer focused, and her mouth had gone a bit slack. "I also like sponge, with raspberry filling," she said dreamily.

"Mabel makes a lovely sponge," Gemma replied, and steered Anne into New Bridge Street.

She was sad when Anne's moment of clarity passed, but relieved that the older woman was no longer speculating about Gemma's love life, or lack thereof. Gemma missed her mother desperately and would have given anything to talk to her about all the things she was feeling, but, although Anne could be maternal, Gemma had no wish to talk to her about things that were private. The old woman's reminiscences had taken Gemma by surprise, though. She had thought that George Ramsey had been the love of Anne's life, but she didn't suppose anyone ever really knew another person's heart or the secrets it kept in order to protect oneself as well as others.

Gemma tried to dismiss the awkward conversation from her mind, but Anne's observations about Sebastian had struck a nerve, and she wondered if Anne might be right about the sort of husband he would make. She also came to a realization that nothing Anne said would change the way she felt, and that a life with Colin sounded very dull in comparison. Gemma wasn't the sort of woman who sought security. If she were, she wouldn't have rebelled against her parents' plans for her future or gone out to Crimea. It had been a harrowing experience, but if she could go back and make the choice all over again she would do exactly the same thing. Perhaps Colin was right, and she was addicted to danger; or maybe she simply wanted to feel alive and make use of her God-given talents rather than spend her days hiding in the drawing room with her embroidery or a book in her lap. And if her choices would bring her pain, then so be it, because she simply couldn't live her life any other way. She didn't want to.

Once Gemma located the address Mary Harbor had written down for her, she guided Anne up the path and knocked on the door. The boarding house looked like the sort of place Gemma herself had vacated only a few months before. The building was far from grand, but it was in reasonable repair and looked well looked after. The step was cleanly swept, the paint wasn't peeling or cracked, and there were lace curtains at the window of what had to be the parlor.

A woman of about sixty opened the door. Her hair was streaked with gray, and her hands looked workworn, but her back was straight, her olive skin looked surprisingly smooth, and her dark eyes radiated friendliness.

"How can I help, ladies?" the landlady asked. "I'm afraid I don't have any vacancies, if it's a room you're after."

"I was hoping to see Miss Bright," Gemma explained. "Is she in?"

"And who may I say is calling?" the woman asked.

"Miss Tate. We knew each other in Crimea."

"Nurse, are you?" The landlady's gaze slid to Anne Ramsey, who was staring into space and humming softly to herself. "And I take it that's your current charge?"

"Yes."

"Well, come in. The street is no place for the likes of her."

"Thank you."

Gemma escorted Anne into the parlor and settled her by the unlit hearth. Anne didn't seem at all put out to be in a strange place. Instead, she examined the framed sampler on the wall and smiled at a figurine of a little dog on the mantel, clearly charmed by the playful puppy, whose nose was slightly chipped. Gemma shrugged off her cape and draped it over the back of a chair, but didn't sit down. She suddenly felt too anxious to remain still.

"Gemma Tate!" Poppy exclaimed when she burst into the room. "As I live and breathe."

"I hope you don't mind me turning up like this," Gemma said as she came toward Poppy, who pulled her into a warm embrace.

"Of course not. I'm so glad to see you. However did you find me?"

"I stopped into Harbor's Drugs yesterday, and your sister and I got to talking. She gave me the address."

Now that she had met Mary, Gemma could see the resemblance between the two women, but, where Mary looked stern, Poppy's smile was mischievous, and her dark coloring didn't make her look forbidding in the least. Her brown gaze was warm, and her dark brown hair was wound into a knot at her nape, but several curling strands had been left loose and framed Poppy's face.

"Did she now?" Poppy said, and laughed merrily. "I'm not even going to ask how my name came up, but I'm glad it did. Miss Bossy Boots manages to do me a good turn from time to time," she added affectionately. "Do sit down. Should I ask Mrs. Sloan to put the kettle on?"

"Oh, yes," Anne piped up. "I'd love a cup of tea."

"This is Mrs. Ramsey," Gemma said. She didn't need to

explain that Anne was her patient. Poppy had gleaned as much, and smiled at Anne.

"Pleased to make your acquaintance, Mrs. Ramsey."

"Likewise, I'm sure," Anne replied demurely.

Poppy stepped out into the corridor to speak to Mrs. Sloan, then returned to the parlor and addressed Anne. "We'll have that tea for you in a jiffy, ma'am. Mrs. Sloan might even furnish us with a few biscuits. I always crave a midmorning comestible, don't you?"

Anne nodded eagerly, but her eyes kept turning toward the ceramic dog.

"Sweet, isn't it?" Poppy said, following the direction of her gaze. "Mrs. Sloan's son gave that to her for her birthday. If it were me, I'd keep it in my room, but she wanted everyone to enjoy it. And, of course, someone dropped it and chipped the poor little chap's nose."

"I used to have a dog just like it when I was a girl," Anne said. "His name was Rabbit, but my brother called him Ratbag. He wasn't very nice."

"No, he certainly wasn't," Poppy agreed, and patted Anne's liver-spotted hand.

They chatted about dogs until Mrs. Sloan brought in the tea tray. Once Anne was supplied with a cup of tea and a biscuit, Gemma and Poppy got a chance to speak without interruptions.

"You're in mourning," Poppy observed, eyeing Gemma's black gown and mourning bonnet.

"My brother. It's been nearly five months."

"I'm so sorry. I remember Victor. He was lovely. What happened, if you don't mind me asking?"

"An accident," Gemma said. She couldn't bear to go into the details, not when she was finally learning to navigate life without her twin, but she still felt guilty for downplaying his death for her own benefit.

"I'm sorry," Poppy said again, cutting across Gemma's sad

thoughts. "Victor's passing was connected to the death of that heiress, wasn't it? I saw something about it in the papers, but I didn't read the full account. It was too upsetting."

Gemma nodded. "He was at the wrong place at the wrong time, and he paid for it with his life."

"Or maybe he was at the right place at the right time," Poppy said sadly, and stared into her tea.

"What on earth do you mean?" Gemma exclaimed.

"My brother-in-law is Presbyterian, and he's always banging on about predestination. Are we ever in the wrong place, or are we precisely where we were meant to be all along?" Poppy asked. "Did we make the decision to answer Florence Nightingale's call, or was it always going to happen?"

"I don't know," Gemma replied. "I was actually just thinking about that and wondering if I ever really had a choice. Sometimes it does seem like everything is preordained, doesn't it? But I refuse to believe that I don't have free will. I chose to come here today, didn't I?" she asked, smiling at Poppy over her teacup.

"Did you?" Poppy quipped. "Or were you led here by providence?"

"It was quite a coincidence that I met your sister, wasn't it?"

"Or maybe it was all by design," Poppy said, wiggling her eyebrows playfully.

They dissolved into giggles, and Gemma felt lighter than she had in days, even though the subject itself was rather weighty and called for deeper analysis.

"How long ago did they take over the shop?" Gemma asked.

"Nearly two years ago now," Poppy replied, and reached for another biscuit. "Mr. Harbor, as he prefers to be addressed, used to work at a chemist's in Clerkenwell but was finally able to afford his own shop when his uncle died and left him the entirety of his estate. I've never seen my taciturn brother-in-law so giddy."

"I suppose an unexpected windfall will have that effect."

"Oh, it wasn't unexpected. Harbor had been waiting for that money for years, and he made good use of it when it finally came to him."

"It's a nice shop."

"They bought it for a very reasonable price. It seems the owner, Mr. Wyvern, died quite suddenly, and there was no one to take over. A distant cousin negotiated the sale."

Gemma refreshed Anne's tea and handed her another biscuit. Anne gave her a vague smile before her attention returned to the little dog once again.

"Mary said you work at an infirmary. Are you happy there?" Gemma asked.

Poppy was the sort of person who made the best of any situation, and had been a welcome ray of sunshine at a time when they had all questioned their sanity and begun to doubt that the war would ever end and they would return home. It had been like a nightmare one couldn't wake from, but Poppy had found a way to keep the ugliness at bay and had made the most of every minute she had away from the ward. She wasn't one to engage in a clandestine love affair, but she had been friendly with everyone and a favorite with the doctors.

Poppy smiled wistfully. "Happy is perhaps not the right word. It's honest work, and it pays the rent. You know how it is with those of us who were in Crimea. The other nurses think we're stuck-up cows, and the doctors never miss an opportunity to remind us of our place in case we should make them look bad or challenge their arcane methods. But it's not all sour grapes. The two doctors who are usually on my shift are young and sympathetic. They genuinely want to help those in their care and, if I can lend a hand, they'll accept it with thanks."

"That sounds like the ideal situation," Gemma replied.

"Or close to it," Poppy agreed. "No matter what they might dish out, it's still better than working with Mary and Levi

Harbor. Those two would have my whole day divided into preapproved segments of genteel industry. Or better yet marry me off to one of Levi's widowed associates. I wonder if those dullards bored their wives to death." She smiled ruefully. "I suppose that sounds unkind, but I simply can't imagine a life with one of those men. When the good Lord was giving out desirable traits, those fellows were waiting in the wrong line."

"What did they get?" Gemma asked, her mouth quirking. Poppy's opinion was a bit harsh but, if she knew her friend, it was honest and probably accurate.

Poppy shrugged. "I honestly couldn't tell you. Excellent digestion?"

The two women laughed, and Anne joined in, even though she didn't seem to get the gist of the joke.

"I do miss Scutari sometimes," Poppy admitted. "It was awful while we were there, and I fell asleep every night dreaming of home, but once I got back home just wasn't the same."

"Or maybe it was you who weren't the same," Gemma replied. She had felt much the same, even though she had been thrilled to come home and had cherished every moment of peace and comfort.

"You're probably right there, Gemma. I came back a different person, and I wanted different things. I don't mind telling you that I thought I'd find a husband out there. All those doctors and soldiers. A handsome officer, whom I'd nurse from the brink of death and get to fall madly in love with me. Except the only reward I got for my pains was chilblains, a nagging cough, and a questionable reputation."

"We really didn't understand what we had signed up for, did we?"

"No, but I'm still glad I went. I miss the camaraderie, Gemma, and the sense of purpose. I'd never felt so alive. I was making a difference, even to those men who died. I made their final moments a bit less lonely. Or at least I'd like to think so. All I do now is take out chamber pots, change bandages, and administer the occasional enema—the highlight of my day."

Poppy's gaze fixed on Anne, who was beginning to nod off. "How long have you been looking after Mrs. Ramsey?"

"A few months. I worked at the Foundling Hospital before that."

"Oh," Poppy exclaimed, and instantly lowered her voice. "Were you there when that poor child was murdered?"

"I was."

"Terrible business. The depravity of some people never ceases to astound me. Is that why you left?"

"I was sacked," Gemma admitted, and felt her cheeks grow warm with embarrassment.

"Sacked?" Poppy's eyes grew round with curiosity.

"I became involved in the investigation and broke a number of hospital rules."

"I'm sure you were only trying to help," Poppy said loyally.

"Unfortunately, Matron didn't quite see it that way."

"They never do," Poppy scoffed. "I broke a few rules myself while in Scutari and, even though I wasn't sent packing, Miss Nightingale wasn't overly pleased with me. The thing is that we're human and, like it or not, we get involved and develop feelings for the people in our care."

Gemma choked up at the thought of Lucy, but couldn't bring herself to tell Poppy about her loss. Talking about the girl was painful, so she pushed down her sadness and used the opportunity to steer the conversation in a different direction. She wanted to help Sebastian catch Esme's and Christopher's killer. Except for him, there was no one to fight their corner, and once the case was closed the troupe would simply move on and the sensational story would be replaced by other headlines and new crimes. There were already new lead actors to take Esme's and Christopher's places, and Gemma was sure their funeral would be a miserly affair, with nothing more than a graveside eulogy and crude pine boxes. Guy Weathers didn't strike her as the sentimental type, so the two actors would be lucky to get a wooden cross to mark their resting places, much less a stone to commemorate their lives.

"Poppy, do you remember anyone named Christopher Hudson? He was wounded, I believe."

Poppy's gaze turned quizzical. "Do you mean Romeo of *Romeo and Juliet* at the Orpheus theater?"

"That's the one."

"Gemma, have you not seen the papers?" Poppy asked carefully.

"I have. That's why I'm asking."

"Why on earth would you want to know about him?"

"I was at the theater when it happened. Mrs. Ramsey's son wanted to take her to a play to celebrate her birthday," Gemma said. She felt the need to explain why she had attended the theater while in mourning, even though she didn't think Poppy would judge her.

"Oh, you poor dear. How awful," Poppy exclaimed. "Murder just follows you round, doesn't it?"

"It would seem so," Gemma agreed.

"I did know Christopher, as it happens. Except he was Bobby then. Bobby Metz. Christopher Hudson is— was his stage name. Funny how a name can make such a difference to the way one is perceived," Poppy mused. "Bobby Metz sounds like a butcher, or a fishmonger. Or a foot soldier. Someone who's of no account."

"Yes, a name can make all the difference to the way one is perceived."

"When I was a girl, I wanted to be called Hyacinth or Gardenia," Poppy said, and chuckled. "I thought it would make me sound aristocratic, and I liked flower names."

"Poppy suits you," Gemma said. "And it's always been one

of my favorite flowers. So, what sort of man was Christopher?" She'd made a mental note of the actor's real name to pass on to Sebastian.

Poppy shrugged. "It's difficult to tell what sort of person someone is when they're scared and in pain, but he did have a flair for the dramatic; that I recall. He could recite entire poems from memory. Imagine my surprise when I bumped into him near Covent Garden Market. We had a nice chat, he told me about his new name and career, and he invited me to come to the play. Said he'd leave a ticket at the front door."

"Did you go?"

"I work six nights per week, and the one day I have off, the last thing I want to do is sit through a three-hour play, and all by myself. It was a kind gesture, though."

"Yes, it was. Did Christopher seem happy when you saw him?" Gemma asked.

"He did, yes. He said it was the life he'd always dreamed of. And there were certain perks that made up for the lack of adequate financial compensation."

"What sort of perks?"

"He didn't elaborate, but I took that to mean that he didn't lack for female companionship."

"Did he mention his leading lady?"

"Not that I recall. Why do you ask?"

"It would seem they were having an affair."

Poppy nodded. "That doesn't surprise me. He was the sort of man who was gratified by his own sexual prowess," she said. "I don't think it was about the woman. For him, it was all about the conquest."

"Did he say anything about his plans for the future?" Gemma asked, wondering if Christopher had been making plans with Lady Argyle, who must have doted on him.

"We didn't talk for that long. I had to get back, and he had rehearsal in half an hour. He only came to the market to buy a few oranges."

"What about General Modine? Did you ever come across him in Crimea?" Gemma tried again.

Poppy nodded. "Oh yes, I met him once and thanked the Lord I never got him as a patient on the ward. Odious man."

"What do you remember about him?"

"He was wounded during the Battle of Inkerman. Took a saber to his left arm. He was brought to Scutari for treatment but refused to stay once Dr. Dean stitched him up. He was raring to get back to his men. I overheard the conversation between him and Dr. Dean while I assisted."

"I suppose that's admirable that he wanted to return to his men," Gemma observed.

Poppy shook her head. "He spoke very rudely of them and said they were like children who'd run wild if their father spared them the rod. He told Dr. Dean he had someone flogged once a week just to keep the men on their toes. He made certain those poor soldiers lived in constant fear, Gemma."

Gemma stared at Poppy, horrified by what she'd heard. Had Esme Royce realized what sort of man she had become involved with? Perhaps she'd never seen that side of General Modine, but Gemma couldn't imagine that a man who flogged innocent soldiers just to make a point could be a caring lover. Had the general lost his temper when he'd discovered that he wasn't the only man in Esme's life, and wanted to punish both her and the man who'd usurped his place? Gemma could easily imagine a man who was capable of needless cruelty murdering two people in cold blood, but she couldn't see him resorting to skullduggery and tampering with theater props. Someone who was as proud as he was vicious would want the world to know that he had meted out justice to a woman who had betrayed him and had killed the man who had dared to stake his claim on what the general considered his property. The motive was clear, but the method didn't fit.

"Did General Modine say anything of a personal nature?" Gemma asked, hoping that the general had been vain enough to keep talking about himself throughout the time it had taken to patch him up.

Poppy looked at the ceiling as she tried to recall that day. "He mostly talked about the battle, but he did say that his wife would probably be forever grateful if he didn't return."

"Really? He readily admitted that?"

"I expect he treated her as cruelly as he treated his soldiers."

"Did he happen to mention her name?" Gemma asked, immediately recalling the entry she had spotted in the poisons ledger. *F. Modine.*

"No, he didn't, but another officer did, now I think about it. He'd overheard General Modine's comment about his wife and told Dr. Dean later that day that he had known Frances Modine before she married the general and that she had been a lovely girl before he'd beaten her into submission."

"Frances," Gemma said under her breath.

"Yes. What of it?"

"Nothing. It's a lovely name."

"Brings to mind someone delicate," Poppy replied.

"Did Christopher Hudson happen to mention General Modine the day you met?"

Poppy stared at Gemma, then laughed and shook her head in obvious disbelief. "Gemma Tate, are you involved in this investigation as well?"

"Only peripherally," Gemma admitted.

"And what exactly does that mean?"

"Inspector Bell, who was with me at the theater and is investigating the murders, is a dear friend."

"Dear friend?" Poppy scoffed, her eyes sparkling with amusement. "Is that what we're calling it?"

"Poppy, I'm in mourning for Victor," Gemma reminded her friend sternly. "So that is what we're calling it until such a time when we can call it something else. *If* it becomes something else," she added softly.

"Forgive me," Poppy said. "That was unkind."

"It's all right," Gemma replied graciously.

It was only natural that Poppy would be intrigued by Gemma's dealings with a policeman, but Gemma wasn't going to discuss her association with Sebastian. For one, it seemed disloyal to give away the details of his work, and for another, her feelings for Sebastian were so fragile and sacred that she couldn't bear to diminish her regard for him by gossiping about their relationship as if it were fodder for entertainment rather than her most cherished dream. She hoped she could make up with Sebastian before their tiff grew into something as solid and impenetrable as a brick wall between them and any relationship became impossible and Sebastian no longer saw any reason to call on the Ramseys so he could see her.

"Where exactly did you see Christopher Hudson?" Gemma asked, no longer bothering to hide her personal interest in the matter.

"On Russell Street. He'd just come out of Driscoll's Drugs." Poppy giggled, then leaned toward Gemma and lowered her voice so Mrs. Ramsey couldn't hear. "He was probably buying condoms."

"Condoms?"

"Oh, Gemma, you're such an innocent," Poppy teased. "Men use them to prevent unwanted pregnancy."

"Of course," Gemma said, but, although she had a vague notion of what Poppy was referring to, she had never seen a prophylactic for herself and didn't think she ever would.

"They don't come cheap," Poppy said matter-of-factly. "Especially the ones that are made of sheep's intestines and are too delicate to be reused. Perhaps Christopher bought the cheaper ones. They're coarse, but I hear they do the job. If his admirers were of a certain age, then perhaps he didn't need them at all and was simply shopping for tooth powder or a bar of soap."

"Esme Royce was with child," Gemma said. "About twelve weeks."

"Was she? They didn't mention that in the papers."

"It's not common knowledge. Mrs. Ramsey's son performed the postmortem."

Poppy's mouth fell open. "Are you serious? You're living with a police surgeon and dallying with a detective? I do declare, I have newfound respect for you, Gemma. Who would have thought you'd turn out to be the most exciting person I know?"

"I'm hardly exciting, and we are talking about the murders of two people. Three, if you count the baby."

Poppy's smile slipped. "You're right. I'm sorry. It's just that, after Crimea, I try to focus on the living rather than the dead. Thinking about all that awful waste of life makes me sick to my stomach. There's nothing more we can do for Esme or Christopher, but you and I are still here, and we have to find some joy in our lives, don't we? Otherwise, what's the point of it all?"

"And do you find it? Joy?" Gemma asked. She wondered if Poppy had ever had a lover. She may not have found a husband in Crimea, but perhaps she had found love and a reason to go on.

"I try," Poppy said, and her eyes brimmed with tears. "I try so hard."

"Gemma, dear, I think I'd like to go home now," Anne said. She looked confused as she took in her surroundings. "George will be worried, and you know how Colin gets when I leave. He's so attached, the poor mite."

"Of course, Mrs. Ramsey. Shall we stop at a bakery on our way back?"

"Bakery?"

"To get a sponge."

Anne brightened. "Yes. A sponge. With raspberry filling."

Gemma stood, and Poppy joined her.

"Gemma, it was so good to see you. Do you think we might meet again soon? Maybe take a walk by the river or have a cup of tea. I get so lonesome sometimes."

"So do I. I would love that. What about next week?"

Poppy patted her on the arm. "I'll check my schedule for next week, and we'll get something fixed up."

Gemma gave Poppy her address, thanked Mrs. Sloan for the tea, and escorted Anne outside.

"What a nice young woman," Anne said once they set off for home. "She'd make a good match for your Mr. Bell. Don't you think, dear?"

Gemma didn't answer, and hoped that Anne would have forgotten all about her matchmaking schemes by the time they arrived at the bakery.

TWENTY-NINE

Sebastian's day began at Scotland Yard. He waited patiently while Lovell upbraided him for not providing him with an update last night, particularly since Lovell was due to see the commissioner that afternoon and needed to be prepared should Sir David wish to discuss the case. Sebastian then filled Lovell in on what he had learned so far.

The superintendent leaned back in his chair and fixed Sebastian with a narrowed gaze. "Arrest Cabot."

"I don't think he did it."

"He's the most likely suspect, and one hundred milligrams would be enough to murder two people."

"Not according to Colin Ramsey."

"What does he know?" Lovell exclaimed. "Has he attempted to murder anyone lately? No, don't answer that," he sputtered. "That man spends his days elbow deep in cadavers. I wouldn't be surprised if he resorted to doing something unspeakable himself."

"That's a vile accusation," Sebastian countered, furious on Colin's behalf.

Lovell waved a dismissive hand. "I didn't mean murder. But

you must admit we have a serious problem with grave-robbing, Bell. No one's loved ones are safe."

"I assure you, Superintendent, Mr. Ramsey does not steal corpses in the night."

"Maybe not, but I'm certain he deals with men who do. He needs subjects for his dissections, and we don't send him nearly enough cadavers to support his lifestyle."

"What lifestyle is that?"

"Do you think I'm deaf and blind, Inspector? I assure you I'm very well informed. Mr. Ramsey uses the bodies we send him to instruct private students, therefore earning a double fee off someone else's misery."

"Mr. Ramsey is an experienced surgeon who doesn't butcher the remains while too drunk to wield a scalpel," Sebastian ground out.

"You will speak of Mr. Fenwick with respect," Lovell bellowed.

"I never mentioned Mr. Fenwick, but I'm glad you knew precisely who I was speaking about."

"Get out!" Lovell hissed. "You've tried my patience enough for one day."

Sebastian pushed to his feet and fixed Lovell with what he hoped was a withering look. "I would thank you not to take your anger out on either myself or Mr. Ramsey, Superintendent. If you find yourself unable to control your emotions, then perhaps your retirement is not as untimely as you might imagine."

With that, Sebastian turned on his heel, walked out, and nearly collided with John Ransome, who had just come out of the break room and was carrying a steaming mug of tea, which he avoided spilling all over himself only through sheer luck.

"Bell!" he exclaimed. "Good to see you, old boy." Ransome looked happy and relaxed, his dark eyes dancing with amusement.

"Congratulations on your marriage, John."

"Thank you. Laura and I returned from our wedding trip yesterday, and, to tell you the truth, I'm raring to go. It would seem I'm not cut out for a life of leisure. Easily bored, I'm afraid," he said as they walked together toward the duty room.

"Surely you weren't bored on your honeymoon," Sebastian teased.

"Of course not, but all that infernal sightseeing is not for me. You've seen one Roman ruin, you've seen them all. And we have plenty of fine sights right here in England. When we build a castle, it doesn't crumble into dust," John Ransome stated loyally. "Laura was in absolute heaven, though, and it made me happy just to see her enjoyment." Ransome's expression softened, and Sebastian thought that he might have misjudged him, and Ransome really did care for Laura Hawkins and didn't just see her as a means to an end.

"I think I might have some news to share with her tonight," Ransome announced. He had the look of a man who was torn between revealing too much and desperately needing to talk about a worry that was weighing on his mind.

"Oh? What news is that?"

"I have a meeting with Sir David scheduled for this afternoon. Change is imminent."

"So I hear."

"We all make choices, Sebastian," Ransome said, "and some choices have the power to destroy our lives. There are things you don't know. About Lovell, I mean."

"I know he's angry and feels betrayed by a man he'd put his faith in."

"Sir David didn't betray him. It was the other way around," Ransome said, and Sebastian could tell from his expression that he was telling the truth, or some version of it. "I can't talk about it. It wouldn't be right. All I can tell you is that Lovell made a grave miscalculation."

"From which you stand to benefit."

Ransome nodded. "Yes, but if promoted I will give it my all."

"I believe you will," Sebastian replied, and meant it.

"Do I have your support?" Ransome asked, his dark gaze demanding an answer.

"You do," Sebastian said before he'd even considered the question. "You do, John."

John Ransome clapped him on the shoulder. "Good man. You won't regret it."

I hope not, Sebastian thought as he walked away. It seemed he had officially picked a side, and he had done so in anger, which was never a good idea.

As he stepped outside, Sebastian realized that he hadn't told Lovell Walt Dickie was dead; but he didn't think Dickie's death would significantly alter the course of his investigation. As far as Sebastian could see, no one had a compelling reason to want the watchman dead.

Unless the old man had known too much to be allowed to live, he amended as he walked away.

THIRTY

It was too early in the day to call on members of the aristocracy, but Sebastian didn't have the luxury of time and wasn't about to waste several hours waiting for a more opportune time to visit Lady Argyle and Lord Gilroy. He found a cab and directed the driver to Lady Argyle's Mayfair address. Lady Argyle might not have a military background or have earned a reputation for cruelty, but if she felt betrayed by her lover and jealous of his new lady she would have motive aplenty for murder. And Lord Gilroy had been backstage as well, and might have seen something the actors had not noticed while they were preparing to go on stage or taking a moment to rest during intermission.

Lady Argyle's house was exactly what one would expect of a widowed aristocrat's town residence. It was large and imposing, and noticeably quiet at a time of day when the servants had finished their morning chores and were probably enjoying their midday meal in the servants' hall. Sebastian was admitted by a young maidservant, who was surprisingly accommodating and took his things without a word of reproach. The woman directed Sebastian to the drawing room, where Lady Argyle reclined on a chaise, a book in her hand.

Normally, the first thing Sebastian did upon meeting a potential suspect was take the measure of the person he'd come to see, but the drawing room was so crammed with gilt-framed paintings, porcelain ornaments of all shapes and sizes, and stuffed birds that he found he had difficulty separating the lady of the house from the ornamental tat that made him feel as if he were under attack. His gaze fell on the stuffed peacock that stared at him with its beady glass eyes, and he couldn't help but note that the peacock and the woman bore a striking resemblance to each other.

"Beautiful, isn't it?" Lady Argyle asked as she followed the direction of his gaze. "My husband brought it from India, and had it stuffed after it died. Couldn't bear to part with it. I briefly debated treating my husband to a similar fate after he passed, but that would have put off callers, and I do enjoy visits from friends," she went on with a coy smile. "Oh, do sit down, Inspector. You're giving me a crick in the neck."

Sebastian settled on the arsenic-green settee and tried not to look at the bird or stare at his hostess. At first glance, Lady Argyle appeared to be in her mid-forties, but, the closer Sebastian got, the older she appeared. Now that he was mere feet away, he could make out the fine lines around the eyes and mouth and pick out strands of silver in the fair locks that peeked from beneath a purple and turquoise turban decorated with a peacock feather. Her gown matched the turban, and the overly embellished neckline displayed surprisingly firm breasts that spilled forth as if Lady Argyle were going to a ball and wanted to ensure that her dance card was full. Sebastian put the woman at around fifty-five, but it was possible that she was older and had taken great pains to counteract the ravages of time.

"I was expecting you," his hostess announced.

"Were you?"

Lady Argyle nodded, then seemed to remember something and reached for the bellpull, which she yanked several times and with considerable force. The same maidservant who'd let Sebastian in rushed into the room and stood before Lady Argyle as if she were on parade.

"Bring us tea and those little cakes I like, and be quick about it," Lady Argyle said imperiously, and the maid sprinted from the room. "This is not a conversation to be had on an empty stomach," she said as she turned back to Sebastian. "I don't normally take luncheon. At my age, one must watch what one eats if one doesn't want to run to fat."

"I don't think you have any reason for concern, my lady," Sebastian replied smoothly.

"Flatterer," Lady Argyle said with a smile and a wave of the hand. "You remind me of him, you know."

"Christopher Hudson?"

"You look different, and you're older and rougher around the edges, but you have that look in your eye."

"What look might that be?" Sebastian asked, thinking he probably wore the glassy look of the unfortunate peacock.

"You have the look of a man who knows precisely who and what he is and feels entirely at ease in his skin. So few people have that sort of confidence. Most men are endlessly comparing themselves to their rivals and cringing as they secretly catalog their failings."

"I don't have any failings," Sebastian replied with a grin.

He found that he liked Lady Argyle's unapologetic direct-ness and refusal to be overlooked. She was the sort of woman who probably used her wit to intimidate her companions and was always at the center of any gathering, mostly because she ensured that she placed herself there.

Lady Argyle laughed at his joke, but the tinkle of amuse-ment quickly turned into delicate sobs.

"I miss Chris so much," she wailed. "And there's no one I can turn to for comfort."

"I'm sorry," Sebastian said.

Lady Argyle nodded and blew her nose delicately on an embroidered hanky, then took a moment to compose herself while the maidservant set down a laden tea tray and poured out. She handed a cup to her mistress, then turned to Sebastian.

"Milk and sugar, Inspector?"

"Yes, thank you."

The maid made him a cup of tea, then smiled conspiratorially before loading a gold-rimmed plate with several bite-size sandwiches and handing it to him. Sebastian smiled in gratitude and sampled a fish-paste sandwich before resuming the interview.

"Can you tell me about your relationship with Christopher Hudson?"

That was the most diplomatic way he could think of to ask what he needed to know, and he hoped Lady Argyle would spare him having to rephrase the question in a cruder manner. The lady nodded and set down her teacup on an occasional table at her elbow.

"I married Lord Argyle when I was seventeen. We were married for nearly twenty-five years and shared three children, but I never felt even a fraction of the affection for my husband that I felt for Chris. When Malcolm died, I simply donned my widow's weeds and hoped the time would pass quickly." Lady Argyle clasped her hands together. "I'm bereft, Inspector. Absolutely hollowed out by grief, and, although I wish I could show the world that I'm in mourning, I would be harming my reputation and bringing shame on my children."

"Were you in love?" Sebastian asked. It was a foolish question and a disservice to this obviously clever woman, but it would be rude to ask if the only thing she had wanted from Chris Hudson was a good rogering.

Lady Argyle smiled sadly. "I was. I am. But, of course, for Chris this was nothing more than a profitable arrangement. I paid his debts, gave him a weekly allowance, and pretended that

I didn't love him to ensure that I didn't drive him away with my neediness."

"It has come to my attention that Christopher Hudson was romantically involved with his costar. Some might say that gives you a motive for murder," Sebastian said.

"Yes, I'm sure some would, but I didn't kill my darling Chris. And he was not having an affair with Esme Royce."

"How can you be so certain?"

"When I invited Christopher into my bed, we agreed on certain—shall we say—conditions. I didn't expect him to proclaim his love for me, but I would not tolerate sharing him with another woman. Of course, Chris could have easily lied to me, but he was an honorable man, and a pragmatic one. The allowance I gave him would not make him rich, but if he were careful he could set aside a tidy sum. No one wants to remain on the stage once they've been relegated to playing old men or Hamlet's ghost. And to be frank, Inspector, Esme did not strike me as someone who would give her affections indiscriminately."

"There's some suggestion that she was involved with Ishmael Cabot as well."

"Don't believe everything you hear," Lady Argyle warned.

"You were at the theater the night of the murders."

"Yes. I stopped by on my way to a musical evening at Lady Dunbar's salon. Chris was happy to see me and promised to come by after the performance."

"How often did you see him?"

"Twice a week. Sometimes he came in the evening and stayed the night, and other times he came in the morning, and we lounged in bed until it was time for him to get to the theater."

"Where are your children, my lady?" Sebastian asked.

A son who was humiliated by his mother's scandalous liaison could easily become angry enough to kill the man, especially when he realized she had been seduced by a fortune hunter.

"My eldest is in Scotland. He never leaves his ancestral home and despises all things English. We see each other only when I visit in the summer. My youngest son died in Crimea. God rest his soul. And my daughter married a penniless French count. She lives at his dilapidated castle and enjoys pressing his grapes." The countess sighed. "I was very lonely, Inspector, and Chris made me happy. I would never do anything to harm him, even if he was in love with someone else and saw fit to go back on his word. Anything he gave me was better than nothing."

"Thank you, my lady." Sebastian stood. He hadn't seen or heard anything that had led him to believe that Lady Argyle had murdered two people. She had a motive and an opportunity, but she didn't display the desire. Despite her brightly colored outfit and sarcasm-laced levity, it was clear that she was genuinely grieving, and, unless Sebastian could find evidence to link her to the murder, he was inclined to leave her to her grief.

"Good day to you, my lady."

"Good day, Inspector." Lady Argyle smiled wolfishly. "If you find yourself short of funds, I would be happy to subsidize your wages."

"Thank you, but an inspector's salary will have to sustain me."

"Touché," Lady Argyle said, and gazed toward the window. Their interview was over.

THIRTY-ONE

Lord Gilroy's residence was a few streets over, and Sebastian was glad to find the man at home and receiving despite the unfashionable hour. His drawing room was not as over-whelming as Lady Argyle's but came a close second, with portraits of dour-looking relations, two large mirrors, gleaming antique weaponry mounted above the mantel, and at least six occasional tables, four of which were topped with sizable urns. Lord Gilroy had to be at least seventy, but he looked fit and spry, and still boasted a full head of hair and a mouthful of teeth, which he flashed in a smile of welcome.

"I was wondering if someone would come," he said once Sebastian had been announced by the butler and invited to take a seat. "I have read about the murders in the papers, of course, but couldn't reconcile the facts with the people I have come to know and like."

"You don't believe anyone at the Orpheus is capable of murder?"

"I honestly don't," Lord Gilroy said. "What possible reason would they have to murder Esme and Christopher?"

"Jealousy, revenge, professional rivalry," Sebastian supplied.

"Pshaw! Human beings are just that—human, my dear man —but to go as far as to poison two people on stage is barbarous. Not to mention incredibly foolish. Esme Royce and Christopher Hudson filled the seats, which benefited everyone involved. They were talented young people who made their audience forget their cares and transported them to a world of make-believe. Not an easy feat."

"I believe you're a great admirer of Serena Winthrop, my lord," Sebastian said.

Lord Gilroy held up his hand to forestall him. "Before you ask any intrusive questions that will embarrass us both, allow me to make a brief statement."

"Please," Sebastian replied, wondering what the old man had up his very expensive sleeve.

"My father passed in May last year. In two months, my official period of mourning will finally be at an end, and I have every intention of marrying Serena. I have already asked for her hand, and she said yes. Serena had no reason to harm anyone." Lord Gilroy smiled indulgently. "Now, you might think I'm not being honest with you. After all, what sort of loving son goes to the theater and romances an actress young enough to be his daughter while in mourning for his dear papa? The answer is a son who had been belittled and bullied his whole life and who would have gladly pissed on his father's grave."

"And how does your family feel about your impending marriage?" Sebastian asked, all the while wondering if Lord Gilroy had actually pissed on his father's grave or if the statement was purely hypothetical and meant to shock. And why had he decided to wait until the period of mourning was over to marry Serena if he didn't care about observing it in the first place?

"I have no family. My parents are long gone. My wife died nearly twenty years ago, and my only son drowned when a ship bound for New York encountered a storm in the Atlantic and went down with all souls on board. I'm seventy-two years old, and I intend to enjoy whatever life is left to me. And when my time comes, I will die happy, knowing that I changed someone's life and offered her a future she could never have imagined."

"That's very generous of you, my lord. So why delay until May when you can marry Serena right now?" Sebastian inquired.

"I'm enjoying our engagement, Inspector. Sometimes the anticipation is a joy in itself, and May is a much nicer time to have a wedding, don't you think? I plan to take Serena on an extended wedding trip to Greece."

"Are there no distant cousins or beloved nephews who might feel cheated should the entirety of your estate pass to a stage actress?"

"My last will and testament will be ironclad, and no greedy nephews will get their grubby little hands on my money. Now, if you still have questions I will be happy to answer them, but, please, leave Serena out of the conversation. She's as innocent as the day is long."

"During your frequent visits backstage, have you formed an opinion of Ishmael Cabot?"

"A melancholy youth, who could use a friend."

"There was some talk of him romancing Esme."

"I have never seen those two so much as look at each other. In truth, I think Esme felt a certain amount of disdain for the young man."

"And Kate Sommers and Nigel Mowbray? They are now the leads."

"If those two had managed to come up with such an elaborate scheme, I'll eat my hat," Lord Gilroy announced. "Nice people, but thick as two planks."

"So, who do you think is clever enough to kill two people in full view of the audience?"

"The only two people in that theater who are devilishly

clever are Ned Bannon and Guy Weathers. I would look to them, Inspector, but, to be frank, I can't conceive of a scenario in which they would want to kill the two people who actually made their little enterprise profitable. The expression 'to cut off one's nose to spite one's face' comes to mind—but what do I know? Could be that Esme and Christopher were robbing them blind or plotting to start their own troupe and leave Ned and Guy high and dry."

"Interesting theory," Sebastian replied. "Did you ever meet Mr. Bonneville?"

"I did. Seemed a decent enough chap."

There didn't seem to be anything more to say, so Sebastian thanked Lord Gilroy and took his leave.

THIRTY-TWO

As soon as Gemma and Anne returned home, Anne retreated to her favorite chair and gazed out the parlor window, her attention fixed on the passersby and the conveyances that trundled down the road. Gemma sat next to her, but her mind wasn't on people-watching or the fine carriages that Anne counted on her fingers as they went past the house. It had been a joy to see Poppy, and Gemma looked forward to spending more time with her friend, but before she could make plans for the future she had to contend with the present, and that meant unraveling the current case.

Poppy had supplied two useful facts. Gemma had known that General Modine was a cruel and controlling man, but she hadn't given his wife any real thought until now. The fact that her name was Frances and that the entry in the ledger at Driscoll's was F. Modine couldn't be mere coincidence. The poisonous substances had to have been purchased by Frances Modine; but the real question was, had she bought them for her husband or for herself? Was it possible that Frances was consumed with jealousy and had intended to murder his lover? Perhaps she had come to her senses and changed her mind, or maybe she had decided on morphine instead of arsenic and laudanum, since it was more potent and guaranteed to get the job done. Frances Modine could have sneaked backstage during the performance, and, if she weren't sure which vial was meant for Esme, she could have poisoned them both. Christopher's life would be inconsequential for a woman who was bent on revenge and refused to be thwarted.

But Christopher Hudson had also patronized Driscoll's. Gemma hadn't seen his name in the ledger, but she had been looking for Hudson, not Metz. Could he have procured the poison? It wasn't beyond the realm of possibility. If he had loved Esme and she had rejected him in favor of General Modine, he might have decided to kill her and then himself rather than go on without the woman he loved. Or he could have had a connection to Frances Modine. What if they had conspired to get rid of Esme but then the plan had gone horribly wrong?

Gemma was pragmatic enough to admit that her theories were far-fetched and it was more likely that Frances Modine and Christopher Hudson had simply gone into the shop to purchase items they had needed at that moment. There was only one way to find out for sure, and Gemma wasn't about to share her suspicions with Sebastian until she knew more. Otherwise, she might be sending him on a wild goose chase at a time when he was already stretched so thin, and he was sure to try to stop her from going. She glanced at the ormolu clock on the mantel, its loud ticking marking another hour she had spent sitting patiently by the window. But there was something she could do.

Morning calls were generally paid between two and four o'clock in the afternoon. It was customary for the man of the house to socialize with the gentlemen who accompanied their wives, mothers, and sisters, but it was also a time for ladies to visit with their female acquaintances and catch up on society news. Some men left the house altogether on certain days, preferring not to have to contend with idle female chatter or salacious gossip. General Modine might follow accepted social protocol and preside over the drawing room for the allotted time, or he might prefer to spend his time on more pleasurable pursuits. From what Gemma had heard of him, she didn't think he would be interested in something so banal as gossip. He was the sort of man who would go to a gymnasium, or take luncheon at his club, where he would be surrounded by men of his own stature and either engage in conversations concerning masculine topics or retire to a quiet corner to read a newspaper or smoke a cigar.

It wouldn't take long to determine if he was at home, and, if Frances Modine was on her own, it wasn't likely that she'd turn away a visitor without at least finding out the reason for the unsolicited call. It was worth a try, and, if Gemma was barred entry, then she would at least know that she had tried and would share the information with Sebastian and leave the rest to his discretion. She had heard Guy Weathers tell him that General Modine resided in Bedford Square. Finding the right house shouldn't prove too difficult.

Having come to a decision, Gemma sprang to her feet and walked out of the room. Mabel had just started preparing dinner and had a pot simmering on the range while she chopped, mixed, and rolled out the dough for the mincemeat pie she intended to make. Colin preferred beef or mutton on Thursdays, since on Friday they usually had fish. Mabel barely glanced at Gemma as she paused in the doorway.

"Mabel, I need to step out for an hour. Would you mind keeping an eye on Mrs. Ramsey until I return?"

"Of course. Lock the front door, would you, Miss Tate? We don't want a repetition of the last time." Mabel shook her head in dismay without pausing in her work. "I shudder to think what might happen if she runs off again. If not for Inspector Bell..." Her voice trailed away, but Gemma knew exactly what she meant. If Sebastian hadn't found Anne, she might have kept wandering until they had no hope of locating her or had died of exposure to the elements.

"I will be sure to lock the door," Gemma promised.

She grabbed the key for the front door from a peg in the kitchen and hurried to the foyer to get her things. Colin had his own key, but he probably would not come up until it was time to dress for dinner, and she fully expected to be back by then. Morning visits lasted no longer than twenty minutes, so, even if she got to see Frances Modine, she wouldn't stay long.

THIRTY-THREE

Gemma found a cab and made it to Bedford Square without incident. She alighted and looked around, surprised that the general resided at such a desirable address. Imposing Georgian terraced houses surrounded the square, and the gated park at the center looked well maintained and inviting, the sort of place one could take a walk without being disturbed by traffic or other pedestrians. It would be the perfect place for someone like Anne, easily frightened and always in danger of getting hurt.

Gemma chose a house at random, resolutely marched up to the door and knocked. A uniformed maid of middle years opened the door and looked at Gemma with the bemused expression of someone who wasn't accustomed to greeting visitors. In fact, Gemma had noticed few carriages, despite the hour.

"Can I help you, madam?" she asked.

"Good afternoon. Miss Tate to see Mrs. Modine," Gemma announced, and smiled in what she hoped was a disarming manner.

"I'm afraid you've got the wrong house, miss," the maid said.

"Oh, I'm so sorry. I've forgotten my spectacles, and when I

checked the address Mrs. Modine had given me I could have sworn it said number four."

"It's forty-one, just there." The maidservant pointed toward the row of houses visible through the still-bare trees of the park.

"Thank you so much. I'm most grateful."

"It's no trouble, miss," the maid said, and shut the door.

Gemma walked sedately toward the side of the square where the Modine house was located. She had hoped she would see someone leaving so she could gauge the situation, but no one came or went from number forty-one, and the glossy black door remained firmly shut, no movement visible behind the ground-floor windows. There was no way to deduce whether the general might be at home or if the Modines were receiving callers that afternoon. To simply walk up to the house and ask to see Mrs. Modine was a risk, since Gemma had no good reason for being there that the general would believe, but to leave wasn't an option. The best she could do was to ask to see the lady of the house and, if the general was at home, pretend that she had made a mistake and got the wrong house once again. Few men would hold an innocent mistake against a flustered female, especially one who was in mourning and whose confusion could be the result of a mind addled by grief.

Gemma drew back when she came face to face with the snarling countenance on the door knocker, then lifted the ring with two fingers and knocked. The door was opened by a stony-faced butler, who looked at Gemma as if she had just dropped from the moon and had chosen the Modine residence for her landing.

"Yes?"

"Miss Tate to see the lady of the house."

"What's your business with Mrs. Modine?" the butler asked.

He seemed surprised, and Gemma wondered if Mrs. Modine didn't receive many visitors, or if the butler was simply taken aback because he'd never seen Gemma before and knew her to be a stranger to the family.

"Is Mrs. Modine unavailable?" Gemma asked.

She hoped the butler would let something slip and forewarn her if there were other callers or if the general was at home, but the butler was too well trained to give anything away and stood his ground.

"I would like to see Mrs. Modine regarding a most noble and virtuous cause," Gemma tried again. She realized she was clutching her reticule to her middle in her nervousness, and did her best not to appear intimidated, but her chances of speaking to Frances Modine were evaporating like morning dew.

"You tiresome do-gooders never give up, do you?" the butler muttered under his breath.

"I'm only here because Mrs. Modine had expressed an interest," Gemma replied brazenly. "I wouldn't dare bother her otherwise."

"What is this worthy endeavor?" the butler asked.

"I'm collecting on behalf of the Foundling Hospital," Gemma said. "It is a most deserving cause, and the hospital's reputation speaks for itself."

"Wait here," the man said, and shut the door in Gemma's face.

She took an involuntary step back and sighed. As soon as the butler informed Mrs. Modine that some woman she'd never met had claimed that they had previously discussed charitable works, she would refuse to speak to her, and Gemma would have had a wasted journey, but she wasn't sorry she'd come. She'd had to try, and the fact that the butler had agreed to check with Mrs. Modine rather than send her away immediately did give her some hope. Perhaps Mrs. Modine regularly gave to charity and would be willing to hear Gemma out.

When the door opened, Gemma held her head high and stared down the butler, who reluctantly stepped aside and permitted her to enter. He wordlessly escorted her to a lovely drawing room, where a woman who was a few years Gemma's senior, presumably Frances Modine, sat before the fire, a shawl draped over her shoulders and a demure cap covering her fair curls. Gemma saw no evidence of morning callers and, more important, no sign of the lady's fearsome husband.

"Miss Tate," the butler intoned.

"Good afternoon, Mrs. Modine. You probably don't remember me," Gemma began, but Frances Modine smiled in welcome.

"Of course I remember you, Miss Tate. Do come in. That will be all, Richardson," she said to the butler, who was still hovering near the door. "Please, make yourself comfortable. Shut the door, Richardson," she called to the butler as he finally turned to leave the room.

Gemma sat down. It wasn't the custom to take a visitor's things when paying morning calls, and she was rather warm in her cape and bonnet, but she didn't expect she would be staying very long. Mrs. Modine had clearly mistaken her for someone else and would realize her mistake soon enough, so she had better say her piece quickly.

"Mrs. Modine, forgive me for barging in on you like this, but I'm working with Inspector Bell, and I have a few questions I would like to ask you."

Frances Modine blanched, her already fair skin turning the color of curdled milk. "You're working with the police?"

"In an unofficial capacity," Gemma hurried to explain.

"How very peculiar," Mrs. Modine said, peering at Gemma as if she were a new addition to the zoological gardens. "So, you lied about collecting for the Foundling Hospital."

"I'm sorry about that."

Mrs. Modine inclined her head in acknowledgment of Gemma's apology, but she still looked perplexed and was clearly trying to work out how to appropriately respond to the unwelcome intrusion. "I presume I'm not under any obligation to answer your questions, Miss Tate?" she asked at last.

"You're not, but I would be most grateful if you did, since the information you provide could divert suspicion from you, and the authorities need not get involved."

"Divert suspicion from *me*?"

Seeing her chances of getting answers grow slimmer by the minute, Gemma plunged in. "You visited Driscoll's Drugs recently and purchased a quantity of arsenic and laudanum. Given that Esme Royce and Christopher Hudson were poisoned, it's important that we rule you out as a suspect."

Gemma suddenly realized that Frances Modine might be unaware of what had happened. If her husband had never mentioned it and she wasn't permitted to see the papers, she would be in complete ignorance.

"Have you heard what happened?" Gemma asked, just to be sure.

"Yes," Frances muttered. "Am I a suspect?" She gaped at Gemma, her confusion obvious. "What have I got to do with their deaths?"

"Anyone who purchased a poisonous substance and came into contact with the victims is a suspect at present."

"I did not have contact with either of them."

"But your husband did. He was at the theater the night Esme and Christopher were poisoned."

"So, I'm guilty by association?" Frances asked.

"No one is accusing you of anything, Mrs. Modine. These are just routine questions."

"Why would Inspector Bell send you if he believes I'm involved? He could have spoken to me himself when he was here."

Gemma wasn't about to claim that Sebastian had sent her, because that would be an outright lie, so she skirted the question with one of her own. "Would you not feel more comfortable speaking to a woman? I find there are some things a woman can't admit to a man."

Frances nodded, and her eyes filled with tears. "Can I rely on your discretion, Miss Tate?" she whispered.

"Of course. This is just a quiet tête-à-tête between two women, nothing more."

"I did know that my husband had gone to see that actress, but I had nothing to do with what happened. I bought arsenic and laudanum for the household," Mrs. Modine replied. "The arsenic was for the kitchen, and I take a few drops of laudanum to help me sleep. I still have half a bottle left. I assure you, Miss Tate, there's nothing sinister at work, and I haven't been anywhere near the theater since my husband took me to see the play in December."

Gemma nodded as if she understood perfectly, then met Mrs. Modine's innocent gaze with one of her own.

"You have a butler, Mrs. Modine, which leads me to believe that you also have several female members of staff to see to your and the general's needs. Why would the lady of the house purchase arsenic for the kitchen and laudanum for herself when she has maidservants to do that? And why would she call at a chemist's shop near Covent Garden when there are a number of respectable chemists within a stone's throw of Bedford Square?"

Mrs. Modine stared at her, all color draining out of her face. "I... I..." she began, but couldn't seem to find the words.

"You either purchased the poison for yourself or for your husband. Which was it, Mrs. Modine?"

Frances Modine dabbed at her eyes with a lace-trimmed handkerchief. "I bought it for myself, and the reason I went to Covent Garden was because I didn't want my husband to know."

"What were you going to do?" Gemma asked. She was surprised that Frances Modine had given up the pretense so quickly, and hoped she could get some answers before the woman realized she could simply throw Gemma out on her ear.

"I was going to take it," Frances whispered.

Gemma stared at the woman before her, shocked to the core by her revelation. "You were going to take the poison?" she asked, just to be clear.

Frances nodded. "I'm afraid I had given in to melancholy and went so far as to acquire the poison, but I didn't have the courage to take it."

"What did you do with it?"

"I hid it in a hat box. I still have it," Frances replied. "All of it."

"What drove you to such depths of despair?"

It was rude to pry, but Gemma suddenly felt terribly sorry for this woman who looked so frightened and alone. Perhaps that was why she had granted Gemma entry. She was lonely and wanted someone to talk to, even if that someone was a complete stranger.

Frances raised her tear-filled eyes, and Gemma knew without a shadow of a doubt that she had told her the truth.

"My life has become unbearable, Miss Tate, and now my latest misfortune is that I'm too much of a coward to set myself free from it."

"I'm sorry," Gemma said. "If there's anything I can do to help..."

Frances shook her head. "There's nothing anyone can do. The moment you marry, you become your husband's property, and he can do whatever he likes. If he calls you horrid names and tells you that you're less than worthless, you have to lower your eyes and nod in agreement, because if you don't he will punish you for defending yourself. And if he takes a riding crop to you as if you were one of his horses, you have to bear it and pretend that everything is all right in front of family and friends, who all think you're so lucky to have made such an advantageous match."

"I'm sorry." Gemma reached out for Frances's hand, but Frances recoiled from her touch. Perhaps it wasn't sympathy she wanted, only understanding.

"I no longer have any family or friends left, so no one will miss me if I'm gone. And once I summon the courage, I will..." Her voice trailed off, but her meaning was clear.

"Do you have any money of your own? Can you get away?" Gemma asked.

Frances shook her head. "I don't have anything save the allowance my husband gives me, and, even if I did run away, Jonathan would hunt me down." She looked like someone who had been sentenced to prison for the rest of her life. "Knowing I have a way out makes it possible for me to get through the day." She wiped her streaming nose and eyes and faced Gemma. "Now, I told you what you wanted to know, so kindly take your leave. I will tell my husband that I've made a donation to the Foundling Hospital, and you will not come here again."

Gemma nodded. "Good luck to you, Mrs. Modine."

"It's not luck I need, Miss Tate. It's courage."

Gemma hurried from the room and crossed the tiled foyer. She didn't wait for the butler to see her out, just yanked the door open and fled. If Frances Modine had told her the truth, and Gemma was in no doubt that she had, the beautiful house suddenly felt like a dungeon that had seen untold suffering and echoed with its mistress's longing for death.

THIRTY-FOUR

Still bothered by his acrimonious meeting with Lovell, intrigued by Ransome's impending promotion, and worried that Gemma was angry with him, Sebastian decided to head to Blackfriars instead of returning to the theater. *Damn Lovell and damn his decree!* he thought savagely as he hastened his step. Lovell could make things difficult for him if he tried, but at this juncture his bite lacked teeth, since he had clearly lost favor with both Sir David and the Home Secretary. It was more important to make things right with Gemma and tell her there was no one in the world he would rather work with and that she was a better copper than most policemen he'd encountered in his fifteen years on the service. She deserved to hear that, just as she deserved his unequivocal apology.

When Sebastian turned into Colin's street, he was surprised to see Gemma alight from a hansom that had left her at the corner. She looked grave, her lips pressed together and a frown line clearly visible between her eyebrows even from a distance. Her gait was unusually slow as she made her way toward the house, and it was clear that she was reluctant to go inside. Despite her obvious despondency, Gemma smiled when she spotted Sebastian coming toward her, and some of her misery seemed to melt away, the worry replaced by relief.

"Gemma, are you all right?" Sebastian asked once they were within speaking distance.

Gemma nodded but didn't explain where she had been or what had happened.

"Can we talk?" he asked.

"Of course. Come in."

"I would rather we spoke in private."

Gemma nodded. "Let me check on Mrs. Ramsey, and I'll come right back out."

She reached out, touched his cheek, and smiled into his eyes, and Sebastian's heart lightened immediately, his foul mood lifting like fog. He watched as she walked up the steps and disappeared inside, then reappeared some minutes later, sans her reticule.

"Mrs. Ramsey is resting, and Colin has yet to emerge from the cellar," Gemma said as they began to walk toward the river.

"I'm sorry," Sebastian said once he'd managed to swallow the lump in his throat. "For everything." He'd forgotten his carefully rehearsed speech and couldn't seem to find the right words to express everything he needed to say, but he was sure Gemma understood what was in his heart. She always did. That was one of the things he loved about her.

"I'm sorry too," Gemma said. "And I feel awful for what I said about you comparing me to Louisa."

"You were right. What happened to Louisa is never far from my thoughts, and I'm terrified of unwittingly putting you in danger."

"You won't."

Sebastian nodded. He didn't want to get into it, but he had to admit that Gemma and Louisa were as different as two women could be. When he'd met Louisa, she had been seventeen, a girl fresh out of the schoolroom who'd had no life experience and had looked to him to teach and guide her in all things. Gemma was a grown woman who'd seen and done more than he ever had and was experienced and fiercely independent. She was aware of the dangers of helping him and could look after herself. She had done it in Crimea and had continued to do so in London. His patronizing attitude toward her had to be infuriating, and he knew he had to let go of his irrational fears and treat her like the equal she was, or he might lose her for good.

"Was that our first quarrel?" Sebastian asked, and was surprised to hear a quaver in his voice.

"Probably, and very likely not the last," Gemma replied.

"I plan to quarrel with you for years to come."

"Is that a promise?" Gemma asked, and her eyes shone with unshed tears.

"You know it is."

"Will you quarrel with me if I tell you that I ignored your request?"

Sebastian sighed and bit back the reproof that sprang to his lips. "And did you learn anything while you were ignoring my request?"

"I may have, but tell me what you have discovered first."

Sebastian reached for her hand and held it as they walked along the river. As far as anyone was concerned, they were just another couple taking the air, and he relished the moment and wished they didn't have to part.

"This case is like a badly written penny dreadful," he confessed, once they had passed a well-dressed couple and their conversation couldn't be overheard.

"Is that a dig at your irritating neighbor?" Gemma teased.

"Not even B.E. Ware could come up with so many red herrings," Sebastian grumbled. "I don't yet know what's relevant, but I think I must focus on Esme Royce rather than Christopher Hudson."

"Go on," Gemma invited, listening intently.

"According to Serena Winthrop, Guy Weathers is in the habit of making free with the female members of the troupe and has gone so far as to threaten them with dismissal if they don't submit, but Esme had steadfastly ignored his advances. It's possible that she had wounded his male pride, but I can't see that Weathers would murder the two people who continuously brought in the audience out of petty jealousy. And he would not be likely to call attention to the murders if he had been the one to poison the vials."

Gemma nodded. "I agree."

"We know that Esme was involved with both Christopher Hudson and General Modine," Sebastian went on. "By all accounts, General Modine was mad for her and would have felt humiliated and betrayed if he found out that his mistress was seeing other men. He had an obvious motive, and an opportunity since he was at the theater on Tuesday evening. He left before the performance began, but that doesn't put him in the clear, since he could have tampered with the vials before he left. Guy Weathers might not have noticed there was something inside the vials when he filled them with brandy."

Sebastian took a deep breath and continued. "It's also been suggested that Esme had engaged in a casual dalliance with Ishmael Cabot. Ishmael admitted to stealing a bottle of morphine from Ned Bannon's office, which he replaced with a bottle of treacle. He claims to have been blackmailed over his relationship with Ned Bannon and told to leave the morphine in a cabinet outside Esme's dressing room. He could have just as easily used the morphine to poison the brandy if he had been rejected by Esme and felt bested by her lover. With Christopher Hudson out of the way, he stands to get better parts and make a name for himself."

"Who does he think blackmailed him, and what exactly is his relationship with Ned Bannon?"

"Ishmael's relationship with Ned Bannon can land him in

jail, and he thinks he was blackmailed by Serena Winthrop, but can't prove that she was involved. And given that Walt Dickie's now turned up dead, it's also possible that Dickie had seen something and had been the one to blackmail him."

"You think Walt Dickie was murdered?"

"Given the state of the man, I'm inclined to think that he died of natural causes; but, knowing that he was in the habit of spying and probably knew more than anyone gave him credit for, I'm not ready to say so definitively."

"Did you search his sleeping quarters?" Gemma asked.

Sebastian shook his head. "It's my understanding that Walt Dickie bedded down wherever he happened to fall. That's the thing with drunks; they're not very particular."

"The evidence against Ishmael is certainly damning. Are you going to arrest him?"

"Lovell wants me to bring him in, but I'm not convinced that Ishmael is guilty of murder. General Modine had a strong motive and opportunity, but to accuse Cabot would be easier, since he doesn't have the money or the reputation that would enable him to beat the charge."

"Are you certain that General Modine was aware of Esme's infidelity?"

"Mona Grady threatened to tell General Modine that Esme was unfaithful and the child wasn't his unless Esme gave her money to go to Lourdes, where Mona believes she will be visited by the Virgin Mary. I only have her word that she didn't carry out her threat."

"I have heard about the visitations," Gemma said. "The Church has yet to determine if they're dealing with a true miracle or an elaborate hoax, but believers have been flocking to Lourdes for months."

"It's probably absolute claptrap, but Mona, who was once a Catholic nun, believes it and thinks that the Virgin will help her find her son, who was taken from her to protect a priest who'd raped her."

"Dear God," Gemma exclaimed. "The poor woman."

"Poor woman?" Sebastian countered. "What sort of nun turns to blackmail? And her language was rather colorful for a woman of God, and I've heard my share of women swearing."

"She could be telling the truth about the boy. Is she a suspect?" Gemma asked.

"I can't see Mona Grady murdering two people, even if she had been blackmailing them both and they had failed to take her seriously. The dead don't pay. But I can see her stealing the brooch that General Modine gave to Esme the day she died. Rubies and emeralds in the shape of a rose."

"If she were to sell it, it might help her get to Lourdes," Gemma agreed. "So where does this leave your investigation?"

"I have a number of suspects, but not enough evidence to make the charges stick."

"Is there anyone else you intend to talk to?"

"I've interviewed Lady Argyle and Lord Gilroy but don't believe they were involved, and I would still like a word with Mr. Bonneville. He'd quarreled with Guy Weathers and was backstage at around the right time to poison the vials, but I can't see a motive for murder." Sebastian turned to Gemma. "All right, your turn."

"I thought it highly likely that the killer had purchased the morphine in the Covent Garden area, so I visited every chemist within walking distance of the theater and attempted to purchase some. I looked over the entries in their poison ledgers when I signed for my purchases in the hope of spotting a familiar name," Gemma confessed.

"And did you?" Sebastian asked.

He was impressed with Gemma's ingenuity but thought her theory too implausible to yield results. The killer was far too clever to make such an obvious mistake—they would have most likely obtained the morphine from a chemist on the other side of town and signed with a false name to eliminate even the slightest risk of detection—but he didn't want to belittle Gemma's efforts by voicing his doubt.

"I didn't see an obvious connection, but an F. Modine purchased arsenic and laudanum not two weeks before. General Modine's wife's name is Frances." Gemma looked at him with something akin to trepidation. "I went to see her, Sebastian."

"You did what?" Sebastian demanded, and instantly checked himself, not wishing to engage in another disagreement. "Were you admitted?" he asked in a softer voice.

Gemma nodded. "She said she bought it for herself. He beats her, Sebastian. With a riding crop."

"The bastard," Sebastian growled. He could believe it all too easily, having seen the bruises on the woman's wrists.

"She said that having the poison to hand helps her get through the day because she knows she can end it all at any time."

"I think I need to have a word with Mrs. Modine."

"What? Why?" Gemma cried. "She can't possibly be responsible."

"Except that she can," Sebastian replied. "A woman named Frances came to see Esme Royce during intermission on the night Esme died." Gemma looked stunned by this revelation, but he had no choice but to continue. "If Frances tried to reason with Esme and asked her to end the relationship with her husband and Esme refused, Frances might have moved on to the second part of her plan. She may have obtained the morphine elsewhere. There are dozens of chemists in London."

"But why murder Christopher Hudson?" Gemma asked, clearly still trying to reconcile the downtrodden woman she had met with this new version of Frances Modine.

"Perhaps she wasn't sure which vial was meant for Juliet, so she poisoned them both. She could have taken the brooch as well, if she had seen it sitting on Esme's dressing table. But even if she was seen by Walt Dickie, he wasn't likely to identify her, and I can't see her coming back to the theater to poison the old man."

"No, neither can I," Gemma agreed. "But there is actually something else. When I visited Harbor's Drugs, Mrs. Harbor mentioned that they'd had a break-in recently. The only thing that was taken was their entire stock of morphine. They did not report it to the police."

"Well, I'll be damned," Sebastian muttered under his breath. "I doubt Frances Modine would break in herself, but she might have paid someone. The general must give her an allowance, so she likely has money of her own."

Gemma nodded. "As it happens, Mrs. Harbor is the sister of Penelope Bright, who was a friend of mine in Crimea. Mrs. Ramsey and I paid a call on Poppy this morning. She had encountered both General Modine and Christopher Hudson, whose real name is Bobby Metz, in Scutari, and recently saw Bobby Metz near Covent Garden. He invited her to come to the play."

"And did the two men ever meet?" Sebastian asked.

Gemma shrugged. "It's possible since they were in Scutari at about the same time. Does any of what I have learned help?"

"You are absolutely brilliant, and you have given me several new leads," Sebastian said.

They had stopped walking, and Gemma looked up at him, her eyes shining with pleasure at his praise. It might have been ill-advised, given that they were in public, but Sebastian wrapped his arm around her waist, pulled her close, and kissed her, grateful for the strangely intimate shield the wide brim of her bonnet provided. The kiss wasn't just a peck on the lips, but a proper kiss that left Gemma flushed and breathless and Sebastian desperate for more, but as usual their affection was curtailed by a lack of privacy, a situation that could not be altered until Gemma came out of mourning.

No one understood the need for mourning better than Sebastian, but he didn't believe that the period of grieving should be determined by the constructs of society. Gemma would grieve for Victor for the rest of her life, just as he would grieve for Louisa, but whereas some people needed to isolate themselves from the world and feed their misery, Gemma was the sort of woman who needed to keep busy and surround herself with people who cared for her. Sebastian might have been able to manage his grief had someone been there to support him and pull him from the brink, but he had no right to suggest that Gemma throw off her mourning weeds and allow him to court her properly.

"I have to get back," Gemma mumbled. Her cheeks were stained a pretty pink, and her lips looked rosy after their kiss.

They walked in contented silence for a while, each lost in their own thoughts, until they reached Colin's door.

"I'll come tomorrow," Sebastian promised.

"I'll be waiting," Gemma said, and hurried up the steps.

THIRTY-FIVE

Inside, Gemma checked on Anne, who was still sleeping, then left the door unlocked and went to fetch her book before settling in the parlor. The house was quiet, and, although she was enjoying the story, she found her mind wandering back to her conversation with Frances Modine. Frances might have lied about her movements and reasons for buying the poisons, but her pain had been real, and Gemma had been able to sense the woman's isolation and fear. The general's unspeakable cruelty to his wife and his men brought back memories as well, of both the wartime years and the time before, when Gemma had still been a naïve girl who believed that people were basically good and that God-fearing men were not capable of inflicting untold pain.

She'd learned quickly that the only way to survive the horrors of war was to keep her head down and find ways to force the awful images from her mind at the end of her shift. She had dreamed of home, preferring to return to a time when both her parents had been alive and she and Victor had been ensconced in comfort and safety. And she had dreamed of London. It had helped her to get to sleep when the dread overwhelmed her. She had imagined herself walking down the streets, and could almost smell the tang of the Thames and hear the church bells that rang out on Sunday mornings. There had been no church bells in Scutari, only the endless rattle of wheels on stone as bodies were carted away to be buried in mass graves.

Gemma's thoughts inevitably turned to Florence Nightingale and the women she had met on the voyage over, and she recalled those last days at home, when she had alternated between excitement, fear, doubt, and hope. Gemma had repacked her trunk at least ten times and had checked items off the list Miss Nightingale had handed out. She had advised them to bring certain things from home, such as soap, tooth powder, supplies they would need when it was their time of the month, and various other bits that would be considered luxuries in a time of war. Gemma had purchased most things at their local shop but had stopped into a chemist's near Covent Garden, when she'd gone to the market to get some potatoes and leeks for the soup she had planned to make, to pick up the remaining items on her list.

She had forgotten all about that day, but when Poppy had mentioned Wyvern's she had remembered the shop. And now, unexpectedly, she recalled Mr. Wyvern as well. He had been a fair-haired man in his mid-thirties whose easygoing manner and warm smile had loosened her tongue, and she had told him about her upcoming voyage and asked for advice. Mr. Wyvern had suggested bringing along a jar of hand cream, since her hands would become red and chapped from constant washing and drying, and he had also added a packet of arsenic to her parcel, pointing out that she might need it to combat the mice and rats that were sure to invade her living quarters. Gemma had been grateful to Mr. Wyvern for both the cream and the poison and had used them up within a fortnight of arriving.

It saddened her to hear from Poppy that he had died, and

she wondered what had happened to his daughter, who had assisted him in the shop that day. Mr. Wyvern had explained that his wife was ill and that his daughter wanted to help in whatever way she could. Gemma could recall the girl's shy smile when she'd handed over her neatly wrapped purchases. And she suddenly recalled something else about that day, and was on her feet before she had time to consider her actions. She had to speak to Mary Harbor.

Just as Gemma was about to put on her cape, Anne Ramsey appeared at the top of the stairs. Her thinning hair tumbled about her face, and her cheeks were wet with tears.

"Mrs. Ramsey, what is it?" Gemma cried as she hung her cape back on the peg.

Anne looked at Gemma imploringly, and it was only then that Gemma noticed that Anne's nightdress was wet and dripping onto the carpet. She hurried up the stairs, took Anne by the arm, and gently led her back to her room.

"I'm sorry," Anne wailed. "I'm so ashamed."

"You've nothing to be sorry for," Gemma replied. "These things happen. Now, let's get you cleaned up."

She filled a basin with water and took out a clean towel and a fresh nightdress. The water wasn't warm, but she thought it was more important to help Anne out of her soaking gown than to wait for the kettle to boil. Cold water would have to do.

"Colin will be angry with me," Anne said, her voice trembling with anxiety and embarrassment.

"Colin would never be angry with you, and besides he need never know. I'll change the sheets and wash them myself."

"Thank you," Anne whispered. "You're so kind to me."

"Nonsense. It's my job," Gemma said, and maneuvered the dripping gown over Anne's head, mindful of the fabric touching her hair or face. "We'll get this cleaned up in no time at all."

By the time Gemma had helped Anne wash, changed the sheets, wiped the floor, and rinsed out the nightdress and the soiled sheets, it was too late to go to Covent Garden. The shop would be closing very soon, and she didn't think it would be right to call on the Harbors at home. She would go tomorrow. It was her afternoon off, so she wouldn't have to rush back.

"What would you like to wear to dinner?" Gemma asked Anne once she had finished with the laundry and hung up the sheets. Anne was still in her bedroom, wearing a clean nightdress and a dressing gown.

"My blue gown. The one with the lace collar."

"Excellent choice," Gemma said, and fetched the gown from the wardrobe. It was Anne's favorite and the one she wore most often.

"You should wear more çolor," Anne said as Gemma helped her step into her crinolines.

"I'm still in mourning, Mrs. Ramsey," Gemma reminded her once again.

"Was it your husband that died?"

"My brother. Victor."

"I don't remember him. Aren't you married to Mr. Melville?"

"No, Mrs. Ramsey."

Anne frequently called Sebastian Mr. Melville, since he seemed to remind her of someone she'd known in her youth.

"Mr. Melville is ever so handsome," Anne said softly. "You should snatch him up before some other woman does, but you won't get his attention in that ugly dress. I have a lovely ballgown I can lend you. It's apple-green and would bring out your eyes."

Anne's ballgown, if it still existed, had to be decades out of fashion, but the thought made Gemma sad. She had never been to a ball or owned a gown worthy of wearing to such an occasion. She had spent the better part of the last ten years in black, first mourning for her father, then her mother, then while nursing in Crimea, and now while mourning for Victor. She missed her brother with every fiber of her being, but what she needed more than anything was light and color, and hope for the future. Gemma closed her eyes and recalled the intoxicating kiss she had shared with Sebastian. Her heart lifted, and she smiled. She might not be ready for color, but she had hope.

Once Anne was ready to go down to dinner, Gemma scribbled a note to Sebastian, then put on her bonnet and cape and hurried outside. There was a cabstand near St. Paul's, and she would pay one of the cabbies to deliver her message. They wouldn't go to Mrs. Poole's specially, but would detour when they were in the area, and leave the note with the landlady if Sebastian wasn't at home.

Having sent her dispatch, Gemma returned to the house and escorted Anne into the dining room, but her mind was still on the case, and she wished she didn't have to wait until tomorrow afternoon to speak to Sebastian. The more she thought about what she'd learned, the more convinced she became of her conclusions, but she wouldn't do anything foolish. She would present Sebastian with the evidence and allow him to make of it what he would. Besides, she could be wrong, and the crucial detail she had recalled might have no bearing whatsoever. She wouldn't find out until tomorrow. Until then, she had a job to do.

THIRTY-SIX

Sebastian's appetite was far from satisfied by the tiny sandwiches he'd eaten at Lady Argyle's, so he walked into the first chophouse he came upon and ordered a fillet of beef and a pint of lager. He needed to organize his thoughts and evaluate what he had learned, and he was too tired and hungry to do that effectively without taking time out to rest and eat. He took a long pull of the lager, then leaned back in his chair, his gaze fixed on the window and the pedestrians walking past, and considered the list of suspects as he applied himself to his meal.

He started with Lady Argyle, because to his mind she was the easiest to rule out. She had struck him as a woman who was worldly enough to comprehend that her relationship with Christopher Hudson couldn't last—she couldn't marry him since she would lose her title, and all her property would revert to her new husband. She might be in love, but she wasn't foolish enough to alienate her children or put herself at the mercy of a man in his twenties who might turn his back on her the moment the ink was dry on their marriage certificate. Lady Argyle had become emotional over what she'd believed was her last chance at love, but Sebastian couldn't see her resorting to murder. She had too much to lose and too little to gain.

Same went for Lord Gilroy. The rich liked their playthings and became cross when someone else wanted to play with them, but if Serena became too much of a liability Lord Gilroy would simply find a new toy. As far as Sebastian could see, he had no motive to kill either Esme or Christopher. The one thing Sebastian had noticed was that both Lady Argyle and Lord Gilroy had seemed skeptical about Esme's involvement with Chris and Ishmael. There could be two reasons for this. The first and most obvious was that the relationships had been kept secret, and the second was that the actors had been nothing more than costars.

The affairs had first been mentioned by Walt Dickie, who was hardly a reliable source and was now dead and couldn't be questioned, and then confirmed by Sid, who might be too young to fully understand what he had seen. And now that Sebastian thought about it, Mona had said that Esme had been in love with Christopher. She hadn't said that the feeling had been mutual or that they had had an ongoing relationship. And she had instantly dismissed the possibility of Esme canoodling with Ishmael. The two women had been close enough to share some of their most private secrets, so Esme had probably confided in Mona, even though Mona had used their friendship to further her own ambitions. It was a despicable thing to do, but, if what she had told him about Brendan was true, then Sebastian couldn't really blame her. He would have sold his soul to the devil to get to his child, so he couldn't find it in himself to judge Mona too harshly, despite what he had said about her to Gemma.

And then there was Ishmael Cabot. The young man had lied, cheated, and compromised himself to remain part of the troupe. According to him, he had been blackmailed, and he had admitted that he had performed illegal sexual acts and had stolen Ned Bannon's morphine. His guilt seemed too obvious, partly because Sebastian couldn't see a compelling motive for murder. Had Esme and Christopher threatened to expose him, he would have had the protection of Ned Bannon and by extension Guy Weathers, who had the final word on who they kept on and would have denied all allegations.

Ned hadn't seemed to realize that his morphine had been switched, but he could have been lying. By threatening Cabot, Esme and Christopher may as well have threatened Bannon, since he could go to prison on a charge of sodomy. Ned Bannon had freely admitted to taking morphine for his pain, but perhaps it was simply a ruse to explain away possession should it come out that the morphine used to kill the two actors had in fact been his.

Walt Dickie might have seen something he shouldn't have, but, given the man's sorry state, the only thing Sebastian could imagine Dickie asking for was more gin, of which he seemed to have a plentiful supply. Unless Dickie had suddenly turned to blackmail, Sebastian saw no reason to silence him.

And then there were the Modines, both of whom had a motive. Frances Modine had been abused and humiliated by a husband who had made her feel worthless. Flaunting a beautiful and very young mistress might have been the final straw. Frances had been seen with Esme on the night of the murders, and, unless there was another F. Modine Sebastian didn't know about, she had purchased poisonous substances for which she had signed with her own name. Having seen that there were two vials of poison in the play, Frances wouldn't be sure which vial was meant for Esme and might have added morphine to both to be on the safe side. Perhaps she had thought that Christopher, being young and strong and considerably heavier than Esme, would not die but would simply become ill.

And then there was her husband. Jonathan Modine had a

reputation for cruelty and violence and would have been furious if he had discovered that Esme had been unfaithful to him. If he had recognized Christopher Hudson—or Bobby Metz, as he had been called then—from Crimea, he would probably have felt even angrier, since competing for Esme's love against a low-ranking officer would be demeaning. And if he'd thought the child was Christopher's and Esme had been trying to pass it off as Modine's in order to assure a comfortable future, that just might have pushed him over the edge.

General Modine had earned a place at the top of Sebastian's list and was followed only by his wife, but Sebastian wasn't ready to charge him yet. He'd met plenty of men like Jonathan Modine, who were too proud, too entitled, and too well respected by their peers to resort to duplicity to satisfy their honor. General Modine was not one to hide in the shadows, nor was he someone who wouldn't take credit for his actions or would throw his life away on individuals he thought beneath him. There was also no physical evidence to link him to the crime, so chances were he'd never be convicted, and Sebastian was sure the general had a judge or two in his pocket.

Having considered the motive, Sebastian turned his attention to the method. Colin and Gemma appeared certain that the weapon was an overdose, which immediately implicated Ned Bannon, Ishmael Cabot, and Frances Modine. However, what Gemma had discovered wasn't to be dismissed. Someone had stolen a large amount of morphine from Harbor's Drugs, which was located close to the theater. Why would someone break into a chemist's and take nothing but morphine unless they needed it to commit murder? The killer had obviously known that the Harbors had morphine and where it was kept, since the shop had not been ransacked or any other merchandise taken. This was someone who had to be familiar with the shop; but, if they were a customer, chances were they wouldn't know what was kept in the back room or where it was stored.

Sebastian pushed away his empty plate and took a final sip of his lager. He had a number of suspects and a few facts, but he had yet to figure out how they all fitted together and who had actually murdered Esme Royce and Christopher Hudson. He had some time until he could safely call on Mrs. Modine, so he decided to return to the theater.

THIRTY-SEVEN

As soon as Sebastian approached the theater, he got the feeling that something was wrong. The doors were bolted when he tried them, and the lamps in the foyer had not been lit, even though dusk had descended and lights were coming on in all the other buildings that lined the street. A handwritten sign displayed in the ticket window advised ticketholders that the evening's performance was cancelled and their money would be refunded in due course. The only way Guy Weathers would cancel the performance and willingly return the money was if something tragic had happened. Genuinely alarmed, Sebastian hurried round the back and found that the back door was locked as well. After he banged on it repeatedly, a pale-faced Sid finally peered through the grille, then unlocked the door and let him in.

"What happened, Sid?"

"It's Ishmael."

"What about him?" Sebastian asked. His stomach muscles clenched with foreboding before Sid had even replied.

"He's dead, sir. Topped himself."

Sebastian was about to ask Sid how he knew that, then remembered that he was speaking to a child and went in search of Guy Weathers instead. He found Rose standing in a darkened alcove. She looked lost and frightened and seemed to breathe a sigh of relief when she saw him.

"Where's Mr. Weathers, Rose?" Sebastian asked.

Rose gestured towards Ned Bannon's office and trailed Sebastian when he strode down the corridor, but stopped before she reached the office, seemingly unsure what to do next. Sebastian found the two men conferring urgently behind closed doors. Their faces were ashen and their movements unnaturally slow as they checked the corridor before allowing Sebastian to come inside.

The windowless office was too dark to see clearly, and the air was thick with a sickly odor. Sebastian turned up the flame on the oil lamp that stood on Ned Bannon's desk and brought it over to the cot, where Ishmael lay on his back, his face serene in death. A brown bottle, exactly like the one that had been filled with treacle, was in his right hand, a brownish liquid seeping into the blanket. Sebastian didn't need to check if it was treacle, since the only thing it would have done was make Ishmael gag. This was either a new bottle of morphine or the bottle he'd claimed to have left in the cabinet.

"That was quick," Guy Weathers said once he'd finally recovered his composure. "We've only just sent Jimmy Milner to fetch a constable."

"I was on my way here," Sebastian replied.

Ned Bannon shot Sebastian a look of contempt. "Why? You clearly don't know anything, or you might have been able to prevent another death. At least now we get to grieve and try to move past this tragedy." He thrust a sheet of paper at Sebastian.

The note read:

I killed them. I'm sorry. I'd rather die on my own terms.

"Is that Ishmael's handwriting?" Sebastian asked.

The note was written in uneven block letters, and the ink was a bit smudged, but Sebastian had no way of knowing how much schooling Ishmael had received at the orphanage, if any, and if he knew how to write in script. The two men stared at Sebastian as if he had just asked them if Ishmael would be getting a royal burial.

"I don't know," Guy Weathers said. "I've never actually seen him write anything."

"Ishmael had lovely penmanship," Serena Winthrop said as she pushed into the already crowded office. "I saw the notes he'd make in the margins of the play."

"He did, yes," Ned Bannon agreed. "But that doesn't mean anything. He was clearly distressed. And those smudges could be tears."

"How long ago did you find him?"

"About twenty minutes ago," Guy Weathers said.

"Did you leave the door unlocked?" Sebastian asked Ned Bannon.

He shook his head. "I thought I'd locked it when I went out to the bank."

"Were there any visitors to the theater this afternoon?"

Weathers and Bannon looked at each other.

"No," Guy Weathers said. "Ned, did you see anyone?"

Ned shook his head.

"Please clear the room," Sebastian said, and as soon as everyone had trooped outside he shut the door.

He leaned against it and shut his eyes for a moment as he tried to block out the din beyond and listen to his instinct. He had no reason to dispute that Ishmael had taken his own life. The evidence was there—the body, the poison, the note, and the motive—but Sebastian's copper's instinct was bucking like an unbroken filly. This was too obvious. Too neat. Why would Ishmael kill himself, even if he was guilty? Sebastian had not accused him, nor had he charged him with anything. Ishmael had had every chance of walking away from this if he kept his head down and waited to see how the case would play out. And if he was guilty of murder, he could have run.

This whole setup reeked as badly as Gustav's beloved sardines after he'd dragged them behind the wardrobe and left the head and fish guts for Sebastian to find, which usually took a few days. Someone wanted Sebastian to think that Ishmael was guilty and close the case now that he had been handed a solution. He walked over to Ned Bannon's desk and sat in his chair. He still needed to speak to Frances Modine, but, unless she had been here this afternoon, the killer was someone who worked at the theater, which also excluded General Modine.

Looking around the room, Sebastian noticed the bottle of whisky and the glass he'd seen on his first visit. It stood atop the cabinet that Ned Bannon used to store his morphine. The bottle was empty, and the glass still had a bit of whisky at the very bottom. Sebastian walked over to the cabinet and sniffed the glass. Beneath the smell of whisky was another odor, and the tiny bit of whisky at the bottom looked too thick to be pure spirits. So perhaps the poison had been in the whisky and not in the bottle in Ishmael's hand. Someone had put it there, another prop used to tell a story. If Ned Bannon had locked his office, then Ishmael might have had a key and let himself in and finished off the whisky. So, who had tampered with the bottle? Was it Ned Bannon, knowing Ishmael would help himself, or was it someone else who was familiar with Ishmael's habits?

Sebastian didn't think the poison had been meant for Ned Bannon, since whoever had murdered Ishmael had placed the evidence in his hand. Or had they not cared who died and Ned Bannon's demise would have done the trick? That was a good question, one Sebastian would dearly love to know the answer to. In the meantime, he had to figure out how to proceed. His first thought was to arrest the lot of them and let them spend the night in the cells, if only to keep them safe from one another, but that wouldn't do. The killer was probably congratulating themselves on throwing him off the scent and was going to let everyone else live. For now.

Sebastian unlocked the door and stepped out into the corridor. Serena and Ned had gone, but several people still milled about and Guy Weathers came striding toward Sebastian, his nostrils flaring with anger.

"I trust you will now leave us in peace, Inspector?" he demanded.

"I don't think there's anything more I can do. Ishmael Cabot murdered Esme Royce and Christopher Hudson."

Guy Weathers nodded in agreement.

"He was probably mad with jealousy," Sebastian added.

"I appear to have misjudged him quite badly," Weathers said with a shake of his head.

"I trust you will see to the body?"

"Yes, we'll see him decently buried, even if he doesn't deserve it. It's not as if we can send him back to his people."

"No," Sebastian agreed.

"Rose, turn the lights on. The play will reopen tomorrow. Tonight, we will rehearse," Guy Weathers announced. "Places, everyone!" he called, and clapped his hands. "Chop-chop!"

"We don't have enough people," Gregory Gorman said.

"We'll just have to improvise and reassign Ishmael's parts," Guy Weathers retorted. "And send the constable away when he arrives, Rose," he called out after the girl. "Tell him he's no longer needed."

"Yes, Mr. Weathers," Rose called over her shoulder.

There was nothing more for Sebastian to do at the theater, so he left by the front door and headed to Scotland Yard. He had to inform Lovell of this new development before he read about Cabot's death in the papers. Sebastian did not look forward to explaining the situation but, even if Lovell was out by next week, he was still his superior, and Sebastian owed him the respect due his position.

THIRTY-EIGHT

The duty room was unusually quiet for a Thursday evening. Normally, there would be half a dozen miscreants and angry constables doing their best not to lose their tempers and belt someone who needed to be subdued. Sergeant Woodward was reading a novel, and Constables Meadows and Hammond were playing cards. Constable Forrest was deep inside a penny dreadful.

"All right, Seb?" Sergeant Woodward asked when Sebastian approached the desk.

"Smashing."

Sergeant Woodward shook his head. "Scorn never bodes well, does it, lads?" he asked the constables.

"Depends on who's doing the scorning," Constable Meadows replied.

Sebastian wasn't in the mood for mindless banter, so he passed through the room and strode down the empty corridor toward Lovell's office. He knocked and pushed open the door. John Ransome sat behind Lovell's desk, a file open before him. He looked up and leaned back in his chair, smiling triumphantly. Lovell's things were gone, and a photograph that used to hang above Ransome's desk now graced the wall. Sebastian had known change was coming—Ransome had told him as much only that morning—but Sebastian hadn't thought anything would happen today. Clearly, he had been wrong.

"Inspector Bell," Ransome said.

"Inspector Ransome," Sebastian replied.

"Superintendent Ransome."

"Congratulations, John."

"And congratulations to you, Sebastian."

Tired of the game, Sebastian pulled out a chair and sat down. "Shall we get down to business?"

"Not yet," Ransome said. "First, I'd like to thank you for not working against my appointment. Those who actively sought to oust me will be transferred to another station tomorrow. And second, my first official act as the new superintendent was to authorize an increase in pay for deserving personnel. You will see a ten percent raise in your pay packet, Inspector."

"Are you trying to buy my loyalty, John?" Sebastian asked.

"I don't need to buy your loyalty. You will either give it or you won't. I do know that you're one of our most capable men, though, and I believe competence should be rewarded. Now, what did you want to speak to me about?"

Sebastian needed to speak to Ransome about Ishmael Cabot's death, but first there was something he needed to know. "You suggested that Superintendent Lovell had somehow betrayed the commissioner."

Ransome inhaled deeply and nodded. "I don't want this getting out, Sebastian. Lovell was a capable superintendent, and he should be allowed to leave with his reputation intact. Do I have your word that this will remain between us?"

"You have my word."

Ransome nodded. "Lovell got it into his head that Sir David was going to replace him as soon as Laura and I became engaged. I won't lie, I had hoped to succeed him as superintendent, but I didn't think it would happen this soon. My father-in-law is a man of integrity and good sense and would not have done anything that would have invited undue scrutiny and criticism. He intended to wait until Lovell retired."

"What changed?" Sebastian asked.

"Lovell requested a meeting with the newly appointed Home Secretary as soon as he was sworn into office, and met with Sir Thomas last week. He accused Sir David of nepotism and asked that he be made commissioner in his stead. That meeting sealed his fate. He was informed this afternoon that I am to be his replacement, and his termination was effective immediately."

"I see," Sebastian said.

He found it difficult to reconcile the Lovell he knew with someone who would allow his suspicions to get the better of him, accuse Sir David, and try to assume his place, but people were at their most vulnerable and unpredictable when they felt threatened. Of all the motives for murder, Sebastian thought that fear was probably the most common. When backed into a corner, some people simply gave up, while others tried to fight their way out, not caring about the consequences or who suffered as a result. Lovell had not murdered anyone, but he had resorted to character assassination of Sir David Hawkins, and had paid the price. The one thing he had feared the most had come to pass as the result of his impulsive decision, and he had been forced to leave in disgrace, his legacy forever tainted.

"Update me on your case, Bell," Ransome said, all business now that the subject of Lovell had been exhausted.

"There's been another death at the Orpheus," Sebastian said wearily.

"Who is it this time?"

"Ishmael Cabot. The death was made to look like a suicide, but I think he was murdered."

"Why?"

"Cabot supposedly left a suicide note saying that he murdered Esme Royce and Christopher Hudson. And then he ingested morphine and killed himself in exactly the same way."

"A neat solution, if it were true," Ransome said. "Walk me through it, Bell."

Sebastian presented the facts followed by his own reasoning, then said, "I think all three victims were murdered by someone who works at the theater. That narrows the pool of suspects, but there's also the possibility that the person who poisoned Esme Royce and Christopher Hudson was paid to tamper with the props. That same person probably murdered Ishmael and staged his suicide in order to close down the investigation."

Ransome nodded. "A clever misdirection, if it had worked. If someone paid this person to commit murder, they're an accessory and will be treated accordingly, but it's the hand that wields the murder weapon that commits the crime. Find the culprit, Bell."

Fixing Sebastian with a meditative gaze, he added, "I became a copper because I wanted to see justice done. I believe in the rule of law, but I also believe that sometimes you have to bend the rules to get your man. As long as the transgressions are within reason, I will turn a blind eye and protect my men at all costs."

Sebastian nodded in understanding and left Ransome's office. They were going to get on just fine, he decided as he stepped into the foggy March night. And he was more than willing to bend a few rules if the situation called for it.

THIRTY-NINE

There was no point returning to the theater. Whoever had murdered Ishmael Cabot believed themselves to be safe and were sure to lower their guard if they thought the investigation was at an end. Tomorrow's newspapers would proclaim Ishmael guilty of double homicide and assign whatever motive sold more papers, since there was no one left to accuse them of slander. The public might initially feel cheated by Ishmael's suicide; people enjoyed seeing their legal system at work, but they might have their satisfaction eventually. The killer was still out there, and Sebastian intended to unmask them and hold them accountable.

And he intended to start by questioning Frances Modine. He didn't think the woman would give up her husband, but there was much to be learned from silence, and from fear. Sebastian found a cab, gave the driver the address, and settled in for the ride. He couldn't help but smile into the darkness. Ransome was a clever devil, much smarter than Lovell had ever been. Come tomorrow, the Yard would become a different place to the one it had been that morning. Those disloyal to Ransome would be gone, and those who had supported his ascension or hadn't spoken out against it would be rewarded. Lovell would be forgotten within a week, and new alliances would be formed. Sebastian wasn't one to join cliques, but he understood the importance of being seen as one of the men rather than an outsider who wasn't worthy of support or respect. This wasn't the sort of job best suited to a lone wolf, and he didn't need to be. Ransome had been clear. He didn't care about the method, only the result, which meant he wouldn't take issue with Gemma's unofficial involvement. Ransome wasn't threatened by a woman, especially since he didn't need to acknowledge her contribution publicly.

Sebastian had also been pleasantly surprised by the increase in pay. Ten percent was substantial, and would make a real difference to his life at a time when he was finally ready to think seriously about the future. The lodgings at Mrs. Poole's had served his purpose at a time when he'd needed a place to lay his head and someone to set a plate of food before him after he hadn't eaten the entire day. But it had been three years, and, for the first time since Louisa's death, he found himself longing for a home of his own. The wage increase was timely, and he wondered if that was precisely the reason Ransome had authorized it. He understood what Sebastian needed and had given it to him in order to ensure his support. Ransome was starting as he meant to go on, and, if he was the sort of superintendent who would support his men and not simply expect obedience and results, he was sure to become a popular leader. Sebastian tended to reserve judgment until he had more facts, but he wasn't one to look a gift horse in the mouth either. His feelings might change over time, but for now Ransome had ensured Sebastian's favor.

Sebastian called out to the cabbie to stop as soon as he approached Bedford Square. He didn't want anyone to see him. He paid the man and walked the rest of the way, keeping to the shadows. General Modine didn't strike him as someone who spent his evenings at home with his wife, and, now that Esme was gone, he would surely be in search of new diversions. At the very least, he would dine at his club or find a card game or a vaudeville performance in some seedy tavern. Sebastian didn't believe for a moment that the general genuinely grieved for his lover, and thought he'd find someone to fill Esme's shoes very quickly. He had openly admitted that he always kept a piece on the side. Sebastian pitied his next conquest, and hoped the woman was intuitive enough to see through the general and take care not to get hurt by him.

It was still early enough that the general might be at home, but hopefully he would be heading out very soon. Sebastian took up a position by the park at the center of the square, melting into the shadows of a tall tree as he observed the house. He was rewarded for his patience in less than an hour. The general stepped outside and climbed into his brougham as soon as it rolled up. He was dressed in evening clothes and clearly headed out for a night on the town. Sebastian waited another ten minutes, then walked up to the door and knocked.

The door opened immediately, as if Richardson had been expecting his employer to return. The butler's face reflected first surprise, then irritation, and he tried to shut the door in Sebastian's face, but Sebastian slapped his hand against the wood and pushed hard, nearly knocking the other man off balance.

"General Modine is not here," Richardson snapped.

"I am here to speak to Mrs. Modine."

"She's not at home to visitors."

"I'm not a visitor. I'm an inspector with the Metropolitan Police, and, unless you are prepared to spend a night in the cells, you will let me in and inform the lady that I wish to see her."

Richardson looked torn. On the one hand, he clearly feared the general's wrath when he found out that the butler had allowed Sebastian to force his way in. On the other, a public run-in with the police might result in the loss of his position due to the embarrassment he'd caused his employer and the besmirching of his reputation, which would be considerably worse than a tongue-lashing from Modine. Richardson made his decision, stepped aside, and allowed Sebastian to wait in the foyer while he trod up the stairs to summon his mistress.

When Richardson returned, he did not offer to take Sebastian's things but bolted the front door instead, presumably in case the general was to suddenly come back. Sebastian suspected that, if that happened, he would be asked to leave by the servants' entrance before the man was permitted to enter his own home. Sebastian was in no mood for an altercation, but the butler's fear didn't bode well for the upcoming interview.

When Frances Modine appeared at the top of the stairs, Sebastian finally understood Richardson's reservations. She moved very carefully and was obviously in pain, and her face barely resembled the woman Sebastian had met only a short while ago. Her bottom lip was split, her left eye was swollen shut, and there were livid welts on her face, neck, and collarbone.

White-hot fury exploded in Sebastian's chest at the sight of her injuries, but there was nothing he could do to help her. There were no laws against beating one's wife, and, even if the woman died as a result of her injuries, the husband wasn't likely to be convicted, since everyone would simply assume she had brought it on herself and had no one else to blame. The woman would be quietly buried, the husband would be exonerated and probably marry again as soon as was decent, and the episode would be conveniently expunged from family history.

Frances appeared to shrink with shame when she saw the shock on Sebastian's face, and her eyes filled with tears. As soon as she reached the bottom of the stairs Sebastian silently offered her his arm and led her into the drawing room, where she gingerly lowered herself into a wingchair as Sebastian shut the door and took a seat across from her. There was no fire in the grate, and only one lamp was lit since the servants clearly had not expected their mistress to come down that evening. They knew what had happened and were likely hiding below stairs, too terrified to get on the wrong side of the general for fear of becoming his next victim. Perhaps he hadn't limited himself to beating his wife and had continued his reign of terror downstairs before going out for the evening.

"Why did he beat you?" Sebastian asked.

The reason didn't really matter, but he had to ask, and Frances didn't bother to dissemble.

"Because I spoke to Miss Tate. Everyone in this house reports to my husband, so even a conversation that takes place behind closed doors is never private. Richardson listens at keyholes, as he's no doubt doing right now."

Frances's voice was thick, and her lip began to ooze blood. She dabbed at it with a handkerchief, but if it hurt she gave no sign, since the pain was probably insignificant compared with her other injuries. Sebastian heard rustling at the door and assumed Richardson had moved out of the way in case Sebastian meant to catch him in the act. He didn't bother to go to the door. Richardson would report to his master, and poor Frances would suffer, regardless of what she said.

"I'm very sorry. Is there anything I can do?"

Frances shook her head. "It's not the first time. I will be all right in a few days. Why are you here?"

"Because I need to ask you some questions, and I implore you to answer them truthfully."

You have the power to put that bastard away and set yourself free, Sebastian thought but didn't say so aloud. Most women were willing to endure all manner of abuse rather than face a life on their own, especially if their husband did not leave them well provided for. An occasional beating was nothing compared to a life of penury, and Frances Modine seemed to have accepted her fate long ago.

"He didn't murder them, Inspector," Frances said softly.

"How do you know?"

"Because I know my husband. He's many things, but devious is not one of them. I can't see him sneaking about backstage and poisoning props. Anything he does, he does openly because he's not afraid of anyone."

"You seem to know a lot about what happened."

General Modine wasn't likely to permit his wife to read the papers, so, unless Gemma had told her about the vials, Frances would have remained in ignorance of the details.

"I found a newspaper in the library and read the account. I needed to know."

"Does your husband give you an allowance?"

"He does, but only because he wants me to look my best for his friends. He doesn't care to be embarrassed by his wife, even though I have humiliated him repeatedly."

"How did you humiliate him?" Sebastian asked.

There was a resignation in Frances Modine that worried him. It was as if she no longer cared what happened to her and was willing to take any punishment as long as she got to have her say. And to speak to a detective could mean a death sentence. Perhaps that was what she hoped for, since then at least she wouldn't have to resort to taking her own life.

"I failed to give Jonathan a son. He does not have an heir to carry on the family name and looks impotent in front of his friends, who have broods of healthy children. There was nothing Jonathan could do, which made him feel even more powerless," Frances explained. "Until now."

"What changed?"

"Esme told him she was with child. That altered everything."

"How?"

Frances's head drooped, and tears dripped onto the satin skirt of her gown. "He decided to get rid of me."

"You think he means to kill you?" Sebastian asked.

"Worse," Frances moaned. "He sent for Dr. Lederer."

"I'm not familiar with the name."

"Dr. Lederer is a dissatisfied husband's best friend," Frances said, her damaged mouth twisting into a gruesome smile. "He will declare a woman hysterical, remove her womb in order to subdue her, have her locked up in some asylum, or arrange for her to die during the surgery if the husband is resolved to be set free. My husband means to be free, Inspector."

"You purchased large amounts of poison. Did you intend to kill Esme Royce to nullify the threat to yourself? Is that why you went to the theater on Tuesday?" Sebastian asked. Frances might have lied to Gemma, but he didn't think she would lie to him. She seemed tired of hiding.

"No, Inspector. As I explained to Miss Tate, I bought the poison for myself. All my life, I have done what men told me to do. I have never made a single important decision for myself. Well, this time was going to be different. If I was to be butchered or locked up, I was going to take matters into my own hands. I would have done so already, but then I realized that I didn't want to die."

Frances sobbed quietly into her handkerchief, and Sebastian gave her a moment to compose herself.

"Why did you go to the theater?" he asked at last.

"I wanted to speak to Esme, to warn her. Jonathan is not to be trusted. I know he made promises to her, but he had no intention of keeping his word. If Esme had a son, he would take the child from her and pass him off as a legitimate heir. And if I raised any objections, a visit from Dr. Lederer would be sure to follow. And if she had a daughter, he'd simply turn his back on them both and find a new mistress. He would not remarry until he was certain he had his boy, for fear of getting another barren wife."

"You had a motive to want Esme Royce dead."

Frances shook her head. "Her death would make no difference in the end. Jonathan would simply find someone else. I can't kill them all. It's much simpler to kill myself, when the time comes."

"Mrs. Modine, surely there's another way."

"Is there?" Frances asked softly. "Shall I show you my back, Inspector? He treats me like one of his soldiers. Every perceived transgression is punished severely. He's beaten me within an inch of my life more than once, then had Dr. Lederer tend to me and try to convince me that it was all my fault, and that my husband would treat me with kindness if only I didn't provoke him so. Dr. Lederer will make me disappear as soon as my husband gives the order."

"I can help you get away," Sebastian said, but he knew what she'd say before she said it.

"And go where? My husband would hunt me down like an animal and kill me after he'd brutalized me to his satisfaction. He cannot remarry as long as I'm alive, so my only value to him lies in my death."

"You can disappear. Start a new life. You wouldn't be the first."

Frances shook her head. "I don't think so."

"Would the general murder Esme and Christopher if he thought they were having an affair?"

Frances shook her head again. She was like a marionette, moving this way and that, no longer caring. "You have to love someone to feel the pain of their betrayal, Inspector Bell, and my husband is not capable of love. If he discovered that Esme was unfaithful, he would simply cut her dead, even if she was carrying his child. He would have no need to kill her or her lover. They're simply not worth the trouble."

Sebastian could believe that and thought Frances was correct in her assessment. He genuinely hoped she would find an alternative to killing herself, but, if holding on to poison provided her with a modicum of control over her life, he could hardly demand that she turn it over. He didn't have that right.

"Where did your husband go tonight?" he asked.

"He had plans to dine with friends at Verey's."

"I know it." Sebastian had passed the restaurant many times but had never been inside. It was an elegant place, and not the sort of establishment one would want to go to by oneself. Perhaps he'd take Gemma one day.

"You can contact me at Scotland Yard if you ever need my help, Mrs. Modine."

"Thank you, Inspector, but I won't be needing your help."

"Can I see you to your room?"

Frances shook her head. "Good evening, Inspector."

"Good evening," Sebastian said, and left her to face the night on her own.

FORTY

By the time Sebastian returned to the boarding house, it was past eleven o'clock. He let himself in using the spare key and tiptoed past the landlady's room on the ground floor. He needn't have bothered. The door flew open to reveal an angry Mrs. Poole. Her hair was wound around leather curlers, and her bosom heaved with indignation as she blocked his path to the stairs.

"This is the second time this week you've broken the rules, Inspector. And let me tell you something. If you don't mind yourself, there will be a reckoning, because things are going to change around here." She was about to admonish him further when the light from her candle revealed what she had initially missed, and she stared at the bloodstained collar and cuffs of his shirt, which were clearly visible despite his overcoat.

"Look at the state of you," she exclaimed. "I expect you'll need me to launder your clothes?"

"If you would be so kind."

"That will be an extra charge, on account of it not being laundry day tomorrow."

"I will gladly reimburse you for your tireless efforts on my behalf, Mrs. Poole."

Her eyes narrowed as she tried to determine if he was genuinely grateful or just mocking her. "You think on what I told you," she hissed. "Mr. Quince has declared himself, and I mean to accept him." She smiled despite her irritation, her eyes alight with joy at the prospect of her impending marriage.

Sebastian knew he should keep his mouth shut, but he'd already crossed several lines this evening, so what was one more? He reached out and took Mrs. Poole by the shoulders, lowering his voice so that only she could hear him in case someone was listening.

"He's not what he purports to be, Mathilda," Sebastian said.

"Take your hands off me," Mrs. Poole whispered loudly. "And what on earth do you mean by that?"

"Just ask yourself who has more to gain from the marriage, you or him."

"Are you suggesting that I'm so disagreeable that the only reason Mr. Quince would wish to marry me is because he has something to gain?"

"Any man would be lucky to have you," Sebastian forced out, "but the moment you marry Mr. Quince, this house and everything else you own will become his. Everything."

"Mr. Quince is not the opportunist you imagine him to be."

"I sincerely hope not, but he's a railway porter, who rents a room in a boarding house."

"And you're a police inspector, who rents a room in a boarding house. What of it?"

"I'm not the one who asked for your hand."

Mrs. Poole exhaled loudly through her nose, much like an enraged bull. "Mr. Quince is a published author, who makes a respectable living from his literary efforts."

"According to him."

"Are you suggesting he's a liar?"

"I'm suggesting you think things through. There's no call to rush to the altar."

"You don't have to allude to my age to prove your point, Inspector," Mrs. Poole said, but Sebastian could see he'd struck a nerve. Mrs. Poole was desperate to be loved, but she was no fool, and the boarding house was her only source of income.

"That is not what I meant, and you know it," Sebastian replied, and hoped she would hear him.

Mrs. Poole sighed heavily and nodded. "Thank you, Sebastian. I know you're only looking out for me. Does that hurt?" she asked as she peered at him over the candle flame.

"Not really. Most of it is not my blood."

"Well, thank the Lord for that. I'll launder your shirt for free," she added grudgingly. "Goodnight, then."

"Goodnight."

Sebastian went up to his room, hung up his hat, and shrugged off his coat. Once he was in his shirt, he rolled up his sleeves, poured water into a basin, and used the hand towel to clean his face and wash the blood from his knuckles. He might not be able to charge Jonathan Modine with battery, but he hadn't been able to walk away and mind his own business after he'd seen what the bastard had done to Frances. Modine hadn't looked any better than his wife by the time Sebastian had finished with him, and he had greatly enjoyed watching the general curl into a ball as he lay whimpering on the ground, his fine clothes covered in muck, blood pouring out of his nose and seeping into the cracks between the filthy cobbles.

Modine had managed to get in a few good punches, but then Sebastian had got hold of his walking stick and used it to beat the smug piece of shit within an inch of his life. The beating wouldn't prevent him from hurting Frances again, but it would even the score a little.

Sebastian flexed his right hand. Thankfully, nothing was broken, and he'd had the foresight to tie a dark kerchief around the lower half of his face and wear a black woolen cap that he'd borrowed from a drunk lounging in a doorway to hide his hair. He doubted the general would be able to identify his assailant, particularly since Sebastian had made sure to shove him into a dark alley. Perhaps the general would come into Scotland Yard tomorrow, and Sebastian could question him at length about the assault and promise to catch the thug who'd had the temerity to set upon such an esteemed personage.

The thought made him smile, which in turn made him wince since his jaw was sore, but on the whole he felt he'd had a very productive evening. Sensing Sebastian's benevolence, Gustav jumped onto his chest as soon as he got into bed, and, rather than push him off, Sebastian stroked his back until they both fell asleep, snoring contentedly.

FORTY-ONE

FRIDAY, MARCH 18

Sebastian reread Gemma's cryptic message, then folded the paper and pushed it into the pocket of his waistcoat. The message had been delivered yesterday evening, but Mrs. Poole had forgotten all about it and only given it to him at breakfast. Gemma didn't leave for her afternoon off until noon, so no harm done. Sebastian had received the message in plenty of time to meet her, and planned to call on Mr. Bonneville in the interim. He hoped the owner of the Orpheus had returned from his stay at the sanatorium and would be willing to answer some questions.

It was one of those rare March days when the sun shone, the breeze was gentle and smelled deliciously of spring, and the sky was blindingly blue. It was a perfect day for a walk and offered Sebastian an opportunity to gather his thoughts. His first concern was Frances Modine, but he could hardly turn up at the Modines' front door and ask to see her. That would only infuriate her husband and make her more of a target. Sebastian hoped that he'd bought Frances a few days' reprieve until the case was solved and he could either charge the general with murder or admit that there was nothing more he could do for her and hope that she found the courage to save herself.

When he arrived at Mr. Bonneville's address, his knock was answered by the same young maidservant he'd met on his first visit. She smiled warmly, then seemingly recalled that she had been chastised by the housekeeper for revealing too much, and the smile slid off her face.

"Inspector Bell to see Mr. Bonneville," Sebastian said.

"Mr. Bonneville is at breakfast, sir."

"Please tell him I need to speak to him urgently."

The young woman seemed conflicted, but then invited him to wait inside and went to inform her master that he had an early morning visitor.

"This way, please," she said once she returned, a few minutes later.

She led him to a cheery breakfast room, where Mr. Bonneville was applying himself to a bowl of porridge. Instead of tea, he was drinking what appeared to be hot water with lemon. The man nodded in greeting and gestured toward a seat at the opposite end of the table.

"Would you like something to eat, Inspector?" Mr. Bonneville asked.

"Thank you, no."

"Cup of tea, then?"

"I won't be staying long."

"Please leave us, Enid," Mr. Bonneville said to the maid, and lifted his cup of hot water to his lips.

Enid picked up the empty plate and dirty spoon and walked out the door, leaving it open behind her, which seemed to annoy her employer. He set his cup down and went to shut the door before returning to the table. The momentary distraction offered Sebastian an opportunity to study the man unobserved. Mr. Bonneville was in his mid to late forties. His thick brown hair gleamed with pomade, and his eyes were the color of dry moss. Although his features were pleasing, he had the gaunt look of a man who didn't get enough to eat on a regular basis, and his face was unnaturally pallid.

"I heard about what happened at the Orpheus as soon as I returned to London," Mr. Bonneville said. "Terrible business."

"There's been another death, Mr. Bonneville. I expect the news will be reported in the evening editions," Sebastian replied.

"Who's dead?" Bonneville asked, clearly stunned.

"Ishmael Cabot. I believe he was murdered."

"How do you imagine I can help?"

"You were at the theater on the night Esme and Christopher were murdered."

"Yes, but I didn't see either of them."

"I was told you had an argument with Guy Weathers."

Mr. Bonneville's surprise was evident. "An argument is a strong word, Inspector. We negotiated the terms of the new contract and eventually came to an understanding. I think Mr. Weathers might wish to rethink his decision to renew the contract now that such a tragedy has befallen his troupe, but I assure you, Inspector, I have nothing to gain from the deaths of the actors. Quite the opposite."

"Mr. Bonneville, are you aware that there are peepholes in all the dressing rooms?"

Bonneville nodded. "I really should have them covered up."

"Why didn't you?"

"To be frank, I didn't learn about them until quite recently. Walt Dickie let it slip while in his cups that he watches Serena Winthrop as she prepares to go on stage. He's a devoted fan. I think he watched Esme too."

"Walt Dickie is dead," Sebastian announced.

"Is he? God rest his soul. The way he drank, he wasn't long for this world," Mr. Bonneville replied matter-of-factly.

"Why did you keep him on?"

"I know I should have asked him to leave, but I felt sorry for the man. He had nowhere to go and would have been dead within a week if forced to sleep rough."

"It was kind of you to let him stay."

"It doesn't cost me anything to help a fellow human being. If I prolonged his life by a year or two, then I'm glad of it."

"Is that why you took in Rose and Sid?"

"Their father was a good man and helped me at a time when I was desperate for relief."

"Relief from what?"

"Pain. Both physical and mental. I lost my wife just over three years ago. We never had any children, and we were everything to each other. Bertha was my love, my best friend, and my keeper. She looked after me since she was seventeen years old." Mr. Bonneville sighed and took another sip of water. "I suffer from a peptic ulcer and must be extremely careful about my diet. Mr. Wyvern was a chemist, and he made me a compound of bismuth that I was to take before every meal. It was Mr. Wyvern who recommended the Lakeview Lodge when he deduced that my condition was chronic."

"What is it they do for you at Lakeview Lodge, if you don't mind me asking?"

Sebastian wasn't really interested in the details of Mr. Bonneville's condition, but, if morphine was used to control the symptoms, that would make Mr. Bonneville a suspect in the murders of Esme Royce and Christopher Hudson. And possibly Ishmael Cabot, since Bonneville might have returned earlier than expected. He had keys to all the doors, and no one would suspect anything if they saw him at his theater.

Mr. Bonneville's face looked pinched when he replied. "Dr. Gordon, who looks after the patients at the Lodge, has come up with a procedure that keeps the symptoms at bay for up to a fortnight. He injects milk into the stomach by means of an enema. The milk neutralizes the gastric acid, and if I keep to a diet of bland foods I suffer almost no acute discomfort between visits."

Sebastian did his best not to envision the procedure Mr. Bonneville had described and to focus on the subject at hand. "Do you ever take morphine, Mr. Bonneville?"

"No, I do not." Bonneville looked thoughtful. "Is that what killed them? An overdose of morphine? I haven't read the papers yet," he explained. "But I have seen the headlines."

Sebastian nodded.

"Strange, that," Mr. Bonneville muttered.

"Strange how?"

"Mr. Wyvern died of an overdose as well. The coroner said it was most likely laudanum and would have ruled it a suicide if he could be sure that the overdose was intentional. In the end, he decided on 'death by misadventure'."

"How long ago was this?"

"About two years now. Rose was fourteen. After Mr. Wyvern died, a relative stepped in and sold the shop. I couldn't let the children go to a workhouse, so I asked if they would like to work for me at my new theater. In exchange, I offered them a room and a wage that would allow them to be independent."

"But not so independent that they could find decent lodging," Sebastian replied, his tone more reproving than he had intended.

"I did what I could for them, Inspector. They're safe and warm and have enough to eat. They could have fared much worse."

"Where was Mr. Wyvern's shop located?"

"Covent Garden. It's now called Harbor's Drugs."

"Do you still patronize the shop?"

"Yes. Why do you ask?"

"No reason." Sebastian studied Mr. Bonneville as he

digested this new information. "Does Rose have a set of keys to the theater?"

Mr. Bonneville nodded. "Rose has a key to every door in the theater. I didn't trust the keys to Walt, but Rose is a responsible girl and makes sure to lock up after everyone leaves."

"Thank you, Mr. Bonneville," Sebastian said, and pushed away from the table. "I'm sorry to have interrupted your breakfast."

"It's no bother, Inspector. I do hope you find whoever did this awful thing."

Outside once again, Sebastian decided to walk to Covent Garden. He had time until he was due to meet Gemma, and, now that the facts were beginning to form a pattern in his mind, he needed to organize them into a clear narrative. Mr. Bonneville had been acquainted with Mr. Wyvern, who just happened to be the previous owner of Harbor's Drugs, and who had died under suspicious circumstances. A large quantity of morphine had recently been stolen from the same shop. That couldn't be a coincidence, not when the Wyvern children were now employed at the Orpheus theater.

Mr. Bonneville had taken the children in and given them a home, but Sebastian didn't think his reasons were as altruistic as he'd made them sound. Bonneville benefited from the bargain, since Rose and Sid served not only as unofficial caretakers but also as his spies. It was possible that the information they'd provided had prompted Mr. Bonneville to rethink the terms of the contract with Guy Weathers, who'd been up in arms about having to surrender a higher percentage of his takings.

But Sebastian didn't think the murders had anything to do with money. These crimes had been motivated by feelings that ran so deep, they could only be managed by removing the source of the killer's suffering. Sebastian had been so fixated on the complicated relationships between the adults that he'd completely disregarded sweet, virtually invisible Rose and eager, excitable Sid, who had been there all along. There was a clear line to be drawn between the Wyvern children, the shop, the theft, and the murders. And the only reason Sebastian could see that Rose would want to murder Esme and Christopher was because she had been in love with Christopher.

But Sid had seen Christopher with Esme; he'd admitted as much. How could Rose, who was passably pretty and afflicted with a physical infirmity, compete with a young woman who shone as bright as the sun and was just as talented? To harbor such intense feelings for a man who thought her invisible and probably treated her with no more consideration than a beggar on the street had to have hurt, especially if Rose had made her feelings known and Christopher had mocked and rejected her.

Hell hath no fury like a woman scorned. Serena Winthrop had used those very words when speaking of the killer, and Rose might very well have been scorned. And who else would take a brooch in the shape of a rose if not Rose? *A rose by any other name...* The quote swam unbidden to the top of Sebastian's mind. Rose. A delicate flower. Except roses had sharp, vicious thorns that tore at the flesh and drew blood. If Rose was the killer, then she had not only disposed of the two people who had hurt her but had probably murdered Ishmael Cabot in order to lead Sebastian away from the true motive and make him think that Ishmael had killed his blackmailers and then taken his own life.

Clever girl, Sebastian thought as he quickened his step. He wanted to speak to the Harbors, but he would be sure to get to the theater before Gemma. He couldn't risk leaving her alone with Rose and Sid.

FORTY-TWO

Gemma arrived at twenty past twelve. She had been able to get away earlier than expected and thought she'd wait for Sebastian at the Orpheus. As long as she didn't make any accusations or ask any leading questions, she was safe, and, if she happened to exchange a few words with Rose, there was nothing suspicious in that.

She had not recognized Rose straight away. Gemma had seen her once, all those years ago when she had stopped into Wyvern's to purchase a few additional items for her journey. She probably would not have remembered Rose at all except that, when the girl had stepped out from behind the counter and gone to fetch a jar of hand cream, she had noticed when she reached up that one of Rose's boots had a very thick sole and the hem of her skirt had lifted past her ankles.

Rose's gait had been almost normal then, the thick sole balancing out a leg that was too short, clearly a birth defect. With her long skirts covering her legs, no one would have realized she had a deformity at all. Without the thick sole, however, Rose leaned to the right with every step, which had to put undue pressure on her spine and hips. She must have outgrown the boots, and had no money to order a new pair that would improve her mobility and conceal the defect she had to be conscious of. Her boots looked old and scuffed, and were too big for her, no doubt castoffs that she had either bought from a rag and bone man or taken off someone who no longer needed them.

Gemma didn't like to think Rose would stoop to robbing the dead, but she was keenly aware of how common it was to come across someone who'd died in the night, especially during the winter months. Prostitutes who did their business in the street often froze to death in doorways, and the river bestowed its grim offerings upon the riverbank. There were plenty who robbed the dead, relieving them of their belongings before they were carted off to the dead houses and buried in paupers' graves, where they would no longer have need of their clothes or shoes.

Strange that Rose and Sid had ended up at the theater, but Gemma supposed they'd got lucky. The children could have wound up on the streets when their father died, or in a workhouse, which would kill them just as quickly, given the horrific conditions and lack of proper nutrition and medical care. Mr. Bonneville had offered the children a place to live, but he probably didn't pay them enough to do much more than survive. It was an act of self-interest disguised as kindness.

When Gemma got to the theater, the front doors were unlocked but the members of the troupe had yet to arrive. The theater was silent, the auditorium seemingly holding its breath and the empty balconies looming out of the darkness like the decks of an abandoned ship. Backstage it was almost eerie, with most of the lights off and the sunlight from the windows blocked by props and closed doors. Gemma considered leaving —she could always wait for Sebastian outside, in the bright afternoon sunshine—but then she heard footsteps from the floor above. Someone was there, in one of the dressing rooms. It wouldn't hurt to check. She could always say she was looking for Sebastian and have a bit of a chat with whomever she happened to encounter. Because none of the members of the troupe had seen her since the night of the murders, when she had attended the performance with Sebastian, they would discount her interest and attribute her presence to her personal relationship with the policeman.

Gemma headed up the stairs and stopped at the mouth of the long corridor, looking about her. The white walls were bare and dingy, the floor was scuffed, and the doorknobs and wall sconces glinted dully in the light of an oil lamp that someone had left on a hall table by the back wall. There were several doors—all on the same side of the corridor—with the actors' names displayed in brass frames. Only one door, the one closest to the end of the corridor, was partially open, and when Gemma approached it she saw that it still bore Esme's name. Gemma knocked and pushed it open without waiting to be invited in.

The room didn't have a window, but sunlight filtered in through a skylight in the ceiling, casting a pool of light on the floor beneath. Rose sat before the mirror, humming softly as she applied a bit of rouge to her pale cheeks. Their eyes met in the mirror and Rose turned, smiling guilelessly, as Gemma entered.

"Good afternoon, Miss Tate," she said.

Gemma was surprised that Rose had remembered her name, but she supposed the girl had a good memory and didn't have much to occupy her mind, particularly during the day, when she had nothing to do. Rose was still wearing the blue gown she'd worn on Tuesday night, but a lovely dress that must have belonged to Esme was laid out on the chaise, ready to be tried on, and Rose's eyes were expertly lined in kohl, the way Esme's had been on the night of her last performance.

Perhaps Rose liked to play dress-up when no one was about, putting on stage makeup and beautiful gowns and twirling in front of the mirror. During those moments, she could be anyone she wanted, and who she seemingly wanted to be was Esme Royce. Or perhaps she simply wanted to be beautiful, the sort of young woman who was admired by women and desired by men.

"Good afternoon, Rose," Gemma replied, and smiled at the girl. "Are you all alone?"

Rose nodded. "Sid went to get us something to eat. I'm hoping for oyster stew."

There was a small table covered with a fringed tablecloth that was set for two. Rose and Sid had clearly made themselves at home.

"What are you doing here, Miss Tate?" Rose asked. She had turned back but was still watching Gemma through the mirror, seemingly unperturbed by her presence. She dipped a finger in the rouge and dabbed some on her mouth, making it appear unnaturally red, then smacked her lips together, as she must have seen Esme do.

"I'm here to meet Inspector Bell. He had a few follow-up questions for Mr. Weathers, and then we were going to take a walk," Gemma improvised. She hadn't expected to find the theater empty and now needed to invent a reason for her presence in Esme's dressing room. "He must be running late," she added unnecessarily.

"Questions about Ishmael?"

"What about Ishmael?" Gemma asked carefully.

"Didn't you know? He killed himself."

"What? When?" *And how?* Gemma wanted to ask, but didn't want to admit to Rose just how interested she was.

Rose completely ignored her questions. "He's nice, Inspector Bell," she said as she turned around again. "Sid is quite impressed with him. He says he wants to become a policeman."

"I'm sure he'll make a dedicated police officer."

"I suppose," Rose replied with a shrug. "Would you like some tea while you wait? Esme had some tasty biscuits." She reached for a tin that stood on the dressing table and rattled it experimentally. "I reckon there are a few left. Enough for you, at any rate."

"No, thank you," Gemma said. She wasn't foolish enough to accept tea from a murderess, not when it could be the last thing she ever did.

"Suit yourself," Rose replied airily, and turned back to the mirror. "Esme had such pretty things. I wonder what will happen to them. I suppose Serena or Kate will take the lot. Ruth is too old and fat to wear any of Esme's gowns," she said spitefully.

"Have you seen a brooch in the shape of a rose? General Modine gave it to Esme on the night she died."

Rose nodded. "Inspector Bell took it."

"Did he?"

"Slipped it into his pocket when he searched the room. I saw him." Rose's narrowed eyes met Gemma's in the mirror again. "Maybe he'll give it to you once the case is closed. I reckon you've never owned anything so beautiful."

Gemma was about to reply, then realized that Rose was probably baiting her, and nothing good could come from disputing her claim that Sebastian had taken the brooch. She suddenly recalled the conversation she'd had with Anne about the girl who betrayed her as she wanted Anne's first love for herself, and thought that Rose probably wasn't as artless as Gemma had first assumed. She probably had an innate mean streak that had grown wider after years of hardship and neglect.

"I think I'll go wait outside," Gemma said. "It's a beautiful day. Have you been out today?"

"Too cold for the likes of me," Rose said, and turned to face

Gemma. "And too crowded. People push me aside if I don't move fast enough."

"I'm sorry. That must be frustrating for you."

"I'm used to it. Sometimes I push them back."

Feeling more uncomfortable by the minute, Gemma turned to leave and came face to face with Sid, who smiled warmly at her.

"Hello," he said cheerfully. "Did you come with Inspector Bell?"

"He's not here yet," Gemma replied.

"Then you must eat with us. There's enough for three," he said as he lifted the crock of stew he carried to show Gemma. "Rose, get another plate."

"There are only two plates," Rose said. "You'll have to eat from the pot."

Sid shrugged. "I don't mind, as long as there's a spoon."

"There should be one on the table. I set it out to serve the stew," Rose replied sulkily. She clearly didn't care to share her portion with Gemma and probably hoped she would leave.

"Take off your things and stay awhile, Miss Tate," Sid said as he bounded into the room, forcing Gemma to step aside to let him in.

Gemma was growing warm in her bonnet and cape, and thought she may as well get comfortable. She took off her bonnet, then unhooked her cape and laid the items on a nearby chair, setting her reticule on top. Sid set the crock of stew on the table and removed his own coat and cap, tossed them on top of Gemma's things, then returned to the table and leaned forward, presumably looking for the extra spoon. He lifted the crock, as if to move it out of the way, then turned quite suddenly. Gemma didn't know what made her take a step back and duck—probably some primal instinct that sensed that she was in danger—but had she not, the iron crock would have collided with her skull.

Gemma cried out in shock, and Sid let out a roar of frustration as the contents of the pot flew in all directions, splattering the walls, soiling Rose's hair, and oozing onto the floor as slimy oysters slid down the wall and landed on the bare boards with a wet plop.

"You idiot," Rose cried as she sprang to her feet and advanced on her brother. "Now look what you've done."

"She knows, Rosie," Sid said resignedly, and grabbed one of the knives Rose had laid out on the table. "That's why she's here."

"If she didn't before, she surely does now," Rose snapped.

She looked horrified, but there was resolve in her eyes that Gemma knew to be love. She would protect Sid no matter what. He was the only family she had left.

Gemma lurched forward, but Rose moved surprisingly fast, cutting her off before she got to the door. Rose slammed the door shut, turned the key, and pocketed it, then stood with her back to the wooden panel, blocking Gemma's only means of escape.

Sid remained where he was, his head cocked to the side as he studied Gemma, the knife still in his hand. A cruel little smile played about his lips, and there was a sly look in his eyes, as if he were deciding how to best deal with Gemma now that she was trapped. All traces of the eager little boy were gone, and Gemma suddenly realized that Sid was probably older than she had initially thought. He seemed taller and broader now that he was no longer stooping, a boy on the cusp of manhood, who'd had to fend for himself for the past few years and was probably more resourceful than anyone gave him credit for. And given how Rose looked at him just then, perhaps Sid was the one who took care of her and not the other way around.

"You nosy cow. You just couldn't leave well enough alone," Sid ground out. "You think I don't know what you've been up to?" He seemed in no rush to charge her, but his hand gripped the handle of the knife with deadly intent.

"It was you," Gemma choked out. Her mouth was dry, her hands trembling with fear. "You killed Esme and Christopher." She still didn't know how a young boy could pull such a thing off, but she was now convinced it hadn't been Rose's idea.

Rose hissed at her brother to be quiet, but he didn't seem to care. He was through pretending, probably because he was safe in the knowledge that Gemma wouldn't live long enough to reveal what she knew.

"I did, yeah. They deserved it."

"Why? What did they ever do to you?" Gemma cried.

She needed to keep Sid talking. The longer it took for him to explain, the better chance she had; but even as she thought that she realized she was grasping at straws. Sebastian wasn't due to arrive at the theater until one o'clock, and Sid obviously wasn't worried about the other members of the troupe showing up. Walt Dickie was gone, and there was no one else who would hear her if she called for help.

"Why?" Gemma cried again.

Sid sneered. "For one, they mocked Rose. I heard them talking, and they referred to her as—what was it they said?—ah, yes, a pathetic cripple, who'd sell her soul for one minute with Chris," he said, his gaze sliding to Rose, who looked like she was about to cry.

"Sid, don't," Rose whispered. "Please."

Sid ignored her and moved closer. "But that wasn't the worst of it. See, Chris pretended to be Rose's friend, and she fell for it. She allowed him to come up to the attic, the gullible little fool, so they could be alone. She thought he was going to kiss her or tell her that he cared for her. I don't blame her, really. Chris was a good actor. Better than most. He could get anyone to believe anything, and he toyed with people for his own amusement. He toyed with Rose."

Rose was crying now; the kohl she had applied had been dissolved by her tears and was running down her cheeks. "Sid, no," she whispered. "Don't tell her."

But Sid couldn't seem to stop. He wanted to boast about what he had done so that at least one person would know how clever he was, and how ruthless.

"Once he went up there, he knew," Sid said, shooting Rose a look of reproach. "He'd seen enough to realize we were running our own little business, and he told Esme. We thought they'd tell Weathers or that idiot Bannon, but they wanted in on the scheme. They wanted half."

"What business were you running, Sid?" Gemma asked desperately.

The corridor beyond the room was eerily silent, no sound of a man's footsteps or the creaking of wood to frighten Sid into letting her go. Even if Sebastian had arrived early, he was probably waiting for her outside or in the foyer and thinking she was late.

Sid smiled. "Rose went through the pockets of the coats that were left in the cloakroom, and I did a little discreet pickpocketing of my own as I escorted people to their seats. They never noticed me—to them I was a faceless lackey—and, by the time they realized their purse was missing or their watch was gone, I was the furthest thing from their thoughts. We were never greedy, mind," Sid added with obvious pride. "This was too good a setup to cock up. Rose would take a few coins, and I would only do one job per night. A watch here, a diamond bracelet there, a ring, or a purse full of notes. And if someone came looking the next day, they never found anything. They could have lost their things anywhere, or got their pockets picked while they waited in line or walked down the street. Happens every day."

"And you fenced the goods?" Gemma asked.

Sid nodded. "We made a small fortune, Rosie and I. Enough to see us through."

"Why?" Gemma asked again.

She knew why, but she hoped Sid would keep talking until his anger fizzled and he couldn't bring himself to murder her in cold blood. But she had miscalculated. Sid's eyes blazed with fury, and he moved a little closer to her.

"When our father topped himself, I was twelve. I promised Rose I'd take care of her. And I have. And we're not going to live like rats, scurrying around in the attic for the rest of our days until we end up like Walt Dickie. No one gave a toss when I snuffed him. They barely noticed he was gone."

"Why did you kill the watchman?" Gemma cried.

Sid scoffed. "Why do you think? He knew enough to tip off that nosy policeman. Like a bloodhound that one." Gemma noticed a spark of respect in Sid's eyes, but his admiration quickly burned out.

"So, what will you do now?"

"We have enough put by to get us a decent place and eat more than once a day." Sid bared his teeth. "Just because that imbecile Bonneville chooses to starve himself doesn't mean other people don't need to eat."

"Sid, please," Gemma pleaded as she took a step backwards and pressed her back against the wall. "I mean you no harm. Get away while you can. Inspector Bell is on his way."

Sid chuckled. "Lucky I locked the door when I came back then, so he won't be getting in, your precious inspector. He'll wait outside, then think you stood him up. And you do mean us harm. That's why you're here. You had to prove how clever you are, Miss Tate. You'd even found your way to Harbor's Drugs."

"How did you know?" Gemma croaked.

"I saw you come out of Driscoll's and walk over to Harbor's. I followed you. I keep an eye on the place." Sid's face was white with anger and his voice strained. "It was to be my inheritance.

And one day, I mean to get it back. Rose and I were practically running the shop after our mam died and our father just gave up. We measured out the medicines and cut the tablets in the back room. We ordered stock and managed the books. And then we were left with nothing. Just like that! It all went to Robin Wyvern, a man we'd never even met," Sid cried, his face twisting with grief. "I begged him to help us, but he sold the shop out from under us and left. Didn't care if we lived or died. We weren't his responsibility, he said. Well, he didn't get to enjoy his ill-gotten gains for long because I killed him."

Gemma sensed that Sid was done talking. He had needed to explain, to get things off his chest, but now there was nothing left to say. The people who'd wronged the Wyvern children were all gone. Robin Wyvern, Esme and Christopher, and Ishmael, who'd been set up to take the blame.

"Why did you poison Esme and Christopher on stage?" Gemma cried, desperate to stall him for even a moment longer.

Sid smirked. "For one, it was fun. And for another, what better time to pick a few pockets than when people are running scared? Made out like a bandit before I went for the police. Couldn't let all that effort go to waste, could I?"

"You're a monster," Gemma exclaimed, and knew she'd made a dreadful mistake as soon as the words left her mouth.

Sid's face twisted with hatred, and he lunged, the knife held before him, the blade pointed at Gemma's belly. He was going to kill her, and it wasn't going to be quick, not if he stabbed her in the stomach. Gemma screamed in terror and tried to maneuver out of the way, but there was nowhere to go. The table that had been laid for lunch was to the side of her, Sid directly in front, with Rose against the locked door behind him. The dressing table, wardrobe, and chaise occupied the remaining space. She was completely boxed in, the furniture no shield against a killer. Gemma shut her eyes, unable to look into the face of the man-child who wished her dead.

As she braced for the searing pain of an abdominal puncture, time appeared to slow. Gemma's limbs felt as heavy as tree trunks, her terror pinning her to the spot. Her innards trembled violently, and her heart was beating so hard she could barely breathe. Oddly, the paralyzing panic seemed to galvanize her thoughts; memories, dreams, and regrets all fought for dominance in those final moments of consciousness, because the one thing she knew for certain was that Sid was not going to let her live.

Was this how it was going to finish, a sudden act of violence putting an end to a life barely lived? The physical pain was still to come, but the agony of loss was just as difficult to bear. Gemma's terrified mind—or maybe it was her heart—cruelly reminded her that she had never experienced the joy of a longed-for marriage proposal, had never known physical intimacy, and had never held her child in her arms. She was nearly thirty, but the things that made life worth living had eluded her and her path was paved with nothing but loss and pain. And now, when she had finally found love, a bitter, angry boy was going to kill her because she had unwittingly backed him against the wall, leaving him no choice but to eviscerate her so that he and his sister would have time to gather their ill-gotten gains and get away.

As the tip of the knife struck the whalebone of Gemma's corset, her last thought was of Sebastian, and how much she wished she'd had just one more moment with him, just one more kiss. She roared like a lioness and blindly pushed against Sid's chest, desperate to keep the blade away from her flesh. Her senses were heightened, her nose burning with the acrid stink of Sid's sweat—or maybe it was her own—the sickening fishy reek of the spilled stew, and the flowery perfume Rose must have dabbed on as she sat at Esme's dressing table. Gemma's hearing picked up every sound, from Sid's ragged breathing to Rose's desperate whimpers. And beneath the animal wail of her own terror, she heard another sound, a muffled scrambling followed by a loud bang.

Gemma's eyes flew open, and she stared in mute horror as Sid was thrown backwards, his mouth opening in surprise and blood frothing on his lips and trickling down his chin. The knife clattered to the floor as Sid fell, his body hitting the floor with a loud thud. Blood from a wound in his chest soaked into his shirt and waistcoat and stained his quivering hand as he tried to staunch the flow. His body convulsed, and his breath came in gurgling gasps as saliva and mucus flooded the airways. Gemma recognized that sound. It was the death rattle, and she had heard it many a time in Scutari when her patients succumbed to their injuries and passed from the world.

Rose shrieked and fell to her knees next to her brother, calling to him not to leave her, but it was too late. Sid's gaze clouded, and a small sigh escaped his bloodied lips as his brief life came to a tragic and violent end. Rose stared at Gemma in panic, probably thinking she could help, but Gemma was pinned to the wall, her entire body shaking with shock as she groped for the corner of the wardrobe, desperate for something solid to anchor her before she collapsed to the floor. Her panicked brain warned her that the shot had come from behind the dressing table, but she couldn't bring herself to turn her head and search for the hole that had to be in the wall.

Gemma's heart thundered, and she could barely hear above the roar in her ears as she slumped against the wardrobe for support. She heard the pounding of feet and then stared dumbly as the door burst open, the wood of the doorjamb splintering as Sebastian exploded into the room. There was a gun in his hand, and his expression was absolutely murderous.

Rose scampered away from Sid's body and cowered in the corner, and, although Gemma couldn't hear her wailing, she saw Rose's mouth open in a scream as tears streamed down her face. She covered her ears with her bloodied hands and rocked back and forth, then slid to the floor and curled into a quaking ball next to the chaise, burying her face in her chest as she wept.

"Gemma, are you all right?" Sebastian's hand was on her arm, and he was shaking her gently, his worried gaze searching her face. "Gemma. Talk to me."

Gemma swallowed hard and nodded. She couldn't bring herself to speak as she stared at Sid's body, and wished more than anything that Sebastian would take her into his arms and hold her until the terror had subsided, but he could hardly turn his back on Rose, whose hand was mere inches from the knife that had fallen to the floor. With Sebastian's help, Gemma staggered over to the chair before the dressing table and sat down heavily. She folded her arms on the table, then rested her forehead on her wrists and shut her eyes. Now that Sebastian was in charge, she could allow herself a few moments of respite to gather her wits about her until she felt able to go on.

There was a commotion outside, and then a wild-eyed Guy Weathers burst into the room. He must have just arrived and unlocked the front door.

"I heard screams. And a shot," he cried. His mouth fell open with shock when he took in the awful scene before him, and he froze in the doorway.

"Mr. Weathers, kindly send a message to Scotland Yard and ask them to send two constables with the police wagon," Sebastian said. He sounded reassuringly calm.

"Of course, Inspector. Right away," Weathers replied hoarsely and fled. His voice carried as he called out to someone to remain downstairs and make sure no one went up.

Feeling marginally more in control, Gemma opened her eyes and turned her head, but couldn't find the strength to lift it or to stand. She watched as Sebastian grabbed Esme Royce's gown from the chaise and threw it over Sid. His legs stuck out, but his face and blood-soaked chest were decently covered. Sebastian poured some water from a pitcher on the table, then helped Rose to her feet and, once she was seated on the edge of the chaise, handed her the cup. Rose drank the water in one gulp and handed the cup back. She appeared to be in shock. Her eyes were glazed as she stared at the wall rather than at her brother's body, and her lips were moving, perhaps in prayer.

Sebastian shot Gemma a worried look, then took Rose gently by the arm and pulled her to her feet. She didn't protest and allowed him to lead her to an adjacent dressing room, where he presumably locked her in so she wouldn't escape. Sebastian returned for Gemma, who was still as weak as a newborn kitten and trembling violently, and helped her up and led her downstairs to Guy Weathers' office. He settled her on the chaise and used a dressing gown he'd retrieved from a chair to cover her.

"Lie still for a while and take deep breaths," he instructed matter-of-factly. "In and out. In and out. I'd give you some brandy, but it may have been tampered with, so I'd rather not risk it."

Gemma was shaking hard, her mind replaying the awful scene in Esme's dressing room in excruciating detail and taunting her with her own culpability. She lifted a trembling hand to her middle and felt about until her fingers located a tear in the fabric where the knife had torn the bodice and had sliced the stiffened linen of the corset to leave a chunk of whalebone exposed. It was that bit of bone that had saved her from getting hurt in the moments before Sebastian had fired on Sid.

Once again, Gemma wished Sebastian would hold her and tell her that everything would be well, but how could it be? A child lay dead. His sister would be hauled off to Scotland Yard to be charged with theft and conspiracy to murder, and then sent to prison to await trial. And Sebastian was probably furious beyond words at what he'd had to do to save Gemma's life. If Sid had lived, he would have been charged, tried, and sentenced to hang, but he would have died by someone else's hand, not Sebastian's, and that was on her.

"Are you angry?" Gemma asked once she was able to formulate words without them turning into sobs.

Sebastian, who'd pulled up a chair and was sitting next to her, nodded. "At myself, mostly. I'm so sorry I was late." He reached for her hand beneath the dressing gown and held it tight.

"What happened to your face?" Gemma asked now that she was able to focus.

"Walked into a door during the night."

"I don't believe you," Gemma muttered. He'd hardly have bruised knuckles if he'd walked into a door.

Sebastian didn't reply. "How did you know?" he asked instead.

"I remembered Rose from Wyvern's, and something Mrs. Ramsey said reminded me just how underhanded young girls can be. I thought Rose had murdered Esme and Christopher because Christopher rebuffed her."

"I also thought it was Rose at first. I even went to speak to the Harbors, who told me that Robin Wyvern, who'd inherited the shop, died shortly after selling up. Poisoned. I was on my way to meet you when I spotted Sid. He didn't see me, so he had no reason to play a part." Sebastian shook his head in disbelief. "I suddenly realized that he must be older than I thought, and stronger. He wasn't a child but a young man, who'd been thrown out of his home and cheated out of his inheritance. Rose is too slow and clumsy to break into a shop and get away unnoticed, but Sid was fit and quick, and knew where the morphine was kept in a shop he'd grown up in. It was him all along."

"You were inside the walls," Gemma said.

Sebastian nodded. "I got in by the back door, and then, when I heard you scream, I knew I had mere moments. I forced the door to Ned Bannon's office, grabbed his gun, and crept

along the passageway behind the dressing rooms. The peepholes were easy to spot from the other side. When I saw Sid go
for you, I fired. I had no choice," he said, and Gemma saw the
toll killing the boy had taken on him.

"You mustn't blame yourself, Sebastian."

"I would kill a dozen people to save you," Sebastian said
wearily, "but I wish I'd figured it out sooner. Sid could have hurt
you quite badly." *Sid could have killed you* hung between them,
the words unspoken.

"I'm all right," Gemma assured him and squeezed his hand
a little tighter. "What will happen to Rose?"

"I will take her back to the Yard, take her statement, then
leave the rest to Ransome."

"Ransome?"

Sebastian nodded, and his expression told her that this was
a conversation for another time.

"I'm so sorry, Sebastian," Gemma whispered contritely. "I
should have waited for you outside."

Sebastian didn't absolve her of guilt, but he lifted her hand
and brought it to his lips, his eyes full of all the things he
couldn't bring himself to say at that moment. They remained
quiet for a time, and after a while the shaking finally subsided
and Gemma's thoughts were no longer muddled. She was warm
beneath the dressing gown and tethered to the moment by the
gentle pressure of Sebastian's hand.

"I will see you home," Sebastian said when Guy Weathers
eventually reappeared at the door to announce that the constables had arrived. "Let me get your things."

Gemma nearly asked if she could come with him to Scotland Yard, then remembered herself and nodded. She felt
unsteady on her feet as she stood, but Sebastian wrapped his
arm about her shoulders and guided her outside. The sunlight
was blinding after the gloom of the theater, and Gemma's eyes
filled with tears when she realized she might never have seen

the sun again. Sebastian must have sensed her distress but didn't bother to offer any platitudes. He found a cab, helped her in, and sat next to her, his arm around her and her head resting comfortably on his shoulder while the conveyance swayed soothingly as it began to move.

Gemma barely recalled the ride back to Colin's house or the rest of that day. All she knew was that she was alive, and Sebastian had saved her.

FORTY-THREE

Sebastian felt a little more in control of his emotions by the time he arrived at Scotland Yard. He couldn't help but think about what might have happened had he not got to Gemma in time, but she was all right, if badly shaken, and he had a job to do. He didn't want to be the one to send Rose Wyvern to the gallows, but he had no choice but to charge her. Even if Rose had not been the one to administer the poison, she had not only known what Sid was up to but had no doubt helped him. She had also stolen hundreds of pounds' worth of money and goods from unsuspecting patrons and had assisted Sid in fencing the items he'd stolen.

When Sebastian entered the duty room, he was surprised to find Constable Meadows behind the desk. The young man smiled apologetically, as if it were his fault he had been promoted.

"Where's Sergeant Woodward?" Sebastian asked.

"Transferred to B Division in Westminster. And Inspector Reece has gone to C Division. I think he'll like it at St. James's," Meadows said. "I'm to be the new duty sergeant. The youngest constable ever to be made sergeant," he added proudly.

"Congratulations, Seth," Sebastian said. "Well deserved."

"Thank you, Inspector Bell. I owe it all to you. You taught me so much."

"Oh, go on with you," Sebastian said, and smiled. "You've earned it on your own merit."

That was only partially true, since, although Seth Meadows was smart and resourceful, he would have never made sergeant as long as Sergeant Woodward manned the desk. It was Seth's good luck that Ransome was cleaning house. Otherwise, he'd have had to wait years to get his stripes. It was good news about Reece, though. Let C Division deal with that prat and see how they liked it.

"Please have Rose Wyvern brought to an interview room," Sebastian said. "I'll just have a word with Ransome."

"He's waiting for you, sir," Meadows said, and called out to Constable Hammond to fetch Rose.

Rose looked like a ghost when she shuffled into the room and practically fell into a chair. She had wiped away the makeup she had worn at the theater, but her skin was stained with what remained of the kohl that had lined her eyes and had run down her cheeks. Her bodice was stained with Sid's blood, and her nails were bitten to the quick. John Ransome arrived a few moments later, eager to oversee his first case as superintendent. Sebastian didn't mind. He would have gladly left the interview to Ransome, but he could hardly admit that this case had nearly pushed him over the edge. Instead, he took out his notebook and pencil and began.

"Tell us what happened, Rose," he said.

He would prefer that Rose tell them her story rather than question her like a hardened criminal. Rose appeared dazed, and Sebastian wasn't sure she had even heard him, but then she started to speak. Her voice was so thin, he could barely hear her over the noise from the duty room, so he shut the door and returned to his seat. If Rose was intimidated to be alone in a room with two men, she didn't show it. She was somewhere else, her gaze as unfocused as if she were drugged.

"We were happy once," she said quietly. "A loving family, and I thought I'd always be safe and loved. But then Mother got with child when I was eleven. The baby was stillborn, and the pregnancy had caused her to develop sugar sickness. Father did everything he could to help her, but there's no cure. She died less than a year later."

Rose wiped away the tears that slid down her cheeks and continued. "Father did his best, but he couldn't cope with his grief. He began to take laudanum to help him sleep, and the doses grew larger and larger, until one day he simply didn't wake up. Sid was so angry. He was convinced Father had killed himself, but I think he was simply desperate for relief. He never meant to leave us."

"What happened then?" Ransome asked.

Rose's exhalation was like a gust of wind. "Father had listed his cousin, Robin, as the beneficiary on his will. He thought Robin would look after us, but Robin didn't want the responsibility of two children. He said I could come and keep house for him, but he had no room for Sid. He was going to take him to an orphanage, but Sid refused to go. He said he'd run away. So we slept in the shed behind the shop until the new owners moved in. It was then that Mr. Bonneville came by and saw us in the street. He said we could work for him at the theater. We were so happy. We thought we were saved, until we saw how dingy the attic was where we'd be living and heard how little we would be paid."

Rose clasped her hands and looked toward the window, her shoulders stooped with defeat.

"Rose, did you know Sid had stolen morphine from

Harbor's and used it to murder Esme and Christopher?" Sebastian asked.

Rose turned back and shook her head. "I honestly believed someone else had done it. They weren't very nice, Esme and Christopher, but they didn't deserve to die. When Sid and I were alone in the attic that night, I saw something in his face, and then I knew it was him." Rose sighed again. "Something broke in Sid when our parents died. I tried to love him, but there were times when I was afraid of him."

"Why did he murder Ishmael Cabot?" Ransome asked.

"Sid took an instant dislike to Ishmael and blackmailed him for the sheer pleasure of it. But then he became convinced that you would solve the case if you hung about long enough, so he killed Ishmael to throw you off the scent," Rose said, turning to Sebastian.

"Did he really see Esme with Ishmael?" Sebastian inquired. Their supposed relationship had never rung true to him.

Rose shook her head. "Esme didn't like Ishmael. Especially not like that. She was in love with Christopher. Sid only told you that to muddy the waters."

"But Walt Dickie had said it first," Sebastian replied.

"Walt didn't know what he saw half the time. His brain was addled with drink. He didn't need to die." Rose's eyes filled with tears again. "I didn't murder anyone, I swear. I know I did wrong, but I only stole from people who could stand to part with a few quid."

"Did you take the rose brooch?" Sebastian asked.

Rose nodded. "It's gone. Sid sold it the next day. What will happen to me?" she whispered urgently.

"Even if you're not convicted on a charge of accessory to murder, you'll spend the better part of your life in prison," Ransome said. There was no pity in either his gaze or his tone.

"I never had a choice," Rose cried.

"We all have a choice, love," Ransome replied, and pushed away from the table. "Charge her, Bell."

Sebastian left Scotland Yard an hour later, after Rose had been dispatched to Coldbath Fields to spend the first of many nights in a cell. Heavy rain had begun to fall, and the street was deserted, the hansoms all occupied as they trundled past, the cabbies looking drenched and miserable as they sat hunched on their elevated perches. Sebastian was in no rush to get home, nor did he think he should call on Gemma. Colin and Mabel would look after her, and it was probably best that he give her a little time to come to terms with what had happened and hopefully put it behind her.

They had solved the case, but Sebastian didn't feel any better for it. A boy was dead, and a sixteen-year-old girl would either be hanged, go to prison for the rest of her life, or get sent down to a penal colony, where she wouldn't last a month, assuming she survived the journey. Not an outcome he had hoped for.

Sebastian had joined the police service when he was eighteen because he'd wanted to keep the innocent safe and punish the guilty. There were days when he believed he was an instrument of justice and prided himself on making a difference, but there were other days when he hated his job and thought that sending countless people to their deaths wasn't really justice, just defensible homicide. This was one of those days, and he knew it would take a long while for him to stop thinking about Sid and Rose Wyvern. But there were things he could do to restore balance to his world. As a plan began to formulate in his mind, he walked faster, suddenly eager to get back to his lodgings.

EPILOGUE
APRIL 1859

Gemma smoothed down her skirts and patted her hair into place before going downstairs. Colin had insisted on a small birthday dinner, but she was in no mood for a celebration. She hadn't seen Sebastian in nearly three weeks and was beginning to think that he was purposely avoiding her. If he failed to come tonight, she didn't think she would be able to get through the evening, or the months that lay ahead. She imagined the coming days echoing with crushing loneliness and the loss of hope. He had every right to be angry, and, although he had said that he didn't blame her for Sid's death and his own part in it, Gemma knew he'd only said that to make her feel less responsible. If she had not gone into the theater by herself, Sid would still be alive, if not for long. But it was one thing to charge someone with a crime, and quite another to take their life.

Sebastian liked to pretend he was strong, but inside he was still fragile, and her actions might have sent him back to Mr. Wu's opium den or on a days-long drinking bender. Gemma would learn to live without him if she had no choice, but she now knew she would never be happy. No other man had ever touched her heart or made her long for the physical intimacy that was part of marriage. She ached for him in a way that left her cheeks burning with shame, and she would do anything to have him back, if just for an hour, so she could beg for his forgiveness and promise that she would never again interfere in his investigations.

She wouldn't even ask him about General Modine, who had been viciously attacked the night Sebastian had allegedly walked into a door. Rumor had it that the general had suffered such grave injuries, it would take weeks if not months for him to recover. Poppy had heard from one of the doctors at the infirmary that the general's recovery had suffered a setback when his wife went out for a walk one afternoon and never returned. Gemma hoped that Frances Modine was far, far away and wouldn't come back to London as long as her husband was alive and had the means to hurt her. She also prayed that Sebastian would not be charged with assault, should his door turn out to have been General Modine's head.

With no reason to keep to her room any longer, Gemma braced herself for a difficult evening and made her way down the stairs. She arrived at the bottom just as someone knocked.

"Your guests are here," Mabel chirped as she hurried to answer the door. She had been cooking and baking all day, and the house smelled of roast lamb with spring potatoes and sponge cake with raspberry filling.

"I'll get it," Gemma offered, and Mabel beat a hasty retreat into the kitchen.

Gemma plastered a smile onto her face, convinced she was about to greet Poppy, but her heart nearly exploded out of her chest when Sebastian walked through the door, a small, neatly wrapped parcel in his hand. He smiled just for her, and then she was moving toward him, her arms encircling his neck as he caught her and held her close, his heart beating against her heaving bosom.

"Happy birthday, sweetheart," he whispered into her hair, and Gemma thought she would die from happiness.

"Where have you been?" she cried. "I thought you were finished with me."

Sebastian's eyebrows lifted in surprise. "Didn't you get my note?"

"What note?"

"I sent it with Hank, Mrs. Poole's boy."

Gemma shook her head. "I didn't receive anything. Perhaps he gave it to Anne, and she forgot to give it to me."

"Come into the parlor," Sebastian said once Gemma had finally let go of him. "I have a present for you, and I don't want you to open it in front of the others."

"You didn't answer my question," Gemma said as they settled on the settee. "Where were you?"

"County Cork."

"Why did you go to Ireland?"

"Because I had to do something good, Gemma. Something to right a wrong."

Gemma shook her head in confusion. "What wrong could you right in County Cork?"

"I found Mona's son," Sebastian said simply. "The local constables were only too happy to help an inspector from London, if only to get me to leave them in peace. Brendan Grady was taken to an orphanage and then given to a childless couple who wanted a boy to help them work their farm."

"Will they give him up?" Gemma asked, amazed that Sebastian would devote his own time and funds to helping Mona find her child.

"I don't know, but Mona is on her way to Ireland and will be reunited with her son."

"She got her miracle," Gemma said, and felt the sting of tears.

Sebastian nodded and smiled, and Gemma could see that he was at peace.

"What did you get me?" she asked as she looked at the parcel Sebastian still held in his hand.

It was wrapped in pink paper and tied with a white ribbon. It was about the size of a book, and Gemma thought Sebastian had probably got her a novel he thought she might enjoy, or maybe a box of chocolates or marzipan. She was grateful he'd got her a gift, but deep down she felt a pang of disappointment. She would have liked something more personal.

"Well, open it," Sebastian said once he'd handed it to her.

Gemma untied the ribbon, carefully removed the wrapping paper, and studied the polished wooden case. Not a book, and definitely not chocolates.

"What is this?"

"Open it," Sebastian said again.

Gemma opened the lid and stared at the contents of the box. She couldn't believe her eyes. Inside, nestled on a bed of blue velvet, was a pistol. It was the smallest firearm she had ever seen, but also the most beautiful. The handle was made of smooth dark wood, and the barrel was intricately carved and decorated with etched images of wild animals. The stamp on the side read *Colt*.

"It's a gold-inlaid Colt 1849 pocket revolver," Sebastian said proudly. "Made in America."

"You got me a gun?" Gemma choked out, still stunned by Sebastian's choice of gift.

"Since you're unlikely to stop meddling in my investigations —and if I'm truly honest, I don't really want you to—I thought you should be able to protect yourself. You might need a bigger reticule, though," he said with a grin that made him look boyish. "It's a thing of beauty, that." He gazed at the gun with undisguised longing, and Gemma wondered how long it had taken him to find just the right model and how much he had paid for it. The piece looked expensive.

"Where did you get this?"

"Doesn't matter where I got it. What matters is that you know how to use it."

"Will you teach me?" Gemma asked.

"It will be my pleasure."

Gemma hastily shut the lid when someone knocked again, and then she heard Colin's voice as he escorted Anne down the stairs. Mabel was already taking Poppy's cape and bonnet and inviting her into the parlor.

"Sebastian, Colin, I would like you to meet my friend, Poppy Bright," Gemma said once they were all assembled.

Poppy smiled shyly. "It's a pleasure to meet you both. And it's lovely to see you again, Mrs. Ramsey."

Anne peered at Poppy as if she'd never seen her before, Colin smiled shyly, and Sebastian shot Gemma a knowing look and stepped back, leaving Colin to welcome Poppy and engage her in conversation.

"I have one more present for you," Sebastian said, so softly only Gemma could hear. "I have arranged for you to see Lucy. The visit will be supervised by Matron Holcombe, and very brief, but you will see for yourself that Lucy is thriving and have the chance to say a proper goodbye."

Gemma's heart soared, and she would have thrown her arms around Sebastian and kissed him if propriety allowed such a wanton display of gratitude. Instead, she smiled into his eyes and reached for his hand.

"Thank you," she whispered.

"You're welcome," he whispered back. "Happy birthday, my darling."

Happy birthday, indeed!

A LETTER FROM THE AUTHOR

Huge thanks for reading *Murder at the Orpheus Theatre*. I hope you were hooked on Sebastian and Gemma's latest case. Their adventures will continue. If you want to join other readers in hearing all about my new releases and bonus content, you can sign up for my newsletter.

www.stormpublishing.co/irina-shapiro

If you enjoyed this book and could spare a few moments to leave a review, that would be hugely appreciated. Even a short review can make all the difference in encouraging a reader to discover my books for the first time. Thank you so much.

Thanks again for being part of this amazing journey with me and I hope you'll stay in touch—I have so many more stories and ideas to entertain you with.

Irina

irinashapiroauthor.com

facebook.com/IrinaShapiro2
x.com/IrinaShapiro2
instagram.com/irina_shapiro_author

ACKNOWLEDGMENTS

I would like to thank my readers for embracing this new series so enthusiastically. My editor, Emily Gowers for taking my writing to a whole new level, and the amazing team at Storm Publishing for their hard work on my behalf.

Made in the USA
Columbia, SC
10 February 2025

53642405R00198